*ROOKIE PATROLMAN PETE WILLIS WENT
OVER BACKWARD AND SLID ACROSS
THE CEMENT FLOOR.*

Seeing the muzzle being leveled at his head, he knew it was over. He shivered once and felt a cold wind envelop him. When the roar came, filling the room, reverberating off the walls, he smiled.

Funny, he had always thought death would be painful. But he felt nothing. Hours seemed to float by before it occurred to him that he was still breathing. The knowledge came slowly. And with it came the pain.

When his eyelids finally fluttered open, he looked directly into the green eyes of his district sergeant. A few feet away, the body of his attacker was sprawled facedown in a pool of blood.

The odor of gunpowder swirled about him to mingle with another smell far more intoxicating. It was the distinctive aroma of a woman. Pete's last thought before losing consciousness was that he had never seen—or smelled—a more beautiful woman than Sergeant Dixie T. Struthers.

Murder is Only Skin Deep

L. V. SIMS

CHARTER BOOKS, NEW YORK

MURDER IS ONLY SKIN DEEP

A Charter Book/published by arrangement with
the author

PRINTING HISTORY
Charter edition/August 1987

ISBN: 0-441-81300-3

Charter Books are published by The Berkley Publishing Group,
200 Madison Avenue, New York, New York 10016.
The name ''Charter'' and the ''C'' logo are trademarks
belonging to Charter Communications, Inc.
PRINTED IN THE UNITED STATES OF AMERICA

10 9 8 7 6 5 4 3 2 1

I wish to give special thanks to Sergeants Jerry Albericci and John Trussler for all the hours spent in patrol cars in the dead of night, for all the stories, good for a hundred novels. A very special thanks is due former Sergeant Hal Lail . . . homicide detective *extraordinaire* . . . pilot . . . private investigator . . . genius. For the information given on toxins and postmortem findings, thanks are due to Dr. Pete Ballard of San Jose State University, and to organic chemist Dr. Alan Olivero. I am grateful to Peg Crites for all the typing, proofing and encouragement. Most of all, I wish to give both love and thanks to my husband, Bill, a great cop and a better husband, and to my four children Debbie, Lori, Jay and Michelle. Their love, laughter and patience make my life happier, my career easier. Special thanks are also due Roslyn Targ, my agent, for her confidence, and Natalee Rosenstein, my editor, for her invaluable assistance, advice and patience.

For Sgt. Bill Sims . . . with love and gratitude for the long walks and pep talks.

PROLOGUE

IT WAS NEARLY dawn and dead quiet as Rookie Patrolman Peter Willis nosed his blue and white beat car around the corner of a deserted intersection. He hated working midnights, hated the hours and the struggle to stay awake. His metabolism just refused to adjust.

And this was the time he hated most. Gliding along deserted streets. Alone. With the city slumbering around him. It was like being trapped in some netherworld. A soft spring mist wrapped the headlight beams of his patrol car in gauze. He was very sleepy.

Pete jerked himself upright behind the wheel, his eyes watering with fatigue and boredom. Damn, he hated it!

But then his training officer had warned him it would be like this. A new rookie always came up with the dregs. No choice of beat, shift, *or* sergeant.

Boy, was that the truth! Here he was, working mids with no partner. His beat was in an old industrial area of the city, with few single-family homes. And, of all the district sergeants he might have pulled, it had been just his luck to get stuck with D. T. Struthers. Just thinking about his direct superior made Pete curse aloud, but then he immediately yawned. Once again his eyes tried to close of their own accord.

There were few restaurants on his beat, and none were

1

open in the wee hours except a small all-night doughnut shop. He turned the car in that direction, knowing that if he didn't get coffee soon he would fall asleep for sure. He would have a couple of cups of coffee, and he would wake up. Then, when he finally made it home, he would lay awake for two hours wishing that the Dunkin D Donut Shop had been closed, too.

Pete shrugged. Maybe, soon, he'd get used to it. Maybe.

For the past few weeks it had become his habit to stop at the shop once or twice during the long night shift to revitalize himself and shoot the breeze with the cashier. Jackie was a nice old broad. Simple. Blessed with a sharp tongue and a sense of humor. And a talent for making incredibly strong coffee.

Rolling to a stop just a few yards from the front door of the doughnut shop, Pete looked through the steamy window and saw that for once he would not be the only customer. A tall man stood facing away from the street, toward the cash register. Jackie was staring up at him.

Pete was never sure exactly what tipped him. Maybe it was the expression on Jackie's face. Or the stiff, unnatural posture of the man. Or, just maybe, Pete was already beginning to develop a cop's nose for trouble. Whatever the reason, he suddenly knew that something was very wrong. His heart began to pump and all thought of sleep was forgotten as he shifted into reverse and eased the patrol car back out of the pool of light.

He saw the gun now. A small, short-barreled revolver pointed directly at Jackie's chest. He jerked the radio mike from its cradle and pressed the transmitting button.

"Comm two, this is 8824." He was almost whispering.

The cool, feminine voice of the dispatcher bounced back at him, and the sound seemed to boom into the night. *"Comm two. I don't quite read, 8824. Please repeat."*

He raised his voice an octave. "Comm two. 8824. Code 33."

"Comm two. Right, 8824. Code 33."

"Requesting a fill for 211 in progress at Second and Keys." This time his voice came out in a croak and he struggled to keep it from quavering. The training he had received at the academy raced through his brain. A description. He had to broadcast a description. "A WMA . . . wearing a Levi's jacket . . . shoulder-length brown hair . . ." His throat felt dry and parched. "I . . . I can see him through the window. He's holding a gun on the cashier." Pete's eyes quickly scanned the street. "No vehicle visible."

Again the dispatcher acknowledged his message, using the same infuriating, crisp, calm tone. He felt as if hours had passed. Years.

Pete swore under his breath. He was sweating. Reaching to the dash, he pushed the electric release switch that held his shotgun in place. The weapon came into his hands. Solid. Reassuring.

A loud snap punctuated the dark as he got out of the car and jacked a round of double-ought buck into the shotgun chamber. There was no way to approach the well-lit shop without being seen. Not unless the man inside simply failed to turn around.

Pete prayed for luck. And a speedy backup.

Coming closer, he could see Jackie stuffing what little money she kept on hand into a pastry sack. A stray lock of gray hair had escaped the net she always wore and hung down against her forehead. Her face was washed white, her lipstick and rouge garish beneath the glare of fluorescent light. Pete was almost to the door before she saw him. Their eyes met through the glass and he tensed, expecting her to cry out in recognition. Instead, she dropped the sack of money.

The thief leaned over her and yelled into her face before bringing his arm up to strike her hard across the temple with the barrel of his revolver. She buckled and slithered down behind the counter.

Pete suddenly lost all fear—and with it caution. Three strides took him through the front door. He took aim and shouted. "Stop! Drop it!"

The man who spun to face him was young, no more than twenty-five. A sparse beard and mustache surrounded his thin, colorless lips. He raised the gun and at the same time, Pete jerked the shotgun trigger.

Nothing. There was no deafening explosion. Just a soundless void. Nothing but silence and the smell of brewing coffee and fresh-baked doughnuts.

Then, from behind the counter, Jackie moaned. Pete yelled, an exclamation of rage and horror. An acknowledgment of his own stupidity. He stared down at the right side of his trigger guard with glazed, unbelieving eyes. The safety was still on.

The first shot fired by the thief caught Pete square in the chest. He staggered back as the .38 caliber round ripped through his jacket and shirt, lodging neatly in the webbed confines of a bulletproof vest. And though it did not penetrate his flesh, the slug bruised him deeply, throwing him off balance. The shotgun slung sideways in his right hand while his left clawed at the slick surface of a glass pastry case. He had no time to steady himself before the pain came. Hot and wet. The second shot seemed to sound after he was already hit.

Almost detached now, Pete looked at the dark stain spreading down the pant leg covering his upper thigh and then up into the face of his assailant.

The young man was ashen, eyes wide and round, but he was also smiling. He appeared to grow taller as Pete felt himself going down. The thief fired again.

Pete's arm dangled against his side, useless. He went over backward and slid across the cement floor. Seeing the muzzle being leveled at his head, he knew it was over.

Rookie Patrolman Peter Jacob Willis closed his eyes and waited to die. He shivered once and felt a cold wind envelop him. When the roar came, filling the room, reverberating off the walls, he smiled.

Funny, he had always thought death would be painful. But he felt nothing. The world around him grew quiet; sounds muted. Almost pleasant. Hours seemed to float by before it occurred to him that he was still breathing. That he wasn't dead at all. The knowledge came slowly, rippling over him. And with it came the pain.

When his eyelids finally fluttered open again, he looked directly into the eyes of his district sergeant. Those eyes were the color of emeralds with minute chips of gold surrounding the pupils. Beneath them was an incredibly dainty, upturned nose. The lips were moving, saying something he couldn't quite make out.

For just a moment he allowed his vision to range past the face hovering above him and then down and across the floor. A few feet away, the body of his attacker was sprawled face down. Unmoving. The denim jacket soaked up a pool of blood.

Pete's head rolled from side to side. He blinked several times. The incongruous odors of gunpowder and yeast swirled about him to mingle with another . . . a smell far more subtle and intoxicating. It was the distinctive, unmistakable aroma of a woman.

Pete blinked one final time, but his last thought before losing consciousness was that he had never seen or smelled a more beautiful woman than Sergeant Dixie T. Struthers.

CHAPTER 1

THE WEATHER WAS fine. Crisp and clear. Free of the industrial debris that so often hung over all 1,355 square miles of the Santa Clara Valley, the broad, sprawling metropolitan area now synonymous with computers and high tech. *Silicon Valley*.

Dixie rolled down the car window and enjoyed the rarity. It was a long ride home, but she didn't mind the commute. During her first two years on the police force, years spent locked in constant conflict with her former husband, she had spent even more time on the freeway. She and Donald had lived in San Francisco then, where they had both been raised. Donald had insisted on remaining there even though Palo Alto, where he still attended classes at Stanford University, would have been the perfect compromise for them both. Compromise was not a part of her former husband's character. His life, he had insisted, was in San Francisco. His social life. His friends. And, most of all, his mother.

Dixie much preferred the commute she now made. Not from San Francisco to San Jose. Not from one seething city to another. She took the opposite direction now, up into the oak- and pine-studded Santa Cruz Mountains.

The decision to leave her husband, to end their three-and-one-half-year marriage, had not been easy. She had loved Donald Struthers. Donald, the armchair philosopher. Donald, with his soft blond hair and beard, and softer brown eyes. Donald the perpetual student, the boy/man whom she had finally realized would never attain adulthood.

But with the pain of divorce, of a dismal, failed marriage well behind her, Dixie admitted to herself that she enjoyed being single. Most of the time. The relationship she shared with Assistant District Attorney Joseph Kirk was satisfying in a companionable, noncommitted sort of way. More important, she had a career that she loved.

The freeway traffic moving toward the mountains was sluggish and lazy, a reflection of the people sitting in their cars. Most of the drivers wore bored, Friday faces, expressions tight with a residue of work-week tensions. And for all her love of career, Dixie was no exception. The muscles in her shoulders were bunched into knots. Her scalp felt tight, and a scowl marred the normally smooth skin of her forehead.

She leaned forward and tuned the car radio to an easy rock station—oldies but goodies. The music of her early high school years still seemed sweetest and best to her ears. Without thinking, she hummed along with Gordon Lightfoot.

"Carefree highway, let me slip away on you . . ."

Realizing how closely the wistful words matched her mood, she shook her head and tried to shrug off the vague depression which had been with her intermittently over the past weeks. As of now, this minute, she was not at work. The prospect of a leisurely weekend lay ahead.

Still, thoughts of work did intrude, and with them a renewal of her frustration. She could not help remembering the excitement she had experienced upon graduating from the police academy more than six years before. The feeling of pride and anticipation had been almost overwhelming. But with the memories came a bitterness, too, a disgust at the path her professional life seemed to be taking.

She had not made her career choice lightly. When she began college, at her mother's urging, she had chosen political science as her major. The first step toward law school. But it wasn't until just after she had received her degree that she saw an opportunity to fulfill her true ambition. A secret dream, unshared but never completely forgotten.

Times were quickly changing. Law enforcement was changing. All across the nation women were being recruited for regular police work. No longer were they relegated only to desks and clerical paperwork.

Following in the footsteps of her father, a police officer killed in the line of duty, and of her paternal grandfather, she applied for a position as police officer.

Donald had tried reasoning with her. Her mother ranted. Her stepfather looked distantly disapproving. Only her half brother, Ryan, and Patrick Flannigan, her retired police officer grandfather, cheered as Dixie became the first female to graduate from the San Jose Police Academy.

Being the first woman on regular duty had given her a unique status, an opportunity to prove to both herself and her fellow officers that a woman could be an effective and capable cop. Not an easy job. Never easy. But, then, she had not expected it to be a breeze, not even in the beginning.

Dixie was a petite woman, especially at first glance. The uniform she wore, an almost exact duplicate of the one worn by her male counterparts, closely fit her trim, muscular legs— legs developed first by ballet and kept supple with exercise. Dressed in the midnight-blue uniform, there was little outward indication of the flat, well-developed abdominals and dancer's haunches, the source of not only strength but agility and grace, that were within.

To Dixie's academy classmates she had been just another "libber," one of those females who just had to stir the shit. And when she did well, not only on written exams but at the pistol range and in physical training, she found herself no more accepted than on the first day. Rather, the washouts, men who proved not to possess the required stamina and aptitude for police work, despised her utterly. Others simply convinced themselves that she did well because leeway was given because she was a woman—a *minority*.

But nothing—not the ranting of her husband, mother-in-law and mother combined—could dampen Dixie's spirit or take away her feeling of pride and achievement. With the exception of the domestic turbulence, her first years on the force had been the best of her life. Gradually, bit by reticent bit, she gained not only acceptance but a grudging respect from her peers.

She was not overly friendly, certainly not social. Dixie was, by nature and by design, a private person. In the beginning she had been married, a status she made no attempt to downplay. After the divorce, she had been surprised at the scurry to win her favor, but when she consistently refused both invitations and advances her professional life once more settled into place. Finally, she felt comfortable with herself, with her job, and with life in general. She moved to the mountain house once used by her mother's family for summer vacations. With slight renovations and upgrading, the chalet bequeathed to her by her maternal grandfather became, more than anyplace had ever been, *home*. At age twenty-six, after only slightly more than four years on the police force, Dixie had felt fulfilled, completely content with her career and life.

And then came the sergeant's exams, the written and oral testing to determine who would make promotion. Yet again, Dixie had faced a choice. She could study, take the exams, join the mad dash to make rank—or she could settle back on her pretty backside and continue to enjoy the status quo. Her fellow cops never knew how much thought she had given that particular decision, how very tempted she had been to cling to the hard-won security of acceptance. In the end, however, Dixie's character, her natural competitiveness, and the same healthy ambition that motivated so many of her peers came to the fore. She tested and she passed. And, perhaps worst of all, her scores put her smack on top of the eligibility list. Within a month she found herself a District Patrol Sergeant, and once more she also found herself ostracized. Resentment ran hot, especially from men who had been tested for the third or fourth time.

For Patrol Sergeant D. T. Struthers there had been no *code 7* rendezvous, no taking meal breaks with other officers. No casual *1087* chats, discussions of various interesting beat incidents. More than ever, Dixie worked alone. And if acceptance had been slow before, it now came at considerably less than a snail's pace, until . . .

Remembering the incident which had recently catapulted her career, Dixie unconsciously winced and shook her head. The scene in the doughnut shop, the horror of looking in and seeing one of her rookies down . . . possibly dying . . . the

armed man drawing down, taking aim for that final, fatal
shot . . .

She still cringed at the memory. Her heart picked up tempo
and she could almost taste the acrid film of fear in her mouth
again. Fear for Pete Willis, and for her own life, too. And
then shooting another human being . . . killing a man . . .

Traffic was picking up, moving faster, thinning until it
zipped up through the rolling foothills. Dixie easily maneuvered her '73 Jaguar XKE along the wide and twisting asphalt
ribbon of road as the Nimitz Freeway turned into Highway 17.
The wind coming through the window kissed her face with
the scent of earth and pine, but for once she hardly noticed.
She impatiently pushed at the unruly tendrils of hair that
escaped from her chignon. Keeping the mass of coppery
auburn curls pulled away from her face was no easy task at
any time, and now the wind played havoc with the hairstyle
she had long ago adopted for her working hours. She wore an
expertly tailored dark blue linen suit and a pristine white
blouse with a ribbon bow at the collar. Except for a slight
peek-a-boo of white lace visible around her knees as she
down-shifted to leave the main highway, there was no frip-
pery about her outfit. She made it a point to look professional, especially now that she no longer wore a uniform.
Soon after the incident in the doughnut shop she had been
transferred into the detective bureau—to the homicide division.

Dixie frowned. *A reward? For saving the life of another
officer? For doing what any other cop would do? For killing
a man . . .*

Her lower lip twitched with irritation. She could not shake
the feeling, the near certainty, that she had been made the
very thing she wished most not to be—a *token*.

The music she had been only half aware of turned to static
as she drove deeper into the hills. She turned the radio off and
once more tried to put the week's aggravation, the frustrations
of her new position, behind her. Above all, she did not want
to think about the man who had so recently become her direct
superior.

Dixie felt her jaw tighten. Lieutenant Anthony Di Franco.
The very name made her clench the steering wheel harder.
She forced herself to relax, taking several long, deep breaths.

As of now, she was off duty. She refused to let him spoil her weekend.

And so she talked to herself the rest of the way home—to little avail.

The landscape had changed slowly, from city to scrubwood and manzanita, and finally to towering pines. There were thousands of homes in these mountains, but most were well away from the highway, nestled in small valleys, banked against slopes and surrounded by trees. In short, most of the homes were like her own. Private.

She had to ease off the speed now, veering onto yet another narrow side road. The curves became sharper and more frequent. The quarter-mile-long driveway leading to her own property was barely wide enough for the car. The Jag hit a pothole and bounced gently before crossing the last barrier. A sturdy old wooden bridge, worn smooth with the patina of passage and time.

Once over the swollen creek, the road abruptly opened onto a tiny meadow. Shafts of fading sunlight slanted through the trees and fell on the house. Like the bridge, it, too, was old and large, the exterior made of aged redwood. A chalet built in the twenties, it had a shingled barn roof and Dutch door. A fresh coat of French blue paint along the eaves and around mullioned windows had given it a gentle and dignified facelift. A huge gray wolfhound bounded off the wide front deck and charged across the meadow, tongue lolling from between massive jaws.

"Down, Poke!"

Dixie had parked in the open garage, but she wisely stayed put. She knew better than to try to emerge through the open car door before the ritual greeting took place. Her five-foot-two-inch frame, even in its current prime condition, was no match for a joyfully hurled hundred and fifty pounds of ecstatic dog.

Poke whirled and whined, pawed and lapped at her face until she managed to steady him with a series of brisk pats. Several minutes passed before they walked back up the drive and entered together.

The living room was deserted, but Dixie could hear the rattle of pots and pans. She inhaled deeply and smiled. Breaded chops. Corn bread. Something with lots of garlic, butter, and onions. And, of course, a dessert. With crust. No less than a three-thousand-calorie meal beckoned her to the kitchen.

A lavish backside greeted her as she and Poke walked into the room. Reversa Green was stooped over, going through a lower cabinet, muttering to herself.

"Never can find one damn thing in this house. Never! What with that old geezer always pawin' around, goin' through stuff . . ."

It was a familiar household theme. Dixie cleared her throat and attempted to bury her smile. She failed.

The amazonian black woman looked around and straightened with a glare. "And just what are you grinning at, Missy? About time you got here. Dinner's almost ready. You think I just stand around here cookin' for my health?"

"Traffic was heavy," Dixie answered, offering the same excuse she did every evening. When she had worked patrol, on swing shift or mids, the initial exchange between them varied, but only slightly.

"About time you pulled yourself out of bed, Missy," Reversa would then say. "Sleepin' all day, out lookin' for trouble all night. Why you have such a job I'll never know, and that's for sure. Whoever heard of a biddy little thing like you becomin' a po-leece. Just look at you, ain't no bigger'n a popcorn fart!"

Dixie's profession was also a main theme, one far too familiar for her taste, especially in her present frame of mind. "Where's Pop?" she now asked, hoping to ward off the remainder of this day's lecture.

Reversa's scowl deepened. She jerked a thumb toward the back door and then returned to her work, still grumbling beneath her breath.

Contrary to outward appearances, the rivalry and constant bickering between the housekeeper and Dixie's paternal grandfather was only a facade covering a bounty of affection. Dixie lived with it, took sides as seldom as possible, and loved them both desperately.

Patrick Flannigan was just turning off the hose he had used to water a small vegetable garden when Dixie came onto the long porch.

"How goes it with the greens?" she called and waved.

The old man looked back over his shoulder at neat rows of lettuce, turnips, and broccoli, vegetables he commonly referred to as his winter crop. "Need another patch job on the fence. Those damn deer are at it again."

Coming closer, he cast a baleful eye on Poke. "And that hound of yours is no help. He wants to play with the pesty critters."

Poke yawned, plopped down beside Dixie, and rolled over on his back. His thick tail thumped against the wooden planks of the porch. She knelt to scratch the woolly, cowlicked ears. "He's not much of a watch dog, I'll grant you, but he *looks* scary."

Patrick grunted and hung the hose on a tree peg. After mounting the steps, he settled into a deck chair, struck a wooden match, and lit the stub of a cigar he had been holding between his teeth. Dixie rested her weight against a porch rail and folded her arms across her chest.

"And how was your day?" he asked. "Things getting any better?"

She sighed, suddenly more weary than ever. "Not much. Di Franco is still managing to keep me out of the way. In a word, Pop, the man can't stand me."

"Oh, come on, honey. Just give him a little time. Some of the brass just take longer than others. Sometimes a body just has to nurse them along. You'll win him over. Remember, it's not personal. It's just that you're a—"

"Yeah, yeah, Pop. I know what you think, but I'm telling you it can't be only because I'm a woman. That just doesn't wash. Females have been in on the PD for too long now. Five and a half years, to be exact."

"Not many of them."

"Wrong, Pop. As of last month forty-two women have been hired."

"Forty-two women and how many hundred men?"

Dixie shook her head. "I still don't think that's it with Di Franco. It's me in particular, something I do, or maybe something I've done. Something I don't realize."

Patrick nodded. "Now you've got it. It is different with you, Dix. Real different. And it'll stay that way for a while.

You made rank, and you're the first woman to do that. I know guys like Di Franco. I'm sure he objected to hiring females in the first place. It was crammed down his throat as far as he's concerned. He's taking it personal. And then what do you do? You go and make promotion in double time. Probably sticks in his craw like hot gravel.''

''Making rank means passing a test, Pop. Since when do brains come in gender? I could understand it easier when I worked out in the field. The guys were a long time learning I didn't have to be six feet tall to hold up my end. But now . . .''

All her frustration came rushing back, throwing a pall over the peace of the evening. The blatant chauvinism of her direct superior was driving her slightly over the edge. During her career she had never once cried *sexist*, never accused anyone of treating her differently because she was a woman, even when she knew that to be the case. She worked hard, minding her own business, sure that if she did the job well everything else would eventually fall into place. But for all her denial, Dixie knew that her grandfather was right. Di Franco was prejudiced against female officers in general, and now, since she was in his unit of command, against her in particular. The situation was wearing as thin as tissue. Within the bounds of pride and good judgment, she had done everything possible to win the man's respect. Still, most of the time she was delegated the semiclerical task of matching fingerprints. Or, at best, tracking down a routine missing person report. It was all the more galling when she remembered her original elation at being assigned to the homicide detail. By no standard could she consider her present duties those of a homicide detective.

''Maybe you should switch tactics,'' her grandfather said. His voice was low and mild. Dark had fallen completely now. Light spilled from the kitchen window, haloing the full head of silvery hair he still possessed. His face was in shadow and Dixie couldn't read his expression.

''Tactics?''

''What I mean is . . . oh, hell, Dix, have you ever considered just letting yourself go? If you're going to be a female, then *be* one, a real one. Who knows, it might even help with Di Franco. A little charm goes a long way. Even with a guy like him.'' Patrick waved an arm at her. ''Just look at you. You pull all those gorgeous Flannigan locks back in that bun getup. Swear to God, makes me think of a peeled onion. You wear your plainest duds to work . . .''

A hot flush crept up Dixie's neck. She opened her mouth to protest, but he cut her off with an impatient chop of his hand. ''Now don't go gettin' your Irish up with me, Dixie T. I've watched you and I've kept quiet. I tell you, you're hiding your best light under a bushel. You've been working hard, girl, trying to make a place for women in a world that's always belonged to men. And you've been doing one helluva job. But don't you think it might be more honest to do it as a *genuine* female?''

Suddenly, the strain of the past weeks took its toll. Dixie shot up straight as a poker, and her temper snapped. ''And just what am I supposed to do, shake tits and ass right to the top? Maybe Di Franco would like me better if I let him grab a handful! Really, Pop, you're no better than the rest! You, all of you, are nothing but a bunch of . . . oh, God, it pisses me off!''

She could hardly believe the words were coming out of her mouth, that she was yelling at the dear, wizened grandfather she loved more than anyone on earth. But almost as hard for Dixie to believe was that he was criticizing her. Patrick was the one man she had always been so sure understood her completely. The grandfather who had kept her spellbound throughout her childhood with his tales of days spent on an old San Francisco foot beat. It had been Patrick, too, who had held her and wept with her when her father was killed, gut-shot by a burglar at the age of only thirty-four. She felt raw, hurt that he seemed not to take her side. Especially now, when it mattered so much.

He sat looking at her, puffing gently on his worn cigar. She could not see his eyes. He spoke, and his voice remained unchanged. ''When you've had a chance to settle yourself, we'll talk darlin'.'' He puffed on the cigar again.

Dixie glared at him, more angry than ever, for now she also felt unutterably silly. Like a chastised and overwrought child.

''I'll go change,'' she said through stiff lips. ''After dinner we can turn on the floodlights and I'll help you mend that fence, but I think we've *talked* quite enough."

She left the porch with as much dignity as she could muster. The screen door slammed shut behind her.

At first glance, the man who stood looking at himself in the mirror resembled Count Dracula. His wet, jet-colored hair swept back from a sharp widow's peak above a pair of dark, glittering eyes. He was smiling at his own reflection. Almost leering.

But closer inspection dispelled the vampirish similarity. There was nothing pale or pasty about his face. His tan was even and rich, his smile a dazzle of white-capped teeth. He stood completely naked, gazing at his equally tanned body, and then looked around the room. His smile broadened to a grin as his eyes took in the black and white marble floors, the expensive furniture and fixtures.

Women. He loved them, each and every bitchy one. There was no end to what they would do, what they would spend to maintain and extend the fragile facade of youth. And there was no end, either, to what they would tell the person who helped them do it . . . shared woes . . . whispered confidences . . . secrets . . .

In one hand, he held a small plastic bottle, an applicator bottle half filled with dark hair color solution. Stepping closer to the mirror, he scowled. This task of keeping up his own image was growing more and more time consuming. But then it was necessary. He could hardly pander what he himself did not possess. His smile returned as he slowly turned to the left and right, flexing his chest muscles. He was in great shape.

Running his free hand down the length of his torso, he examined his chest and pubic hairs with minute care, frowning with concentration as his eyes sought and found the tiny, telltale silver strands. He dabbed the color solution onto his body with quick flicks of his wrist, wincing slightly at the smell. For some reason there seemed to be more sting this time. His skin itched and burned.

He left the room, padding back almost immediately. His bare feet made soft slapping noises against the floor. He looked at himself one last time, stretching and yawning, not in the least bothered by the temporary absurdity of his appearance. He was used to the ritual, a necessity of his present circumstance. As he walked past a row of dressing rooms, he thought again of all the women he served.

Whores. They were all whores in one way or another, using their looks and bodies, panting and sniveling, withholding favors until they managed to have things their own way. He had heard them talk, listened to their complaints, watched them smile and laugh over their victories. He saw each one of them now. Each face. Beautiful and plain. Bored and animated. Deep down they were all the same. And without exception they were also *rich, rich, rich*.

Just beyond the dressing room was a metal door, painted white with a brass bar which he pushed down. The door latch clicked loudly, sending hollow waves of sound into the huge room beyond.

He looked around and once more his dark eyes glinted with satisfaction. He never tired of viewing the world he had created. The house. The grounds. The sheer luxury of it all. Before him now was a pool, surrounded by a garden atrium, complete with tropical palms and a waterfall that splashed musically into a steaming pool.

Paradise. His own private heaven, for tonight at least. Soon, Bobby would come, and then, perhaps, they would take time to share . . .

He closed his eyes for a moment, willing a spurt of excitement under control. This would be a special night. He would make it special, for himself and for Bobby, too. A night to remember.

He had taken only a few steps toward one of the many lounge chairs when the first rolling wave of dizziness hit him. He thrust out one arm, nearly falling. He bent forward, putting his dye-covered head down almost to his knees. A film of sweat popped out on his forehead, and suddenly he was gasping for breath.

His first thought, even before the panic set in, was to get to a telephone. He needed help. An ambulance. He needed an ambulance right away. And with that realization the panic did indeed come. He straightened, his eyes rolling in disbelieving

fear, searching for the phone that he knew hung on the wall
behind him.

But just as he was about to turn, the pain began, screaming
through his body. He bent in half. He hurt. Oh, God, how he
hurt! His chest. His arms and legs. It was as if bolts of
electricity were being pumped through his arteries, into every
vein, each tiny corpuscle. Had he been able to breathe, he
would have screamed.

He pitched forward, stumbled, and managed to right himself. He staggered to a lounge, weaving like a drunkard.

For just a moment, no more than an instant really, the pain
receded as he fell onto the chair. He caught his breath and
heard it rattle in his throat. And in that instant he felt another
jolt of surprise that this could be happening to him—who took
such care to stay healthy, to be fit and appear young.

He had to get help!

All at once he could not remember where the phone was,
or if there was one at all. So great was the next onslaught of
pain that he hardly knew where he was. An agonized groan
tore from his mouth. He began to gurgle as the mucus drained
into the back of his throat. His nose was running. His eyes
wept. Pain thundered through his head, keeping time with the
rapid, almost unendurable rate of his pulse. His chest rose
and fell as he struggled to breathe. His heartbeat shook him
from head to toe.

He was only vaguely aware of the simultaneous need to
vomit and relieve himself when he felt someone touch him.
His first reaction, even with the pain, was relief—a flutter of
hope that help had arrived in time for his salvation.

It was hard to see. So very hard. Even his eyeballs seemed
to hurt. His mouth opened and closed, sucking in air like a
beached fish. Still he managed to mouth the words.

Please! Oh, God, in heaven, please, please, please . . .

He was jerked from the lounge chair, pulled onto the cold
tile of the floor. He hit hard, but the pain grew no worse. To
hurt more than he already did was impossible. His limbs
twitched, his arms and legs. Something, someone, gripped
his ankles.

The world grew black, but the pain refused to fade in kind.
His body quivered and shook, wreathed in a macabre sort of

prone dance as his head rolled back and forth. He slid along the floor.

He felt himself half lifted, shoved and pushed, and suddenly the world was all a wet, wonderful warmth. The sharp edge of pain receded slightly as his body was enveloped in the soothing warmth of hot, bubbling water. He opened his eyes, blinking rapidly, his eyelids and the muscles of his face twitching in spasm.

He looked up and was just able to see the face hovering above him, a face he recognized at once. His mouth opened again in a final, silent, futile plea for mercy as he was pushed beneath the surface of the water. He did not know when he was dunked the second time, or the third. The pain was gone. But he was dunked nevertheless. Again and again and again.

High, keening laughter echoed around the huge room, reverberating from damp mosaic walls.

CHAPTER 2

THE TELEPHONE RANG. And for Investigator Herb Woodall, at that moment, it was the most jarring, irritating sound in the world. He slouched lower in his chair and kept his eyes glued to the television, intent upon a boxing match he had waited for over two months to see. The evening newspaper was scattered around his ankles.

His wife's head poked from around the kitchen doorway. "It's for you, Herb."

He ignored her.

"*Herbert*," she repeated. "It's Tony."

If his five-year-old daughter had not been playing just a few feet away, Herb would have cursed. Instead, he groaned and pulled himself up. As he came into the kitchen, Janice handed him the phone and smiled. It was a smile completely devoid of sympathy. Smug. Janice hated boxing.

"Yeah!" he barked into the mouthpiece of the phone.

"Sorry to disturb your evening, Herb."

"Good, then don't." He and Tony Di Franco had known each other too long for him to stand on ceremony, or feel intimidated.

"No choice." The voice on the other end of the line dropped an octave, taking on an official tone which clearly established their respective ranks and at the same time let him know this was strictly a business call.

The unacknowledged signal was one Herb responded to without rancor. "What's up?"

"I've got two bodies," the lieutenant answered. "Brooks and Delaney have a tech crew at the first scene. You and your little sidekick better report to the other one."

Herb looked at his watch. "It'll take us at least forty-five minutes to get in. Did you try reaching Spatlin?"

"Affirmative. No luck. And Davis is sick . . . again. I'm afraid this one is yours."

Herb scribbled down the address as Tony gave it to him. "Is it dirty?" he asked.

"Not so far as I know. The beat officer reported a probable heart attack or an overdose. At worst, it's a suicide. But it happened over in the Los Palamos district and you know what that means. The body was found in a hot tub."

"Can't get much cleaner than that."

"Nope." There was a pause. "You think Struthers will be okay?"

"Haven't you called her yet?" Herb asked the question, but he already knew the answer. Lieutenant Anthony Di Franco, usually a stickler for department protocol, refused to follow proper pecking order where Dixie Struthers was concerned.

"No. No, I haven't, Herb. I'll let you take care of it. But forget that. You didn't answer my question. Will she be okay?"

For no reason he could clearly define, Herb felt annoyed, but he kept his voice carefully neutral. "She's been with the unit long enough. I'm sure she'll be glad to finally give it a go."

"There's no *go* to this. I told you; at worst it's a suicide." There was a distinct edge to Tony's voice now. "The powder puff can show up on the scene and soothe the RP. The death was probably reported by one of those rich-bitchy types. Come to think of it, Struthers might be real good at that sort of thing. No way for her to get into trouble, either. But keep an eye on her all the same."

"For chrissake, Tony, Struthers is the sergeant. Besides, she's a good cop. Good reputation. Why not ease up a little?"

Tony's voice dropped another decibel and turned frigid. "You've been a real good sport about working with her, Herbie, but let's not get carried away. She's not going to be around for long."

He couldn't quite let it go. "I still say she holds her own. It wouldn't hurt to give her half a chance."

"She's a woman, Herb. Do you hear? They've put a goddamn pussy sergeant in my unit."

"Aw, come off it, Tony. You sound like Big Chief Wounded Bull. There are plenty of women on the force now. Or haven't you noticed?"

"Not in my unit."

"It had to happen sooner or later. You might as well get used to it. Things are changing. That's just the way it is."

"Not in my unit."

"Better Struthers than some of the other—"

"Not in *my* unit!"

"You're beginning to sound like a broken record, Tony." Lieutenant Anthony Di Franco hung up.

Janice had stayed in the kitchen, listening to the exchange. Now she followed Herb into their bedroom. She sat on the edge of the bed while he changed clothes. "Sounds like Tony doesn't much care for your new partner."

"More like my boss, Jan. Like I told Tony, she's the sergeant."

Janice shrugged. "You work together. It's just like being partners."

"Yeah, I guess." He pulled off the tattered sweatshirt he was wearing and replaced it with a clean dress shirt.

"And Tony doesn't like her."

"Not much."

"You never talk about her, you know." She ran a hand over their bedspread, smoothing invisible wrinkles, and then began to pick at a loose thread. Her head was down. "You always talked about your partners, told me about them. Just things, you know."

Herb was too busy putting on his slacks to cue in to the expression on her face, to the way she avoided looking at him. And to the innocuous, far-too-soft voice. "Haven't had much chance to get to know her yet," he answered. "As a matter of fact, I'm not sure anyone knows her too well. She's the quiet type."

He worked a belt through his pant loops and weighted it with the necessary paraphernalia. Spare ammunition clip. Cuffs. Badge. Last, he snapped on the neat elkhide holster Janice had given him for Christmas and loaded it with a 9mm Browning. "I'll tell you one thing, though; that little lady has a great pair of legs. *Great!*"

In spades, it was the wrong thing to say. Janice's head snapped up and fire shot from her hazel eyes. "You shit!"

Herb turned to stare at her, genuinely surprised. To him, Janice had always been the cop's ideal mate. In addition to being attractive and bright, she was self-sufficient and a good listener. She was also blessed with a sense of humor which seemed nowhere in evidence at the moment. Her round pixie face was flushed bright red. And if she had not been so obviously enraged, Herb would have sworn she was on the verge of tears. But that was not his wife's style. Not at all. Janice was not the crying type.

He gave her a lopsided grin. "Actually, she's kinda skinny."

His perfect mate continued to glare.

Stepping away from the closet, he crossed the room and sat down next to her. When he touched her at first she was rigid, but in the next instant she went all soft in his arms.

"I love you," he whispered into the top of her hair.

Eight years ago those three words had come with great difficulty. He had slowly learned the art of giving from the girl now resting her head on his shoulder.

Janice spoke against his chest. "I heard she killed a man. For a woman, that seems . . .''

Abruptly, Herb let go of her and stood up. One of his jaw muscles twitched. "That's right, baby, she killed a man. Goddamn unfeminine thing for her to do, too. She blew some scumbag away, and because she did there's still a cop walking around. Going home each night."

Janice looked up at him. He could see tears clearly in her eyes now. Her lower lip quivered slightly. "I'm sorry, Herb. I didn't mean it the way it sounded. It's just that . . . that you never talk much about her. Here you are, with her all day,

and you never . . . hardly ever talk about her at all. She's
with you all the . . . I saw her once. She's pretty.''

In all the years they had been married, Herb had never
known her to be jealous, not in more than a teasing way. But
at the moment, after eight years of mutual fidelity, all he felt
was irritation. His eyes slid toward the radio clock sitting on
the nightstand and he went back to the closet.

"Wear the tweed," Janice suggested. "It goes best with
those slacks.''

Herb pulled a solid blue sport coat from a hanger and
stuffed a nondescript tie into the pocket. 'I've got to call
Struthers. Hope she's a fast dresser.''

He didn't turn around, but he knew Janice was right behind
him as he returned to the kitchen and picked up the phone.
The fight was still on in the other room. The voice of the
commentator grated on his nerves.

A cork bulletin board was mounted above the telephone,
and on it, next to a piece of kindergarten art work, was a
scrap of paper. It bore the name STRUTHERS, with a phone
number and address. The number was local. Three years
before, Herb had opted to take his family out of the Santa
Clara Valley. Away from the soaring crime rate. Out of the
smog. Still, he estimated it would take a good twenty minutes
to reach Dixie's house. He dialed, wishing he had called
before getting dressed. If he had, perhaps the extra few
minutes would have changed the scene in the bedroom; perhaps his stomach would not be full of angry knots.

"Damn," he muttered, listening to a busy tone.

Janice took the phone from his hand and pressed down the
receiver. "Go ahead. I'll keep trying until I reach her.''

They stood looking at each other. She moved closer. Herb
bent and brushed his lips against the soft nape of her neck.

"I'll leave the porch light on," she whispered. "Be careful.''

Dixie let the water run until bubbles began spilling over the
beveled edge of the claw-legged tub. Enveloped in heat, her
muscles relaxed. She much preferred the gently sloping back
and narrow confines of the ancient fixture she now reclined in
to the esthetically pleasing, nonfunctional bathtubs found in
most modern homes—or, heaven forbid, a shower stall.

Her eyelids drooped. She was nearly asleep, and her mind danced from image to image. She let herself drift, not wanting to dwell on anything. Not the argument with her grandfather, or the tenuous, unspoken peace they had made while working together in the garden after dinner. Certainly not about Di Franco. And, most of all, she wished not to think of the call she had just received from her mother.

Rose Klein Flannigan Marks considered it her duty to telephone once a week, like clockwork. And, like all other duties, she dispatched this one with straightforward efficiency. Not for Rose the namby-pamby approach. The career choice of her only daughter met with her most hearty disapproval, and after nearly six years she still refused to accept it with equanimity.

First, there had been that short, altogether-dreadful-and-unsuitable marriage to Donald Struthers. A male gold digger. That's what Rose had called him. To her he had been nothing but a layabout, a professional student who was very likely after the family fortune. And then, as if the marriage was not already bad enough, Dixie had joined the police force. Rose loathed her daughter's career choice—despised everything about it. Above all, secretly, the very idea of police work terrified her. And what Rose hated or feared, she set about lampooning.

The weekly conversations with her mother had become, for Dixie, tedious at best. At worst, and all too often lately, they were downright unpleasant.

"We want you to come tomorrow," her mother had said this time. "In fact, we insist. At least your weekends are free now; you can stay over. There will be several people you know. Ryan is having a few friends, and your father's bringing home a new man they've just taken into the firm. He's just perfect for you, dear. Attended Harvard . . .''

Until Rose really got rolling, Dixie had been almost tempted to accept the invitation, no matter how stridently given. Just maybe the weekend would turn out to be pleasant. Certainly she missed Ryan, her younger brother. She had not seen him in almost a month. But then it had come, as she knew it would. First the gibe about her work, and then the older and deeper pain. Franklin Marks was *not* her father. To hear him referred to as such set her teeth on edge, just as it always had. And the matchmaking had been the last straw. Harvard be damned!

There was a slight leak in the bathtub faucet. The slow, rhythmic drip of the water was almost hypnotic. When the phone sounded from her bedroom, it took Dixie a moment to mentally shift gears. Her skin was bright pink as she came out of the water and reached for a towel. The ringing stopped and she stood there, calf-high in water, praying her mother had not called to renew their argument.

Reversa's voice called from the hallway. "There's a Mrs. Woodall on the line, Missy T. Says she's calling for Herb or some such. Better haul your little buns outta there. I'm sure you're plenty wrinkled by now anyhow."

Dixie smiled and shook her head. To a casual observer, Reversa Green would have appeared to possess all the amiability of a cornered grizzly. But in this house she was known and loved too well to fool anyone. Reversa was a true armadillo, all scales and iron on the outside, a heart of pure mush on the inside.

Tracking water and bubbles across a thick, dusty rose-colored carpet, Dixie picked up the extension next to her bed. A pleasant, rather shy-sounding voice informed her that Lieutenant Di Franco had called Herb Woodall, who would in turn arrive on her stoop within minutes.

After thanking Herb's wife, Dixie gently hung up. At last there was a case, a *real* case.

Once the realization sank in, she moved. It would take her ten minutes just to dry her hair, she thought, making a mad dash back into the bathroom. But in less than half that time, she was not only dry from crown to toes, her face was also lightly made up. She stood in the closet wearing a slip and camisole of mauve-colored lace. Lingerie was one of the few things Dixie purchased to please herself alone, not to fit the mold fabricated by her profession. The hidden parts of Dixie, both in her taste in clothing and in her personality, were ultrafeminine. She loved the feel of satin and lace—the essence, the sweet, fragrant *whisper* of femininity.

She was just reaching for a tailored blouse when she recalled her grandfather's words. Was it true? Had she been doing what she saw so many of the other female officers do? Without meaning to, had she gradually begun taking on pseudomasculine postures and mannerisms in an attempt to disappear, to blend in with her male counterparts? She had observed other women doing so too often not to worry about herself. Her eyes swept around the large, walk-in closet. More and more these days her wardrobe seemed dominated by tailored suits, blouses, and shoes that bordered on austerity.

Though it rankled, she suddenly realized that her grandfather had spoken a very unpleasant truth. Ever since leaving the patrol division, where she had been required to wear a uniform, she had purposefully dressed down. And if she had not actually become swaggering, she certainly had done everything possible to deemphasize her womanhood. Perhaps it reflected an unconscious wish that if she dressed down, appeared almost somber, she would be taken more seriously—by the public, certainly, but most of all by her fellow officers . . . and her new boss.

Dixie heard the doorbell chime and made a decision she would have no time to recant. Her hand hesitated for only a second before selecting a soft V-necked cashmere she knew would subtly drape over her breasts. The creamy color of the sweater beneath the camel's-hair suit she chose next would combine to convey a businesslike effect without sublimating her sex in the least. Quickly, she clasped on a strand of pearls, gold and maybe earrings, and a thin gold bangle.

Standing before a full-length mirror, Dixie began to smile. After drying her hair, she had automatically pulled it away from her face. Now she plucked out the combs and shook the mass free. Burnished curls cascaded around her face and shoulders in a riot of freedom. A new kind of happiness, an almost forgotten satisfaction, bubbled up inside her.

"To hell with you, Di Franco," she whispered, laughing at her reflection. "To hell with you!"

When she came down the stairs a few moments later, she was hard pressed not to laugh again. Her grandfather's jaw dropped. Slowly, the startled expression gave way to one of pleased amusement, and finally he grinned from ear to ear.

"Just getting to know your partner here," he said, indicating Herb. "Good man, if I'm any judge."

Dixie's mood faded somewhat. Trying not to let her sudden discomfort show, she walked toward the man who sat resting his weight on the arm of a large wing chair. Over the past six years she had carefully managed to keep her private life well separated from the job. After her divorce, before meeting Joe Kirk, the few dates she had were never with other officers. Whenever possible, she kept her work conversations on a strictly professional level. Now, seeing the curious, almost startled expression on Herb's face as he sat looking around the room reinforced her conviction that she had been correct in doing so.

"Ready?" she asked.

He nodded and stood, still looking around at the polished oak floors, richly designed oriental rugs, and an array of furniture obviously built to last for generations. She had almost managed to get him to the front door when Reversa came bustling in from the kitchen.

"Now, just you wait one minute, Little Miss Tu—"

"We've got to go, Reversa. We're in a hurry." Dixie cut her off in midsentence and threw her a look that might have killed a less hearty soul. If there was one thing she did not intend to have bandied about the police department it was her middle name; the first caused comment enough. With peripheral vision she saw Herb's brows raise in question.

"Well, ask me if I care one bit, girlie!" The housekeeper held out a large Thermos. "But I made this coffee and you're sure as blazes gonna take it!"

Dixie grabbed the bottle, mumbled a hasty good-bye, and literally bolted through the front door.

Neither she nor Herb spoke as he turned his car and headed down the perilous driveway. The silence remained thick and unbroken until they were off the summit and onto the freeway. They had almost reached the city limits when he looked at her and smiled.

"Pardon me, Sarge, but what a name! Why do you suppose parents would do a thing like that?"

Her frown deepened. "Really, Herb, I don't know that it's any of your—"

"*Reversa?*" His voice held a note of incredulity.

Dixie faced forward again, half sighing in relief. Against

her will, she almost started to smile. "Her father wanted a boy."

For a long moment Herb looked nonplussed, but then he began to laugh. "Don't tell me. Her father wanted a boy, but instead . . ." Dixie was laughing, too. They finished the sentence in unison: ". . . but instead he got the *reversa*."

The remainder of the ride into the city turned out to be more fun than either of them had anticipated.

CHAPTER 3

LOS PALAMOS WAS a misnomer. A small community unto itself, it was tucked into oak-covered foothills well beyond the sprawling squalor of the city's east side. Many of the residents were descended from old, established families. They lived insular lives upon golf greens and tennis courts, surrounded by the reassuring warmth and acceptance of Los Palamos Country Club. Homes ranged from large stone or adobe mansions to spacious ranch styles. The wealth in this district was not new. Not flashy. Not the slick, plastic rich so often associated with California in general and the silicone boom area in particular. The money here was *old*. Like the political influence. Old and subtle, but most definitely evident.

For all the rampant growth and swelling population around them, the Palamos residents still thought of themselves as sophisticated rurals. That glittering, cosmopolitan jewel in the Upper Bay was never referred to as *Frisco*. Not here. Here in Los Palamos, San Francisco was quite simply and irrevocably *The City*.

There were no lights on over the tall wrought-iron gates Dixie and Herb drove through. A high stone wall surrounded what at first appeared to be a private estate. A blue and white beat car was parked in front of the main house, and it wasn't until the two homicide detectives got out of the car and approached the door that they saw the sign. An unobtrusive brass, it read MYSTIQUE DE LA FEMME.

The reporting party, Bobby Todd, was dressed in a red-and-white-checked Esprit shirt unbuttoned almost to the waist, with a white tank top beneath. A wide Gucci chain glowed against his tanned throat. His white designer jeans were snug enough to show each curve and twist of his well-developed physique. Every few seconds he gnawed at the edge of a manicured fingernail.

"We were supposed to go to a party," he said. "I called about five and everything was fine. Fine." His expression was bewildered. "I still can't believe he's really dead. A heart attack, for God's sake—Charles just wasn't that old. It seems imposs—"

"We haven't established the exact cause of death yet, Mr. Todd," Herb corrected in a professional monotone. "We won't know for sure until someone from the coroner's office gets here. Maybe not then."

Herb held a neat clipboard and took notes. It was expected. Every now and then he even used them. But those notes were not nearly as reliable as the small tape recorder silently unwinding in his coat pocket. No sentence or nuance of this or any interview would be lost.

"Were you aware of any health problems Mr. Bouchard might have had?"

"None." Bobby Todd shook his head and his glossy mane of blond hair shimmered in the light.

"To your best knowledge was he on any sort of drugs or medication?"

"Oh, Lord, no! The man was an absolute health nut! A real pest about it, too."

The questions were routine and Dixie listened with only half an ear as she moved quietly around the reception area. The other half of her attention was tuned to the muttered exclamations of her escort, the patrolman who had met them at the door.

"A friggin' beauty parlor! Can you believe it? My wife couldn't afford to breathe the air in this place, much less get her hair done." Officer Howard Smith was a tall, rangy man

with a prominent Adam's apple that danced up and down
above his uniform collar as he talked. "A friggin' beauty
parlor. Damn!''

Dixie nodded. The establishment they were in, however,
was far more than a beauty parlor. The chandelier and carpets
in the reception room alone had obviously cost a fortune.
There was no trace of eye-irritating solutions in the air. Upon
entering, rather, one was immediately assailed by the fra-
grance of hothouse flowers. Bouquets were dotted around the
room—on the petite cherrywood reception desk; beside the
Louis XIV chairs; next to the gilded mirror that dominated
one entire wall. Dixie spent a moment admiring the artful
subterfuge of that magic looking glass. Tipped at a slight
angle and softly lighted, surrounded by creamy peach-colored
walls, it could not but produce the most flattering possible
image.

She turned to Smith. "Is the pool outside?"

The officer shook his head. "No way. It's inside, in back.''
He pointed toward a set of double oak doors which stood
partially open.

Dixie looked through into the main salon. Space-age hair
dryers. A switch in decor to early Art Deco. More mirrors.
She took three steps in that direction only to be stopped as
Smith gently touched her upper arm. He cleared his throat.

"Excuse me, Miss . . . er . . . Sergeant Struthers.'' He
looked toward the foyer, where Herb was still questioning the
RP, and then back again. "I think maybe you better wait.''

It was a phenomenon she had grown accustomed to but still
found slightly aggravating. Her rank notwithstanding, it was
always assumed that her male partner or counterpart would
take the lead. She watched as the patrolman left her and
approached Herb Woodall. The two men stepped away from
Bobby Todd and spoke in low tones. Smith gestured toward
the salon doors, his Adam's apple bouncing excitedly.

She mentally shrugged and walked back to the reception
desk. There, a large appointment book lay open, and her eyes
quickly scanned the exposed page. It read like a *Who's Who*
from the society column. Her brows arched slightly as she
saw the day's last three entries. They were penned in small,
neat script: *4 p.m.—Holmstead. Enriquez. Hobden.* The names

were synonymous with power, politics, and money . . . with a capital *M*.

Patrolman Len Carey shivered. The pool area had been designed as one vast Roman atrium. The room was not cold, but it was damp. Lights reflected up from the depths of the Olympic-size swimming pool. Turquoise shadows danced off the walls. Large potted plants loomed around him, indirectly lighted from behind. It was just plain *creepy*.

No body floated in the pool. The only sound was the soft splashing of a small waterfall as it emptied into the spa. Carey refused to look in that direction. Perched on the edge of a chaise longue, he lit another cigarette and tried not to imagine that the cobalt eyes of a corpse were staring at him. Instead, for perhaps the fiftieth time, he determined to request a new car partner.

It was just like Howard to go off and leave him here. He wished the son of a bitch had at least been able to find a switch for the overhead lights before running off to meet the homicide team. More light would help a little—maybe.

Suddenly, his wish was granted. The room came to life as a bank of lights snapped on and poured down from a lip recessed just beneath a giant skylight. The metal door clanged loudly and Howard Smith came in, followed by a woman.

It took Patrolman Carey several seconds to recognize his former boss. He had never seen Sgt. Struthers dressed in anything but a midnight-blue uniform, an almost exact duplicate of his own—minus the bumps, of course. But he didn't remember her being so feminine, and especially not so sexy. She nodded and he forced himself to quit gawking.

"Found the lights." Smith grinned.

Dixie let her eyes take in the mosaic walls, pool, and elaborate fixtures only briefly before coming to rest on the spa.

Carey swallowed hard. "Could've been an accidental overdose."

She walked the last yard or so and looked down. The two patrolmen shuffled their feet, and she fleetingly wondered if it was the sight of death that made them nervous or the condition of the corpse in her presence. The body was nude.

"The coroner or one of his guys should be here any minute," Patrolman Carey said. He had an almost irresistible urge to put himself between his former sergeant and the gruesome sight sprawled below them. But then he remembered. It all came back to him in a series of frozen frames. Sgt. Struthers getting into an ambulance with Pete Willis. The body in the Dunkin' D Donut Shop with its face blown away. This was bad all right, but not that bad. Not nearly.

Unwillingly, Carey let his gaze range downward. He shivered again. There was something so fucking vulnerable about a naked man, dead or alive. Dead was worse.

Surrounded by the opulence of Mystique de la Femme, the corpse seemed more macabre than it might have otherwise. Flecks of vomit clung to the gaping mouth. Trails of mucus shone from beneath the nostrils. Death had ultimately robbed the body of its former rich, even tan. Without the suffusion of living, coursing blood the flesh looked sallow, the face yellow and pasty. Most of the body was submerged. It floated gently in the 110-degree heat. The dead man's head was tilted back, propped against a slab of simulated lava rock. The warm waterfall lapped gently down over his right shoulder. But it was his hair that caught and held Dixie's attention. Hair that had been wet but was now dry, spiked on end. Very dark and dull.

She knelt at the edge of the spa and leaned forward to get a better look. She saw it clearly then. A berry-colored stain ran around the edge of the hairline. The top of each ear was darkly mottled.

"Dye." She said the word softly.

Patrolman Howard Smith snorted disgustedly and swore. "Figures!"

Dixie didn't think it figured at all. Not a single gray strand showed on the thickly furred chest. The victim's genitals were floating just above the surface of the water, and the pubes surrounding them were also dark. Almost black.

Dixie looked again at the lifeless face of Charles Andre Bouchard, knowing all at once that he had been a man of great vanity.

Dixie and Herb stood watching as a homicide tech team

milled over the atrium. One detective was scraping a small penknife along the seam of a floor tile where drops of hair dye had been found. Another snapped photographs while a third knelt by the corpse, taking fingerprints. Two ambulance attendants stood nearby, talking quietly, both wearing expressions of boredom. Waiting.

Bouchard's body was out of the water now, zipped into a black rubberized body bag, all except for the hand being used for fingerprint identification. The tech rolled one digit and then another across an ink pad. The head coroner was also there, standing close, cheerfully scribbling in a small notebook.

"That guy's a ghoul," Herb whispered. "Swear to God, look at him. Really enjoys his work."

It was a well-known fact that Dr. Jason Wittenhaur did indeed love nothing quite so much as the prospect of a challenging autopsy. Dixie still paled whenever she remembered the first one she had seen him perform. The tiny buzz saw used to open the skull of a slain robbery victim had haunted her sleep for weeks afterward. Each police academy class was required to view Wittenhaur's specialty as a part of the curriculum, and Dixie suspected that he relished shocking the recruits with as gruesome a spectable as possible. Rumor had it that at least one cadet in every class accommodated the good doctor's sense of humor by fainting dead away.

The pathologist finished writing, closed his notebook with a snap, and joined Dixie and Herb. His cherubic face was wreathed in a smile. More than a little plump, he stood only a few inches taller than Dixie.

"You can get your search warrant," he said. "This is no accidental. The whole deal smells to high heaven." He looked delighted.

"Then it wasn't a heart attack?" Herb never could manage to look directly into Wittenhaur's twinkling blue eyes.

"Might be, but I seriously doubt it. Too much drainage." The pathologist's smile widened as Herb cringed. "Same for an overdose."

"There were no wounds," Dixie said, remembering the body as it was being pulled from the water. "No obvious lumps or bruises, either. What's your guess?"

Dr. Wittenhaur sobered and pulled himself up to his full

diminutive height. "I never *guess*, young woman. But once you obtain a warrant I would be very interested in getting a sample of that hair dye."

He looked back at the body, which was now being lifted onto a gurney. "I think it highly unlikely that a man giving himself a full-body color treatment would decide to take a dip."

"Holy shit!" The exclamation came from Herb.

"Oh, my, yes. It's not that unusual, you know. I see it often enough. Everyone wants to cheat Old Man Time." Wittenhaur was beaming again. He rubbed his own hairless crown. "Doesn't work, of course. They all come to me in the end."

"When will the autopsy be scheduled?" Dixie asked, trying to keep him on the subject. She had noticed the beads of perspiration standing out on Herb's forehead.

"First thing Monday morning." Wittenhaur looked at his watch and then around at the elaborate facilities of Mystique de la Femme. "I'm half tempted to wake my wife and tell her about this business when I get home. She's been pestering me for two years to let her come here and get herself done up. And, I must admit, it really is quite something. Had himself a going little concern, didn't he? Oh, my, yes!"

The coroner walked away shaking his head, still half smiling, and Herb visibly relaxed. "Do me a favor, will ya, Struthers? If I ever get myself snuffed, don't let that canoe maker anywhere near me!"

Now came the frustration of waiting. Herb had put in a call to the on-duty district attorney, who in turn would call a drowsy-eyed stenographer. Eventually, a judge would be jarred awake and cajoled into giving a signature for the warrant. It would be nearly daylight before a legal search of the premises could begin. Patrolmen Len Carey and Howard Smith had been instructed to cordon off the house before going off duty. The RP, Bobby Todd, had been allowed to leave. One of the techs had gone for doughnuts and now they all sat in the reception area drinking Reversa's coffee and dropping crumbs onto the plush carpet. Only Herb remained standing, gazing out a window.

Dixie watched him and wondered, not for the first time, if he would prove to be a friend or simply a watchdog. Di Franco's watchdog. Considering how things had been going lately, the odds seemed better than even that this case, her first real one, would be snatched right out of her hands.

Headlight beams hit the front windows. For a moment, Dixie thought she saw Herb smile, but when he turned toward her his expression was serious. He sounded annoyed. "We have company. Looks like reporters. Nosy bastards seem to get wind of everything."

"What do you expect when someone gets bumped off in Los Palamos?" one of the techs muttered, wiping crumbs from his lap and standing up. "Did you get a load of that appointment book? Now we are really talkin' some bucks!"

But Dixie was concentrating on Herb. He had been the only one near a telephone since their arrival. She stood and came up beside him. Looking through the window, she saw two men opening the rear door of a van. One began mounting a video camera on his shoulder.

"Guess you'll have to talk to them." Herb most certainly was smiling now. He turned and their eyes met. "Go get 'em, Sarge. It's your ball game now."

CHAPTER 4

ANTHONY DI FRANCO sat hunched behind the clutter of his desk. Red-rimmed eyes and the dark shadow on his lantern jaw gave evidence of a night without sleep. Just outside the glass cubicle that served as his office, Jake Spatlin moved around on tiptoe, grateful for the mud-colored carpet that cushioned and all but obliterated the sound of his footfalls. He held little hope that his unit commander would remain immobile for much longer. Any minute now, Di Franco was going to explode like a volcano. And Jake knew only too well who was going to get spewed all over.

Shit! Jake cursed himself. If only he had stayed home last night! Then it would have been him and not that Struthers broad who was sitting pretty up there in Los Palamos, posing for the TV cameras and lapping up the publicity. The Bouchard case was going to bring a lot of publicity. Handled right, it could be great for a career.

Silently, Jake swore again. This settled it. That damn Lucinda was taking up too much of his time. Too much effort. No female was worth this kind of trouble.

Sergeant Jake Spatlin had spent every night of the past two weeks trying to score with the head nurse in the emergency room at Valley Medical Center. Expensive dinners. First-run movies. Even flowers and a live stage play, for chrissake!

Nope, he decided, no uppity-assed little broad was worth

what Di Franco was getting ready to dump on him. Not even Lucinda. Lush Lucinda. Round. Gorgeous. Smooth skinned. *Almost* white.

Not that Jake really gave a rip about white girls, or so he kept telling himself. He'd had a few, and more often than not they proved a disappointment. But Lucinda offered the best of both worlds. Skin that glowed a deep ivory. Full, well-defined lips. And eyes . . . Lord, those eyes! They promised primitive nights filled with the excitement of drumbeats!

"Well, well, well. Who *have* we here? I believe my eyes behold none other than Sergeant Spatlin. And I *do* believe yo' ass is grass."

The voice was gratingly familiar. Jake spun around to glare at Dody Bangor, the secretary who had served the homicide unit for the past three years. Her lips pulled back from her teeth and stretched into a wide, decidedly nasty grin. "If'n I was you, *boy*, I'd run fer da hills."

He wanted to slap her right through the bay window that dressed one entire side of the Police Administration Building. Instead, he straightened his spine and forced his face into an expression of hauteur he was far from feeling at the moment. "Go play with yourself, Ms. Bangor—if you can stand the company."

Dody exhibited her high regard for good office decorum by flipping up the slender middle finger of her right hand. It was a sign that could not be seen from the lieutenant's office.

Jake ground his teeth. Everyone seemed to think Dody was a dream. She typed ninety words per minute; was a veritable whiz on the computer. She could mentally file, and then recall at will, suspect descriptions and MOs she might only have thumbed through several months before. Invaluable. That was good ol' Dody. Invaluable to everyone but Jake. On the rare occasions when the two of them were alone together, the curvaceous, Alabama-born blond made no secret of her loathing. She missed no opportunity to let Jake know that to her he was and would forever remain just another uppity California nigger.

Screw her, he thought. She was just a secretary. A nobody. He watched her stroll casually into Di Franco's office. She left the door standing open and he could hear her sultry voice switch gears, soften to only a slight Southern slur. "Good morning, sir. Is there anything you need before I get started? Coffee, maybe?"

Jake knew what she was up to. She just had to stir the shit pot. It wasn't enough that Di Franco sat there like a stone, wearing an expression appropriate to a ritual black mass. No siree, that wasn't exciting enough for Dody. She had to push and prod, poke at the lieutenant like at a sleeping crocodile in hope that he would come to life and rip someone limb from limb. And since Jake was the only one in the office, Dody knew exactly who that someone would be.

The tactic proved successful. Di Franco straightened in his chair. His eyes scanned the outer office until they came to rest on his on-call detective, the very same man who should have been available to take the Bouchard case. Dody looked coyly over her shoulder, smiling sweetly. And then it came. A bone-rattling, glass-shattering bellow.

"Spatlin!"

Jake tried to fix a pleasant grin on his face. If there was one thing he knew for sure, it was that he owned an award-winning, knock 'em dead smile. But this time it didn't work. This time his facial muscles refused to cooperate. The flash of white teeth in his ebony face appeared more a grimace than anything remotely resembling a smile. Sweat trickled down the back of his neck, dampening the collar of his salmon-colored dress shirt. He walked toward the lieutenant's office with the timed steps of a man entering the gas chamber. He was just through the door, doing his level best to ignore the gleeful, carnivorous gleam in Dody's blue eyes, when his reprieve came.

There could have been no two people on earth Jake was more
delighted to see at that exact moment than Herb Woodall and Sergeant Dixie T. Struthers.

Tony Di Franco came to his feet with an agility that belied his hulking two-hundred-and-three-pound frame. A sweeping wave of his arm sent Dody and Jake tumbling back into the squad room like a pair of bowling pins.

He had not missed the relief on Jake Spatlin's face, and at any other time he might have been secretly amused at the impact of his own authority. But at the moment it would have taken a great deal more than seeing Jake turn a dull shade of gray to provide amusement.

After meeting Herb's eyes with a fleeting but withering glare, Tony fixed his full attention on the petite figure of Dixie Struthers. The headache he had been suffering for hours became more intense. His teeth clamped together and ground slowly back and forth. The pit of his belly felt like it held a puddle of battery acid.

Why him? he wondered. Of all the divisions in the dick bureau where they might have dumped Struthers, why had they picked his?

The burning in his gut worsened. Bob Fox was responsible for this. Tony knew it for sure. *Fox.* That posturing, self-important asshole who now held the post of Chief of Detectives had harbored a grudge for years. And this was just like him. What a low-down, fucking way to get even!

Lieutenant Anthony Di Franco went to the door.

If there was one thing more feared by the homicide team than the roaring bellow of their unit supervisor, it was his soft-spoken command. When Di Franco's gravelly voice dropped to little more than a hoarse whisper, punctuated with uncharacteristic courtesy, it was a sure sign that the recipient thereof was in deep trouble. Herb needed no extrasensory perception to know that he was in very deep trouble indeed.

"Do you have just a moment, Inspector Woodall?" Di Franco spoke with almost no movement of lips, his tones rolling in honey. And though his question was directed at Herb, his eyes remained unblinkingly fixed on Dixie. "I know you and your partner are pretty wrapped up, but if you can spare a little time there are a few things you and I need to go over."

The squad room was silent. The figures of Jake, Dody, and Herb stood in frozen tableau. Only Dixie managed to maintain a facade of studied nonchalance. The lines of her face remained carefully smooth and unperturbed. Actually, she wanted to laugh. Sing. Lift her skirt and dance a jig! Instead, she took off her jacket and sat down at her desk, striking a pose so deceptively demure that Di Franco's eyes narrowed to slits.

The phone rang and everyone in the room jumped. Dody was on top of it in a split second. The secretary's eyes danced excitedly from Di Franco to Dixie and back again. Her expression read like an open book. *Hell's bells! This might be even better than watching Spatlin get his black ass chewed up one side and down the other!* "It's for you, Sergeant Struthers," she said aloud. "A reporter from the *Mercury News*."

Herb inwardly cringed at seeing the spatulate thumb his superior jerked over one shoulder, a silent command to follow. In all the years the two had known each other, Herb could never remember seeing the expression Tony now wore. This was not simply a token show of the famous Di Franco temper. Tony was more than just annoyed.

For a moment, Herb actually felt afraid. He liked working homicide. He had worked toward being in the unit for years. It was what he had always wanted. A picture of himself working a west-side beat through long, quiet midnights loomed in his mind. His stomach churned uneasily.

But then, following Tony into the command office, Herb squared his shoulders and inhaled deeply. He released the air from his lungs in a long steadying breath. Before snapping the door shut behind him, he caught a look from Dixie. She was talking into the phone, but the unspoken gratitude, the warm camaraderie that sparkled from the depths of her green eyes, made it all seem suddenly worthwhile. He smiled at her, braced himself, and turned.

"You shit-heel!" Tony was sitting now, the expanse of his desk and piles of reports separating them. For all the vehemence of his words, his tone was still dangerously low, nearly a monotone. "You're a traitor, Herb. A friggin', back-stabbing traitor. That's the only word I can think of at the moment. But you can bet there are more."

Herb sat without invitation and rested one ankle across the opposite knee. Damned if he was going to give those vultures out in the squad room any idea of just how uncomfortable he felt.

"What did you expect me to do, Tony?" he asked. "Struthers is the ranking officer. You know that, even if you don't like it. Anytime an incident goes down in Los Palamos it makes the news. You know that, too. Besides, she photographs a hell of a lot better than me. Prettier.''

It never hurt to inject a little humor into a bad situation, he thought, but then, looking at Di Franco, decided maybe it did.

Tony's face was turning a florid red. He had been tilted back in his chair, but now he sprang forward. His body lurched halfway across the desk. "Don't give me that crap. Someone *called* the media, and it wasn't Struthers!" His voice was rising, gearing up to be heard throughout half the detective bureau. "I have a connection or two, Herb, or have you forgotten? I know who made that call to the television station." His face darkened to purple. "You're damn right I know the somebody who made that call. And that somebody is gonna pay dearly! You hear me! *Pay!* Come time for shift change, that shit of a somebody is going to find his traitorous ass behind the wheel of a shiny black and white!"

For a minute, Herb thought Tony was actually going to come completely across the clutter of paperwork and fasten a pair of ham-size fists around his throat. Instead, the lieutenant flopped back. His face and posture went suddenly weary. The air seemed to leave his body all at once. His arms dropped limply to his sides. "Yeah, I know who called in the cameras, the publicity. But what I still can't figure out is why; why did you do it, Herb? Why?"

Herb hated the guilty feeling that came over him. Partly because he didn't think he should feel guilty, but more because he knew that with Di Franco there was no way of knowing whether or not the injured tone was real or feigned.

"Look, Tony,"—he kept his voice steady—"this is going to be one hell of a case. I feel it in my bones. You gave it to Struthers yourself. Remember? True, you figured it for a big zero, but you gave it to her all the same. Regardless of what you think, it was a smart move. The publicity will be good for the unit, and what's good for the unit is good for you. The media will eat it up. Female cops get a good break with the press. Remember when that gal who's working vice—"

"You're forgetting one thing, Herbie." Di Franco cut him off. "Struthers might muff it. We could get away with blowing a homicide investigation on the east side. Maybe. Nobody gives a rat's ass when some local beaner stabs one of his brothers. Not for long, anyhow. But we both know that anything going down in the Palamos district is a whole different story. Hell, the mayor lives up there. When a body gets itself bumped off in Los Palamos, people, important people, get nervous. They're going to want action, Herb. Not tomorrow or the next day, but yesterday. And it won't be your cute little partner they come after when things go sour.''

"Dixie will do okay." Up until that moment, Herb had harbored a few lingering doubts of his own, but suddenly he believed what he was saying. "She's got style, Tony. I get the impression that Los Palamos and the kind of people who live there are nothing new to her. She'll know how to deal with them better than either you or I could. At least give her a chance to prove she has what it takes. If she doesn't cut it, you can always pull her off the case."

Di Franco's lips drooped at the corners. "*Su-u-ure* I can. The papers would just love that, wouldn't they? You're full of it, Herb, full of it like a Christmas goose. You didn't just stab me in the back when you made that call. You jabbed it in right to the hilt and then twisted the blade. No matter how the Bouchard case goes, I lose. If that female out there blows it, I catch the heat. If she comes up smellin' like a damned petunia, it's worse, because then I'm stuck with her."

"That might not be as bad as—"

"Screw you, Herb!" Di Franco's hand came up and slammed across the desk, sending papers flying in all directions. The glass-paneled walls quivered. "Listen up real good, Herbie. The way I look at it you've about washed yourself up in this unit. Come shift change you're out the door—but to where I haven't decided yet. You stay on top of this and I just might put in a good word for you. Otherwise, *old friend*, you best buy yourself a king-size tube of Preparation H and a heavy jacket."

Di Franco calmed himself, and his voice once more went all silky soft. "From this minute on, Herb, you and the powder puff are going to be inseparable. Amos and Andy. Mutt 'n' Jeff. Bonnie and Clyde. Got it? If she so much as sneezes, you're going to let me know exactly how many germs are dumped into her little lace hanky. What you know, *I* know. Got the picture?''

Herb felt sick. Di Franco went on, mapping out what he expected to be done on the Bouchard case. But Herb's attention wandered. He kept visualizing how Janice would look when he told her—*if* he told her. She had hated it when he worked midnights on patrol. Though she had never made a fuss, he knew she worried and waited and slept poorly until he was in bed beside her, safe and sound. The worry would be intensified now that he had to drive back and forth over the twisting roads just to get home. After an all-night shift, he would be dog tired.

If Janice had one failing as a cop's wife it was that she had a tendency to conjure up visions of terror. She saw bad guys lurking on every darkened city street after eleven o'clock at night.

Danger. It wasn't something Herb thought about often. He could deal with danger, and even fear. During his career he had met plenty of situations which left him with a mouth like cotton and a pressing need to relieve himself. No, the risk was not what turned his insides sour. It was fear of boredom. If he was sent back to patrol, Di Franco would make damn sure he did not get assigned to an east-side beat, one where a patrolman could count on a certain number of heavy calls. No such luck.

Herb expelled a deep sigh. He would deal with his dilemma later. His entire career had been aimed toward becoming a detective, an investigator first, and someday, perhaps, a part of command. But for now there was only the Bouchard case.

Out in the squad room, he could see Dixie sitting at her desk, absorbed in the report she was writing. She didn't even look tired. Her face was intent. Rays of sunshine slanted through the window, turning her hair a bright, shimmering copper.

Funny. Half listening to the persistent, emphatic drone of Di Franco's voice, Herb suddenly couldn't decide which troubled him more, the fact that his own career seemed to be crumbling down around his ankles or Dixie's new trust in him. He had seen it in her eyes the night before, as they went about searching the crime scene. Trust. Respect. The beginning of a friendship that promised to be a cut above the ordinary.

Dixie wasn't easy to get to know. She always seemed to keep a part of herself hidden. And for some reason that Herb did not stop to analyze, he realized he wanted the friendship her eyes had promised. There was something decidedly special about Sergeant D. T. Struthers. She brought out instincts, feelings, in Herb of which he had remained unaware until only a few hours before.

It wasn't just sex, either. Not that, after giving the idea a full thirty seconds of hard consideration, he would mind. But he knew, too, that his feelings for her were more complex. For the first time in his life he really wanted to be friends with a woman. *Friends!* The idea startled him slightly. He had always thought of himself as a man's man—the kind of guy who needed and wanted a pleasant, attractive woman as a wife, a mother for his children, as a helpmate and lover, but . . .

Di Franco's last comment broke through Herb's thoughts and brought him back to earth with a thump. The lieutenant's voice was more reasonable now.

". . . for the sake of friendship," he was saying. "After all, we go back a long way. And maybe, just maybe, if you can close this case yourself, there's a chance for you to stay right where you are. You solve this one, Herb. Not with her, but in spite of her, if you get my drift. And make sure it looks that way. I don't want her going off on her own. Remember that. From now on your name is *The Shadow*. Do we understand each other?"

Herb nodded. The sour feeling was back in his stomach. He felt like he might throw up.

Yes, he thought, Dixie trusted him now. And that was just too damn, stinking bad . . .

CHAPTER 5

THE CAR WINDOW was down and the cool air, alive with a heady aroma of madrone and pine, assailed Dixie's senses. She rested her head against the back of the seat and closed her eyes. She was glad that Herb drove, for exhaustion was finally beginning to set in. But though she was physically lagging, her brain remained busy. Her thoughts leaped from scene to scene like a ping-pong ball. Once again she saw Mystique de la Femme. The corpse of Charles Bouchard. The reporters with their banks of lights, microphones, and cameras. And, last of all, she remembered Di Franco and his spine-shriveling fury, all of which he had directed at Herb.

Methodically, she began to sort and categorize both her thoughts and the series of vivid images flashing through her brain. She concentrated for a few moments on each and then filed every thought neatly away for consideration at a later time. This mental process came so automatically that it never occurred to her how unusual it might be. Such organized psychological data sifting had been an integral part of her character for longer than she could remember. During her school years, high school and college, she had honed her natural tendency to "prioritize" to a fine art.

The Bouchard case she temporarily put aside, knowing that she could take no immediate action. In order to effectively plan the investigation, examine the bits and pieces she had

thus far gleaned, she needed to be alert and wide awake,
definitely not her condition at present. Di Franco, however,
was a different matter. Her closed eyelids fluttered in annoyance just thinking about him. The man was a total ass, that
was all there was to it; a braying, chauvinistic, nasty-tempered
ass. And of all the things she did not like about her superior,
his slithering, roundabout approach topped the list.

Why didn't he come right out with it, she wondered. If he
had a problem with her being under his command, why didn't
he just say so? To her directly. Face to face. Knowing that
sooner or later she was going to have to brave the bull in his
pen, she wished Di Franco would just say what he wanted to
say, come right out front—for both their sakes. The under-
cover pirouette they had been doing since the first day she
arrived in the homicide division was driving her nuts.

A weary sigh escaped Dixie's lips. She felt Herb's glance
touch her and then turn back to the road again. Now, Herb
was worth a little in-depth thought, she decided. Nothing
could have surprised her more than the support he had so
poignantly displayed at the crime scene. Until then she had
just about pegged her companion as being Di Franco's hand-
selected hatchet man. A spy and watchdog. Obviously, she
had misjudged him, but his present silence was unsettling.

Opening her eyes, she shifted slightly to one side and
looked at him. He was, she thought, a handsome man. He had
a full head of thick, sandy-colored hair and a sincere, Huckle-
berry Finn sort of good looks which appealed to her. She
liked his laid-back manners and the mischievous twinkle she
sometimes observed in his changeable blue eyes. Herb Woodall,
she decided, would be a valuable ally . . . *if* he ever made
up his mind to become her friend.

Not for the first time, she wondered what kind of relationship Herb shared with Di Franco. Someone had mentioned
that they were once car partners, a fact which could mean
everything or nothing at all. Riding in a patrol car together,
depending on one another, could draw two cops together for a
lifetime, or make them mortal enemies. Watching Herb and
Anthony Di Franco in the squad room, Dixie saw evidence of
neither hatred nor intimacy, but then she knew she probably

wouldn't. Cops were notoriously tight-lipped about their personal lives and relationships.

Dixie looked at Herb again. *Tight-lipped.* That certainly painted an accurate portrait of him at the moment. He had not spoken more than a dozen words since skulking out of Lieutenant Di Franco's office, and Dixie felt a twinge of guilt. Di Franco had dumped all over Herb. She had not been able to decipher the verbal specifics of their discussion, but Di Franco's intermittent roars and apoplectic complexion had given credence to a very foul humor. Had Dixie thought for an instant that intervention on her part might lessen Herb's predicament, she would have walked right in on their conversation. But it would not have made the least difference, she knew. If anything, interference from her would have escalated the situation and increased tension in the already overcharged squad room.

Poor Herb. His boyish grin was nowhere in evidence at the moment. A scowl creased his forehead and his mouth was pulled down at the corners. He looked positively grim.

When they arrived at Dixie's house, he did not turn off the car motor. Nor did he smile as Poke came streaking down the driveway, jumping and twisting like a cowlicked clown. Herb's features remained set in stone. Most disturbing to Dixie was the studious way he had avoided looking at her ever since leaving Di Franco's office.

"Herb." She spoke his name almost shyly.

"Yeah." He kept his eyes forward.

"I'm sorry about Di Franco. I know it must have been on my account that . . . well, I know you went out on a limb for me. I want to thank—"

"No big deal." He cut her off. Reaching across, he opened her side of the car.

Dixie put down a feeling of annoyance at his coolness. She touched his arm and felt the muscles beneath her hand tense. "Damn it, Herb, look at me!"

Their eyes met, his a dark smoky gray, hers wide and inquiring.

"It's a very big deal to me," she said. "The Bouchard case is going to be a hot one, Herb, and until it's solved we'll be living in each other's pockets. Just for the record, I want you to know that I'm glad you're my partner."

His lips turned up ever so slightly. Certainly not in a smile. Rather, it was a wry twisting of his mouth that had no effect whatsoever on the rest of his face. "Amos and Andy, that's us."

He began revving the motor and shifted gears, obviously impatient to be gone. "Get some rest, Sarge. See you bright and early Monday."

She got out and stood watching as his car disappeared into the shadow of redwoods. Absentmindedly patting Poke on the head, she frowned.

Luckily, she was not able to hear the mutterings of her partner as he pulled back onto the main highway. Herb Woodall alternately cursed himself and Di Franco all the way home.

The remainder of the weekend sped by. The weather was pleasantly mild, and on Sunday Dixie worked beside her grandfather in the garden. She related the details of the Bouchard case to him one at a time. Giving voice to her thoughts as she pulled weeds helped to clarify things in her own mind. Her grandfather was a good listener, the perfect sounding board, and he interrupted only to ask pertinent questions. When they had finished in the garden, they sat on the back porch drinking Reversa's aromatic coffee from thick ceramic mugs. Meanwhile, Dixie jotted notes in a small spiral notebook, a list of things she would begin doing the next day. *Check crime lab report. Attend autopsy. Background checks on Mystique de la Femme patrons. Interviews with salon employees* . . .

Her perfectly arched brows lowered into a scowl of concentration. Finally, not quite satisfied, she handed her notebook to Patrick. After perching a pair of wire-rimmed glasses on the end of his nose, he gave the list his full attention.

"Seems like a fair start." He nodded, handing it back. "But I have a gut feeling about this case, Dix. It's potentially a very dirty business."

"Why, because of the overtones?" Her question was far

from idle. Above any other person she knew, Dixie respected Patrick's opinion. "Because the RP might be gay?"

"*Gay*." Patrick, in many ways a very old-fashioned man, scowled. "Never have been able to understand that word. Makes me wonder about folks nowadays. Gay used to mean *happy*." He shrugged and then continued. "Well, whatever you call it, even in my day there were homosexuals in San Francisco. Not like now, maybe, not large communities, but small ones certainly. And, naturally, there were murders in those communities every now and again. Crimes of passion, I guess you'd have to call them. Stabbings. Shootings. Almost always gruesome. I wouldn't be a bit surprised to find out that's what you have here at this Mystique. A crime of passion. If I was you, I'd check out your RP, Bobby Todd, real careful like. That little twit might well be your culprit."

Dixie tried not to smile. Effeminate Bobby Todd might be, but he was a far cry from being a "little twit." The well-developed physique she had observed while Herb was interviewing Todd gave evidence that he probably worked out many hours each week, very likely right on the premises of the salon.

After obtaining a search warrant, Dixie and Herb had gone over Mystique de la Femme with minute care. The tech crew had accompanied them every step of the way. The entire building had been only slightly less breathtaking than the main floor. The San Francisco salons frequented by Dixie's own mother were elaborate and complete, offering every imaginable service, from facials to hairstyling, pedicures to manicures. But even those did not compare with the plush establishment in Los Palamos.

Their search had begun on the third floor, in Bouchard's private apartment. It was not lavish, not overdone, and certainly not gaudy. Contemporary furniture, upholstered, simple to the point of being spartan, sat surrounded by mocha-colored walls. Carved moldings formed baseboards and trim. Beautiful paintings graced the walls, portraits mostly, many of children, and one of a male nude. The remaining decor was provided by leafy plants, glass tables, and artful lighting.

Only the bedroom stood out in garish relief. Dixie had gasped as she opened the large double doors, for the entire room seemed not in keeping with the personality of the rest of the apartment. Plush beyond imagination, it was an *embarras de richesses* that might well have jumped straight from the pages of a Harold Robbins sex fantasy. The floor was laid with a carpet of blood red, and the mirrored ceiling caught the vivid hue, bouncing it back with claustrophobic brilliance. Upon entering, Herb groaned and rubbed his stomach. One of the techs burped, bowed from the waist, and swept out his arm. "Welcome to hell, folks!"

The description seemed apt enough, for the room was dominated by a gigantic four-poster water bed, all draped in shiny black satin. Each of the bedposts was set with a wide brass ring.

Herb whistled and then snapped his fingers. "I've got it! The crime is solved. The interior designer done it; walked in here, saw the room, and killed Bouchard on the spot. I say it's a case of justifiable homicide."

But beyond some rather bizarre manifestations of Bouchard's outlandish sexual preferences, the bedroom held little if anything in the way of evidence. The closets were neatly hung with both masculine and feminine attire in a range of interesting sizes. These were matched and complemented by the frothy lingerie in bureau drawers. Other cabinets were stacked with everything from rainbow-colored ostrich plumes and clove-scented massage creams to a veritable stockpile of vibrators, complete with imaginative appendages.

At one point, Dixie opened the cover of a black lacquered Japanese photo album only to snap it quickly shut again upon viewing the contents. If was full of painted pictures and postcards rather than photographs. She was just barely able to fight off a blush, and it was with a tremendous sense of relief that she finally preceded the men in a search of the lower floors.

Short of formal plastic surgery, it was hard to imagine what a woman might need to bolster her beauty and self-image that Mystique de la Femme did not provide in abundance. A dry sauna, fully equipped gym, dance studio, and massage room dominated the second story. There were also two small day rooms where a patroness might catnap before continuing her regimen. Quite simply, the Los Palamos client could walk through the discreet but impressive doors of Mystique de la Femme and spend an entire day toning and primping whatever lavishments she might have to work with. There was even a small health and salad bar conveniently located on the first level.

But beyond the wonderful luxury and fixtures, the entire place was pristine clean. Not a drawer undone or a stick of furniture out of place. Only the supply room, just off the main salon, contained anything in the least suspicious. That one small room, no more than a shelf-lined cubicle, however, caught and held Dixie's complete fascination. Sitting on the narrow Formica counter were three partially empty bottles of hair color, a plastic container of creme developer, and a large, nearly depleted application bottle. The gleaming porcelain sink contained two surgical gloves, both with the fingers stained with dark purple, almost black splotches.

Holding the bottles precariously at top and bottom, one of the techs had balanced them next to a thick piece of slotted cardboard. Another tech wired them securely in place to prevent breakage or spilling. The secured bottles were then set upright in a small box for transportation to the crime laboratory. The gloves were picked up with forceps and dropped into individual evidence bags.

Now, sitting peacefully on the porch with Patrick, Dixie still had the same suspicions about those bottles. The same excitement still gripped her about the pending investigation. In her mind, she was sure the black dye found on the victim had caused his death. But the *who*, the challenge of discovering who and why, hung before her, gleaming like a forbidden fruit.

"Yep," Patrick said, holding the small of his back as he came to his feet. He stretched and yawned. "I'll give you two quarters to a dime that what you have here is one of those crimes of passion. Messy maybe, but easy."

Dixie also stood but slowly shook her head. "This time I'm going to have to disagree, Pop. A crime of passion, as you call it, would have been much more messy. A stabbing. Shooting. Strangulation. Bludgeoning. An enraged murder. This was premeditated. The man or woman who killed Bouchard *planned*, with all the creativity of a Borgia."

. They entered the kitchen together, pausing at the sink to wash and dry their hands. And while they cleaned up they continued to discuss the different aspects of the case. When they took their respective places at the large round oak table in the kitchen, Reversa loomed over them. She plunked down a soup tureen.

"I swear, Poke is better company than the pair of you. A regular couple of ghouls! How in blue blazes is a body to eat with all the talk going on around here? Blood 'n' guts. Stabbin'. Shootin'. I swear! From mornin' 'til night!''

"It's all part of the job,'' Patrick argued, but was unable to finish before she interrupted him with a derisive snort.

"Job! What job? The only job I can see *you* got around here is pokin' your nose into my business. And as for the missy, why, she's got no business being in her business.''

Sitting her ample behind on a chair, Reversa began ladling thick, creamy soup into their bowls, well peppered with large bits of clams and flavored with leeks and butter. She disgustedly shook her head one last time. "Poison, my foot!''

CHAPTER 6

O-O-diethyl-O-p-nytrophenyl-phosphorothiate.

It had the ring of science fiction. A rocket fuel for Flash Gordon's bullet-shape spaceship. But there was nothing fictitious about the substance. The pale yellow liquid that had been found laced into the murder victim's Sable Sunset hair color formula was very real and highly toxic. A pesticide. Not a garden variety snail zapper, and frightening when you realized that it was a substance commonly used on crops.

Looking at the preliminary crime lab report, Dixie felt a moment of grim satisfaction. She had been right about the mode of death. Poison. Slow. Hideous. Bouchard had suffered terribly as the pesticide seeped into the pores of his skin and scalp, attacking his central nervous system. And had it not been for the telltale stains around his forehead, the damp, vividly hirsute chest, it might well have been assumed that he died of a heart attack. Even in retrospect the symptoms were not unlike those of a mass coronary. Vomiting. Defecation. The spasmodic convulsions and rasping breaths might also have been induced by a drug overdose.

Dixie wondered if the murderer had stood watching Bouchard's agony, his final death throes.

A shadow fell across her desk and she looked up to see Herb leaning over her shoulder. His eyes were scanning the report. He finished and then shuddered.

"I have a friend who does crop dusting," he said, "a real daredevil type. I used to think it would be a gas. You know, swooping down over the fields in one of those old Stearman biplanes. Snoopy and the Red Baron. But according to this report pilots have been killed while working with this zero, zero, diet . . . diethy . . . oh, shit, this *stuff*."

"Zero, zero, diethyl, zero, p, nytrophenyl phosphorothiate." The cumbersome formula rolled smoothly out of Dixie's mouth. "More commonly known as E 605." She gave Herb a dead-pan expression and then wrinkled her nose and stuck out her tongue. "Get your own report, Woodall. It makes me nervous to have anyone hang over my shoulder."

He moved back but not before taking a deep whiff of her perfume. She looked and smelled fantastic, he thought, wondering why the whole room wasn't staring at her. And then, almost immediately, he wondered why *he* was. Maybe he was losing it, letting the silly argument with Janice get to him. Or maybe he was going through an early midlife crisis. He mentally shook his head and looked around the squad room. All was normal.

Jake was on the phone, talking to his partner. "This is the third time you've had the flu this month, Davis. Yeah, yeah, Mike, I know ya got four kids who all go to school and bring home a ton of germs, but . . . listen, Davis . . . yeah, but listen . . . well, for chrissake, then put the brats in quarantine, 'cause I've had it with carrying your share of the fuckin' load!" He slammed down the receiver.

The two senior investigators, Pat Delaney and Bill Brooks, were absorbed in the task of sorting through mug shots, trying to find a picture that matched the description of their stabbing suspect.

Two murders in less than four days. The week was off to a rip-roaring start. Everyone was busy and a bit cranky, suffering a case of the Monday morning grumps. All the same Herb wondered if they were blind. To him it seemed that his partner had undergone a rather drastic metamorphosis, and he knew it wasn't just his imagination. The outfit Dixie wore was a departure for her, and in fact from the attire of any female cop Herb had ever seen. When not working in patrol, the female officers most often wore suits or tailored separates that severely played down the least hint of frivolity. Until now it had always been the clerks and secretaries who caught his attention. Dody Bangor wore everything from jumpsuits and low-cut dresses to supersnug designer jeans. Just watching her bend over a file drawer was to have an electrifying experience, the aftermath of which often lasted for hours.

But Dixie?

Again Herb shook his head, as if to clear away a fog. He had always thought of Dixie as pleasant-looking. He knew she was intelligent. *Chic* even, with a really nice figure. But before the Bouchard murder he simply never thought of her as . . . as . . . well, hell, the lady was a mind blower!

Her hair was down again. The mass of curls around her shoulders looked as soft as silk and slightly mussed. She was wearing a dress, not a neat shirtwaist but an honest-to-Pete *dress*. Emerald green. Like her eyes. It was what Janice would call a *wraparound*, with navy piping down the neckline and around the cuffs. When she leaned back in the chair and crossed her legs, as she was now doing, the lace of a navy blue slip was just barely visible.

Sweat broke out on Herb's forehead. He sat down at his own desk and forced himself to concentrate on the picture of Janice and Amy he kept under the plastic cover of his desk blotter. What was the matter with him anyway? Janice was great, his perfect mate. His daughter was the cutest kid in her class, in the world. So why did he keep playing peek-a-boo with the smooth lines of his partner's calves?

Herb looked down and stared hard at the photograph of his family. Very hard.

Another investigator came through the door. The men in the squad room looked up, nodded, and went back to their work. Larry Thorton worked down the hall, in Sexual Assault Investigations. He was a mooch and a clown. Clowns often become tiresome and Thorton had long ago worn out his stash of bad jokes. He was carrying a styrofoam cup. "Hey, you guys got any sugar . . ."

His voice trailed away as his eyes fastened, unblinking, on Dixie. "*Sh-u-u-u-gar!* I'll say you do!"

Herb's head snapped up, and without realizing it he narrowed his eyes.

Thorton headed for the coffee table, strolled actually, taking a long meandering route behind Dixie's chair. He craned his neck, taking in the gentle slope of her cleavage. Next, he passed Herb, ignoring, or perhaps not noticing, the scowl. Stooping low, he began singing in an exaggerated stage whisper. *"Oh, I wish I was in Dixie . . . Hoorah! . . . Hoorah! . . ."*

There were snickers from the other male detectives, but Dixie didn't move. Herb saw the flush creeping up her neck, the anger in her green eyes.

Thorton loved getting a laugh, and he was blatantly pleased with himself as he reached for a box of sugar cubes. He scooped several into his cup. "I'll bring these back later. Always nice to visit."

Still leering at Dixie, he did not see Herb stand up, nor pay much attention as he approached and filled his mug with steaming coffee.

"Saw your television debut, Sergeant Struthers." Thorton leaned against the table, obviously prepared to stay and chat. "You take a great picture, honey. Maybe you and I oughta . . . *Damn!*"

A howl erupted from the sex investigator's throat as hot coffee soaked through to his skin. Dropping the cup he was holding, he pulled the fabric of his shirt away from his body. Sugar cubes danced across the floor. "Why don't you watch what the hell you're doing, Woodall! Shit, that hurts!"

"Sorry, Larry." There was no trace of repentance on Herb's face as he put down his empty mug and picked up a handful of paper napkins. "Here, let me give you a hand. Guess I'm still half asleep." He dabbed ineffectually at the splattered shirt and paisley print tie.

"Never mind! Jesus! This shirt cost me thirty bucks. Now I'm gonna have to go home and change!" Thorton stomped out of the squad room, forgetting the sugar cubes altogether. His ranting could be heard long after he disappeared.

The squad room was dead quiet. Delaney looked at Brooks. Dody looked at Jake. And for the first time the latter two seemed to enjoy a moment of wordless communication. Their eyes telepathed an identical conclusion. *Uh-oh!*

A small sigh of regret fluttered from Dody's pouting lips as she turned back to her typewriter. Too bad, she thought. Herb was a real cutie—a hunk. She had hoped that someday, maybe soon, she would find a way to offer him a taste of some real Southern Comfort. But from the look of it, D. T. Struthers had the man all wrapped up. Hog-tied and ready for market!

Herb poured himself another cup of coffee and ambled back to his desk wearing a self-satisfied smirk. But he still refused to look at Dixie, directly at her, at least. Not once since arriving had he allowed his eyes to meet hers. And, watching him, Dixie decided that her partner was a very hard guy to figure. He had spilled the scalding contents of his cup all over Larry Thorton on purpose. She was sure it had not been an accident. Just as she was certain that Herb had made a quick phone call to the television station at the crime scene. And yet, she still had the distinct feeling that Herb didn't care for her much. It was almost as though he felt obligated to act chivalrously, and resented the need.

Suddenly, Dixie was annoyed. There was no time to worry about Herb right now. If having her as a partner proved a burden, he would just have to live with it for a while. She had not asked for his heroics—not at Mystique de le Femme and not this morning. His inflated sense of masculinity was his own problem.

Standing, she glanced at her watch. "Dr. Wittenhaur should be about ready," she said. "We probably ought to get over to the county morgue."

For one perverse moment she exulted in the green pallor of Herb's face, but her malice was short-lived. Viewing an autopsy was not exactly on the top of her favorite duty list either. She smiled and kept her voice casual. "Hey, don't sweat it. Why don't you go over and see what else they've turned up at the lab while I take in Wittenhaur's little act. No reason for us both to get sick."

Herb's brows lowered, forming two angry juts over his eyes. "Don't worry, Sarge, I won't faint. Scout's honor." His tone was sharp and cool, each word clipped. "I'm not in the habit of leaving my dirty work to a woman—even when she is my *superior*."

Dixie felt her jaw tighten. There it was again, his high-handed regard for her gender. His attitude was beginning to grate against her nerves. *Really* grate!

She straightened her skirt and adjusted her belt. The challenge her grandfather had proposed, she decided, was going to be even more difficult than she had anticipated. She wanted to take his advice, wanted to keep every thread of her femininity intact. But somehow she was sure that had her hair been pulled back in its traditional bun, had she been wearing a nice authoritarian blue suit, the morning would have gotten off to a far better start.

Watching her put on her raincoat, Herb felt much the same way. No female on earth should be that beautiful—and certainly not a female cop!

He followed her out of the building and, almost of their own accord, his eyes measured the tiny girth of her waist, registered the graceful sway of her hips. Herb cursed himself for a fool.

The stainless steel surgical table, with its trim of gutters and convenient drain apparatus, gleamed beneath the bright lights. The pale body stretched upon it was stark. Pathetically vulnerable. The thickly matted chest hair and inky pubes were vivid against white flesh. Charles Bouchard had looked inglorious indeed floating in the sweltering waters of his spa. But now, about to be probed inside and out, examined in grisly detail by the impersonal eyes of Dr. Wittenhaur, he was stripped of any personal dignity he might ever have possessed.

A county crime photographer moved quietly around the perimeter of the autopsy table. A strobe blinked as he snapped a series of preliminary pictures. The photographer chewed gum and wore a bored expression.

Dangling from the ceiling was a microphone that recorded the pathologist's voice as he began to tick off the vital statistics of a once living, breathing human being. "Charles Andre Bouchard . . . white male adult . . . five feet eleven inches . . . one hundred and seventy-eight pounds . . . approximately sixty years of age at time of demise . . ."

An incredibly quick flash of the scalpel pared the victim's

torso with a huge, bright and bloody Y. Herb barely made it to the restroom before throwing up.

A California driver's license showed the deceased to be forty-seven, a fact that had been completely ignored by Dr. Wittenhaur during the autopsy. The pathologist never took anyone's word for anything. And while Dixie and Herb also suspected that Bouchard was less than honest with the Department of Motor Vehicles, neither judged him to have been more than in his early fifties. In this particular instance, however, both the educated guess of the pathologist and the DMV had missed the mark. Charles Andre Bouchard, A.K.A. Charlie Phelps, had in actuality been murdered at the age of sixty-six, a fact confirmed by the computer readout from CII. More than that, the state investigative agency had traced a vivid and colorful past for the proprietor of Mystique de la Femme.

Born in Louisiana, the victim had a rap sheet which began in New Orleans when he was only eighteen and encompassed three states and multiple crimes. Extortion. Assault. Soliciting for a lewd act. Bigamy had been the last, a crime for which he was charged in Los Angeles County. Unbelievably, he had been convicted only once in his life. The first charge of extortion had gained him five years of hard time. In all other cases, he had been acquitted.

"Cut loose every damn time." Herb shook his head in disgust. "But it sure makes a person wonder how he came up with the dough to open a joint like Mystique de la Femme, doesn't it?"

"Makes me wonder about a whole lot of things," Dixie said. She put down a second rap sheet, one much less weighty, on Bobby Todd. "Todd's clean, though; just one arrest for *duce*."

A single drunk driving arrest hardly made the man a prime murder suspect, but then neither would a spotless record eliminate him.

Dixie tapped her lower lip with her pen. "Look, why don't we see if the guys in the Intelligence Unit have anything on Bouchard. You're right, it doesn't make sense that a man with his record could open a place like Mystique. We're obviously missing something. The money had to come from somewhere. Maybe he was *connected*.''

Herb's brows lifted. "Organized crime?"

She shrugged. "Who knows? He had to be connected to something or someone. That little parlor of his cost at least a million. And that's a conservative guesstimate. A man with Bouchard's background couldn't just lay his hands on that kind of money. He's backed by someone. There's the other thing, too; with all those arrests, why just one conviction?''

"Misunderstood?"

It was Herb's first feeble attempt at humor in hours, and Dixie smiled. "Oh, no doubt."

They both lapsed into silence again. The tension between them remained. In the wake of the autopsy, they had decided to forgo lunch. Still, after talking to Dr. Wittenhaur, stopping by the crime lab again, and getting the computer readouts on Bouchard and Todd, the regular work day was almost at an end. Outside, the sky had turned leaden. A head of dark clouds was billowing in from over the Santa Cruz Mountains, forerunners of a storm. Dody had taken off work early, and the other investigators were still out in the field. Di Franco had not shown himself all day—a minor windfall which was noted and appreciated by both Dixie and Herb. The office was quiet.

"Well, *Sarge*, where to next?"

Dixie's spine stiffened and she tossed her pen down on the desk. "Will you please stop it! In case you haven't noticed, I've got a name."

He wore a deceptively bland and innocent expression. "Sorry. Didn't know you were sensitive about your rank."

"I'm not," she snapped. "I've earned the title, but it's just a little formal for office use, don't you think? Unless maybe you'd like to be called *Investigator Woodall* . . . or maybe *Detective Woodall* . . . or, if you're so into titles, maybe— "

"Uncle!" Herb threw up his hands in mock surrender. His mind was going in two directions at once. He wanted to hold onto his irritation, but on the other hand, he liked the way her nose bobbed up and down when she got ticked off. She had freckles, too, just a few, but clearly visible under the light sheen of her makeup. He wanted to find something wrong with her but couldn't, no more than he could stay angry. "You win. Herb will do just fine . . . Dixie."

She felt her shoulders relax, and the smile she gave him was easy and genuine as she answered his initial question. "I think we should start by interviewing the women who had appointments with Bouchard the afternoon he was killed. Those were some pretty heavy-duty names. Todd's initial statement should be gone over again, too, as soon as possible." She looked at her watch. "We still have a couple of hours. Maybe you could go see Todd while I start up in Los Palamos. The Enriquez address is a matter of record. Think I'll begin by paying a call on our beloved city councilman."

Herb's mind was working furiously. That's all he needed, for Dixie to go off on her own. If Councilman Enriquez got into a snit and called Di Franco to complain, or worse yet called the chief, Herb knew his ass would play grass to Di Franco's lawnmower.

"Why don't we stick together, at least for today?" His voice sounded lame, even to him. "Two observations are always better than one, especially in a case like this. Mrs. Enriquez was probably just in getting her hair done for a campaign dinner. I remember hearing about one, and I'm pretty sure it was that night. Two C notes, if I remember correctly, to help Enriquez run for the state senate." He was afraid he was talking too fast and slowed down. "It won't take us long to interview Mrs. Enriquez. Then we can pay our respects to Mr. Todd. Whadda ya say?"

Dixie leaned back in her chair and crossed her legs. Making a temple of her fingers, she gave him a long, steady look. He was wearing a charming, lopsided grin. Or was it just sheepish?

"Whatever you say, Herb. You've been at this longer than I have."

Once more they donned coats and left the squad room, this time with Herb taking the lead. Dixie watched him, the easy walk, the tilt of his head, and wondered for the hundredth time where he was coming from, why she kept getting mixed signals from him. One minute he was like a cornered bear, and the next Sir Galahad in a business suit, and every now and again, just a plain nice guy, a good cop and a good partner. Much of her discomfort came from her obvious inability to size Herb up. Over the years, with most people, she had developed the skill to do so rather quickly, especially with men. The ability to concisely peg members of the opposite sex was not something she thought of on any real conscious level. Rather, it was just something she did, perhaps out of the age-old feminine instinct for self-preservation. Now, being unable to understand Herb made her uneasy, for she could only remember one other time in her life when a man's character had completely eluded her. Like Herb, her former husband had also been an enigma at first, a man with genuine charm, seemingly capable of great intellectual depth. And Donald Struthers had given her a merry, deceptive, very painful time of it.

As they reached the car, Herb turned and smiled at her again, the same lopsided, little-boy smile that she was growing to like and hate all at the same time.

"You drive," she said, tossing him the keys. She knew her voice had grown curt and cool once more.

The Enriquez residence was a sprawling ranch-style structure which sat less than three miles from Mystique de la Femme. Nestled against a hillside and surrounded by two-plus acres of manicured lawn, flower beds, and eucalyptus groves, its grounds also included a white-fenced corral and paddock, servants' quarters, and a four-car garage. A gnarled oak of gargantuan proportion grew up out of an inner courtyard, spreading its bristling arms protectively over the red tile roof. In keeping with the councilman's public image, the facade of the house was Spanish, plastered in simulated adobe. Intricate wrought-iron grillwork dressed the windows, each and every one wired to a sophisticated alarm system.

Albert Enriquez was a champion of the people—*some* people. Young for a politician, he was energetic, eloquent, and a *Californio* in every sense of the word. His boast that his Mexican forefathers had helped civilize the valley was true, at least in part. The Enriquez family had indeed been among the first families to settle in the huge Santa Clara basin; they had *not* been Mexican. However, to say that one was Spanish simply was not in vogue. For an up-and-coming political figure to admit that his ancestors were the exploiting conquerors of the *Indios* would have been tantamount to standing on a street corner in Tel Aviv and proclaiming Hitler close kin. In truth, there was but a smattering of Latino blood left in the Enriquez family line. But fortune had blessed Albert Enriquez with soft brown eyes and a thatch of wavy black hair. He helped nature along by keeping his skin darkly tanned and cultivating a dark mustache. When he addressed a cause, it was with all the impassioned charisma of Pancho Villa.

The first raindrops fell just as Herb turned the unmarked squad car into the long, winding driveway of the Enriquez estate. By the time he and Dixie got out of the car and to the front door, it was coming down hard. A dark, stately woman, obviously of true Mexican heritage, answered the door. Her glance flicked quickly over their dripping coats and shoes and then out at the unimpressive conveyance they had dared to arrive in. Her expression changed only subtly, but that change said all that was necessary, and more. No one of any great importance would arrive at the councilman's stoop in a buff-colored Dodge sedan. A slight lift of her finely arched brows indicated that her original conclusion was not altered after they identified themselves and asked to speak with the lady of the house.

"Mrs. Enriquez is busy at present." Her carefully modulated voice bore a faint accent. "There are to be guests tonight."

"Our business won't take more than a few minutes," Dixie answered. A cold wind was at her back and her teeth were beginning to chatter.

The woman hesitated a moment longer, then stepped back to allow them through the front door. She left them standing, dripping, on the mosaic tile of the foyer.

The motif of the house had been carried through beautifully. Arched doorways and large potted palms in multicolored handwoven baskets set off paintings of adobe huts and wide-eyed children. Bright Navajo rugs had been hung as tapestries. From somewhere deep within the house came the soft, musical splash of an indoor fountain.

Shaking the moisture from his coat, Herb looked around

and whistled. "It must be rough—don't know if I could take living like this."

Dixie smiled but made no comment. She knew he would not have understood if she told him there were more important things in life—much more important things—than opulent surroundings. Without knowing what her life had been, he would think her incredibly banal and clichéd. Still, she knew the cliché to be true. The home where she had been raised after her mother's remarriage to Franklin Marks far surpassed the one they were now in. Dixie had not been happy in the Marks mansion.

Muted voices sounded in another room and moments later the woman who had initially greeted them returned, followed by Albert Enriquez. He approached them immediately and extended his hand to Herb. "You'll have to forgive my secretary," he smiled. "Christina is a bit zealous in guarding our privacy."

The woman named Christina also smiled. Faintly.

"Actually, it's your wife we wish to see, Mr. Enriquez." Dixie held out her hand. "I'm Sergeant Struthers, and this is my partner, Investigator Woodall."

Councilman Enriquez had addressed his greeting to Herb, but now he turned toward Dixie. He clasped her hand warmly, lingering only slightly too long before releasing it again. "Ah, yes, I remember seeing you on the news. A shame about Mr. Bouchard. Am I to assume you are here because my wife occasionally visits his salon?"

"Yes, sir. We know that she had an appointment at Mystique de la Femme just an hour or so before Mr. Bouchard was killed. There are a few questions we'd like to ask. We hope she may be able to help us."

"I can understand, of course, and I'm sure she will be delighted to help in any way she can. But as Christina has told you, we are expecting guests soon. My wife is quite busy at the moment and I don't believe—"

"Al! Shame on you, darling!" Judith Enriquez entered the foyer wearing a lounging robe of royal blue silk. Her blonde hair had been pulled into a thick cluster of curls on top of her head and tied with a matching ribbon. The damp tendrils framing her face indicated that she had just emerged from shower or bath. "Don't leave these nice officers standing. I'll talk to them in the living room." She turned to her husband's secretary. "Christina, my dear, perhaps you'll ask Lupe to bring in some coffee."

As she swept forward and clasped Herb's hand, he decided that coffee was certainly in order, especially for the councilman's wife. The sweetness of talcum powder and perfume were not sufficient to mask the odor of alcohol. And her eyes were bright. Too bright. Sparkling blue.

"I'm sure that Sergeant Struthers will be happy to come back tomorrow, Judith." Enriquez put an arm around his wife's waist.

"As a matter of fact, sir, it would make things a little difficult. Our business won't take long, I assure you." Dixie began unbuttoning the front of her coat, smiling directly at the councilman's wife. "Is there someplace I can put this? I'd hate to get water stains on the furniture. My, what a lovely home you have here . . ."

Following her lead, Herb also removed his raincoat and handed it to Christina, who had as yet made no move to send for coffee as requested. He also saw the hooded look that passed from the secretary to her employer.

"Charles was such a dear. Why, I've lost fifteen pounds in the last three months. Can you believe it? I guess a crash diet would get quicker results, but as Charles always says . . . excuse me, *said* . . . 'pounds lost steady and slow are pounds slow to regrow!' " Judith Enriquez giggled. "Now, isn't that cute? Dear, dear Charles. He always had the cutest little sayings."

"Did you know Mr. Bouchard well?" Dixie was doodling swirls and squares in the small notebook she held open. She knew Herb had a tape going, but it made little difference in any case. So far the woman they were interviewing had said nothing at all worth noting. She had been pacing back and forth over the brick-colored carpet, gesturing expansively with her hands, talking constantly without saying a thing.

"Oh, yes!" she bubbled. "I saw him two or three times a week. Going to Mystique makes a person feel so good about herself. Of course, Charles couldn't always take care of me personally. But all the boys are good. Especially Michael. He's the salon manager. Such a nice man. Very nice."

"But you didn't socialize with Mr. Bouchard?"

"No, not really." There was another giggle before she sat on the arm of her husband's chair, draping one arm across his shoulders. "Charles wouldn't have mixed too well with . . . well, with the rest of our *friends*." She put a heavy, almost sarcastic emphasis on the last word.

Albert Enriquez shifted his weight and recrossed his legs. "What my wife means, Sergeant, is that our social functions often revolve around community obligations or charities of one kind or another. I don't believe Mr. Bouchard was terribly interested in such things."

Dixie nodded. "You had a late afternoon appointment with Mr. Bouchard on the day he was killed, Mrs. Enriquez. Did he take care of you then, do your hair perhaps?"

The other woman blinked several times. "Well, yes—I mean, no. I did have my hair done. We had a dinner engagement that evening. But Charles doesn't do hair. He has to be free to oversee things and make suggestions. He has"—once more she corrected herself—"*had* wonderful ideas about how a woman should look. He had everyone on an individual improvement program. Very specialized, you understand. He took everything into consideration, just everything. You know— personality, life-style, background, age—just everything."

"But you did see him on that day?" Dixie asked. "I mean, see him physically?"

"Yes, I told you, I did see him."

"And did he seem upset about anything?"

"No." There was no hesitation in Mrs. Enriquez's response. "Charles was always delightful. I don't believe I've ever seen him angry or upset." Her eyes turned misty. "I'll miss him terribly, you know. Mystique is one of the best things to happen to Los Palamos in absolute years!"

"I'm sure you'll miss him." Dixie closed her notebook and stood. "We appreciate your cooperation, Mrs. Enriquez, and you, too, Councilman. I know our visit has been an inconvenience, but we'll be talking to all three of the women who were at Mystique that afternoon. There was a Mrs.

Hobden, I believe, and . . .'' Dixie scowled and began flipping back through the pages of her notebook.

"Holmstead," offered Albert Enriquez. "Judith mentioned seeing Kathryn Holmstead. She and her husband are close friends of ours." He stood and looked down at his wife. "It's almost five o'clock, Judith. If you don't start getting dressed, you'll never be ready by seven."

The dismissal was polite but pointed.

CHAPTER 7

"YOU'LL BE HOME for dinner?" Janice's voice came through the receiver slightly distorted by distance.

Herb transferred the phone to his left ear and reached for the latest lab report on the Bouchard case. "Yeah, I'm just now leaving. Is Amy still up?"

"Yes, but she probably won't be by the time you get here. It'll take you at least an hour to make it over the summit in this rain. I just heard over the radio that there have been two accidents on Highway Seventeen, and there was a mud slide at . . ."

He was only half listening. His eyes scanned the fingerprint results from the crime scene. None had been picked up from the bottles of hair color solution, no sight of the loops, whorls, and tinted arches that so uniquely identified a person from cradle to grave. Bouchard's prints had been lifted from the insides of the rubber gloves.

"Herb?"

"Hmmm."

"I was just thinking, maybe Dixie would like to come for dinner. I mean, she doesn't live that far from us and . . ."

That snapped him back in a hurry. *No,* he thought, *no way!*

Dixie was clearing her desk and he swiveled his chair so that his back was to her, lowering his voice. "Nice thought," he lied, "but it's too late."

"She's already left?" From Janice's tone it was hard to tell whether she was relieved or disappointed.

"Yeah. Look, I've gotta go. See you." He didn't wait for her good-bye. Rain beat against the huge glass windows in a persistent and accusing treble. *Shame on you! Shame on you!*

When he turned around, Dixie was looking at him, her eyes searching his face. "Everything okay?"

"Fine." His voice sounded sharper than he intended, and he tried to gloss the rudeness over with a smile. "Sorry. This weather really gets to me. It's a long drive home. Usually I don't mind the commute, but at times like this I wonder why we ever moved. The little two-bedroom place we used to have over on Twelfth Street would look awful good tonight."

"I suppose so, but the trip still seems pretty convenient to me. I spent my first two years on the force hauling it up and down the peninsula from San Francisco."

It was the first time she had talked about herself in any personal way, and Herb suddenly wondered why. Come to think of it, there were a lot of things about D. T. Struthers that didn't seem to add up. The place she lived in for one. For all its modest exterior, the chalet was large and extremely spacious. Not the kind of place a cop could normally be expected to afford on salary alone. The furniture he had seen on his one and only visit had been old, antique mostly, or pieces from the thirties. Not the kind of junk scrounged and refinished, either, but heavy oak and mahogany pieces which had cost a small fortune even when new. She was no longer married, so there was no financial help there, not unless her ex was very well-to-do and paying spousal support. Somehow Dixie did not strike him as the kind of woman who would file suit for alimony. She seemed far too independent for that, too self-sufficient. And, perhaps, too proud. Her grandfather was obviously retired. And then there was the rather bossy black woman, Reversa. Herb smiled remembering the name of Dixie's . . . servant?

"You're originally from San Francisco?" He kept the question carefully off-handed, somehow sensing that if she suspected his curiosity she would snap shut like a clam.

"Yep, born and bred, except for the time I was away at

college. And even that was pretty close to home." She did not mention Stanford University or the law career she had originally planned. She locked her desk drawer and stood up, putting on her coat. Herb resisted the impulse to help her.

"My grandfather was on the San Francisco police force," she added, with an unmistakable touch of pride in her voice. "Guess you could say I've got a law-and-order heritage. My dad was killed making an arrest when I was still quite young." Her face didn't change, but there was something in her eyes, a sudden hardness that said more than words.

They walked out of the squad room and got into the elevator. The rain had turned her hair slightly fuzzy and most of her makeup had been washed away. "We'll get on that Todd thing tomorrow," she said. "Too bad he wasn't home."

Herb nodded. "Funny. For some reason I figured him for a poor boy. I've seen the type before. Fancy clothes, jewelry, but living in a hovel, just barely keeping it together. Of course, it was no giant surprise to learn he still lives with his mother. The Rose Garden district is real upper crust. Most of it. Affluent. The kid must be a real disappointment to his mother, though; she didn't seem to fit the stereotype at all. A nice lady."

Dixie was looking at him strangely. "What stereotype is that?"

Herb shrugged. "Oh, you know, bossy . . . domineering . . ."

The elevator door opened and he dropped the subject. But he hoped Dixie wasn't that *other* type—the nice, liberal, live-and-let-live type. The gay issue, the supposed new morality, rubbed Herb's fur the wrong way. And he did not want to discuss that sort of thing with Dixie—even if she was a cop.

In spite of the weather the front lobby of the police station was full of citizens filing or requesting accident reports; suspects who had appeared for voluntary booking; people posting bail for traffic violations. Phones rang constantly, to be picked up by uniformed officers, many of whom were on limited duty status because of injuries which kept them temporarily off the streets. Their present duties were coveted by no one.

Herb nodded to the officer guarding the solid wooden gate separating hallway from lobby. A lock buzzed and snapped open, allowing Dixie to precede him through.

"Sergeant Struthers!"

They turned in unison to see the beaming face of Peter Willis. The patrolman had been perched on a stool behind the information counter, but upon seeing Dixie he stood. A slight grimace of pain wrinkled his forehead as he put his weight on his leg, but the expression of discomfort was fleeting, lost almost completely in his obvious pleasure at seeing his former boss.

Dixie held out her hand in greeting. "Glad to see you back, Pete. I was beginning to wonder if maybe you were bribing those doctors. How's the leg?"

"Great! They did the last surgery six weeks ago. This weather doesn't help, but you can't have everything. I should be back on regular duty in another couple of weeks."

Herb watched them and tried to imagine how Willis felt. Stories about his shooting had circulated all over the department and the tales were more or less colorful depending on the narrator. As with all such department scuttlebutt, there was a broad range of attitudes and interpretations. A shooting never went down without a ream of second guessing. And cops were harsh judges, tending to analyze any given situation according to how they thought they themselves would react. Herb had listened as they talked about Pete Willis.

"Stupid ass didn't release the safety on his shotgun . . ."

". . . heard him broadcast that night. Kept his head pretty damn good for a rookie."

"Shit, man, if it wasn't for Struthers he would have been dog meat! She blew that sucker away just as he was coming in for the kill!"

To have your life saved by a fellow officer was something no cop could ever forget or repay. A lifetime debt. But how much more complex the debt and emotion if that officer just happened also to be a female? Herb wondered. Pete Willis stood six feet four inches tall, with mountainous shoulders and a barrel chest. Dixie was all of five two. Soaking wet and wearing combat boots she *might* weigh in at one hundred six pounds. The picture of her making the cavalry charge which had saved Willis's life was slightly ludicrous. Herb tried to visualize her hoisting a short-barreled shotgun and killing a man but couldn't. Yet he knew she had done exactly that. Delaney, the detective who investigated all police shootings, had talked about the incident at some length.

"She was rattled afterward," he had told Herb. "But she didn't come unglued like some guys I've seen. She objected like hell when we insisted on calling a doctor. That shotgun nearly ripped her arm off. The doc said she would be bruised for a month."

But if Pete Willis felt any embarrassment about having his rear end saved by a female, it certainly was not apparent from watching him now. Rather, it seemed to Herb that Dixie was the uncomfortable one as she turned away from the counter and started for the door. She was silent and, walking beside her, Herb decided the best comment he could make was none at all.

Bobby Todd in his own home was not the same young man who had talked to Herb in the foyer of Mystique de la Femme on the night of the murder. Seeing him, it was hard to decide which image was the facade.

His mother was an attractive woman in her late sixties, and once again it had been she who answered the door. After greeting Herb and Dixie politely, she led them through a spacious older home and out into the backyard where a small studio had been built. In contrast to the house, it was starkly modern, a round stucco hut with chimneylike arms sprouting from the roof in all directions. For all its jarring appearance, the design was easy to understand once inside. Each appendage to the building was fitted with a cone window. The top of the studio had also been cut away and replaced by a large bubble skylight that allowed light to spill into the structure from every angle.

Mrs. Todd was a gracious woman, obviously proud of her only child and, as Herb had remarked, she in no way fit the stereotype mother associated with many homosexuals. Nor had Bobby been raised without the influence of a strong father figure. Widowhood was a relatively recent condition for Ruth Todd, one she bore with quiet dignity.

"Robert always encouraged Bobby to pursue his talent," she said. Her eyes studied the easel her son was presently at work on, an oil in pastel colors portraying a girl asleep on a flowered hillside. "His gift is something few people are blessed with, a gift it would be sinful to waste, don't you agree?"

It was more than courtesy that prompted Dixie's positive reply. The canvases propped around the studio, all of living subjects, displayed a touch of genius. Herb walked around the room. From time to time he stopped in grudging appreciation of what he saw. In truth he was a bit surprised.

The real surprise, however, was not Todd's talent. It was the man himself. Wearing a flannel shirt and a pair of paint-dabbed denims, there was not a whisper of gaiety about him. His movements were brisk and decisive as he stood cleaning a set of brushes.

"Charles and I were supposed to attend a party together that night," he told them again, closing one eye and contemplating the pointed tip of a brush. "He said I would be able to meet some people from one of the New York galleries there. That contact would have been invaluable to me."

Completely cooperative, he continued, reiterating his earlier statements. His tone and bearing now made his relationship with the deceased seem little more than a casual friendship. While talking, he moved about the studio, putting away solvents, flipping through a large sketchbook. All the nervousness displayed during the first interview seemed to have evaporated, and with it the faintly feminine overtones in his speech. He spoke confidently, in a rich baritone. But at no time did he meet the eyes of either detective.

The questions Dixie interjected were at first cursory. To delve into the relationship she suspected between this man and Charles Bouchard seemed somehow unthinkable with Mrs. Todd standing in the room. The older woman's face was serene and her bearing completely unruffled. There were questions which needed asking, but to Dixie the situation also seemed to call for tact. She tried first one approach and then another without ever quite coming to the point, aware all the while of Herb's growing impatience. No longer engrossed in the studio, her partner stood leaning against one wall. His arms were folded across his chest and he was watching Bobby Todd with unwavering concentration. She was on the verge of trying yet another tactic to get to her subject when he took matters out of her hands.

"Bouchard's body was naked when you found it, isn't that right, Todd?"

Ruth Todd blushed, but Herb went on without giving Bobby the chance to respond. "He was giving himself a dye job—right down to the genitals. Did he usually go into the pool area after that sort of thing? For that matter, did he usually swim in the buff?"

Todd froze for a moment and then slowly closed the sketch pad he was still holding. "I really wouldn't know, Officer . . . Woodall, isn't it?" He looked at his mother and smiled. "Perhaps it would be better if you went back to the house, Mom. I really hate for you to hear about this kind of thing."

His mother seemed only too anxious to comply. "Of course, dear. This whole thing is so grisly, I must say. And terrible, really terrible. Charles seemed like a very nice man."

She looked at Dixie. "I do wish Bobby hadn't been the one to find him like that. It's bad enough to have a friend killed so violently, but the publicity is going to make it all the worse. An artist, a fine artist like Bobby, really shouldn't—"

"I'm sure everything will work out fine, Mrs. Todd." Dixie gave the woman her most encouraging smile. "It's amazing how quickly people forget about this sort of thing."

The studio was quiet as Ruth Todd turned to leave. Just before opening the studio door, she gave her son a long, worried look but said nothing more. When she had gone, Herb returned his full attention to the artist. "Will the real Mr. Todd please stand up?"

His voice dripped sarcasm. "I think we've beat around the bush long enough, don't you? We all know what kind of relationship you had with Bouchard, so let's get on with it. I want to know everything there is to know about the man—how long you've known him; exactly why you were at the salon that night. The whole thing, Todd."

Herb was pushing things and he knew it. He tried to tell himself that it was Todd, the man's suspected sexual preferences, that aggravated him. The truth, however, was that he had crawled out on the wrong side of the bed that morning— after a night punctuated by dreams that made him feel like a heel. A rotten husband. A rotten father.

Dixie was a little surprised by the tension she saw in Herb. Normally he used a laid-back approach, never pushing too hard, getting information through a series of seemingly innocuous questions. The night before, while at the Enriquez house, he had been almost reserved. For some reason this business with Todd seemed to have him breathing fire.

But the artist had neatly recouped his aplomb. Strolling to a canvas chair, he sat down and crossed one ankle over his knee. "Am I to expect a third degree now, Officer Woodall?" His tone was light. "I've told you, not once but twice, why I was at Mystique. We were supposed to go to a party, and I don't believe I'm required to tell you what party. I see no reason to drag other people into this mess simply because they were kind enough to extend an invitation to someone who got himself murdered."

"So there *was* no party."

"So, as I said, I don't feel obligated to tell you about it."

Herb leaned over the man. "Fine, Todd, because in that case you're going to have a real good time handling this all by your little lonesome. You were at the scene of the murder. When we arrived, you were in a highly excitable and agitated state. There was no one else on or near the premises. You have no one to corroborate your time of arrival. In short, dear, you're the only closet queen we've got." He could hardly believe the words had slipped out of his mouth. His face turned a deep red, which only served to make him appear more angry.

"Herb." Dixie spoke softly but her warning was clear. His blunt manner had possibly served a point until now, but she saw no reason for slurs, or antagonizing Todd, even if he was a suspect.

Herb straightened and glared at her. Inwardly, he was beginning to feel a genuine sense of panic; worse, he felt like a fool, a bumbling rookie. But rather than backing off, as he knew he should, he plunged on, angry at himself, and at Dixie for the effect she was having on him. "Ah, for chrissake, Struthers! If this isn't just like a female cop! Just when I'm beginning to have a little hope for you, you go and turn into some kind of squeamish bleeding heart. How long are you going to coddle this jerk-off? We both know what he is . . . the kind of game he and Bouchard had going. And just because he's got a nice little mama—"

Both of Todd's feet came down on the floor with a loud thump. His upper body swayed forward. He was no longer smiling. "If this is your good guy/bad guy routine it's not going to work, Sergeant." He, too, was glaring at Dixie. "I'm afraid television has blown your cover on that one. And if you insist on playing games, perhaps it's time I called an attorney."

"This is no game, Mr. Todd." Dixie felt trapped between a rock and a hard spot, sandwiched into a definite no-win situation. She was furious with Herb, but he was her partner. She could not leave him hanging. "You may not like my partner's methods, but I think you would do well to answer his questions. I'm sure there will be no need for an attorney . . . unless, of course—"

"Damn it, I've answered your questions, several times!" He looked up at Herb's glowering face. "Perhaps I was a little flip, but the truth is I'm not sure exactly where that party was supposed to be, only that it was in San Francisco. Other than that everything happened just as I told you the first time. Charles had all kinds of contacts. He had been making noises for a long time about knowing some big shots from the New York art scene. I don't need to tell you what that could mean for me. He kept promising some introductions, and finally it looked like it was going to happen. I agreed to pick him up at eight. The door was open, and I went in. When I saw he wasn't in the main part of the salon I went looking for him. I found him, and that's all there is to it." He felt the pocket of his shirt. "Damn, I need a smoke!"

To Herb's amazement, Dixie opened her purse and produced a pack of cigarettes which she shook toward Todd. She also brought out a small gold lighter. Herb was sure she didn't smoke.

Bobby Todd inhaled deeply. "I usually don't light up in there. Too many flammables. Besides, it's not good for the paintings."

"Your work is beautiful." Dixie indicated the work on his easel. "Do you use models?"

"Sometimes." Obviously relieved to change their topic of conversation, the artist stood and moved to the painting. "This model doesn't even know she is one. I snapped a picture of her in Vasona Park with my telephoto lens."

The studio grew quiet again, and when Dixie next spoke it was very softly. "How did you meet Bouchard, Bobby? Were you doing a portrait of him?"

"No." Todd tried to smile but failed. "I met him in a park, too. In San Francisco."

Dixie heard the disgusted noise Herb made deep in his throat and rushed on before he could renew his assault. "Did he help you with your art? I mean *really* help. I would think he could have put you in contact with quite a few prospective clients."

"Actually, that's not the kind of help I need. My work sells relatively well locally. I needed, still need, more wide-range exposure. A good exhibition in San Francisco could lead to national attention, the right kind of contacts. Charles promised me that and more." Todd began pacing back and forth. "Charles was full of promises."

Still frustrated but in better control, Herb asked the next question, doing his best to assume a neutral tone. "And how long had you and Bouchard been . . . friends?"

Todd looked suddenly weary. His earlier confidence was gone. "Look, I'm not going to deny that Charles and I had a relationship. It wasn't, *isn't*, my normal thing, but with him it was the only way. The guy was strange—he swung both ways—but I wouldn't consider anything he did straight. He never really hung around with other . . ." He hesitated and flushed. "He never hung around with other gays, at least not openly, not like so many do. The guys who work at Mystique are straight, too, as far as I know. That's what he told me.

Charles was heavy into *seduction*. I don't think he cared if a
person was male or female. He liked new meat; you'll excuse
the crudity. He also liked *young*. And he would do anything
to get what he wanted. I had something he wanted. He made
promises, and at the time it seemed like a fair enough swap."

"And was it?" Dixie asked the question quietly.

For once Bobby Todd looked directly into her eyes. "If we
had made it to that party it might have been." He ran a hand
through his sun-shot hair and gazed around the studio. There
was true grief on his face, but not for Charles Bouchard.

"What in the hell is the matter with you, Woodall?" Dixie
pulled away from the Todd residence, heading the car toward
Los Palamos. Her face felt as if it was set in stone. Her jaw
ached from clenching her teeth.

Herb ignored her. The secret vow he had made not to look
at her legs again was getting harder and harder to keep. He
felt downright mean, and guilty as sin. He had always considered himself a good cop, a totally professional investigator,
but he had blown it today—royally. He had needed something, anything, *anyone* as a target for his frustrations. Unfortunately, Todd had been handy.

He wished he could just leave work and go home. Make
love to Janice. Play with Amy. He wished Dixie would not
wear perfume.

"Listen, Herb, I'm not sure how the burr got up your
behind, but—"

"Look here, Struthers, I'm sorry if I insulted you back
there. I wasn't cool. I don't feel so cool today. But could we
just can the sergeant's chatter? Maybe in the future it would
be better if you just do your thing, and I'll do mine, okay?"

"Damn it, Herb, we're not supposed to be doing our own
thing. We're partners, remember?"

"Yeah, Mutt 'n' Jeff. Jekyll and Hyde."

Dixie felt like she was beating her head against concrete,
and suddenly decided she didn't give a damn whether she got
through to him or not. This whole business with him and with
the homicide team in general was getting ridiculous. Di Franco
with his spider-and-fly games; Herb with his menopausal

moods. If there was one lesson she had learned early in her profession it was that she could not force acceptance. Some of her male counterparts would resent her for as long as she remained with the police department, until she retired. It was a fact of life. There was nothing she could do about it except perform as well, or *better* than, any of them. If Herb decided to shut her out she would just have to find a way to work around him and get the job done anyway. The Bouchard case was the best chance she would ever have to prove herself in homicide, and at the moment she was almost beyond caring if she had to do so alone. She would work with her partner or without him.

"Look out!"

A battered Chevrolet seemed to come out of nowhere, materializing as a solid mass of nicked and dented red metal, streaking across the intersection. Dixie slammed on the brakes and felt the squad car begin to fishtail, rear wheels skittering over the slick pavement.

"Cut to the left!" Herb's voice reverberated in her ears. "To the left, damn it, to the left!"

She cut to the left. *Hard.* The car slid sideways, front wheels bumping over the curb of a sidewalk, scraping a lamppost before it dove into a thick hedge and nestled to a stop. The engine burped and gurgled and finally died. The red Chevrolet was nowhere in sight.

Had Herb's stomach not been gripped by a wild series of flip-flops, had there not been a sudden and very uncomfortable pressure on his bladder, he might have taken time to weigh his next words. But he didn't. They were out of his mouth before he even knew what they would be. "God save the world from women drivers!"

Dixie's hand came off the wheel. Slowly, she turned toward him, the pale marble of her face smooth and expressionless. She sat perfectly still. Only her eyes remained vividly alive. The wide pupils seemed to dilate, expand to meet the glittering golden chips surrounding them.

There was no plausible explanation for the ripple of apprehension that bristled the hair at the nape of Herb's neck during that fleeting yet somehow interminable instant. And it was not until she restarted the car and eased back onto the wet street that he realized he had not been breathing at all. After catching up by inhaling and exhaling deeply, he decided the delayed intake of oxygen must have made him lightheaded. Suddenly, he wanted to laugh—at her, at the situation, but most of all at himself.

Still, he could not quite shake the feeling that he had just made a close, almost kissing acquaintance with death . . . and *not* because of the accident.

CHAPTER 8

HERB AND DIXIE stepped into the cool, crisp air, leaving the velvet beehive of Mystique de la Femme behind. Just as they closed the salon door, a dazzling ray of sunshine broke through the clouds. The view was spectacular. A large pine shimmered like a Christmas tree on the sloping lawn, its branches wreathed in teardrops of moisture. Drenched in damp but sunny brightness, the grounds around the mansion were an almost blinding green. Giant camellia bushes bordered the high iron fences, the new blooms providing a riot of mixed pinks and reds.

No one in the Santa Clara Valley could remember a year with more rain. And the snow level, normally reserved only for the surrounding mountain peaks, had dropped this spring, bearding the tops of foothills in white, startling in contrast to the new grass and poppy-dappled knolls below. Though breathtaking, the scenery was a dichotomy, at odds with the throbbing, hurry-scurry of life in the valley.

Less than half a century before, San Jose and the surrounding suburbs had been little more than small communities set amidst a literal sea of blossoms, a sight which every spring had brought people from all over the state. Individually and in group tours, those people had traveled for miles just to gaze down upon a wonderland of orchards which stretched farther than the eye could see.

And now, from their lofty vantage point, Herb and Dixie could see it all. But the orchards were gone, their snowy splendor long since replaced by the mushrooms of IBM, Lockheed, Fairchild, and thousands of other electronics plants. Each industry in turn was neatly encased by mile upon mile of urban sprawl. Gone forever the farmer; there to stay the aeronautical and electrical engineers. The mainstay of the valley was no longer plums but software—the space-age technology for an entire nation, the entire world. Santa Clara was now only a synonym for silicon, a Pac Man Paradise with computerese as its second language.

Gone, too, were the days of the friendly deputy sheriff and the jovial but slightly stupid neighborhood cop. The men and women presently filling the ranks of the police department were a new breed, all professionals with college training. Most had degrees in Police Science or the Administration of Justice. Dixie and Herb were no exceptions. They were not standing on the stoop of Mystique de la Femme simply by happenstance. Both were highly trained and educated toward exactly that moment in time, Herb only slightly less than Dixie. And what she had in additional education, he made up in hard experience. By all reckoning they should have been the perfect team, a fact blatantly belied by their respective facial expressions.

Upon their arrival at the salon, both had been surprised to see the establishment open. When they announced themselves, the receptionist went immediately to seek out a Mr. Michael Dreyfus, stylist extraordinaire and salon manager. Short and stocky of build, he was good-looking in an athletic sort of way. Even white teeth. Rugged features. The slacks he wore were tailored and the shirt casual, opened at the collar. He was the kind of man who would have seemed equally at ease in tuxedo or tennis shorts. Upon introduction, he gave Dixie a long moment of appreciative perusal, accompanied by a handshake that was just a shade too warm and lingering. But it was Herb to whom he addressed his conversation.

"I got a call from Max early Sunday morning," he said. "We both thought it best to keep things going here. It hasn't been too bad. Most of our appointments have shown up.

We've had a few questions we couldn't answer, and the atmosphere has been a little subdued. Otherwise, I almost hate to admit, it has pretty much been business as usual.''

His reference to ''Max'' had provided Dixie and Herb yet another surprise. They knew about Max Hobden. Almost everyone knew about Max. He was a beefy, self-made millionaire, a true success story. A recent article had appeared in the Sunday supplement of the newspaper extolling his achievements, but nothing had been written to indicate that he owned part or total interest in so exotic an enterprise as Mystique de la Femme. To date, his only known connection to the lavish establishment was his wife's name in the salon appointment book.

Garbage. That was the Hobden specialty. Garbage and maintenance. The disposal and janitorial empire he had conceived some twenty years before had fortuitously coincided with the boom in California industry, making the former Ozarks boy a very wealthy man indeed.

But this discovery of Bouchard's silent partner was the only real enlightenment after a full afternoon of interviews. Michael Dreyfus and the rest of the Mystique staff seemed collectively unable to offer any motive for Bouchard's murder.

There was a masseur team, a brother and sister from Oslow, with the unlikely names of Olga and Ernst. The two spoke little English. In addition, Dixie had interviewed four hairstylists, two males and two females, leaving Herb the manicurist and the young, pretty receptionist.

While Charles Bouchard might have bedazzled the rich patrons of his salon, he had evidently fraternized with his subordinates very little. A stylist named Gregory had described Charles as an *okay guy*, a rather ambiguous personality profile in which his coworkers concurred. All agreed that the pay was more than fair and the tips fabulous. In short, the culmination of three hours of exhaustive interviews was a relative zero. Through it all Dixie and Herb had spoken hardly at all. Now, standing in the waning sunshine, both were glad to leave Mystique and more glad that the shift was near an end. Dixie could hardly look at Herb without feeling a fresh spurt of anger, and so she avoided looking at him at all. For his part, in the back of his mind, Herb kept trying to

convince himself that he really had been in the right. Maybe
Di Franco knew what things were about after all—maybe
broads as cops was a lousy, stinking idea.

The strained silence remained between them as they returned to the car. A wide area of paint had been scraped off
the right side of the automobile in its altercation with the
lamppost, and it was necessary for Herb to put his back into
getting the passenger door open. He jerked and strained while
Dixie settled herself behind the wheel. Her fingers drummed
an impatient tattoo against the dash and she stared straight
ahead as he tugged and swore under his breath. Finally, an
exasperated heave achieved his end, but it also sent him
sprawling backward. In the next instant he found himself flat
on his posterior, his pants soaking up a mud puddle. He
glared into the car, and for a moment he thought Dixie was
smiling, the self-satisfied smirk of a tabby cat. But the glance
she turned on him in the next instant lacked any trace of
humor.

"The door's sprung now," she tersely informed him. "You'll
have to hold it closed until we get back to the garage."

Cursing under his breath, trying to hold the door closed,
Herb found the ride downtown cold and breezy.

The news had reached Di Franco before they could get into
the squad room to fill out an accident report. He was waiting.
Arms folded across his chest like a malevolent totem, he
greeted them with something akin to joy in his eyes, a glint
that made his swarthy smile somehow more sinister.

"Wet weather's rough, huh, Struthers?" His lips stretched
wider. "Anybody ever tell you we're short on cars in this
unit?"

Incredible, Dixie thought, but she could actually remember
a time when the man now grinning at her had seemed sexy.
The very idea made her stomach turn.

"A car pulled in front of me." She hated having to explain
herself, especially to him.

"You're trained to act in an emergency, Struthers. There
are accidents and then there are *accidents*."

Suddenly, he was the disappointed father, and Dixie disliked him more than ever, knowing the act was a total sham.

His voice was condescending, as if he spoke to an imbecile or a child. His brows pulled together in a pained frown. "Don't misunderstand me. I know some things can't be avoided. When a hot chase goes down, cars can get pretty banged up. I've been in a few of these myself. Happens in the patrol division often. Part of the job."

"Wait a minute, Lieutenant—"

"No, you wait." He smiled again. "A lady called the complaint desk this afternoon to say some nut had plowed up part of her hedge and then just drove off and left it. Luckily, she got a license number."

Dixie inwardly cringed. *Hit and run.* Was that what he was after? If so, there would not be much she could say. The anger—no, the *rage*—she had felt toward Herb immediately after the accident had left her deaf, dumb, and nearly blind. Mostly dumb, she decided . . . as in *stupid*. The hedge had not looked damaged. The city lamppost had remained intact. Still, had she been thinking clearly, Dixie knew she would have gone to the door of the house and then driven straight back to the PD if the situation posed a problem. Looking sideways at Herb, she was sure he must be enjoying her discomfort no end. But to her embarrassed surprise, he chose that moment to step forward.

"Wait just a damn minute, Tony. The hedge gave way when we hit it. I tell you it was fine. As for the accident—"

It was the last straw for Dixie. She wanted no help from Herb, no more macho heroics for him to resent. She spun around and glared at him, her temper near the breaking point. "Back off, Woodall! I may be just an inept woman driver—an inept female cop—but when I need your help I'll sure as hell let you know!"

His mouth snapped shut as the smile reappeared on Di Franco's face. The lieutenant looked from one detective to the other. "Come now, we shouldn't have a family spat over a little thing like this."

Dixie wondered if her teeth were going to survive the beating they were taking as she ground them back and forth. Her jaw ached.

"As a matter of fact, Herb's right." Di Franco's voice had taken on honeyed tones and he was quite obviously having himself a ball. "The patrolmen who went out to the scene of the accident said that hedge was perfectly okay. The RP was pacified. But we still have a little problem here, don't we? There are four cars in this unit." He held up the appropriate number of fingers. "Now we have three." One finger dropped.

Dixie wished her heart would quit pounding. She wanted to say that she would use her own car, but it was useless. The insurance problems involved made such a simple solution impossible. There was nothing for it but to stand there, like the fool she was, and take whatever Di Franco decided to dish out.

"Tell you what I'm gonna do, Struthers. I'm gonna go into the captain's office right now and tell him we gotta rent another vehicle. I'm also gonna tell him why. You can take it from there. He's a real nice guy. I'm sure he won't mind the drain on our budget. Maybe he'll even let you pick out something real cute. A pink Rolls maybe."

He was whistling happily as he strolled from the squad room. Dixie went slowly to her desk and sat down. She was pale and silent but composed as she put away reports and locked the drawers. Herb stood where he was, rooted to the mud-colored carpet, his slacks still clinging to his backside, feeling like the biggest horse's ass in town.

Patrick looked at his only grandchild, and he didn't like what he saw one little bit. In all her twenty-nine years, Dixie had never seemed so downright discouraged, down in the mouth, as down on herself as she was right now. And it was the latter which bothered Patrick most. There had been times enough in her life when Dixie was upset or hurt. When the lounge lizard she married began to show his true colors, as Patrick had known he eventually would, she had been cut to the quick. But even during that emotional tempest she had managed to hold her own, to keep her equilibrium. Until now her fierce pride and the inherited Flannigan temper had served her very well indeed.

But she is down on herself tonight, Patrick thought, and that's the worst kind of down a body can be. How he wanted to get his hands around that Di Franco's throat! It was impossible to imagine that the bastard didn't know he had the cream of the crop in Dixie. Why, the girl had the blood of three generations of cops running through her veins. *Irish* cops!

Thinking of the Flannigan generations never failed to bring Patrick's own pain and sorrow back to him. The keen edge of grief was gone now, but all the time in the world could pass without him getting over the loss of his Jimmy. James Francis Flannigan.

Looking across the living room, Patrick's eyes misted as they fell on the figure curled into one corner of the huge living room sofa. Dixie's shoulders were hunched. Her face was a study of misery and self-disgust. Every few moments she ran splayed fingers through her thick mop of hair.

My little girl, his heart called silently to her, don't you know you are the very best? Just like your daddy. The same auburn hair. The same firm jaw and stubborn honesty. Above all, the same courage.

Jimmy and Rose and Dixie—in his mind's eye Patrick saw the three of them clearly, the way they *had* been, walking along the winding pathways of Golden Gate Park. Laughing and playing together. Spreading a picnic basket. He was convinced then, as now, that there could have been no finer family this side of Dublin.

Thinking of Rosie made him smile. Rose Klein, the flower of San Francisco. Dixie had inherited a steel spine on both sides of her family tree, not that he would ever admit it aloud. Rosie's own father, that blustering, Southern-born baboon, with his uppity ways, never thought Jimmy half good enough for Rose.

Sean Klein had been a hard man. A wealthy man. But even Patrick had to grudgingly admit that the man's riches had been very hard won—won with his own nimble brain and a pen meaner than Hades itself. Problem was, Sean never could forget where he came from. The fact that he had been born in Charleston and descended from an old plantation family gave him an overinflated opinion of himself. No matter that his own parents had been dirt poor. They, too, had come from landed gentry. It made no difference to Sean that he had needed to use brawn, muscle, and bone to get into Notre Dame. Once there he had learned more than football. It was a good trick on the Yankees, a very good trick indeed. While they hoorahed their heads off, watching as Sean Klein drove hard through the center line, he had used their scholarship to learn—and later to implement his own grand plan. And journalism became his brutal tool.

Patrick had never learned exactly what brought Sean, Dixie's maternal grandfather, to the West Coast, but there were few people from San Francisco to Los Angeles who had not read his scathing quips. All the savagery once displayed on the football field inevitably found voice in the written word. As owner and publisher of several California newspapers, he retained his position as editor and chief of the *Peninsula Herald* until the day he died, some five years before. But throughout his life he had remained forever a transplanted Charlestonian. The home which had produced Rose was grand, a white-pillared edifice right from the pages of *Gone With the Wind*. The Tara of Saint Francis Wood. Magnolia and dogwood. A completely black staff. Sean had insisted on it all, and Patrick had been surprised that the pretentious attitudes had not rubbed off on Rose, Sean's only child.

But Rosie had made her stand, had married Jimmy Flannigan in spite of everything, bless her heart. And she had been a good wife up until the day Jimmy was gunned down.

But just look at her now! Patrick snorted. He had no use for the man who had stepped into his Jimmy's shoes. Franklin Marks was a snob—a blown-up, posturing, self-inflated snob of a man, in Patrick's opinion. And, unfortunately, Rosie seemed to fit in only too well. She had married the man, given him a son, and become everything her father originally expected her to be. To Patrick it seemed that she had put Jimmy far from her, and he could never forgive her that. It wasn't that she had remarried. Being so young and pretty, having Dixie to raise, he had expected her to take up the threads of her life. No, it was whom she had chosen to marry and what she had become that rankled. And the fact that she seemed to be always trying to remold Dixie.

Over the years, a distance, something very close to enmity, had grown up between Patrick and Rose, and all too often Dixie was their battleground. The fighting had come to a climax on the day she decided to enter the police academy.

With that memory Patrick allowed herself a small, tight

smile. Oh, what a Donnybrook it had been! Donald Struthers, the rotten coward, had gone running off to his mother's house, leaving Dixie to fend for herself. And poor old Franklin Marks had just stood there flabbergasted, with his mouth hanging open, watching his own son stand right alongside Patrick and Dixie. A good boy, Ryan, not a bit like his stuffy sire. Yes, a grand day indeed, everyone yelling, Rosie screaming her brains out, losing all her classiness. How the Irish fur had flown!

And not once had Patrick regretted his own decision to stick by Dixie—not, at least, until this very moment. She looked so small and vulnerable sitting there on the sofa, so completely miserable. The captain had been real rough on her, with Di Franco's urging to be sure. A day's unpaid suspension from duty. It wasn't the pay that troubled Dixie—of that Patrick was sure. It was the blot on her spotless service record. Yes, he had seen Dixie suffer before, but he could never remember seeing her like this. Not ever.

Dixie lay in bed. A lonely bed. Moonlight spilled into the room. On the sloping hillside just outside her window, she could see a small doe mincing through the underbrush, lifting her head cautiously from time to time, testing the clean mountain air with quick, gentle sniffs.

That's the way I feel, Dixie thought. I forever tiptoe toward my goals, toward success. Always careful. Forever cautious of my every step. I've chosen a man's world, and this is the price.

"Dixie Flannigan, you're feeling sorry for yourself!" She spoke the admonition aloud, with only the night to hear.

Funny, she thought, for years now her name had been Struthers and yet she still thought of herself as a Flannigan. Donald had not made much impact on her life after all, not when she stopped to think about it, something she rarely did anymore. There were moments, though, like now, when she longed to be able to curl into a man, feel a pair of strong arms around her. Tonight she would have liked to cry and rant and rave, knowing there was someone who loved her and would be on her side, right or wrong. Someone stronger and more capable than herself.

Donald Struthers had not been strong. No character. That was the way Patrick chose to put it, and Dixie knew he was right. Donald had been a mama's boy. Dixie's mind shrank from remembering the terrible fights with Donald, the silent contest of wills between herself and his mother. It was all water under the bridge now, part of the nearly forgotten past. Dixie was not sorry for the choices she had made, not then or since. She might not be the attorney her mother had wished her to be, but she was satisfied with her life in most ways. She had everything she needed and more. Patrick was a good companion. Reversa, who had been with her mother's family for over thirty years, was a jewel, a constant source of love and amusement . . .

Not for the first time, Dixie counted her good fortune. The very roof over her head had been bequeathed to her by Grandfather Klein. The furnishings had been in her family for years. At one time the house had been a summer retreat, a lovely patch of peace for all of them. She had romped in the surrounding woods, abandoning herself to the beauty and freedom. Now it belonged to her alone. She had brought Patrick here in his old age—and Reversa, who adamantly refused to be separated from the girl she had all but raised. Yes, Dixie thought, still watching the doe move lightly about the hillside, this is a good life. I'm lucky.

Her brows drew together. A man, the *right* man, would make her life complete, but love simply had not happened to her yet. Not the kind of love she dreamed of. She thought of the one man she dated on any kind of regular basis. Joe Kirk was an Assistant District Attorney; he was smooth and cultured and interesting; a man who believed in justice and honesty. He was a satisfying lover. But she knew only too well where he was going and was not at all sure she wished to tag along. That's what it would inevitably become, for Joe was headed straight into the political arena. The handwriting was on the wall. And life as the wife of a politician held little appeal for Dixie. Joe would change. It was inevitable. The two of them would be forced to lead a fishbowl existence. She would settle into the role of an attractive appendage to her husband's career.

Dixie shook her head violently. The very idea made her

feel suffocated. No; Joe Kirk was a nice, stimulating companion, but his chosen path was not for her. She had her own life and her own career, less glorious to be sure, but full of challenge.

Kicking off the blankets, Dixie rolled onto her side, putting her back toward the moonlit window. *Challenge*. For a woman police officer, that was an understatement. And she had muffed it!

Somehow she had to get this whole suspension thing and her dubious position in the homicide unit into some kind of perspective. She had screwed up, she reminded herself, but she could not help wondering if the same discipline would have been meted out to a male officer. Probably not, she decided.

So? Her mind posed the question.

There was redress, of course. The attitude of Anthony Di Franco was no secret. She could seek her revenge in the form of a sexual harassment petition. Other female officers had done so when backed into a corner, both with and without valid justification.

The idea remained with her for little longer than it took to think it through. She was not going to cover her mistakes in that way. Cries of sexual harassment and racial prejudice were beginning to wear more than a little thin, with her as much as with anyone. There was only one thing for her to do. She would have to accept her own mistake, as well as whatever else Di Franco had to pass out. There would be no cop-outs for Dixie T. Struthers.

Suddenly, she was drowsy. Another day was coming. *Her* day. Strangely enough, she felt very little residual animosity toward Herb, no more than faint annoyance. She simply did not understand. Something was eating at her partner, and she was almost surprised to discover how much she cared for Herb Woodall, both as a partner and as a friend.

Peace replaced the restlessness that had been with her for the past few weeks. She began to drift toward sleep, a myriad of seemingly unconnected images whirling through her mind. Di Franco. Herb. Bouchard. Joe Kirk.

Perhaps it was the face of Joe Kirk, and the possibility of becoming a politician's wife, that caused her to focus on an image of Judith Enriquez. She saw again the nervous hands, the artificially bright blue eyes. Even in her near sleeping state Dixie shuddered at the idea of such a life for herself. Just as sleep claimed her, she renewed her determination. Sooner or later, she feared, Joe Kirk would no doubt want to find himself another girl.

CHAPTER 9

THE HOBDEN HOME was not in Los Palamos, but if it had been it would have held its own very well. Monte Sereno, an exclusive community nestled between the suburbs of Los Gatos and Saratoga, was not as old and established as Los Palamos; the homes were more modern in design, more obviously *nouveau riche*. Still, it evidenced a world few people would ever know or be able to afford. Mrs. Lola Hobden made do very nicely with the forty-five-hundred-square-foot tri-level home purchased by her husband.

The weather had cleared and it looked as if Spring had come at last to the Santa Clara Valley, a balmy California Spring. When the two detectives knocked on the Hobden door, Lola herself appeared. She wore a pair of faded jeans and sweat shirt, holding a wallpaper paste brush in one hand. Mousy hair was pulled away from her face and covered with a cotton scarf, a style that accentuated a rather sharp nose. Eyeing the proffered badges, she simply shrugged and swung the door wider.

"Figured you'd be here sooner or later," she said. "Come in. I'm doing Max's game room so you'll just have to talk to me while I work. I've only got an hour or so before I have to stop."

Herb and Dixie followed her through a spacious corridor and down a flight of stairs into a large open room. A long mahogany bar dominated one wall, a lighted Olympia sign blinking on and off over the mirror behind. It was indeed a man's room from end to end. A masculine playroom, complete with billiard and poker tables, both set beneath colorful Tiffany-style fixtures. A drop cloth covered the parquet floor along one wall and on it sat a stepladder, drip pans, and a long cutting table. Several rolls of wallpaper were stacked to one side.

"Ask whatever you need to ask," Mrs. Hobden told them. She set to work at once. Her strokes were long and even as she applied fresh paste to a strip of paper. "I want to get this done before tonight. It's my 'sorry' present to Max. I've only got another hour or so before I have to pick up my grandson at nursery school."

" 'Sorry' present?" Dixie decided at once that she liked this lady. There was energy in her short, overweight figure, and a straightforwardness in the way she looked through her pale blue eyes.

"Oh, hell yes!" The other woman chuckled. "I have to get Max something at least once a month just to let him know that *I* know what a bitch I can be. The fight last week was over his latest hobby." She indicated the wall behind her with a tilt of her head. The two strips of paper she had already hung were covered in a design of old biplanes—red, blue, green, and yellow on a tan background. It made Dixie dizzy to look at the design for more than a second or two at a time. The colors were near blinding in their brightness.

"Seems to me like just learning to plain ol' fly oughta be enough for anyone," Lola continued. "I hate going up in any kind of airplane, much less doing loop-de-loops. And it's not as if Max is a kid anymore. But I didn't have to remind him that he's almost fifty-five. God, he hates it when I do that!"

Bringing the ends of the paper together, she mounted the ladder and began working the top corners into place. She looked over her shoulder at Herb. "Since you're just standing there maybe you could give a hand. Just pull the bottom down straight."

Herb obeyed without comment and they worked in silence for several minutes while Dixie watched. When Lola seemed satisfied and came off her perch they stood back together to admire the result.

"Nice," Herb said. "Great room."

Lola flushed happily and then set to work rolling out the seams, smoothing away small pockets of air. "Max spends a lot of time down here. The whole damn place is full of 'sorry' presents."

"Stunt flying is supposed to be a kick in the pants," Herb assured her, walking around the room. He stopped to run his hand along the gleaming surface of the bar. "I have a friend who does it as a sideline, at fairs and exhibits. His regular job is crop dusting."

She quit working and turned to look at him, but he went on without seeming to notice. "Art's supposed to be one of the best there is, around here anyway."

"That's the guy who's teaching Max!" Lola wagged her head at the coincidence. "Art Cochran, right?"

Herb smiled. "Yep. Now I'm sure you don't need to worry about your husband, Mrs. Hobden. Scares the blazes out of people to watch Art, but he sure knows his business."

"No sense in worrying, even if I do. Once Max gets something into his fat head nothing can stop him. You can do me a favor, though; will you tell your friend to go a little easy—just teach Max enough to make him happy?"

"Sure." Herb looked at Dixie but his expression didn't change. "I'll be seeing him soon anyway."

Lola Hobden smiled, a smile that made her seem almost pretty. She laid her tools aside. "Why don't you two come upstairs while I put on some coffee? I could use a break."

She was more relaxed now, more open, and Dixie realized they had been given a go signal. But she also knew that the most important piece of information had already been given and received. The substance which killed Bouchard, E 605 in its shortest form, had been easily purchased at one time, but such was no longer the case. A farmer might possibly purchase it through a licensed dealer, but its use was pretty strictly limited to crop dusters.

Lola chattered on, oblivious of the excited undercurrent passing between her guests. With the mention of her patronage at Mystique de la Femme she laughed outright. "Do I look like I go to a place like that? Hell, I don't have the time. Don't think I'd fit in too good anyhow. No pedigree." She laughed again. "I went over there to pick up the books for Max. He owns about seventy-five percent of the joint, and he keeps pretty close tabs on what happens there."

"Did you know Mr. Bouchard well?" The question came from Dixie.

"Hardly at all. Didn't want to, either. Don't know what it was about him, just gave me the creeps being in the same room with him. Things like that don't bug Max, though. The guy had a money-making idea, and my Max is all for making money."

She looked around at the kitchen, the brick indoor barbecue, the sparkling, all-electric fixtures, and sighed with obvious satisfaction. Her eyes then went from Dixie to Herb. "Nothing wrong in that, now is there?"

Herb could not decide if his elation was due to the success of the Hobden interview or because of the change in his partner. It was good to see Dixie animated again, to hear her voice. For a while he had wondered if she would ever speak to him again unless forced to. After her meeting with the captain two days before, she had thrown him one long, steely glare and then left the building without a word. He had not learned about her suspension until the next morning.

That day had been miserable. He had known he was dragging his feet, not really pursuing the investigation like he should, while he had the chance to do so alone. In fact, beyond a follow-up on Bouchard's background, he had done next to nothing. That morning, when he related the details he had obtained to Dixie, she had been interested but hardly overwhelmed. She simply nodded and scribbled some notes into the little notebook she always kept handy.

His first impulse had been to get angry all over again. Just like a woman to pout, he had thought. But on giving it a moment's consideration, he realized that pouting was not necessarily a feminine trait. If he had pulled that one-day suspension over a stupid, fractionally damaged hedge, he, too, would have been royally pissed.

In the end, he had decided, they could bat Bouchard's

background around at a later time. Maybe by then Dixie would show a little more enthusiasm. One thing was sure—the proprietor of Mystique de la Femme had certainly lived a charmed life up until the day his luck ran out. Evidently, the only time his own charm hadn't worked was when he was convicted of the single crime in New Orleans. In that particular case his wealthy, middle-aged victim had obviously preferred admitting an indiscretion to her husband than to pay up. But from that point on Charles Bouchard, a.k.a. Charlie Phelps, had quite clearly honed his style to a fine art. The bigamy charge in Los Angeles had ended in acquittal because one victim took flight in order to avoid testifying against him. His prior record read pretty much the same. From the time Charlie Phelps walked out of the gates of Louisiana State Penitentiary at the age of twenty-six he had not served a single full day behind bars. The myriad traffic violations and charges of solicitation for a lewd act, bigamy, and assault had all ended in citations, fines, probation, or acquittal.

Yes, thought Herb, good ol' Charlie had been incredibly blessed with good fortune, until last week.

"Where to next?" Dixie asked. She had pulled a compact from her handbag and was powdering the end of her nose, seeming not to care in the least that he was watching her. "Shall we go to Hobden's office or pay a visit to the illustrious Mrs. Holmstead?"

"Max gets my vote. I'd like to talk to him before he sees his wife."

She snapped the compact shut and slipped it back into its place beside the two-inch .38 caliber revolver she carried. "Very well, James. His office is at the corner of Capitol and Almaden. Drive on."

Herb cringed. "Look, Dix, you can drive if you want to. All this horse shit about—"

"For shame, James!" She looked at him coolly for a moment before the corners of her lips turned up. Her eyes danced with lights he had never noticed before. "Whatever would Papa Bear say if he knew you were trying to shirk your responsibility?"

"Okay, okay, enough already!"

"Besides"—she put on a pout—"I don't like Fords. I thought for sure we would get that pink Rolls Royce."

They drove in silence for nearly five minutes before Herb spoke again. His tone was conversational, elaborately casual. "I was reading some traffic statistics the other day—you know, the kind of stuff they send around the PD all the time. I wonder where they come up with their figures?"

Dixie sounded as if she was only half listening. "From the Highway Patrol, I guess."

"Yeah? Well, someone oughta call those turkeys. According to them women have fewer accidents and receive fewer tickets than men do. What a pile of bunk!"

Herb was more than rewarded by the bubbling laughter that suddenly filled the car. He grinned, feeling like a man just leaving the confessional—forgiven.

"Sorry, Mr. Hobden isn't in right now." The secretary looked at their badges with round eyes enlarged yet more by a pair of glasses. "Is it one of our people again? If so, maybe I can help."

"Thank you, Miss—"

"Lorry. Deborah Lorry."

"Thank you, Miss Lorry, but we really need to see your boss." Herb gave her a taste of his down-home smile. "You know how it is."

The girl sighed. "Oh, yes. The guys who work here are nice, really they are. It's just that a few of them can't seem to stay out of trouble for very long at a time. Seems like every weekend it's something."

"Like to have a good time, do they?" Dixie asked.

The secretary didn't answer at once. Her owl eyes quickly took in Dixie's blue silk blouse and white suit, the tightly fitted skirt with its front pleat. Disapproval registered on her face as she smoothed the sweater draped over her own straight torso. "Sometimes it's things like that, but not always."

She gave her attention back to Herb, who was now resting his weight on the edge of her desk. Her cheeks dimpled. "Max, that is, Mr. Hobden, is just an old softie. He believes in giving everyone a fair shake. When Project M.O.R.E. sends him a man, he almost always gives the guy a chance.

Usually works out pretty good, too. But every now and then . . ." She shrugged.

Dixie and Herb were both familiar with the M.O.R.E. organization ("Method of Rehabilitation—Employment!"). It was one of the more successful organizations established to give help to ex-cons.

"Is it Manuel Ortiz who's in trouble?" The secretary blinked rapidly, and her lower lip trembled ever so slightly. "Max said he used to be a real rough character. He's our newest man. So nice-looking." Her face was unhappy.

"We're really not at liberty to talk about it just yet, Debbie," Herb drawled. "Do you have any idea when Mr. Hobden will be back?"

Dixie managed not to roll her eyes heavenward when the girl smiled at him again. Old Herbie was really on a roll today! First it had been Mrs. Hobden; now it was Miss Lorry . . . *Debbie*. And the grin he wore was enough to fertilize a whole prune orchard!

"I don't think he's coming back today," the secretary answered, gazing up at him with admiring eyes. "He has some sort of flying lesson or something." Her smile widened and Dixie was almost sure she winked. "Can you come back tomorrow?"

"I can hardly wait to see you put all that blarney to work on Kathryn Holmstead," Dixie said once they had regained the car.

"A little courtesy never hurts." Herb gave her a look of offended martyrdom.

"Oh-ho!" she crowed. "If that was a little, I'd hate to see a wheelbarrow full. My God, Herb, the poor girl won't have to put sugar on her Post Toasties for a week!"

Herb gave her a little-boy grin. "You're just jealous."

She laughed. "No doubt. But just to show you how magnanimous I can be, I'm going to let you handle Mrs. Holmstead, too. Maybe I'll learn something."

"No way!" The smile was gone in a flash, replaced by a look of mild panic. "I've heard all about the Holmstead woman, and broads like her give me the jits. Honest, Dix, I've done my share today, and I'll be happy as a clam just watching, listening, and running my trusty recorder. An observer all the way. Time for you to start earning your keep.''

All bantering aside, it was not hard for Dixie to understand his reticence. Kathryn Holmstead wouldn't be easy, not for anyone, and especially not any cop. A former model, the woman was beautiful, rich, and, quite recently, rabidly anti-police, an attitude which coincided neatly with the arrest of her twenty-year-old son for drunk driving—and the subsequent citations she and her husband received for contributing to the delinquency of a minor. In this case it had been plural—fifteen minors. Evidently, John G. and Kathryn Holmstead had seen no reason why they shouldn't throw a little bash for a few of the Los Palamos youngsters, all drinks supplied. And to date, after posting bail for their son, the two had filed false arrest charges against at least one of the officers who had been forced to break up the party. This in addition to numerous calls to the Internal Affairs Division charging police brutality and harassment.

Driving into the Holmstead estate was like entering an armed camp. Private security guards were posted without and within. Dogs included.

''There's been a lot of trouble with reporters,'' the guard at the gate explained after checking their identification. ''I guess it's all right for you to pass, but I'm going to call ahead and let her know you're coming.''

Pulling halfway through the gate he opened, Herb waited for him to relay the message.

''Oh, shit!'' crackled a feminine voice in reply. ''Tell the jerks I'm out for the day!''

Giving the flustered guard a smile, Herb accelerated smoothly past.

Looking at the sleek body stretched out on a webbed deck chair, it was almost impossible to believe that Kathryn Holmstead had given birth to any child, much less one who was nearly grown. The tanned expanse of abdomen showing between the scraps of pink bikini was flawless, with nary a stretch mark in sight. Likewise the high, rounded breasts. Likewise the slim, lightly muscled thighs. She did not bother to sit up or turn her head as Herb and Dixie approached. One of her arms slowly raised. She adjusted her sunglasses and relaxed again.

The pool she rested beside was nothing short of Olympian in its irregular porportions. A waterfall cascaded into a spa at one end. The entire area was more than a little reminiscent of Mystique de la Femme, but on grander scale by far.

"Whatever you have to say can be taken up with our attorney." Her voice was flat and nasal, at odds with the hauteur of her classic face. "You'll find him at my husband's office."

"We're investigating the death of Charles Bouchard, Mrs. Holmstead." Dixie saw no reason to mince words. "You were there on the day he was murdered."

The only indication that she had heard was a tiny vertical crease just over the bridge of her nose. "I go to Mystique every Tuesday and Friday afternoon. I kept my appointment last Friday. I always keep my appointments."

"So we understand." Dixie felt sure the eyes hidden behind those dark glasses were busy now. Very busy. She took out her notebook and began once more to trace the series of squares and circles that kept her hand moving. "And how did you find Mr. Bouchard that day? Upset, perhaps, or nervous?"

"Charles was Charles, that's all."

"Meaning?"

The honey-colored legs swung around as Kathryn Holmstead sat up. She took the glasses off, exposing eyes that were a luminous midnight, so dark the pupils seemed undefined. A straight waterfall of blonde hair fell nearly to her waist. "Meaning exactly what I said, Officer."

"Sergeant Struthers," Dixie offered. "This is my partner, Investigator Woodall."

"Very well, Sergeant Struthers." For once, Herb's nod and lopsided smile went completely unacknowledged. "Charles Bouchard was an ass-kissing faggot, but he knew his business. He checked my weight, clucked appropriately, and put me through the paces. Gregory did my hair and Angie applied my makeup while Chestine did my nails. Charles approved it all with his usual imbecilic murmurings. I left the salon around five-thirty."

A door slammed and a young man appeared from around

the corner of the pool house. He was tall, bronzed, and blond. "Mother, Dad just called, and he said . . ." His voice died away at the sight of Dixie and Herb.

For just a fraction of a moment, Mrs. Holmstead's features softened. "These are policemen, Jason." Her mouth quirked in amusement. "Or perhaps I should say police *persons*. You were saying, dear?"

The boy's eyes darted from his mother to the detectives. "Dad said to tell you the Enriquezes won't be able to make it tomorrow night."

"That's too bad. I'll call Judith."

"It's a bummer," her son agreed. "I was sure hoping that Michelle—"

"Thank you, Jason." Kathryn Holmstead's voice had turned cool again.

Jason looked from face to face once more and then, without further words, he ran to the edge of the pool and dove in. His lean body sliced almost soundlessly through the calm surface.

"A nice-looking young man," Dixie commented, watching him lap gracefully back and forth.

"Will that be all?" The other woman stood and slipped her arms into the sleeves of a white terrycloth robe.

"Almost. Can you tell me who else was at the salon that afternoon?"

"I can tell you who I saw—Judith Enriquez and her daughter, Michelle."

Dixie stopped doodling. "Her daughter?"

"Yes, Michelle was there, but she wasn't having anything done. I think she might have gone in for a quick swim but nothing else." Stepping into a tiny pair of sling pumps, Mrs. Holmstead started for the main house, leaving Dixie and Herb to follow. "There was no one else. Mystique is usually quiet late in the day. I prefer to book my appointments then for that reason. Now, if you'll excuse me."

Before they could reply, she opened a set of French doors and closed them behind her.

Dody Bangor was just leaving as they entered the squad room, and when the phone rang she swore and looked at her watch.

"Go ahead," Dixie said. "I'll get it."

"Thanks." The secretary arched her back slightly, thrusting out a pair of very large breasts. " 'Night, Herb."

Dixie shook her head and picked up the phone. At first she thought she had a bad connection. The only sound coming over the line was a sharp crackle. It stopped abruptly and the sound of distant music came through. And then a voice. Soft and feminine. "Sergeant Struthers, please." The words were slightly slurred.

"Speaking."

"There were tapes, you know."

Dixie was not sure she had heard correctly. The music grew louder again, much louder. "Pardon me?"

"There were tapes, you know, and they will show . . ." The caller giggled. "I've just made a poem! Get it? *There were tapes, you know, and they will show who killed the fucker Bouchard.*"

Dixie motioned Herb to a phone. "What tapes are you talking about?"

"He kept tapes. That's what I'm telling you. Tapes."

"What kind of tapes, Miss—"

The voice was slower, less distinct, and the music came on louder still. ". . . he got it right from their own mouths, he said. *Stupid cunts.* That's what he called them. All of them."

"I'd like to talk to you about those tapes. Can we—"

"I'm going to write it down . . ." The phone crackled loudly. ". . . *killed the fucker Bouchard.*"

There was a sharp click and the line went dead. A second later Dixie and Herb found themselves listening to the unwavering drone of a dial tone.

CHAPTER 10

AFTER THE BOMBSHELL phone call, dinner seemed in order. To try and quit for the night, shut off their brains, and settle down to a relaxing evening at home would have been futile. Dixie telephoned a disgruntled Reversa. Herb let Janice know he would be working late, without mentioning dinner one way or the other.

Original Joe's served the best Italian food in town. The old family restaurant still placed importance on style and grace, service with a flair, in spite of a decided lack of ambiance. To the unaccustomed, it was at first jarring to see tuxedo-clad waiters moving about the plastic upholstered booths, zipping back and forth behind an old-fashioned counter where chefs cooked over open grills and antiquated stoves. Only the huge potted plants, carpets, and soft lighting saved the restaurant from looking like a five-and-dime soda fountain. But once seated under the unfailing ministrations of a waiter, all was forgotten but the cuisine, the delectable aroma of bubbling sauces, garlic-drenched pasta, and home-baked sourdough bread.

But on this particular occasion the food and mouth-watering smells served only as a backdrop. Uppermost in both their minds was the weird and disjointed phone call.

"Maybe it was the receptionist," suggested Herb. "If some kind of blackmail was going on at Mystique she probably would have known, or maybe she wasn't supposed to and found out by accident.''

Dixie nodded as the waiter placed a heaping platter of shrimp scampi before her. ''But if it bothered her so much, why wait until now? And don't forget there's another young woman now, the Enriquez girl. Her mother never mentioned her being at the salon that day. The Hobdens have a grandchild; maybe they have a daughter, too. The list could be endless.''

They ate in silence for several minutes, Herb unbuttoning his vest to make room for the veal scallopini. ''Could be the receptionist was afraid to say anything. Bouchard had one arrest for assault about four years ago. No conviction, but we both know that doesn't mean anything. I think it has to be someone on the salon premises, someone who wants to help but is afraid. I can't see a kid knowing about tapes, or being blackmailed. The Enriquez girl would be too young for that sort of stuff.''

''There are too many loose ends, Herb. The first thing we should do is go back over the salon. A second warrant might be a little hard to get, but I think Joe Kirk, one of the DAs, will help us on that. We've missed something. I feel it in my bones.''

''More background checks, too, I think. Max Hobden for one; now maybe his secretary, too.''

''The pilot, Art Cochran?''

Herb shook his head emphatically. ''Not a chance. I've known him all my life. A smart ass sometimes but clean as a whistle. It wouldn't hurt to talk to him, though. I intended to anyway. He's the only person I know who might be familiar with your E six-o-whatever. I thought of him as soon as I saw the lab report.''

The discussion continued right through the spumoni, as both detectives thought aloud, sharing their ideas. Herb prided himself on the orderly progress of his own mind, but he was little short of amazed to realize that Dixie's functioned like a data processor. Her little notebook was almost a joke. He had always believed her intelligent, known she was a good cop. But too often good cops made only mediocre detectives. It took more than intelligence to bring a case to successful prosecution. Above all, patience was a necessity, often in gargantuan doses, and the humility to occasionally plod from time to time, to work slowly from point A to point Z, being absolutely certain to miss nothing in between. Dixie obviously had all the qualifications.

Finally, they were both quiet. The coffee was strong and delicious. Dixie looked at him across the table, her eyes catching and holding the flicker of candlelight.

"Not a bad day." She smiled and Herb silently cursed the increased tempo of his circulatory system.

"Holmes and Watson all the way." His voice was wry.

Her brows came down into a mock glower. "Oh, yeah? Who's Holmes and who's Watson?"

"I take it back—Holmes and Holmes."

"Or, God forbid, Watson and Watson!"

Suddenly tired and slightly punchy, they laughed longer and harder than the quip warranted.

It was dark as they walked to the back parking lot. Both Dixie and Herb felt tired but satisfied. Herb waved and stood watching as she went to her car and unlocked the door. He was loosening his tie, just about to turn away when he heard her call over her shoulder.

"Hey, Woodall."

"Yeah, Struthers."

"You hot on barbecue?"

Her back was toward him, and it bothered him that he couldn't see her face. "Only if the meat's not burnt to a crisp."

She did turn now, and he saw a quick smile. "I'm a crummy cook, believe me, but Reversa does one bang-up job. Why don't you and Janice come next Sunday, and bring Amy along. Pop would love it."

"How about you, would you love it?"

"Don't push it, Watson. Let's say I'd *like* it."

Herb hesitated, wondering how good an idea it was to put Janice and Dixie in such close proximity. Then, suddenly, he realized that Dixie must also have hesitated. To his knowledge she had never invited another officer into the seemingly closed circle of her private life. To pass up the opportunity, to forgo seeing her as a friend, was ridiculous.

"You're on. I'll check with Janice just to be sure and confirm tomorrow."

She nodded and waved one last time before getting into her car.

That night, driving home, Herb felt better about himself than he had in quite some time. Janice would meet Dixie. They would all become friends. And he would have to pull his act together. Good, he told himself, *good*. He wondered why, while doing the right thing, feeling good about himself, he also felt that he was losing something.

The bouncy little receptionist at Mystique de la Femme simply did not fit the scenario that Herb had tried to imagine for her. When they arrived at the salon the next morning, her entire posture radiated a unique blend of poise and vitality. Her smile was bright and her eyes clear, with no hint of hangover or the lethargy often produced by drug abuse. Her smile did waver when she learned the reason for their visit, however, finally dissolving into a tiny frown.

"This is going to be most inconvenient," she said, running a long plum-colored fingernail down the page of her appointment book. "We have a heavy schedule today. I don't see how we can do it. I'm sure you understand how upsetting it would be if our patrons saw you rummaging through drawers and cabinets and peeking under chairs while they're being *done*."

"We realize it's a bit disturbing, Miss Severson." Herb's voice was courteous but insistent. "But we do have a warrant."

"Well, I'll have to go get Michael." She stood reluctantly and started toward the main salon. "He'll probably want me to cancel our next appointments." She looked at her watch. "Damn, Mrs. Silva and Mrs. Martin are probably already on their way. Michael isn't going to like this one little bit!"

She was absolutely right. Michael Dreyfus was most unhappy. He came into the reception area with long strides, totally devoid of the relaxed gregariousness he had greeted them with on their previous visit.

"Really, Sergeant, this is just too much!" His angry eyes only skimmed Dixie this time. No twinkle of appreciation. "We have a business to run here, in case you haven't noticed. You'll have to come back after closing hours. Surely you can wait that long.''

"I'm afraid we can't, Mr. Dreyfus," she replied. "We also have a business to run, and in order to do so we need your employees in attendance. I believe we may have more questions for them when we finish the search."

"I still say it's ridiculous. If you'll just tell me what it is you're searching for, maybe I can help. We can all save trouble that way. Unless, of course, my cooperation would interfere with your police rules?"

"Come to think of it, you might be right." Dixie gave him a long steady gaze. "We're looking for electrical outlets, Mr. Dreyfus. You know, in unusual places, the sort one might use for taping conversations, *private* conversations. The kind of tape recordings that might be used for—"

The salon manager held up his hand. There was no mistaking the sudden pallor of his skin. Color drained from his face. He looked at the receptionist, who was at her desk again, staring back at him with curious blue eyes. "When Mrs. Silva arrives, please show her upstairs, Megan," he said. "Olga is waiting for her."

The girl nodded and feigned great absorption in her appointment book, but her ears were almost glowing as her boss turned back to the waiting detectives.

Dreyfus swallowed with difficulty and moistened his lips. "Let's go into the office."

Following him through the foyer and down a short corridor to Bouchard's former office, Dixie noted the mottled skin on the back of his neck. The casual carriage and studied nonchalance he had once exhibited were nowhere in evidence. His gait was stiff, his hands doubled into fists at his sides. By the time he seated himself behind the Louis XIV desk, he had still regained only a minimum of composure. His eyes were slightly glazed and his lips pale. His carotid artery throbbed in jerky, irregular thumps that could be plainly seen on his neck. He seemed to have some difficulty getting out his first sentence.

"Look . . . Charles had a thing going here, that's true enough. I mean it wasn't *my* scam . . . I never approached anyone, I . . ."

"But you did handle the recordings." Herb began playing the heavy this time. His voice was intentionally curt. "And you got a percentage."

"No!" Dreyfus came halfway out of his chair.

Dixie walked to the front of the desk. "Mr. Dreyfus, I must inform you; you have the right to remain silent. You have the right to have an attorney present for questioning. If you cannot afford an attorney"—she ignored Herb's barely muffled snort—"one will be provided by the court free of charge. If you choose to speak, anything you say can and will be used against you. Do you understand?"

The salon manager sat down heavily and ran shaking fingers through his hair. "I didn't get a percentage."

"Does that mean you understand what I've just said and are willing to talk to us?" As they entered the room Dixie had seen Herb reach inside his suit pocket. She knew the recorder was going.

"Will it help me if I talk to you now?" Some of the color was returning to his face. "I mean, I haven't done that much, not anything really terrible. I never threatened anyone. No money ever got to me."

"We can't make promises." She took a chair, crossed her legs, and extracted the omnipresent notebook she didn't really need. "But whatever cooperation we receive will go on the record and be taken into consideration."

"Did the fact that you didn't get any money make you unhappy, Dreyfus?" Herb was seated, too, now, his thumbs hooked over either side of his belt, a pose which separated and held his jacket open. "Surely you got something for your effort."

"I make a damn good salary here, Investigator Woodall, better than I could anyplace else, unless I was willing to move to L.A. or New York."

"It all amounts to the same thing. Hobden pays you an exorbitant salary for being his snoop."

"Wait a damn minute! I never said anything about Max Hobden. He's got nothing to do with this!"

"You expect us to believe that the man who owns three-quarters of this flesh factory wasn't in on the fringe benefits?" Herb laughed derisively. "Come off it, Dreyfus. The guy didn't make his millions by being deaf, dumb, and blind.''

"Look, I'm telling you the truth. Max was a patsy, just like everyone else. Charles had him by the short hairs, too. Bouchard had a friend with similar setup down south, a woman I think. Only her salon must have catered to both sexes because I know she caught Max at something, something he didn't want his wife to find out about. Maybe he propositioned a masseuse, for all I know. Whatever she caught him doing, she must have owed Bouchard a big favor because Max is the one person I know for sure he had something on. He used to laugh about it all the time.'' Dreyfus waved an arm around him. "You can see the results. Charles didn't give a shit about running this whole operation, not the regular business end. One-fourth was all he needed. One-fourth. A place to live and the freedom to conduct the operation exactly as he pleased.''

"How many of the women coming here have to pay a . . . how shall I put it . . . a *bonus*?''

The other man rubbed his hands over his face. "I don't know. It could have been just a few, or most of them. You can't believe the things women will talk about in a place like this. It's worse than a confessional, or better, depending on how you look at it.''

"But you don't know who was forced to pay up? I think that's a lot of crap, Dreyfus.''

An indignant flush crept up the salon manager's neck. "I'm telling you the truth,'' he repeated. "I set up the system and turned it on each day. We used several large spools and Charles always took them off. I don't know how he worked things from that point on. But I'll tell you one thing; if you're looking for someone who wanted Charles Bouchard dead, I'm sure you won't have far to look. He was a bastard. Mean as a snake when he turned off the phony charm.''

"What about you, Mike?'' Dixie put the question to him softly. "Did you hate him, too?''

He met her eyes. "Hate isn't a good word, Sergeant. Charles disgusted me. Whenever possible I avoided being near him because he made my skin crawl. I think most of us here felt that way.''

"Did any of the others know what was going on?" Dixie went on with the questioning while Herb continued to study the other man.

"They weren't supposed to, but I've wondered how they could help suspecting. Charles coached us constantly. He was always giving us pep talks about how women like to relax when they come to Mystique, how they want to lay back and get things off their chests. He even made suggestions about how we should listen and the kinds of leading questions we should ask when an opportunity presented itself. 'You've all gotta be like the three monkeys.' He used to say it all the time. 'A patron can tell you whatever makes her feel good, and you're gonna hear no, see no, speak no. It's all part of the Mystique service.' Sometimes it even went a little further than listening. I overheard part of an argument he had with Gregory, our head stylist, once. His voice was raised and I was standing out in the hall. 'If she wants to grab a handful of cock every now and then, let her, damn it! It won't kill you!' " Dreyfus looked at Dixie apologetically. "Sorry, but that's the way he talked when patrons weren't around."

"Which patron was he talking about?"

"Judith Enriquez, I think, but I can't be absolutely sure. She comes in a little gassed up every now and then. She was Gregory's last appointment that day. The argument happened around five, but we had been super busy. It might have been one of his earlier appointments."

He stood up. "I don't guess there's any way you can wait until later to go over the place. I'll be glad to hold everyone here and pay them overtime. You've got my word I'll still be here when you get back."

"And plenty of time to turn off your cute little surveillance, too, huh, Dreyfus?" Herb reinjected his sarcasm into the conversation, just to stay in character.

Michael Dreyfus sighed deeply. His posture was weary as he led them to the door and then on into the salon.

The system was neither little nor cute. In fact, it would have done the CIA or the KGB proud. An elaborate network of thin wires had been laced through the walls of the main salon and all the upstairs rooms, excluding only Bouchard's private apartment, the foyer, and reception area. In some cases, the small microphones had been seeded behind a plant or wall hanging, or under a lamp shade. But most often they appeared as innocuous air vents in styling chairs, no bigger around than a dime, or as a part of the regular intercoms conveniently set up at each station. In the same way the system had been easy to install in the pool area. The large two-way intercoms used to call patrons to phones, or announce that their masseuses were ready, were in reality working nonstop, picking up every laugh, every nuance spoken, and sending the conversations intact back through the insidious wires where they were recorded on tapes slowly unwinding on a machine hidden behind a camouflage of cabinets in the supply room. Not even the shower rooms or the lavatories were exempt. Charles Bouchard had been a very meticulous man.

The honesty of Michael Dreyfus was borne out in one fact, at least. When Herb and Dixie uncovered the system it was turned off. There were no tapes on the spools.

If any of the Mystique employees suspected the existence of the listening equipment they most fervently denied it now, and as Dixie and Herb went from one stylist to another, asking questions, many of the ladies being "done" turned a sickly puce. The hardest of the employees to interview were the blond giants, Olga and Ernst. Using first one tactic and then another, the detectives tried to determine whether or not the pair might possibly have provided extended services to the rich women who came under their vigorous ministrations.

Finally, through a series of broken sentences and hand gestures, Olga seemed to catch their meaning.

"No!" she cried, shaking her finger in Dixie's face. "No *lovey-dovey*! Only *rub*!"

There was a quick exchange with her brother, who came to his full six-foot-six height with a face twisted into an apelike grimace of offended pride. "Ya! *Rub*! Only rub!" His hands kneaded the air in front of him and then balled into ham-size fists that caused Herb to pale slightly and step back several paces.

When they came back down the curving flight of stairs, Michael Dreyfus was waiting for them, a light sports coat thrown over his arm. Dixie and Herb looked at each other.

"My attorney has been called," he said. "I didn't want to talk about it over the phone, and I assumed I would have to meet him downtown anyway." He looked like he was going to offer his wrists to be handcuffed at any moment.

"Put your coat away, Dreyfus," Herb snarled. "We're not taking you anywhere. Not that I wouldn't love to, seeing as how you're so anxious."

"But . . . but I thought . . ."

"You thought wrong. We have no victim at this point, Dreyfus. But don't you worry. It won't take us long."

"You mean to say . . ." A smile spread over the salon manager's face.

"Exactly." Herb sounded disgusted. "No victim—no crime."

Dixie had the front door open, and Herb was right behind her when Dreyfus spoke again.

"Sergeant Struthers, I don't suppose you could . . . uh . . . er . . . keep this out of the papers? Some of our patrons would be . . ."

Dixie and Herb walked out of the door, laughing.

The luminous dials on the car clock showed nearly ten-thirty as Dixie turned the Jag onto the narrow dirt road leading to her house. It had been a long day, and yet she wasn't in the least tired. Her mind went over the events of the last few hours with vivid clarity.

As she and Herb had expected, a newspaper reporter was lurking close by when they filed their search warrant for Mystique de la Femme. A short time later, following his nose, the same reporter saw the equipment which had been painstakingly removed from the exclusive salon and booked into evidence in the Bouchard murder case. It took no genius for him to put an intriguing picture together.

But the real highlight of the day had come late in the afternoon, while she and Herb were filling out all the necessary forms. Two reporters came charging into the squad room. Lieutenant Di Franco had been on his way out when a cameraman brushed past him without so much as a glance, making a beeline for Dixie.

Normally cameras made Dixie nervous. She did not like

having members of the press hanging over her shoulder. But giving that particular interview had been a pleasure. It had been easy to smile. The reporter asking the questions had no way of knowing that it was not the tape recording system found at the exclusive Los Palamos salon, or even the break in the Bouchard case, that put such sparkle into her eyes. It was the face she saw over the reporter's shoulder. Frozen in the doorway stood her lieutenant, his face florid, the rims of his eyelids red. She could almost see plumes of smoke billowing from his nostrils. Once more, Anthony Di Franco looked like an enraged bull. But this time it was the sweetest sight Dixie could remember seeing in a very long time.

Remembering Di Franco's helpless rage, she was still smiling as she drove along. The lighted windows of her house were just barely visible through the trees when she was forced to slam on the brakes. The Jag rocked to a stop just inches from a fallen tree. The trunk of the pine was not terribly large, maybe no more than eighteen inches in circumference, but it was long. The limbs were thick and close together, forming a barrier of spiky needles across the road. A cursory glance told Dixie there was no way she could move the tree without help. For a moment she considered honking her horn several times to alert Patrick of her trouble, but quickly changed her mind. He was probably already in his robe. There was no need for him to come out into the chill night air. The best he could do tonight was walk her back to the house.

After extracting a flashlight from the glove compartment, she switched off the motor and opened the car door. She inhaled deeply. The forest at night never ceased to amaze her with its changes. She found the heavy, almost primeval aroma of damp moss and the furtive scurryings of small creatures fascinating. The beam of light she rotated around her hardly pierced the wooded depths. It was cool, and she pulled the light sweater she wore closer around her. An owl hooted from somewhere above her.

She quickly saw that if she were to try and step over the log her hair and clothing would be snagged. The last thing she wanted was to walk into the house looking like the Wreck of the Hesperus and scare the blazes out of Patrick and

Reversa. The lectures would be endless. The only solution
was to leave the road and circle around.

In spite of the day's warmth, the ground was still damp and
soggy. The heels of her shoes sank deep into the mire,
throwing her slightly off balance. She swore softly, held out
her arms, and then gasped as the flashlight beam fell on the
severed tree trunk. The shock of what she saw caused her to
lose her equilibrium altogether. She slipped again and fell
sideways, the flashlight flying from her hand. Though the
spill had not been painful, her heart was hammering against
her ribs. Her eyes were wide, struggling to adjust to the
velvet blackness around her.

This was no accident! The realization shuddered through
her. In the split second before she went down she had clearly
seen the exposed stump with its level top neatly sawed away.
And in the next instant she heard the sound. Stealthy. Cautious. Someone moving through the underbrush. Very close.

The familiar surroundings became suddenly threatening.
The towering redwoods no longer seemed proud sentinels but
conspirators giving shelter to the stalking menace. She fum-
bled for her purse, her fingers stiff and unwieldy as she undid
the clasp. She had the two-inch Detective Special halfway out
of its holster when she was knocked back, crushed beneath
the hurtled weight of a man. She could smell the musky scent
of her attacker, feel the heat of his body. And though he was
not tall or particularly heavy, he was powerfully built. The
purse was caught between them. Her hand felt like it was
trapped in a vise as the metal clasp bit into her wrist. Her
skirt rode up the back of her legs as she thrashed, struggling
to free herself. A pair of strong hands laid siege to her throat,
fingers pressing harder and harder, cutting off the air, shaking
her head back and forth like a rag doll's.

There was no breath left for screaming, but even had Dixie
been able she knew no one would hear. The house was too far
away. Darting spots of white and red danced behind her
fluttering eyelids. Blood pounded in her ears. She could feel
her body going limp, and at the same time the weight on top
of her shifted slightly.

It was enough. At last able to move one arm, she brought it
up and clawed at the shadowy face above her. Her nails raked

flesh, opening a bloody wound along the surface of a stubbled jaw. Her attacker loosened his death hold to grab at her wrist.

Air came rushing into her lungs, giving her the strength to push at the iron chest pressing against her. The man fell back but only slightly. For just an instant her throat was completely free.

She felt the blow coming before his fist actually made contact. Pain shot through her left cheekbone, slicing through her eye, straight to the center of her brain.

Even in her agony, Dixie recognized a chance, the only chance she might have. Panic fled in the face of her will to survive. She brought her knee up. *Hard.*

A scream of mingled pain and rage pierced the night as the man rolled away from her, clutching his groin. He swore in a guttural voice.

Scrambling away on all fours, she dragged her purse with her. The hand that had been pinched was numb, and her fingers simply would not cooperate as she tried once more to extract the small revolver.

But her assailant had no way of knowing the extent of her incapacitation. He was on his feet now, bent nearly in half, limping back into the cover of trees. She saw only the outline of his body, the hunched shoulders, the curve of his neck as he stumbled once and then disappeared. Fallen branches broke and crackled under the heavy tread of his feet and finally died away. The woods grew quiet once more. Crickets resumed their mating songs. But the only sound Dixie heard from that moment on was the rattle of her own breath.

Her shoes were gone, her clothes mud-soaked and bloody when she gained the house only a few minutes later. The startled faces of Patrick and Reversa were little more than blurs as she sank to her knees on the living room floor.

CHAPTER 11

"HOBDEN WAS AT home playing poker." Herb sat on the long back porch with Dixie. "There were three other men there, as well as his wife and another woman. It's airtight, Dix. He wasn't the one who jumped you. As a matter of fact, much as I hate to admit it, he seemed like an okay sort, real down to earth."

His eyes went across the expanse of garden to a shady spot beyond, where Patrick Flannigan was pushing Amy back and forth on a makeshift swing. That's the best kind, Herb thought, a thick rope with an old tractor tire tied to one end. He had one himself as a boy. Every now and then a patch of dappled sunlight fell on his daughter's golden head as she laughed and called out to her mother. Standing beside a large open barbecue pit, Janice waved and then resumed her conversation with Joe Kirk. The scene was peaceful, pleasant to the eyes, soothing to the spirit. Easier on both by far than looking at his partner.

Herb had tried to convince Dixie to postpone this get-together, to rest for another day before returning to work, but she had insisted they come. When he continued to argue with her over the telephone, a note of desperation had crept into her voice.

"Please, Herb. I feel fine and I *need* the company. I just keep thinking about it." Her voice had quavered, not much,

but enough to let him know what she must be going through.
"Besides, it will give us a chance to catch up. I've been
going half crazy. Hope Janice won't mind a little shop talk."

Janice didn't mind. She wasn't the type. Herb looked at his
wife and once more realized how lucky he had been in his
marriage. She was wearing Levi's and a knit top, her body
small and compact, only slightly too heavy at hips and thighs.
Her hair curled naturally around her face, and even from
where he sat her eyes looked bright blue, catching the afternoon light. He could not count the times she had sat through
hours of shop talk, war stories, his own and that of other
officers, when he knew damn well she would rather have
been dancing or visiting with other wives. Janice was a great
girl.

Not for the first time, Herb determined to find a way to
deal with the conflicting emotions that had filled him over the
past weeks. He owed it to Janice. And Dixie.

"You're sure the times matched, Herb?"

He turned and looked at the woman next to him. The sight
made him wince. There was a small butterfly bandage just
below Dixie's left eye, an eye almost unrecognizable, surrounded by puffy black and purple bruises. The marks on her
throat were still vivid, chilling reminders of the horror she
had lived through. He was startled by the warm chuckle that
suddenly bubbled up out of her. She was smiling at him, her
good eye twinkling mischievously.

"Don't be so woeful, Pard. I'm not going to look like this
forever."

"Jesus, Dix, I still can't believe it! I'd like to kill the son
of a bitch who did this!"

"You're not the only one. God help the poor sap if Pop
ever lays hands on him. Between him and Joe and you, he'll
be buzzard bait before he makes the jailhouse door."

"Poor sap, my ass!"

"Settle down; it's not your problem. This place is out of
our jurisdiction, remember? The Santa Cruz sheriff's office
will take it from here."

Herb made an uncouth flatulant sound, evidence of the
friendly rivalry between city cops and county officers, depu-

ties. "Yeah? Well, they're going to get a little help on this one, like it or not. Just call it professional courtesy." He took a deep gulp from his bottle of Killian's Red. "I wish I knew for sure whether or not this was connected to the Bouchard case."

"No way we can be sure at this point." She frowned and immediately cringed, touching the corner of her eye with cautious fingers. "I realize we have to check that theory out, but it must have been just some kook, with me as a haphazard victim. A nut. Otherwise, it doesn't make any sense at all. We don't even have a good firm lead on the Bouchard thing."

"Oh, we have leads all right, too darn many leads. They're sprouting like cabbage leaves, Dix. It's beginning to be more a question of who didn't kill the 'fucker Bouchard' than who did. Hobden. Todd. God only knows how many of Mystique's clientele."

"I still keep coming back to that phone call, Herb. We've got to find those tapes. I can't believe Bouchard would get rid of them."

"No, but the killer might have. Probably did."

She sighed. "Yes, and our caller seems to know an awful lot about them. Whoever that young woman is, she's not hinged right. She's on drugs, booze, something."

"I agree. She sounded young to me, too. I keep thinking about the possibilities. Megan, the receptionist. Or Deborah Lorry, Hobden's office girl. The call could have come from either of them. And then there are the ones we haven't had a chance to interview yet."

"Like Michelle Enriquez."

Herb nodded. "I keep thinking about that one. In fact, I went back to the Enriquez place Friday while you were off. No one was home except the housekeeper. She said the family was gone for the weekend. A ski trip to Lake Tahoe. Evidently they have a cabin up there."

"A modest little place made all of logs, no doubt."

"Hey, you two!" The voice of Joe Kirk broke into their conversation. It was an orator's voice, deep and resonant, easily carrying across the backyard. "These coals are about ready. Cut the talk, and tell that good-for-nothing Reversa to bring on the beef.''

''You just hold your britches on, Mr. Big Shot Lawyer. I'm comin' just as fast as these ol' legs can carry me.'' Reversa stamped out of the kitchen door carrying a platter of thick New Yorkers. Casting Dixie a reproving glance that belied the worry in her eyes, she grumbled. ''Couldn't decide whether to cook yours or hang it on your face, Missy Tu—''

''Reversa!'' Dixie nearly squealed in alarm. ''Don't you *dare* do it, Reversa Green! If you use that name I swear I'll choke you! Every time I have company you just glory in pulling out all the skeletons!''

The black woman closed her mouth with a snap, but her frown deepened. ''Have it your own way, Missy. But I swear I never knew a body to be so sensitive. It was your Grandma Klein's name, and a pretty one, too.''

Herb and Dixie stood and walked out into the yard, Dixie ignoring his curious stare. Just before they joined the others, he leaned over and half whispered into her ear. ''I've always wondered about that, Dix—the *T*, I mean. Partners shouldn't have secrets.''

''T is for Trixie,'' she said in a sing-songy voice. She didn't look at him.

''*Dixie Trixie?*'' Herb sounded incredulous and then narrowed his eyes. ''An out-and-out lie.''

Dixie laughed, a rich warm sound that brought quizzical looks from Janice and Joe Kirk. ''Absolutely,'' she whispered back, ''but far, far more palatable than the truth, I assure you.''

Dawn was just breaking, sifting a soft pink glow through the bedroom window. Dixie got up slowly, careful not to disturb the figure stretched out beside her. Joe had never spent the night with her before, not here in her own home, with Patrick and Reversa sound asleep beneath the same roof. And though she feared no redress or censure from either her grandfather or Reversa, she was surprised at her own acquiescence to the notion. The wine was probably responsible in small part, she decided, and the lighted fireplace, and the relaxed atmosphere that followed a very enjoyable day. With the departure of Herb and his family, Patrick and Reversa had also tactfully retired, leaving her and Joe alone. The romantic glow of the fire and nature had accomplished the rest.

Normally their lovemaking took place at Joe's home, a minimally spacious condominium not far from downtown. It was much more convenient, but even then Dixie never stayed all night.

Last night had been special, or perhaps her needs had been special, more intense than usual. It had been reassuring, having him near, feeling his arms around her even after he had fallen asleep—a very special kind of closeness: his rough chin nestled against her collar bone; the smooth, silky texture of his lower abdomen; the hardness of his chest and thighs. He was a beautiful man.

As if her thoughts had been spoken aloud, Joe's sooty lashes parted and he smiled. "I had better get out of here before Reversa discovers my immoral presence and beats me about the head and shoulders with her broom handle."

"Do you have to be in court today?" Dixie pulled on her robe and started for the bathroom. In her case, she knew it was going to be an extra-long day. She had dozed only intermittently, and a slight headache caused by the attack still niggled at the back of her brain.

Joe threw his legs over the edge of the bed. "Yeah, this afternoon. The public defender is a real asshole, too. It's a rape case, but the victim is retarded. I'm not sure how well she'll hold up under questioning."

It suddenly occurred to Dixie how bizarre the conversations that she and Joe shared might seem to other people. *Normal* people. Lovers, or husbands and wives, who got up in the morning and went to work at an office, or stayed home to keep house, or attended board meetings.

Rape. Burglary. Murder. Assault. These were events as common in their lives as eating and sleeping. Theirs was not your everyday dialogue, but perhaps not your everyday love affair, either. She remembered the negative feelings she had been having about her relationship with Joe and now tried to push them all aside. He was so good-looking, such damn good company . . .

There was a brisk knock on the door. "Hey in there! You better get yourself downstairs, Mr. Big Shot Lawyer, unless you plan on wearin' them old worn-out jeans to work. Breakfast in ten minutes, and I don't call twice!"

"Oh, shit!" Joe blushed to the roots of his dark hair.

Dixie could not help laughing at his discomfort. It was the first time she could remember seeing him in less than complete control.

"Reversa's harmless," she assured him, "but you better get a move on anyway. She might indeed trounce you if breakfast gets cold."

She went into the bathroom and was leaning over the tub, pouring bath crystals under the running tap, when she felt his arms come around her waist. He pulled her up, nuzzling her neck before turning her around to face him.

"I could grow accustomed to this," he murmured, tracing a finger lightly along the line of her battered cheek. "Only thing is," he kissed her forehead, "I don't know if I could live down hanging around with such an *u-u-ugly* girl. You look like a boxer."

He stepped away from her and moved to the sink, still naked. She loved his lack of modesty, his free, almost arrogant stride.

"All a part of the job," she replied.

His eyes met hers in the bathroom mirror. "*That* could always be remedied."

The smile on his face did nothing to lessen her conviction that he was not really joking, and slowly the soft, dreamy haze of the morning began to evaporate.

Herb and Dixie arrived in the police parking lot at the same time. When they entered the squad room they found Bobby Todd waiting for them. The artist looked at Dixie's face and his eyebrows shot up.

"For cryin' out loud! How does the other guy look?"

"I'd give a lot to find out," she answered lightly, but the expression on her face and the sudden steely glare emanating from Herb sobered their visitor immediately.

"I read about that business at Mystique," he said, "and I think I've got something you want."

Dixie looked at him closely, almost afraid to hope. "The tapes?"

When he nodded, she led him to a chair beside her desk and invited him to sit. Walking back to a coat tree which stood near the door, she was just about to hang her jacket when her partner nudged her gently. She followed the direction of his eyes and saw the reason for his concern. Just outside, lounging on a bench in the corridor, was a reporter. Dixie recognized the man at once as one of the more innovative and persistent journalists on the newspaper staff. And he was already craning his neck, frowning as Dixie quickly turned her profile away from him. The last thing she needed now was publicity. If discovery of the tapes was broadcast it might very well scare any potential witnesses away. And her face . . . good Lord, her face!

"Get rid of him," she hissed.

Herb turned abruptly and greeted the man, who was even then coming to his feet, heading in their direction. As Dixie walked back to her desk, she heard her partner talking in a bluff voice, telling the reporter about the case, relating all the grisly details which had been hashed over in the headlines at least a dozen times already. Still, Herb managed to tantalize the man with a tiny morsel here and there. Dixie expelled a breath of relief as she returned to her desk.

She looked at Bobby Todd. "You brought them with you?"

He nodded. "I have them in the car. But I want to make one thing clear right now. I didn't have anything to do with what went on at the salon. I didn't even realize what I had until after I read the paper. A few weeks ago Charles gave me some boxes to store for him. He said it was just some books and records and junk. I thought it was kind of funny at the time because it seemed to me that he had all the space he needed. I thought it was so funny, in fact, that I opened the boxes after he left. Not very nice, maybe, but safer. I didn't want anything there that might put my mother in a bad situation. But it was just like he said, books and records, and tape recordings, the kind you play on spools. I just closed the boxes back up and put them over the rafters in our garage."

"Did you listen to those tapes after you read the paper, Bobby?" Dixie looked into his eyes.

"Listen? Sergeant Struthers, the last thing in the world I want to know about is whatever got Charles killed. The tapes don't fit my player, and even if they did I wouldn't have listened to them. If I'm recorded on any of them the worst you can learn is what you already know, and I don't care enough to get upset about that now."

"He wasn't blackmailing you?"

Todd shook his head. "No. Perhaps he planned on doing so later, but right now it wouldn't have done him much good. My mother has some money, but I don't—not yet. Charles knew that."

"You would if anything happened to your mother. And, from what we're learning about the man, I don't think Charles Bouchard was necessarily above that kind of thing, do you?"

"Maybe not, Sergeant, but I am." He leaned back in his chair and looked at her. There was unhappiness in his face, but a kind of aloof pride as well. "You don't think much of my scruples, do you?"

"Does it matter?"

He gave her a small, tight smile. "Not in the least."

A patrolman went to the car and helped carry three large cardboard boxes into the squad room before Todd left. Most of the boxes were indeed filled with books, old and musty, some of them spotted with mildew. Each was gone through, however, in hopes of finding additional evidence, a ledger sheet or list of some sort. There was nothing.

Dixie and Herb saved the tapes for last, taking them into one of the interrogation rooms where the sound would be absorbed by brown carpeted walls and acoustic ceiling. They were excited as they sat down at the table and started the first reel, but very soon their elation was replaced by boredom and gloom.

The recordings had been made at Mystique, all right. There was no mistaking the background noises: hair dryers, music, the hiss of styling chairs, pool sounds, the slap, slap of Ernst's or Olga's powerful hands, showers running, toilets flushing. But the information on the tapes was useless. Shreds of conversation. Snatches of gossip. They recognized a few of the voices. One conversation in particular caused them to lean forward in hopeful expectation.

"I couldn't believe it." The nasal twang belonged to Kathryn Holmstead. *"Jeff's mother must be shattered. Why, just last week he was at our house because he and Jason were planning a camping trip."*

The other woman was crying, sniffing every second or two. When she spoke, Dixie and Herb looked at each other and nodded.

The voice of Judith Enriquez quavered. *"How could he do such a thing, Kathryn? My God, suicide! He and Michelle were so cute together. For her to find him like that was awful. Awful!"*

"I don't think it was suicide, Judy. The paper said it was an overdose. These fucking kids nowadays just have to keep experimenting. A little grass is one thing, or even coke in small doses. But the rest is just plain stupid. If I ever found out Jason had messed with heroin I'd ship him off someplace. And I do mean fast!"

Judith Enriquez sniffed several times in rapid succession. *"Michelle keeps saying he killed himself. She's hysterical half the time. Al finally decided to call a doctor for her."*

The conversation was interrupted by a man's cheerful voice. *"Come, come, ladies! We'll never drop those nasty pounds like this. No salad for either of you until I see a little sweat!"*

"Charles?" It was Kathryn Holmstead.

"Yes, dear?"

"Go screw yourself."

Except for a drunken giggle from the councilman's wife, that ended the tapes. Dixie turned off the player and sat back in her chair. She sighed.

"My sentiments exactly," Herb grumbled.

Dixie kept looking at the reel, her face thoughtful. "Why bother to keep this stuff at all?"

"I think the creep was just in love with his own voice. You noticed he was part of almost every sequence. He liked listening to himself—vocal narcissism."

"Could be." Dixie stood and smoothed a cease in her skirt. "I still think it's time we paid a visit on the youngest

Enriquez. It strikes me as odd that her mother failed to mention she was at the salon that day.''

"Probably didn't think it was important.''

"Probably, but I think I'll ask anyway.'' Dixie was still frowning. "Do you remember reading anything about that boy, Jeff, they were discussing?''

"I quit taking the paper six months ago, Dix. Too depressing.''

CHAPTER 12

"To be frank, I'm getting just a bit weary of all this, Sergeant." Albert Enriquez stood in the doorway of his home, his annoyance obvious. "This is beginning to feel like harassment."

"Sir, we're sorry to impose upon you." Dixie tried to smile. The effort made her eye hurt. "But this is a homicide investigation. I hardly think our single visit to your wife was harassment. Our questions are routine but necessary."

"One previous visit, Sergeant? It's my understanding that you've been here twice. My housekeeper tells me that your partner paid a visit while we were away."

Enriquez was dressed in casual clothes, shorts and a Hawaiian print shirt. Every moment or two he looked over his shoulder, as if anxious to return to patio or pool. "My wife isn't home in any case. She's gone to the city for some shopping. So if you'll excuse me."

"It's your daughter we wish to speak with—Michelle, isn't it?"

The councilman's face flushed a deep angry red. "What does my daughter have to do with this?"

"She was at the salon with your wife, was she not? As we told you before, we need to interview anyone who saw Charles Bouchard that afternoon."

"Oh, for crying out loud, what difference can it make?

She's only a child, and she hardly knew the man. There's nothing she can tell you that would help your investigation in the least.''

"I'm sure you're right, Councilman Enriquez. But we still have to make sure. Sometimes the smallest things, little details, make all the diff—''

"Well, it will just have to wait, Sergeant.'' He cut her off and began closing the door. "Michelle is with her mother, and I'm sure she won't be up to talking when she does get home. My daughter hasn't been well lately.''

In the next instant the detectives found themselves staring at the bold Spanish designs carved into the oak door he slammed in their faces.

"That asshole!'' Herb raised his arm to knock again, but Dixie stopped him.

"Leave it for now. We'll come back tomorrow morning'' —her eyes twinkled—"and tomorrow afternoon . . . and tomorrow evening . . . until we find Miss Enriquez able to receive visitors. In fact, I wouldn't be a bit surprised to find out we have to talk to one family member or another quite a few times. Of course, we have to be careful not to *harass* anyone.''

Returning to the car, Dixie went to the driver's side and slipped behind the wheel without a word, something she had not done since her altercation with the hedge. Di Franco had strongly inferred that she should be a passenger for a while. Unable to use much peripheral vision, she didn't see Herb's brief hesitation before he took the passenger seat. They sat in silence for several moments. When she made no move to start the motor he cleared his throat.

"What's wrong?'' His tone was elaborately casual.

"You're really going to let me do it, aren't you?''

"Let you do what?''

"*Drive*, dummy!'' She pointed to the swelling around her eye. "No one with a shiner like this has any business behind the wheel of a car. What kinda cop are you anyhow?''

"Now, damn it, Dixie! I know how sensitive you've been lately, especially about . . . oh, hell, there's just no pleasing—''

Seeing the red creeping up his neck, she couldn't contain her laughter any longer. A series of giggles built into a roar of laughter which left her face hurting and the rest of her almost too weak to change places with him. "Besides," she chortled, "you have the only set of keys."

Herb gave her the smallest of all possible smiles. "Yes, I know."

The slim equestrienne didn't appear until they were nearly off the estate grounds. Just as their car neared the gate, Dixie looked out over the pasture and spotted a girl on horseback galloping toward them.

"Look! How much would you care to bet that's Michelle Enriquez, fresh in from San Francisco."

Herb pulled the car up close to the white rail fence and braked to a stop. "Sure makes it look easy, doesn't she?"

He was right. The girl looked like she had been born in a saddle. Her sleek roan was moving at top speed across the grassy field. She was like a part of the horse. She sat almost perfectly straight, with thighs relaxed, only her knees giving balance and stability. Unlike Judith Enriquez's carefully lightened coiffure or Albert's jet-black locks, the girl had hair the color of rich chestnut. She drew closer, and Dixie saw that her eyes were a golden brown. A rosy complexion gave her the appearance of robust health.

"Hello!" She called to them as she reined in her prancing mount.

Dixie waved through the open window and started to get out.

"Daddy's not going to like this," Herb mumbled, but he, too, emerged.

"You must be the cops . . . er . . . police officers my parents have been talking about." The girl flashed them a smile and leaned forward in the saddle to offer her hand. "I'm Michelle. You've been up to the house?"

"Yes," Dixie answered, "to see you, as a matter of fact."

"Really? Well, why didn't you wait? I was just coming in."

After quick consideration, Dixie decided on a blunt approach. "Your father seems to think you're in San Francisco, Michelle. Shopping with your mother?"

"Oh." Michelle twisted in the saddle and shaded her eyes, looking down the long drive toward the house. When she turned back she was smiling again. "Don't mind Daddy. He's just being overprotective. He's always like that."

"It doesn't matter. We can talk now," Dixie suggested. "That is, if you feel up to it."

Michelle's face registered a moment of irritation. "Of course I feel up to it. And I don't mind at all, even if I can't help much. I'm sure I can't."

"You went with your mother to Mystique de la Femme a couple of weeks ago, is that right?"

"Oh, yeah, on the day the owner was killed. I read about it in the papers. Mom was really upset. God, she spends half her life there!"

"I shouldn't think a girl as pretty as you needs to go to a place like that very often." Herb used the lazy drawl Dixie had come to expect when they were questioning females.

Michelle Enriquez turned a cool look on him. "No, I don't go often, hardly at all. Mom gets lonely once in a while, and I tag along just to be with her. The last time, Mr. Dreyfus, the manager, let me swim while I waited."

Her young face grew solemn. "The only time I go for myself is when something really special comes up, a prom or a big dance or something."

"Did you see Mr. Bouchard when you were last there?"

"Oh, sure. He was gushing all over Mom and Kathryn, just like always. What a geek! All those gold necklaces and that silly dyed hair, ugh!" She tilted her head to one side. "Guess the dye got him in the end, huh? Too bad. Mom's really upset, especially since the other thing got discovered. I can hardly believe it. The old poop was a blackmailer, too! Dad's been going out of his skull just thinking about how much time Mom spent there. He says the last thing he needs is to have his business blabbed all over the place. He told—"

The sound of a car coming down the drive caused her to stop speaking and frown. Her pretty mouth turned down at the corners. "That bitch!"

Dixie and Herb turned, following the direction of her gaze, a look so hostile that it reshaped the lines of her face, turning it older, almost hard. A white Cadillac was approaching.

"She just loves it when Mom's gone!" The words hissed out of Michelle's mouth. "I'd like to kill her! Half the fights they have are her fault, the stinking greaser!"

The big car pulled to a stop and Christina, secretary to Councilman Enriquez, emerged in all her tall elegance. She favored Dixie and Herb with a swift, withering glance before giving Michelle the full impact of her snapping dark eyes. "Your father is beginning to worry." She carefully enunciated each word. "You do not usually take so long to exercise El Bravo."

"His name is Death Song." The girl's face was pale, her lips thin. "And I'll go back to the house when I'm damn good and ready."

"You are ready now, Michelle. If you do not go at once your father will become still more worried and call Dr. Benson. Is that what you wish?"

It was clearly a threat, but Dixie and Herb were nevertheless surprised at Michelle's reaction. She jerked the reins so violently that her mount whinnied and reared. Then, raising her right hand into the air, she gave Christina the ultimate gesture of contempt before galloping away.

The face of the secretary remained undisturbed and unchanged as she got back into the car, but she did not pull immediately away. Quite obviously she intended to go nowhere until the two detectives beat a hasty retreat.

The attack on Dixie still weighed heavily on Patrick's mind, so that now he found himself in the depths of a dark depression, a cloud of gloom hanging over his head. It was almost like a replay, ripping the scab off an old wound. Not since the death of his son could he remember feeling such rage, a slow smoldering rage that burned him up inside. And yet, in a way, this was even worse. Jimmy had met his death in the line of duty, in the age-old battle of cops and robbers, out on the streets. As horrible as that had been, in Patrick's mind there was a certain cleanliness about it. Not like the slithering, cold-blooded attempt against Dixie.

The most frustrating part of all was having, now and over the past few days, to suppress his emotions. To roar and

stomp and get blind drunk like he wanted to would only have
caused Dixie more aggravation. After the doctor had left
them, and after sitting beside Dixie through the night, Patrick
had forced himself under control, saved his bellowing until he
went to remove the tree from the road.

No ax had been needed. With the undulating cry of a
banshee Patrick had taken hold of the bristly blockade and
lifted it with his two hands. Branches had scraped against his
face and arms, pine needles gouging his eyes, as he hefted the
thing from the roadside and threw it down. Then came the
hatchet—not an ax, which would have made dismantling too
easy and swift. Just a small hatchet.

Yes, for lack of a more satisfactory release, Patrick had
given vent to his fury on that innocent pine, hacking and
tearing, growling and uttering some of the most colorful
obscenities to pass an Irishman's lips. He had literally made
kindling of the tree.

Passage of the weekend had helped very little. Only for the
short while he played with young Amy Woodall had he been
able to put the incident partially out of his mind. But in the
end, even Amy's slightly tilted hazel-blue eyes had only
served to make him remember Dixie as she had been, the
sweet child and grown woman who had always held his heart
in the palm of her hand. Patrick felt suddenly old and helpless, helpless to protect the person he loved most. Dixie was
the core of his life, of his soul, and yet she had nearly been
killed right beneath his nose!

And seeing Joe Kirk's face over the breakfast table that
morning had done nothing to bolster his lagging spirits. Joe
was a right enough man but not, Patrick was convinced, the
right man for Dixie. Heaven knew she needed someone, but
not a man so self-centered, not a man who put ambition
before all else. To Patrick's way of thinking Joe Kirk, like
Donald Struthers, was nowhere near good enough for his
granddaughter.

Now, sitting at the kitchen table, brooding over a cup of
coffee, he wore a face like thunder. Reversa came to stand
over him, also scowling like a black Juno as she refilled his
cup. "Are you just gonna sit here all day and grow moss on

your backside? If you are just say so, and I'll go pull out the vacuum cleaner myself. Four times I've asked already and—"

"Will you just hush, woman. I said I'll do it, and I'll do it!"

"Don't go raisin' your voice at me, you ol' paddy!" Reversa's baritone rattled the kitchen windows. "This business with the Missy isn't my fault, and I can't say as I'm feelin' too fit myself. Like to kill someone is what I'd like to do!"

Poke, lying beside the table, raised his head, gazed at them, and then snorted twice before resuming his morning nap.

Patrick was staring at Reversa, looking not so much at her as through her. "Look here," he finally said, "I'll do the floors, but first I'm taking a walk. I have to do something or bust, and I wouldn't be one bit surprised to find out those deputies overlooked something."

The argument, as with most arguments between the two oldsters, was over before it really got started. Reversa eased her bulk into the chair opposite him. "Oh, yeah? Like what?"

"Hell, could be anything—tire marks, maybe, or footprints."

Reversa shook her head. "Nope. I heard Officer Woodall tell Mr. Kirk there wasn't a thing. They went back and checked themselves yesterday. Didn't find nothin' but alotta busted branches."

"Well, I'm for checking *again*!"

His jaw came forward and his face settled into the stubborn lines Reversa knew only too well. She sighed and stood up. "I'll go get my sweater. Those woods are still cold."

"You'll do no such thing. I don't need you breathing down my shirt collar every step of the way. Poke will be company enough."

Still, after she left the room, he sat waiting, halfheartedly sipping at his sixth cup of coffee. It was a short wait. In less than two minutes she reappeared. Standing in the doorway, she held out his own moth-eaten cardigan.

The woods were chilly but not unpleasantly so. With spring the ground was beginning to dry, leaving a soft bed of leaves and pine needles. They moved through lush, waist-high ferns, stepping over sprouting toadstools and budding wildflowers, careful to avoid the rife and ever-present clusters of poison oak. From time to time Poke would bound ahead to search out his old bone haunts.

The abundant ground cover made it easy to understand why no footprints had been found. Rain or no rain, the natural compost would have absorbed the outline of boot or shoe, bouncing back like a sea sponge. But a car was something else again. There should have been marks, wide swaths cut through the foliage into the soft earth beneath. Dixie had seemed positive there had been no vehicles parked along the highway that night, and yet, even in her befuddled state, she had thought she heard a motor start up and then speed away.

Patrick and Reversa walked for what seemed like miles that afternoon. Beginning at the edge of the winding highway, they worked their way backward to within yards of where the attack had taken place. They found nothing.

Sometimes the two argued, but for the most part they simply talked, each describing in detail just how he or she would deal with the filthy villain who had dared put hands on their beloved Dixie.

They combed not only their own property but a good half mile on either side. Still they found no sign that a vehicle had been driven off the main road. Obviously, the assailant had parked a good way off. He must also have been cautious and patient in the extreme, probably laying in wait for several hours until Dixie arrived home.

It was nearly dusk when Patrick and Reversa finally gave up. The incongruous pair walked along the pavement of the road, glancing at the occasional passing motorists in morose silence. Usually the traffic was sparse but now, with commuters returning from work in the city, the vehicles came by in small bunches.

They were almost back to the unpaved road leading to the house when they heard the whine of a motorcycle gearing down to approach a curve. They waited and soon the lightweight frame of a Honda Scrambler appeared and streaked past. The driver raised one hand in brief greeting and then was gone, leaving Patrick to stare thoughtfully after him.

"I wonder," Patrick said. "Why, of course, it *has* to be!

A bike is pretty lightweight. The man was on a motorcycle, Reversa, I'm sure of it!''

The housekeeper gave him a sideways look of sympathy, knowing how hard it was for him to do nothing, and worse to come up with nothing that could help his granddaughter. For Patrick it was worse than for most. He was a former policeman, a man of action, and now to find himself helpless was driving him near crazy. For once she spoke to him gently. ''There's nothing to tell you that, Mr. Flannigan, not one blessed thing. You just gotta face facts. This is work for the police and not the pair of us.''

Instead of arguing, Patrick just nodded, but his face was suddenly so downcast that Reversa wanted to kick herself. She searched her mind frantically for some way to bring a bit of his spirit back.

''Of course, it could have been a motorcycle, but it doesn't surprise me none that it took you so long to think of it. You were so sure it was a car, and once you get something into that skull of yours you get just like a deaf and blind man. I never saw such a mule in all my life!''

She was huffing indignantly, and seeing the irritation on his face she hurried on. ''If you want to know the truth, I don't think you know what you're doing anyway. You ain't a po-leece no more. Next time you go gettin' one of these bugs up your cranny I'd appreciate it if you'd just leave me out of it. Floors never are gonna get cleaned. My legs feel like they're about to drop right off! I'm too old for this nonsense, and if I'm too old, you're sure as shoot too old. Crazy to go stompin' around like this. Why, just look at you huffin' and puffin' like the old geezer you are. It'd help a world if you'd stop smoking those smelly ol' dog turds you call see-gars, too. I been meanin' to talk to you about that; I can't hardly stand the stink no more.''

Reversa felt like she would run out of breath herself at any moment, but she plunged on. ''Why, it's just a wonder anybody can put up with a man like you, much less Miss—''

Patrick's roar was enough to uncurl her hair and turn it the color of cotton. ''Did I ask you to drag your fat self along, woman? I did not! Fact is, I'd rather be swallowed up and trapped in the bowels of purgatory than to be taking you anywhere!''

They turned onto the long driveway leading home, yelling the whole while at the top of their lungs. And so engrossed were they in battle that neither saw the battered red Chevrolet cruise slowly to a stop on the highway behind them. They did not feel the malevolent gaze that pinned their retreating figures nor see the maniacal smile that flashed across the driver's face.

CHAPTER 13

DIXIE AND HERB sat at their respective desks, desks which sat facing one another. Both were deeply absorbed in reading and reevaluating all the notes and reports on the Bouchard case.

The squad room was quiet as the other detectives also used their first hour on duty to catch up on paperwork. There was a certain peace about the scene. Over the past weeks, especially since the attack on Dixie, there had been a subtle change in the attitude toward her in the homicide unit.

Dixie had noticed the change, and though she would much have preferred acceptance through achievement, it was comforting to know that she belonged to the unspoken brotherhood. Cops did not like seeing other cops attacked. It made them angry in a peculiar "don't get mad—get even" way which could, and often did, prove deadly to anyone who chose to make a police officer a target.

Dixie had no way of knowing that the acceptance she sensed was prompted by more than just the attack upon her. Her male counterparts were not all prejudiced, nor did they collectively support Di Franco's attitude toward female officers. But they did watch, very closely, waiting to see whether or not, in their judgment, she had the "balls" for homicide investigation. And what they had seen to date was an officer who worked as hard as anyone. She was not squeamish. She did not seem overly sensitive or easily insulted. To their mutual surprise she had not balked or filed a grievance over the suspension ordered by Di Franco. And, on top of everything else, she had been knocked around real good.

Jake Spatlin, so often without his regular partner, was now almost envious of Herb. He had even considered trying to woo Dixie away, taking her for his own partner when shift change rolled around, the time when all new assignments were posted.

In short, the general conclusion reached about D. T. Struthers was that she was a hardworking, conscientious cop who took her share of responsibility and risk without bitching. Moreover, she and Herb seemed to be developing themselves into a harmonious and well-oiled investigative team.

Had Dixie been privy to this last conclusion she would have been more than a little surprised. She and Herb were frustrated. To them, the Bouchard case seemed to be moving with all the speed of molasses uphill. It was like being trapped, snagged in a net of red herrings.

Perhaps they should be grateful, she thought. All too many homicides were devoid of leads. Others were too simple, a stabbing or a shooting with a dozen witnesses. Still, the calculated murder at Mystique de la Femme led in so many directions that at times it seemed as if the whole world might have "dun it."

As if reading her mind, Herb looked up from the report he was perusing. "You know, Dix, we really haven't begun to explore some of the possibilities. Charlie Phelps, for instance. It's just possible that someone from his past, someone who knew him as Phelps, came out of the woodwork. Maybe one of the women he married down in L.A." He shook his head. "I still can't figure out how a guy can get away with a gig like bigamy for more than a couple of days. If I started being gone from home half the time, even for a week, Janice would be on me like a hound. Hell, she'd have me up a tree and in the stew pot before another woman could kiss me good night."

The other investigators were listening now, and Delaney nodded. "My wife, too. Jesus, I'd be dead meat!"

The conversation continued on, comfortable, lapsing into a discussion of home and hearth. Wives and children. And it was into this warm, companionable atmosphere that Di Franco walked. He came out of his own office and looked around. As fate would have it, Dixie was just chuckling at something Delaney had said. Di Franco frowned as he approached her desk. "See you're healing up, Struthers. For a while there you looked like a freight train ran over you."

Dixie wondered if he expected a polite thank you for the compliment.

"How's the Bouchard thing going?" he asked. "Notice we haven't had any press around lately." He grinned, and for some reason she was reminded of a Doberman pinscher; the man was all half-lowered eyelids and gleaming teeth. "But I have heard from the mayor. Our first lady is getting just a little antsy about having a felon loose in her own neck of the woods."

"We've got some leads," Dixie answered, knowing damn well he had already read every report, every scrap of paper cut on the case. His question was designed for one thing only, to make her look bad.

"Care to share them?"

Some perverse streak in Dixie's nature suddenly came to the fore. Leaning back in her chair, she crossed her legs and daintily tugged the hem of her blue and white Swiss dotted dress down over one knee. "Well, since we all know you keep track of every little thing in here, and don't need to be brought up to date, I guess I can trot right over to city hall and *share* with Ms. Mayor. I just didn't realize you thought my reports were that good."

For several heartbeats the squad room was silent. Dody stopped typing. Di Franco's eyebrows dropped almost even with his eyes. Bill Brooks, Delaney's partner, was the first to release a slightly contagious snicker.

Inwardly, Tony Di Franco did a slow burn. More and more lately, he felt like he was getting the shit end of the stick where Struthers was concerned. If he came on heavy now, over a little joke, he would come out the loser. It would look like he had no sense of humor at all—which he did not, not when it came to Dixie. He couldn't believe what was happening to his unit . . . how his men seemed to be accepting the little . . .

He swallowed what was on the tip of his tongue and forced a smile. "Cute, Struthers, very cute. Now how about you and your sidekick here getting down to a little serious police work. Think that might be arranged?"

It took a few minutes for the squad room to resume its normal pace after Di Franco returned to his glass cave, but Jake Spatlin finally left for an interview with his in-custody shooting suspect. Delaney and Brooks had gotten themselves another stabbing over the weekend and were grumbling good-naturedly as they walked out of the office. Dody Bangor's mind was far from the reports she was typing, already leaping ahead to her covert luncheon date with Larry Thorton. She looked forward to finding out just how much ol' Larry really knew about sexual assault.

Dixie stood up, holding a small stack of papers in one hand. "I'll be right back," she told Herb. "I need to make some copies of this stuff. I can take it home tonight, give it all a little more thought."

He nodded. His mind was still on the little scene with Di Franco. Looking into the lieutenant's office, he knew in his guts who was going to pay the price for his partner's levity. His stomach churned.

All at once, Di Franco looked up. His eyes locked with Herb's as he reached for the telephone. He slowly swiveled back and forth in his chair, half smiling.

Herb's phone rang, and he didn't have to wonder who was calling. Slowly, he picked up the receiver.

"Hello, buddy." The deceptively soft voice caressed Herb's ear. "I'd like to see you before you go off duty tonight."

Without a word, Herb nodded and gently hung up.

Dixie's mind was doing its thing again, a mini global search, a sort-and-select which allowed her to categorize her thoughts into logical sequence. The process was made faster than usual by Herb's silence as he nosed their newly retrieved buff-colored Dodge out of the parking lot.

"I don't think we're going to come up with anything on your Charlie Phelps theory," she said. "It just doesn't fit. For one thing, Bouchard, or Phelps if you will, had been here for nearly four years. I can't picturue anybody from his unsavory past being able to stroll free and easy into Mystique, much less get access to the supply cabinet. Besides, that's one hell of a long time to carry a grudge, especially one hot enough to end in murder.''

Herb was looking at her strangely. For a moment she thought his mind was somewhere else altogether, but then his face cleared. ''Not so long if you were being constantly reminded, Dix. There is one person who knew Bouchard in the good old days, someone who probably hated his guts.''

''Hobden.''

''Yeah, Hobden. No matter what he says, I'm sure Bouchard had something on him, something pretty heavy duty.''

''But he wasn't even in the salon that day, remember? From what you said about your interview with him, he was high, high in the sky with your buddy, Art Cochran.''

''His wife wasn't.''

Dixie looked at him thoughtfully and then shook her head. ''I don't think so, Herb. I have a hard time picturing Lola Hobden committing murder.''

''You're so sure?''

She answered slowly. ''No. You can't be completely sure about anyone, but why would she—unless she knew about whatever supposedly took place in Los Angeles? And if she did know, why would Max have kept paying Bouchard off? It's another big fat circle.''

''This whole damn case is a circle.'' Herb sighed. ''I've got more suspects running around in my head than Carter's got liver pills. Judith Enriquez. Kathryn Holmstead. One or both of them could have been a pretty juicy meal ticket for Bouchard. Todd might easily have gotten pissed off because our victim was not coming across with the promised art connections. Any one of the Mystique employees might be suspect. They certainly had the most opportunity. Michael Dreyfus, for instance. Damn, I tell you the list just goes on and on.''

Dixie knew how he felt and decided not to heap additional aggravation by expanding his list with her own. He had probably already thought of the other possibilities. Albert Enriquez. Ruth Todd. No one connected with the people

Bouchard had hurt could be exempted—not if vengeance had been a motive.

"We've got to find those other tapes, Herb. If nothing else, they will help by process of elimination."

"Or give us a dozen more suspects."

They rode in silence, each lost in speculation. It was quite some time before Herb finally pulled the car onto a side street and stopped. He shifted into park and turned to her. "I say we go back to square one and cover our ground again. We can start with Hobden this time."

"Him or her?"

"Maybe we'll luck out and get them both in one fell swoop. What say we go by and say hello?"

"Very well—drive on." She gave him a nod and an imperious wave of her hand. "So nice to have a chauffeur."

"Hey, Struthers." He grinned. "You ever hear that everyone likes a little ass, but no one likes a smart one?"

"Often." She grinned back.

The silence between them was comfortable as they drove. From time to time Herb gave her a quick sideways glance and then concentrated on the traffic again. He still was not able to sort out his feelings for her, but at least he was better able to cope. Janice no longer seemed worried about the situation, though perhaps she should, for to look at Dixie for any length of time still had the same disquieting effect on his system. At times it was all he could do not to grab her and try for a taste of those soft lips. Every now and again he would wake in the middle of the night, with his wife sleeping contentedly beside him, and wonder what it would be like to reach out and rub a hand over his partner's hips. The fantasies were less frequent now, though, and he kept hoping that soon they would be expunged by the deep friendship growing between them.

Herb inwardly wagged a head at himself. A few weeks ago he would have been furious at her for her antics with Di Franco. A fleeting smile passed over his face—a regular kamikaze, that kid. Unfortunately, it was going to be old Herb who took the heat for her sense of humor. But better for her than for anyone else who came to mind. Truth be known, he loved her sense of humor . . . and her laughter . . . and her courage . . .

Love?

A strange word to describe the way a cop felt about his partner, but as close as Herb could come to analyzing his feelings for Dixie. The problem now was to sort out just what kind of love he was feeling. Looking at her once more, he wondered if he ever would.

Monte Sereno was beautiful. Spring had painted the yards in color. Wide manicured lawns were ringed and bordered with every imaginable variety of flower. Camellias. Fuchsias. Daffodils. Tulips. Homes sat well away from the hilly streets, dappled by the shade of huge oak trees. Few, however, were as inviting in appearance as the Hobden residence. With outer walls of gray flagstone, it had the sprawling grace of a much older home. No one looking at it would have guessed that its foundations had been poured less than four years before.

The two detectives were not surprised when Lola answered the door wearing cut-off jeans and a bikini top. Her hair was uncovered this time, but no less casual, pulled back into a long single braid. A riot of stray ends danced around her face, a face freshly tanned and still slightly red along the bridge of her nose. She held a platter of sandwiches.

"Why, hello." She smiled. "Haven't done a single 'sorry' present since the last time you were here, officers. Max has been good as gold. Come on in, I'm just making some iced tea to take out by the pool. I kept our little Davey home from nursery school today, just so Max can play with him. They're outside."

Plump and barefooted, she kept up a constant round of chatter as she showed them through the house and into the backyard, an area that approximated half a football field. A huge kidney-shaped pool dominated only a far corner of the expanse and was completely enclosed behind a high cyclone fence.

Max Hobden was bouncing a little boy on his lap, but when he looked up and saw them coming his smile disappeared. Putting his grandson down, he patted the child's backside, encouraging him toward an elaborate play area which had been built nearby.

"But I don't wanna, Paw! You said we were gonna go *fwimmin*!"

"I sure did, Davey, and we will, in just a little while. But first I need to talk to the lady and man, okay?"

The tot gave Dixie and Herb a long resentful stare before reluctantly nodding and then skittering away to the jungle gym.

Hobden came to his feet. "Hello again, Officer Woodall. Nice to see you, but I thought we had pretty much covered everything the last time we spoke. What's the problem?"

"Don't be an old grump, Max," Lola scolded. "Invite our company to sit while I go get some tea." She put the platter of sandwiches down on the patio table and started back to the house.

Her husband shrugged and indicated a pair of lawn chairs. "By all means, sit."

Max fit the description Herb had painted for Dixie. Tall and rangy, with slow, almost awkward movements, he was the very picture of an unaffected good ol' boy. One could easily see him on some ramshackle porch with a corncob pipe jutting from between his teeth. Only his eyes were incongruous, a light, shrewd, and steely blue.

"We haven't met," Dixie said, extending her hand. "I'm Sergeant Struthers."

The palm which clasped hers ever so briefly was even more at odds with the man. He had a limp, moist grip that made her want to use a handkerchief.

"Oh, yes," he said. "You must be the little lady who had the run-in. Pleased to meet you."

"Run-in?"

He smiled a smile which she saw did not reach his eyes. "Didn't someone jump you not too long ago? Heard you got pretty roughed up. Hard on a little gal, I'd imagine."

Dixie curbed her irritation. "I'm surprised you heard. I didn't think it made the papers."

"Oh, it didn't. Your Chief of Police is one of our neighbors. He and his wife were over a few nights ago. When I mentioned your partner here, he told me about what happened to you. A nice guy, Tim. I like him alot."

Nice? Chief Timothy Quinn probably was a nice guy, but it

was not an adjective most police officers would have used to describe the man who had taken the reins of power in the department some eight years before. Quinn was a dynamic, hard-hitting man who brooked no insubordination from his troops. A former New York City cop, he had come to San Jose in the wake of a shaky administration, and he had made some enemies, as well as friends, along the way. Internal battles raged as he established the wide perimeters of his authority. Cops were notorious mavericks, and Quinn kept them effectively, firmly corraled. And whether the man was nice or not, whether he was liked or hated, he was *respected*.

Hobden turned a baleful eye on Herb. "After talking to Tim the other night, I got to wondering about some of those questions you poked at me, young fella. Like, for instance, where I was on the night Miss Struthers here got pushed around."

His seemingly casual use of Chief Quinn's first name was pointed, but if he expected an excuse or apology he was disappointed. Neither of the investigators reacted.

"Have you thought about some of the other questions?" Herb's gaze was level. "I've got a funny kind of nose, Max. Over a period of years I've learned to pay attention to it. Right now it's talking to me, and I'm listening. You say you met Bouchard in L.A.?"

"Yes, I told you that when you were here last time. That's where Lola and I lived before we came up to your neck of the woods." Hobden's voice was still folksy, but his eyelids went suddenly half mast. "I also told you that his name wasn't Bouchard then. His real name was Phelps. He was working as a salon manager in one of those fancy places down there."

"Why do you suppose he changed his name?"

"If you wanted to open an exclusive joint, the kind that would attract a certain type of clientele, would you stick with a handle like Charlie Phelps? He wanted something different, *frenchy*."

"My nose is still pestering me, Max. I can't see a smart cookie like you doing business with a flake. And Phelps was a flake; he had a record as long as your arm. With your resources I can't believe you didn't know that before you took him on as a partner."

Hobden stood up, and now he was scowling. "I could give a rat shit about what you think. In my life I've dealt with all kinds of men. People come to me all the time with ideas. If they have something solid to offer I give it a try."

He looked at Dixie apologetically. "Sorry for the language, Miss, but I don't have to listen to this. In fact, unless I'm served with a subpoena, I don't believe I have to answer any questions at all. I've wanted to show a little courtesy, be a good citizen and all that. But frankly I'm getting fed up with your partner and his talking nose."

Dixie had been studying his profile while he talked, looking at the shape of his face and neck, matching it against the shadowy figure who had attacked her. The comparison drew a blank.

"Mr. Hobden, if Charlie Phelps was blackmailing you, this would be a good time to tell us about it." She looked into his eyes. "Because if you don't and something comes up later, it isn't going to look so good. There's already a chance you'll be roped into the extortion thing that was going on at Mystique."

"Damn it, I've already told your bloodhound here that I did not know one thing about what Charlie was up to. Not one fucking thing!" Max's good manners, and his down-home charm, were taking a beating. "Like I tried to let you two know, I've got a few friends in this town. And the next time you step a foot onto my property without the authority to back up your questions, I'm going to have your jobs. Got that, *Miss Sergeant*? Now get the hell out of here!"

Lola approached them, and upon seeing her husband's face, hearing his booming voice, she dropped the tray she was holding. Ice-filled glasses rolled across the lawn. The frosty pitcher landed upside down, contents forming a large amber puddle against the green.

"Stop it, Max! You're gonna get a stroke if you don't quit doing this!" She looked at Herb and Dixie. "What's going on here anyhow?"

"You never mind, Lola. I told them to get out, to get off my property, and by God I want them gone! Right now!"

The little boy named Davey came running up. He seemed

amused by all the commotion. He was grinning from ear to ear, jumping up and down. "Now can we *fwim*, Paw, huh?"

Max froze in the midst of his tirade. For several long seconds his eyes played over the small figure of his grandson. He appeared not to breathe. And then his face twisted into a grimace. He sat down heavily.

"Please, go." His voice came out in a croak. "Please just go and leave us alone."

Lola was pale. Her bovine complacency had disappeared as she led Dixie and Herb back toward the house. They entered the kitchen and were almost through the room when she turned around. Her lips were compressed to a thin line.

"I guess you'll have to know." The words came out slowly. "Max didn't kill that man. He didn't kill that rotten son of a bitch. He didn't blackmail anyone, either. He . . . he . . . wouldn't dare." She began to shake violently. "I'm sorry, but I've just got to sit. I'm . . . I can't hardly . . ." She stumbled to a chair and sat down. Her hands clenched into fists on top of the table.

"Maybe we should do this later," Dixie offered. "We can come back when you're home alone and not so upset. Or you can meet us somewhere, if it would be easier."

"Nope." Lola shook her head. "If I'm gonna say these terrible things, it's gotta be now. Later I might not—"

The back door opened abruptly and a man stepped into the room. He was a young Mexican, in his mid-twenties perhaps. His upper torso was bare and glistening with sweat. A red cotton bandana was tied around his forehead, holding back a shock of black hair. A ring of keys dangled from his wide leather belt and he was wiping his hands on a soiled cloth. He might have been good-looking except for the threatening and unpleasant expression on his face.

"You need help, Mrs. Hobden?" His speech was accented.

Lola looked at him and then quickly away. "You go back to your work, Manuel. I'm . . . I'm just fine."

He didn't move but stared fixedly at Dixie and Herb. "Mr. Hobden says maybe I should help show these people—"

"I said I'm fine." Lola was still shaken but also different somehow, more tense and tightly coiled. "I saw some stragglers on those shrubs out front. They need clipping back."

''The boss said—''

She came to her feet with an energy that nearly knocked
the detectives aside. Her chair tipped and hit the floor with a
bang. There was nothing of the submissive wife, the sweet
grandmother in her stance now. ''Listen here, you. Max
might be the big cheese when you're mopping floors and
dumping dirt around one of his places, but this is *my* house.
Now get your ass out of here or you won't have any boss at
all!''

Manuel Ortiz turned a deep purple. His hands knotted the
cloth he held into a tight ball. But he moved all the same.
Backward.

''Not that way.'' Lola pointed a blunt finger. ''I said the
front needs trimming—the *front*. And don't go thinking you
can run back and snitch me off to the *boss*. Like I said,
Manuel, this is my house. *Mine*.''

With one last impudent stare at Dixie and Herb, Manuel
slid by Lola and left the room. A moment later the front door
slammed.

Lola was breathing heavily, her ample breasts rising and
falling. ''I'm getting mighty sick of that little weasel. Thinks
just because he's good-looking, because I let him . . .''

Color rushed into her cheeks. She left the sentence unfin-
ished. ''Max is just going to have to get someone else to help
out around here.''

The mention of her husband's name seemed to bring her
back to earth with a thump. Looking at the detectives, she
exhaled deeply and picked up her fallen chair. ''Please, sit,''
she invited; doing the same. And then, in a low, strained
voice, she began to talk.

It was a grimy little story she told, one which kept Dixie
and Herb from looking at each other and both feeling more
than a little sick. Max Hobden had indeed been guilty of a
crime, one that many people considered as heinous as murder.

''And he still thinks I don't know,'' Lola said at last. ''If
he knew, he'd probably go out and kill himself. Sometimes,
when I'm lying in bed at night, I think about it all and wonder
if maybe that would be best—for him to just go kill himself.
He acts like he wants to die anyhow—sometimes. Every time
he goes off flying I wonder if he'll ever come back.''

Her eyes narrowed and glittered, transforming her face. "But then I think about it some more and I know it's much better like this, better when he's here, and better yet when I treat him extra nice. I always feel rotten when I lose my temper and start screaming at him, calling him filthy names. Max deserves for me to wait on him hand and foot. He deserves to look at Davey every single day of his life. He hurts more that way. Do you know what my favorite thing is? When Max is home at night I like to sit with Davey in my lap, telling him stories 'bout his mama, how sweet she was, how pretty and gentle."

The malice in her voice was chilling. "When my Sandy lay in that hospital bed dying, when she told me what Max had done to her, what he had been doing to her for years . . . I didn't want to believe her. I thought I must be hearing wrong. 'Mama,' she says to me, 'Daddy did it to me all the time. He talked real pretty to me before he did it, and then real mean. I was so afraid to tell you, Mama. I was afraid you would hate me forever. He said if I told you he would kill me. I was so afraid!' "

Tears were running down Lola's face. "That's what my Sandy told me," she whispered.

Dixie's stomach was doing flip-flops. "Why didn't you go to the police, Mrs. Hobden?"

"Sandy was gone. Would that have brought her back?" Lola shook her head. "No, this is the best way. And Charlie Phelps helped a lot.

"Sandy didn't want to live at home anymore. She never did too good in school, not after she was nine or ten. That's when it started with Max . . .

"Anyway, she decided she wanted to do hair, you know, become a stylist. And she was real good at it, too, or would have been. She went to work as an assistant in the same salon where Charlie was a manager. The money wasn't so great to start out, her being just out of school and an assistant and all, but she knew it would get better. Sandy didn't want any help from us, didn't want Max taking care of her. At the time, I couldn't understand. I thought she was being just plain old stupid stubborn, proud, like her dad . . ."

Lola's mouth turned down. "Not hard for you to guess the

rest, I don't suppose. Right after Sandy left, I found out she was pregnant. Nothing I could say or do would make her tell me who had done it to her. The only thing she'd say was how she would take care of the baby by herself. She sure didn't want our help. The lady who owned the salon was real good to her. She let Sandy work as long as she could, and then she took my girl right into her own home. She seemed so healthy, Sandy did; who could have guessed what having Davey would . . ."

Lola Hobden blinked several times, but then she began to smile. "It must have been when she lived with that lady that Sandy let the truth slip out, the truth about her daddy. The lady told Charlie then, I guess. Women always liked talking to Charlie. He was a real good listener." The grin she continued to wear, one that spread from one side of her face to the other, was far from pleasant. "Yep, a *real* good listener."

Lola walked out to the driveway with them. The malice was gone from her face, replaced by a haggard weariness which made her look very old. Just before turning away, she bent and spoke to them through the open window on Dixie's side of the car.

"You know, even with all that's happened I think there must be a god somewhere. You saw my Davey. He could have been born sick or retarded, but he isn't. You could see how bright he is—you could see that right away, couldn't you?"

The still afternoon air was punctuated by the loud snip of pruning shears as Herb backed slowly out to the street. Neither he nor Dixie spoke for a very long time.

CHAPTER 14

HERB COULD READ Art Cochran's mind. The barely concealed smirk was little different than it had been in high school. The stunt pilot looked like a shit-eating Cheshire cat. Sylvester ready to pounce on Tweety Bird.

But while Herb could read his friend's mind like a book, he wasn't at all sure what was going on in the mind of his partner. He didn't want to believe, *refused* to believe, Dixie was falling for the line of bull Art was ladling out.

"Oh, sure," Art was saying. "I've had several female students. Not for stunt flying, though. I'm real selective about that. To be honest, most women don't have what it takes."

Herb suddenly felt better. *That's right, good buddy,* he thought. *Just keep it up with the sexist remarks. Any minute now you'll have her eating out of your hand!*

"You ever think about taking lessons?" Art asked.

"For stunt flying?" Dixie was smiling brightly, and Herb felt his spirits dip again. She really was eating it up!

Art cleared his throat. "Well, no, of course not. Just regular lessons, getting a pilot's license. You're the type, I think. Flying can be a real gas. You'd love it."

"Oh, I do." She flashed Art Cochran a row of straight white teeth. "I got my AMEL when I was eighteen. Unfortunately, I don't get to use it much these days, or not as much as I'd like. My grandfather had a Beech Baron. The family

153

still keeps it at Buchanan Field. When I lived in the city I used to fly it quite often. Lately, though, I've felt lucky just to get up for my instrument ratings.''

Art looked like his ego had just been stabbed with a hat pin—totally deflated—and Herb wanted to crack up. For the past twenty minutes his former high school sidekick had been playing his fly-boy role to the hilt, throwing out jargon he knew damn well most people would not understand. And Dixie had listened with rapt attention, seemingly enthralled.

Herb remembered very well how crazy all the girls had been about Art, but his popularity had not stopped with just the girls. Art was simply one of those characters you could never forget. Even as a kid, when he did something semi-rotten, which was often enough, you couldn't stay mad at him for long. There was something so damn engaging about his cheesy grin and devilish, twinkling eyes that you shrugged it all off, just laughed and shook your head. He had not changed. Art quite obviously took life as one vast joke, and to be around him for any length of time was to be convinced that he was right. There was a mischievous quality about him, a little-boy-under-cover aspect that even Herb knew was irresistible, especially to women. Moreover, Art was the only man Herb had ever met who could boast about himself for hours on end and manage to make his listener feel privileged to be listening.

But at the moment Art was wearing an expression Herb had never seen before. Looking at Dixie, the pilot's face was intent. There was something in the air between the two which almost visibly crackled. Art's lively blue eyes met Dixie's, and it was as if they were engaged in silent conversation. A communication which excluded the world about them.

All at once Herb felt like he had been rabbit-punched just below the sternum. ''Can we get back to Max Hobden for a minute? If I remember correctly, that's why we came all the way out here in the first place.'' He knew his voice had come out in an irritated whine.

Dixie turned to him. A tiny frown momentarily creased her forehead and then disappeared. She looked at her watch. ''You have a point. If we don't hurry we're going to get stuck in traffic.''

They were sitting at the Red Baron. The restaurant was a local favorite, especially with small-aircraft pilots. Located on the second story of the Reid–Hillview Airport terminal, the place was a virtual shrine to its namesake, Manfred Freiherr von Richtofen—the Red Baron. Coming up the stairs, the first thing customers viewed was a scaled replica of the World War I German Albatross C-III. In the restaurant proper, large models of old biplanes hung suspended from the ceiling. The menu advertised such catchy appetizers as the Zeppelin Sandwich or the Sopwith Camel. And for all the airport's diminutive size, the restaurant's giant control tower windows overlooked one of the busiest private airfields in the nation.

Art looked from Herb to Dixie with speculative eyes and put down his coffee cup. "What I have to tell you about Max Hobden doesn't amount to much. I've been taking him up for lessons for nearly two months, but I still don't know him very well."

"In his own plane?" Dixie asked.

"No. Right now he's got a Bonanza, but a craft like that is no good for stunts. He says he wants a biplane. In fact, he's asked me to check around for him. But between you and me, the whole idea is a little ridiculous. His nerves are good enough maybe, but he's too old. His reflexes are slow. It would be different if he had been flying all his life, but he hasn't. He'll never be good enough for exhibitions."

"Then why do you suppose he's doing it?" Herb put in. "Seems like a pretty way-out thing to take up so late in life."

"I asked him the same question. In fact, I almost didn't take him up at all. But when he insisted it was just for his own enjoyment, I decided what the hell." Art grinned. "To be honest, the money he offered was just too good to pass up. The guy flies well enough, and if he gets his jollies doing a few slow rolls out over the Pacific, I guess it's his life. So far, the stuff we've been working on together is relatively tame."

"He ever show any interest in crop dusting?"

"Not much. It comes up once in a while, of course, over a drink when we've finished the lesson. After all, it's what I mainly do for a living."

Dixie was looking out the windows. A bright blue and

white biplane was parked on the runway apron. "The Stearman," she asked, "is it yours?"

"I hope to tell you!" The pride in Art's voice was genuine. "I did most of the modifications myself. A whole lot of orchards got dusted to pay for that little baby."

"Do you keep your other plane here? I assume there is another one."

"Yes and no. Yes, there's another plane, but no it's not here. I keep both of the planes over at Watsonville. I live over there because that's where I get most of my work, except for instructing." Watsonville was a small town about thirty miles away, a farming community.

"Have you ever taken Max Hobden there, just to show him around?"

"Never." Art was looking at Dixie in that uncharacteristic way again. "Look, it's none of my business, but I think I know what you're getting at. I've been reading the newspaper articles. For what it's worth, I think you two are barking up the wrong tree. Hobden isn't the type, at least not for my money. He's a weird bird in some ways, but not a murderer. In the first place, he's never been near my equipment. And in the second, a guy with his kind of dough wouldn't have a hard time paying someone else to do his dirty work."

"My conclusion exactly." Herb's tone was sarcastic. He knew he shouldn't throw his next barb, but he couldn't help himself. And he sure as hell didn't want to examine his motives. "How much did you say he was paying you for those *lessons*?" The emphasis he put on the last word was hardly subtle.

Art's reaction only rankled him further. The pilot threw back his head and laughed so loudly that people began turning in their seats. "Oh, that's rich—now I'm a hit man. Herbie, Herbie, Herbie."

"I'm glad you think it's so fucking funny!" Herb was really glowering now, and he looked at Dixie for support. All he got was a blank expression.

"I don't think your investigation is funny, buddy. But what I do find amusing is . . ." Art looked at Dixie and then away again. He shrugged. "Oh, hell, never mind. What I started to say was, if I were you I'd be thinking about some of those

Los Palamos people. A few of them must own land over by the coast, for pleasure or investment. I know some of them keep their planes at the airfields in both Watsonville and Castroville from time to time, at least. Crops have to be dusted. And, like I said, most of the land over there is farm land. That could give plenty of access for what you're looking for, right?''

Art stretched and yawned. "Remember, too, I'm the only duster working this area. Several of the pilots, keep equipment and pesticides at the same place I do, and the others over at Castroville."

"Thanks, Cochran. I might never have thought of that on my own." Herb stood up. "Come on, Dix. It'll be time to go off duty before we can get back."

To his surprise, Dixie didn't move. There was a whisper of silk as she crossed her legs and looked out the window again. "You go ahead, Herb. I'll catch up with you in a couple of minutes."

More than a couple of minutes passed.

Five? Ten?

Herb was just about to get out of the car and go back inside when he saw them come through the door together. The afternoon sun fell on Dixie's hair, turning it the color of ripe acorns. She stood talking to Art for several more minutes and then waved good-bye. She was smiling, but as she neared the car her brows drew together, straightened, and once more Herb had the feeling that she had slipped on a mask, one almost without expression.

Forcing his own face into a caricature of good humor, he reached across to open the door for her. "A real bullshitter, isn't he? Takes forever to get away from that guy sometimes."

Dixie slid in without looking at him, and her very silence seemed to fill the car, making him suddenly claustrophobic. The back of Herb's neck felt hot and he knew that his face was red. Guiding the car out of the parking lot onto the expressway, he hoped she would continue to keep her eyes forward, at least until he could get himself under some kind of control.

Damn! He swore at himself. He was acting like a fool! He hadn't been like this when he met Joe Kirk. Even when he and Janice and Amy pulled away from the house on the night of the barbecue, leaving Dixie and Joe standing alone together in the driveway, he had experienced no more than a fleeting twinge of envy.

All his smug self-analysis of the morning seemed to have suddenly disappeared. The tension was with him again, a tight ball of fire in the middle of his gut. He wanted to stop the car and grab her by the shoulders, shake her until her teeth rattled—or kiss her. Instead, his brain worked furiously to come up with some neutral topic of conversation, anything to tear down the barrier he felt resurrected between them.

"What do you say to going over to see Enriquez again before going back to the office?" he asked. His voice sounded too hearty. "Maybe see if he has any property along the coast."

The sun was a huge orange globe sinking behind the mountains. Dixie put on a pair of sunglasses to shield her eyes from the glare. Her tone and posture were uncommunicative. "I don't think so, Herb. Councilman Enriquez wouldn't exactly come forth with his private finances, I'm sure. Besides, I'm beat. I think I'll just run over to the coast on Sunday and see what I can find out on my own—also on my own time, of course."

"Hey, there's no reason to do that. We can go together on Monday. Or, if you're anxious, I'll just go with you on Sunday and we can rack it up to comp time."

She shook her head, still without looking at him. "Thanks anyway, but this time I'm combining business with pleasure. Art's offered to take me up in the Stearman."

The car swayed crazily as Herb turned onto the freeway ramp doing nearly fifty miles per hour. Congested rush-hour traffic formed a solid wall in front of them, and he was forced to slam on the brakes. Tires squealed and the smell of burning rubber filled the car. It was just the excuse he needed to let loose a string of obscenities.

It had been more than three weeks since Dixie had worked up the nerve to walk more than a few hundred feet from the house, and her own cowardice aggravated her no end. She loved taking an evening stroll whenever she could, walking through the woods with Poke. But since the attack her own property had become threatening. Now, after the nerve-rattling day, she really needed to stretch her legs and think things through.

Suddenly, she refused to be victimized any longer. For as long as she could remember she had roamed these woods whenever the mood struck her, and she was not going to stop just because of some nut!

Taking a lightweight jacket from the coat closet, she whistled softly to Poke. "Come, boy, let's get some fresh air."

The dog lifted his head from giant paws and his tail beat against the floor. He tilted his head to one side, as if in question.

She pursed her lips and signaled to him again. "I'm not kidding, Poke. Come on. Time for your mama to quit playing chicken."

Patrick entered the room. "Oh, no you don't! You're not going out there alone, not yet! Just hold your britches on while I get my sweater."

Dixie sighed, knowing it was senseless to try and stop him, but she tried anyway. "Oh, com'on, Pop. I work all day without a bodyguard. I just need a little quiet time to do some soul searching. Why don't you stay and keep Reversa company?"

Patrick crammed his arms into the sleeves of his lint-covered cardigan. "That's like asking me to cozy up with a boa constrictor, Dix. If you need quiet, I'll be quiet. But I'm going. As for Reversa, I don't know why you keep that old bat around. She's got a mean streak that'd stretch from here to Dublin!"

Dixie sighed again, rather loudly, but Patrick simply went to get a flashlight. Once they were off the deck, moving along the driveway, she automatically matched his stride while Poke ran ahead. The night was clean and mild. The sound of their footfalls soon blended with the chirps and scratchings of the night, allowing her a small measure of peace.

Peace. She wondered if she would ever know such a thing again. She was confused. For once her thoughts lacked clarity. They were all jumbled and mixed and battering against one another until she had a headache. She didn't feel up to analyzing. And yet, her nature being as it was, that's exactly what she began to do.

Damn that Herb, she thought. Seeing him today, the way he acted, had been like being struck by a thunderbolt. All at once his bouts of moodiness made perfect sense, a very uncomfortable kind of sense. During the interview with Art Cochran, Herb's feelings for her had stood out like a sore thumb.

But what to do? Possibilities leaped into her mind only to be discarded one at a time: she could go to Di Franco and request a new partner; she could request reassignment to another division . . .

No, no, no! Dixie mentally shook her head. Somehow she was going to have to work through this thing with Herb. In her years in the department, she had never met an officer she liked as much as Herb Woodall. For all his grump and bluster, he was not only a good partner, but a lively and humorous friend. His mind worked much like her own, and to her way of thinking they had all the ingredients for a potentially phenomenal investigating team.

Blast him!

She and Patrick were almost past the spot where the attack had taken place when a set of headlights washed them in glare. The lights were smaller than normal, low and close together.

"If I'm not mistaken, that's Joe Kirk's car." Patrick waved. "Were you expecting him tonight?"

"No, I wasn't, and I've never known him to come without telephoning first. I wonder what's wrong."

"Just can't stay away, I'd say," Patrick grumped, and Dixie couldn't tell whether he was joking or not. The Datsun 280Z rolled to a stop next to them and the window came down.

"Hi." Joe smiled out. "Don't look so worried, I've come bearing a gift. A warrant was issued for Michael Dreyfus; he was arrested tonight."

"He had the tapes!" Dixie's doldrums dropped away like magic. "I've got to call Herb. This is what we've been waiting for!"

"Hold it." Joe lifted a protesting hand. "I didn't say the tapes had been found, did I? I said Dreyfus has been arrested—extortion and conspiracy charges."

Dixie's spirits took another nosedive, and her face showed it.

"Boy, you really know how to bring a guy down," Joe chided. "Here I drive for miles just to make you feel good and you stand there looking like you swallowed a mudball."

"Sorry." Dixie worked up a smile.

"I should hope so. Come on, you two, pile in. I can already taste whatever Reversa fixed for dessert tonight."

Dixie perched on Patrick's knee for the return trip, her nose almost pressed against the inside of the windshield. Poke loped alongside the car, barking and snapping at the tires.

Five minutes later Joe was sprawled in a comfortable armchair, minus his shoes and suit jacket, his vest unbuttoned, slicing deep into a piece of lemon meringue pie. "Yep," he said between bites, "extortion and conspiracy. We've got a victim."

"Judith Enriquez?"

Joe eyed her dubiously and she abruptly closed her mouth. She must really be losing her grip, she decided, to let go with something like that. Joe might be one of the good guys—a district attorney—which categorized him as an attorney in a white hat, but talking to him about certain aspects of the case was still out of line.

"No, not the wife of our charismatic councilman," Joe answered, "although I'd love nothing better than to see Enriquez on the hot seat. A real slippery sam, that guy, not to mention a democrat. No, it was another woman who came into our office this afternoon. I don't know why she didn't go to the police department. Probably because she felt more comfortable with us lawyers." He flashed Dixie a smug smile. "Anyway, she had a recording with her. Bouchard gave her one to keep, probably just to impress upon her how easy it was to make copies, and to let her know he meant business. I tried to get you after we finished the interview with her, but it was too late. You and Herb had already gone off duty."

Dixie waited, wondering. *Kathryn Holmstead?*

"Her name was Lucille Pearlman," Joe said. "To be

honest, I felt real sorry for her. She was a relatively young woman, married to an older man whom she obviously loves. She's been married to him for over ten years, too, and I doubt, even with the age difference between her and her husband, that she's done another wrong thing in her life. A real innocent. The genuine article.''

"What did Bouchard catch her at?"

"It wasn't catch so much as *trap*. The recording was of Mrs. Pearlman and Charles Bouchard playing games in one of the day rooms, presumably after hours.'' Joe shook his head. "The guy was a real pro, I'll give him that. It sounded as if he had slipped something into her health shake. He had her moaning and groaning, repeating almost everything he said. It was like listening to a skin flick.''

"That,'' Dixie mused, "would make me mad enough to kill.''

Joe set his plate down. "Forget it, honey. I'm sure it won't wash, not with this woman. Her conscience was driving her crazy just over her infidelity. *Adultress*. She kept using that word. She couldn't wait to get it off her chest.''

"If she has such a tender conscience, why do you suppose she waited so long to come forward? She had to have seen the papers, heard the news.''

Joe's eyes met hers. "Because Mr. Pearlman, *Judge* Pearlman, died four days ago.''

Patrick and Joe sat talking politics, but Dixie's mind wandered, tripped back over the day, backward and forward, always dancing around the time she had spent at the airport. She barely listened as Joe Kirk's voice rose an octave.

". . . that's malarkey, Mr. Flannigan. We need the Strickland Bill. It's a unique piece of legislation, and if . . .''

Sitting on the floor next to Joe's chair, Dixie drew up her knees, hugging them to her chest. Closing out all else, she finally allowed herself to dwell in full upon the memory of Art Cochran.

Bullshitter. That's what Herb had called the pilot and at first Dixie would have agreed. Art was cocky. It had amused her to observe his almost swaggering self-assurance. He was, she had decided, the sort of man who could con his way through life. But there was more to him than at first met the eye. He was not simply a modern rake.

She wasn't sure at exactly what point her feelings about him began to change. It wasn't just his looks, the lean, well-muscled physique, or even his face, which seemed always to have a smile lurking just beneath the surface. Something drew her to Art Cochran in a way that she had never been drawn before. And she knew it went far beyond externals. In his own unique way, Art was handsome, but the world held no shortage of charming, handsome men . . .

She threw a quick glance up at Joe, the perfect example. Joe Kirk was not only good-looking, he was fantastic. Every time they went out she saw women turn for a second look, and a third, and a fourth. There was something about the attorney, his jet-colored hair and deep blue eyes, that drew feminine attention like bees to a hive. To most women he would have been far better-looking than Art. And yet . . .

"I guess I'd better get going," Joe said. "You look like you're about to fall asleep."

Dixie started almost guiltily. To her surprise Patrick was gone and most of the lights in the house had been switched off, indicating that Reversa had also retired.

Joe reached out, gently pulling Dixie up onto his lap. His lips were warm and seeking, and she knew he hoped for an invitation. She slowly broke the embrace, stood, and held out her hand.

"It is late. Come, I'll walk you to the car."

CHAPTER 15

HERB COULD FEEL Janice watching him. Her face was quizzical and a little confused. He wanted to sit down and be still, settle himself, but he could not, not for more than a few minutes at a time.

Amy played nearby, seemingly absorbed and content with a new doll. Janice pretended to watch her favorite television program, occasionally even laughing at the antics on the screen. But the sound of her laughter rang just a bit hollow. Herb could almost feel her worry hanging in the air around them all. Her eyes kept sliding toward him as he stood and moved restlessly around the family room.

"How come you're mad, Daddy?" Amy suddenly piped. "Did Mommy *overdo* at the store again?"

When no answer was forthcoming, she looked at her mother, a studious frown stamped on her small heart-shaped face. "Daddy's a grump."

Herb turned and glared at his daughter and then his wife, a growl hovering in his throat. He forced himself not to yell.

Janice stood. "Daddy is not a grump, darling. He's just tired. Come on now, put your doll away. It's time for your bath."

"Oh, poop!" Amy used the latest addition to her vocabulary.

Herb snapped at her. "We'll have none of that, young

lady. When your mother tells you to do something, you do it! Sassy little girls are ugly!''

''Herb!'' Janice gave him a look that made him feel like Attila the Hun and opened her arms to a tearful Amy.

''Aw, shit!'' He turned and stomped into the kitchen. Sitting down at the table, he tried to throw off the blue funk which had been with him for the better part of two days. The sound of running water came to him from the bathroom, along with the sound of Janice's most motherly voice, soothing the injured feelings of their daughter.

To hell with Dixie Struthers! Herb paced back and forth, silently cursing himself. This nonsense had to stop. First thing in the morning he would go see Tony and ask to be reassigned— A.S.A.P. Working with a broad day in and day out was a pain in the ass anyhow.

He sat down hard on a kitchen chair and put his head in his hands. His temples throbbed. There was no way he was going to ask for another partner, and he knew it. Not a chance. And he also knew that Dixie was no broad. She was a lady and the best damn partner he had ever had. And worst of all, the strain which once more existed between them was his fault, not hers.

For two days now they had worked side by side, speaking of nothing beyond the investigation at hand. Pretending everything was normal. And though Art Cochran had not been mentioned, he stood between them. Herb kept seeing his friend, thinking of how the two of them had looked at each other, and with the memory an unwanted rancor turned his mouth and stomach sour. The truth was he could think of little else as he and Dixie went about retracing their steps in the Bouchard case. The fact that they seemed to be making zero progress did nothing to lighten Herb's mood.

Public interest had been rekindled by newspaper headlines. After receiving Dixie's call telling him of the Dreyfus arrest, he had gone out for a paper, something he almost never did these days, and sure enough, the Pearlman thing had made front page. Herb's eyes had quickly scanned the article:

How Many Victims?

*Assistant District Attorney Joseph Kirk announced
late yesterday afternoon that charges are being leveled
against a Los Palamos hair stylist, Michael J. Dreyfus,
in connection with the Mystique de la Femme blackmail
scam. According to the D.A., the salon manager is
being charged with extortion and conspiracy for his
part in crimes allegedly committed by recently deceased
Mystique owner, Charles Andre Bouchard. The first
break in this highly publicized case came when Mrs.
Lucille Pearlman, who resides in the exclusive Los
Palamos area, came forth with a tape recording used to
extort money from her. Supposedly, Bouchard, himself
the victim of a bizarre murder . . .*

Herb had groaned upon reading the article, for with the
Pearlman testimony public interest and publicity had become
almost constant. Di Franco was being inundated with phone
calls, and as a result he was snapping at Herb's ass with all
the ferocity of a cornered pit bull. But for some reason Herb
had not yet figured out, the lieutenant never included Dixie in
his tirades. In fact, Tony Di Franco seemed to go out of his
way to avoid Dixie, waiting until she was nowhere in sight to
pounce on Herb with both feet.

Tony Di Franco was a chicken shit. He knew damn well he
might end up with a sex discrimination suit if he kept on
badgering a female officer . . .

The phone rang just as Janice came into the kitchen, but
she made no attempt to answer it. Hearing the grating trill and
seeing the expression on his wife's face worsened Herb's
already foul mood. This time he did growl as he stood. He
jerked the phone off the hook. "Yeah!"

"My, my, aren't we in a chipper mood tonight."

The sound of Dixie's voice caused the muscles in Herb's
shoulders to tighten still more, but his tone softened and he
smiled. "Sorry, Dix. What's up?"

"It's probably nothing—at this point I don't want to pass
any bets. Do you have a tux?"

"Pardon me?"

"A tuxedo, Partner; do you have one?"

"Are you kidding? I rented a tuxedo when Janice and I got married and haven't worn one since, thank goodness."

"Well, go rent another one, before Saturday night. Bobby Todd is making the big time, a full-blown debut of his work at the Stanford Plaza in San Francisco. After the exhibition his work will go on exclusive display with the Forsythe Galleries. I think we ought to be on hand for this debut, don't you?"

"I don't know much about this sort of thing, Dix, but I really don't think a couple of flatfoots like us can expect to receive engraved invitations."

"We have invitations, and you're right, they are engraved."

"Who did you threaten?"

"Shame on you. I'll have you know I came by these invitations legit. Absolutely."

"I see. You mean to tell me that Todd just sent you—"

"Of course not. My mother gave them to me. She thought I might be interested in some of our rural talent. She didn't know anything about Todd's connection with the Bouchard case. In fact, she doesn't know anything about the case at all."

"Oh, I see, and she just automatically figured your big dumb partner would want to go to an art exhibit. Or am I to be disguised as your date?"

The line went silent for a moment. "Neither. Mother is one of the people in charge of the exhibition. I just asked her to let me have four invitations."

"Four?"

"I hope you don't mind. I just figured it would be less conspicuous if we went with our . . ." Another pause. "Oh, hell, Herb! It certainly won't hurt to make a social out of it, do you think? I'll bet Janice would love—"

"Okay, okay. You don't have to bite my head off."

"Sorry, it's just that I've already asked Joe, and I would hate to have to—"

"It's okay, Dix. I said it will be fine. Janice will love it." Herb tried to fight down the feeling of elation that washed over him upon hearing Joe's name instead of Art Cochran's. "Only thing is . . ."

"Well?"

"Do you think the department will reimburse me for the dress my wife is going to have to buy?"

Dixie made an obscene noise and hung up on him. Herb smiled and put the phone down. He was still smiling as he turned toward his wife.

Janice was sitting at the kitchen table now. Her eyes searched his as he relayed Dixie's invitation and briefly explained its significance to the investigation. He finished and then frowned at her prolonged silence.

When she finally did speak, her voice was soft. "Sure you want me along?"

Guilt caused a pain to shoot through his chest, and he was about to snap at her again when he noticed her hand. She was clutching the edge of the table, her fingers tightly curled. The knuckles on either side of her gold wedding band were stark white.

Herb reached down, uncurled those fingers one at a time, and slowly lifted her icy hand to his lips. "Very sure," he murmured, vowing yet again to stop playing the fool.

Mrs. Rose Klein Flannigan Marks adjusted a centerpiece on one of the buffet tables. Her graceful hands deftly rearranged the huge spray of pink rosebuds, ferns, and baby's breath. She stood back, looked at the flowers, and nodded her satisfaction.

Soon the room she was now in would be filled with people, other gallery owners sizing up the competition, art connoisseurs and critics, approximately two hundred and fifty people. But all was quiet now. Bobby Todd stood in one corner speaking to Milton Forsythe in tense whispers. Next to him was his mother, her arm looped protectively through his. Ruth Todd was dressed and coiffed beautifully, wearing a long gown of smoky crepe de chine that maximized her silvery hair and blue eyes. She would be just fine, Rose decided, with relief. Too often an artist's relatives were an embarrassment at these functions.

Milton Forsythe had worked his usual genius on the exhibit. The walls were draped in soft pastels which complemented but did nothing to distract from the perfection of

Todd's work. A few large leafy potted plants, the white carpeting, and soft lighting completed the desired effect.

"I'm going to buy *The Waif*. If Harry doesn't get it for me, I'm not going to speak to him for a week, much less sleep with him!"

Rose turned to look at her best friend, Samantha Helgrow, and decided that such a punishment would probably delight Harry, Sam's long-suffering mate. But Sam was right about the painting; it was one of the best on display. To purchase it now would be a keen investment. In five years Todd's work would easily bring ten times the price paid for it now.

"Come look at it again, Rose," Samantha urged. "And don't you dare drive the price up by getting Franklin to bid on it, too!"

With arms fondly entwined, the two middle-aged women walked across the room and paused before the painting. To look at *The Waif* was to reach out and touch the essence of life. Like all of the Todd paintings, it was of a human subject, in this case a little girl with straw-colored hair and a woebegone expression that tugged at the heart. Perched on the front steps of a dilapidated shack, the child's only clothing was a tattered undershirt and a pair of dingy panties. A swath of belly was exposed between the two bits of clothing. Her hands, sticklike arms, and face were marred by dirt. She was sucking her thumb. The viewer was trapped and drawn into the child's eyes, great beseeching pools of hazel brown.

"Doesn't she just give you chills all over?" Samantha spoke in an awed whisper. "It just makes you want to . . . to . . . Oh, my! Perhaps I oughtn't to buy it. Just looking at it makes me feel guilty somehow."

"Then by all means don't buy it, Sam." Rose was used to the dramatics of her friend and the affectionate scolding came naturally. "And *do* keep from crying now, won't you? Mascara will be all over your face."

Rose pulled her friend along, looking at several other paintings. For herself she decided that she preferred the one entitled *Spring Dreams*. The girl asleep on the hillside made her think of Dixie as she had been while still in high school. Sweet and yet somehow vulnerable.

Shrugging her shoulders to relieve a sudden burst of tension, Rose realized that underneath all her activities that evening, supervising the arrangements, talking to Samantha, she had been looking toward the door, waiting for her daughter to arrive. It had been too long.

And this time I really am going to keep my mouth shut, Rose vowed. I'll be nice all night long even if it kills me!

"This one is very nice, too," Samantha said, looking at the picture Rose intended to purchase. "I don't believe there is anything quite as appealing as a girl, a gangly soon-to-be woman, hovering in that delightful netherworld of pubescence—do you, Rose? I hate every one of them."

Rose broke into a chuckle. "Oh, Sam, whatever would I do without you? Life would be just too damn boring."

A warm hand touched Rose's arm. She turned and smiled up at her husband as Samantha waved to someone across the room and drifted away.

"Well," Rose asked, indicating the painting, "what do you think?"

Franklin frowned and rubbed his chin. "Doesn't this fellow of yours do landscapes or anything? I'll bet he could be really good, if he pushed himself a bit."

"Oh, really, Franklin!" Rose snapped, and then looked up to see the smile lurking in his gray eyes. She took his arm and leaned lightly against his shoulder. "So you will try to get it for me?"

"Could I do otherwise without being badgered to death?"

"Of course not."

He cocked his head to one side. "It does rather resemble her, doesn't it?"

"Yes, rather." Rose looked toward the door again. "People are already arriving. I hope she hasn't changed her mind."

"Quit fussing, dear. Dixie will get here. But will you do me a favor, just a small one? Don't start hounding her the minute she comes through the door."

Rose dropped his arm as if she had been burned. *"Hound!"*

"Now, Rose, don't go getting up on your high—"

She lowered her voice, but her spine had stiffened. She nearly hissed at him. "That isn't fair, Franklin. I only want what's best for her. Patrick has spoiled that child rotten. Yes, and my father, too, God rest his soul. Maybe if he hadn't left her that house, so convenient, so utterly unsuitable. Oh, really, Franklin, you're her father, and you don't even try to help!"

The warmth left his eyes. "No, Rose, I am *not* her father. I would be if she would allow it, but that won't happen because you insist on forcing . . ." His voice died away, and he expelled a weary sigh. "I love you very much, my dear, but you can be a most vexing woman at times. Sometimes I think Patrick was—"

"And don't you dare mention that Patty Flannigan to me! If it hadn't been for him and all his fancy stories, Dixie would never have done such a stupid thing . . . no, and maybe not Jimmy, either!" Rose lifted her stubborn chin and walked briskly away from him, her earlier noble resolves evaporating in a cloud of anger.

"I hate this thing! Makes me feel like a friggin' robot." Herb ran a finger around the inside of his collar. "I tell you, I hate it!"

"We all *know* you hate it, Herb." Janice's voice was mild. "You've said so at least ten times. And I think you embarrassed the poor waiter by carrying on like that."

"I don't care. He looked silly in the one he was wearing, too!"

Joe Kirk was driving. He laughed and tipped Dixie's Jag over the precipice of another hill.

Herb continued to grump. "And these damn San Francisco streets are enough to make a guy suck up seat covers!"

Dixie turned and looked at Janice. "Is he always so easy to get along with?"

"Only since he started working with you."

Janice spoke with laughter in her voice, but almost immediately she flushed and clamped her mouth shut. Staring at his wife, Herb also turned a mild shade of crimson.

Dixie faced forward again, fighting an uncomfortable feeling in the pit of her stomach. She felt that she must say something or have the remainder of the evening spoiled, tense and uncomfortable for all of them. She laughed and hoped it sounded more genuine than it felt. "Yeah, it's rough being outdone by a female from dawn 'til dusk. It can really work on a guy's nerves.''

Joe saved them all with a chuckle. ''Probably gets more of it at home, too. Herb doesn't have a chance. In the good old days a fellow could go to work and expect escape. Not any more. Take my job for instance—the place is crawlin' with broads.''

''*A-h-h-h.*'' The two women regaled him in unison, and he yelped as Dixie jokingly pinched his arm.

Only Herb remained quiet as they entered the underground parking garage and emerged back onto the street on foot. A light fog shrouded the sidewalks, wrapping the streetlights in gauze, softening the outline of the Stanford Plaza. When they entered the lobby, Dixie dropped back a couple of steps and spoke to Herb in a low conversational tone. ''Did you bring your recorder? We might want to use it.''

''I've got it.'' His voice was still gruff.

''Good, now, *smile*, will you? Don't you know de rich folks is happy, happy, happy all de time?'' She lifted her hands, palms out, framing her face Al Jolson style, the silly grin totally at odds with her formal attire.

And when she began dancing a jig across the marble floors of the Stanford Plaza foyer it was too much for even Herb to resist. He started laughing out loud as Joe corraled her with mock severity.

Janice expelled a sigh of relief.

Ryan Marks spotted his sister immediately. Normally he hated being dragged to the endless social and charitable functions his parents attended, and he made every excuse to avoid them. But tonight was different. It had been nearly two months since he last saw Dixie.

He worked himself through the crush of bodies around the buffet table, setting down a glass of punch as he went. He needed both hands free for the hug he was about to deliver.

''*Sis!*'' He scooped her up as if she weighed nothing at all and crushed her against his chest.

''Put me down, you gorilla!'' Dixie laughed up into his young face. ''I know you don't like to hear it, bro, but you seem to grow inches every time I'm away from you.''

"Then you oughta see me more often." Ryan grinned back.

Except for the same lively, dancing eyes, Ryan and Dixie looked nothing alike. At eighteen, he was tall and heavily muscled. His hair was dark and styled into one of the new half buzzed, modified punks that his mother abhorred. Dixie was a unique combination of Jimmy Flannigan and Rose Klein, while Ryan, except for the wild hairdo, was the spitting image of his own father. A young Franklin Marks right down to the nibs. This resemblance, however, went no farther than surface appearance, for the fiery blood of Rose and Sean coursed through Ryan's veins, all but obliterating the staid genes of his father.

"Look, Dix, you gotta talk to Mom for me. She's off on one of her toots again. She wants me to sit still and let this guy paint my picture. Can you believe it? I swear, I'll go mohawk first. I'm not about to—"

"Will you settle down?" Dixie grabbed his arm and turned him around. "I'd like you to meet some friends of mine. This is Joe Kirk, and my partner, Herb, and Janice, his wife."

Ryan fixed his attention on Herb at once. "You're a cop, too? Oh, great, Mom is going to have an attack!" He seemed to find the idea highly amusing. "Don't mind her, though. She's not as mean as she looks, honest."

His comment hardly prepared Herb for the woman who approached them a moment later. Rose Marks was even shorter than her daughter, her frame slender and elegant. Only a few threads of gray shimmered in the upsweep of her jet-colored hair, and her arresting blue eyes were surrounded by thick lashes.

Dixie repeated her round of introductions, omitting only that Herb was her partner, an oversight which Ryan was about to correct when she tread, none too gently, on his toes. Her precaution was well timed, for almost at once the older woman sniffed disdainfully.

"It's so nice to know you've acquired some decent friends, dear. When you asked for those invitations I was afraid you might show up with some of your hooligan associates. The last thing needed at this affair is a bunch of howling policemen!"

She gave Joe a hard, suspicious stare. "You *aren't* a policeman?"

Joe was laughing as he shook his head. "An attorney."

Rose visibly brightened, so much so that she forgot to scrutinize a very red-faced Herb, who was just on the verge of telling her that he was a garbage collector.

Two spots of color appeared high of Dixie's cheekbones, but she said nothing. The argument with her mother was too old and too bitter to air before her friends.

Rose wanted to bite her own tongue until it bled. But she could not help herself. She hated seeing the suppressed hostility in her daughter, but more than anything she hated knowing that Dixie was out on the streets, looking for criminals now, . . . for *murderers*. She blotted out the memory of the night Patrick had come to her door, his eyes red with weeping . . . of Jimmy, lying in his casket . . .

"I think you'll really enjoy this exhibit," she said, slipping her arms through those of both Joe and Herb. "As I told my daughter, the artist comes from your area. Look for the one entitled *Spring Dream*. My husband has agreed to purchase it for me, and then I'm going to commission Mr. Todd to do a portrait of Ryan." She favored her son with a disparaging glare. "If he'll just let a hair or two grow back on his head."

Ryan rolled his eyes and looked at Dixie in a mute plea.

"Let's find Franklin now so I can introduce you all," Rose continued. "He's always pleased to meet Dixie's friends. He's a real dear."

Yes, she thought, Franklin was a dear. She loved him in a quiet, companionable way, but without the searing passion of her first marriage—and, thankfully, without the daily fear.

Glancing sideways, Rose looked at her daughter's face and in so doing saw once more, quite against her will, the proud Irish countenance of Jimmy Flannigan.

Getting close to Bobby Todd proved no small challenge. The roundabout route they were forced to take soon paid unexpected dividends, however, for standing close to the buffet table, hips thrust stylishly forward, was Kathryn Holmstead. She lifted a champagne glass to lips of vivid magenta. The blue sequined gown she wore was form-fitting and cut nearly to the cleavage point in back, revealing a length of curved spine and lightly tanned flesh which had the men behind her drooling into their goblets.

"Oh, no, darling," she was saying. "I wouldn't have *The Waif* on a bet! Not that it isn't superlative, mind you, but who wants to see those hungry little eyes gobbling up every ounce of caviar one tries to enjoy! Good Lord, it would leech the taste right out!"

Her twangy drawl elicited a moment of subdued, slightly embarrassed laughter, for there was little argument among those assembled that *The Waif* was the finest painting Todd had yet produced. More than that, Mrs. Holmstead of Los Palamos was quite obviously intoxicated.

"Would you mind getting some champagne, Joe?" Dixie smiled at her date, but her attention was already fixed exclusively on the former model and socialite. Herb had seen the woman, too, and together they edged casually closer, listening, while Janice stayed with Joe.

"I think I'll get Jon-Jon to make an offer for the one called *Retirement*," Kathryn Holmstead continued. She was swaying slightly. "I just love that one, don't you? The old fart working in his garden? The colors are superlative, I tell you, *su-per-la-tive*!"

People began moving back and drifting away, exchanging glances, until her only audience was the tall, slightly bald and bespectacled man at her side. She looked up at him, squinting. "Whatcha say, Jon-Jon? Shall we buy the *Old Fart* for your den?"

"Please, Kathy, we ought to start for home. It's getting late." He touched her arm tentatively but she jerked away, spilling the contents of her glass.

"Late? Damn, John! We just got here and I'm gonna . . ." The rest of her sentence died away and her eyes narrowed to slits as she recognized Dixie and Herb.

"Well, well," she slurred, "if it isn't the Keystone Kops in person."

Dixie was wearing a mint-colored silk clasped with a small emerald broach, Grecian style, over one shoulder, allowing the remaining folds to drape down almost to her knees. The fabric covered a pair of wide, floor-length trousers. In effect it was a gown, with all the comfort of slacks. Mrs. Holmstead obviously thought the creation amusing, for she approached Dixie and lifted one edge of the flowing fabric, testing it between her sharp-nailed fingers.

"I do like your new uniform, darling. You simply must tell me who—"

"Kathy, you're making a scene." John Holmstead was more adamant now, taking her arm firmly in hand. His wife attempted to pull away again and upon finding herself trapped, pulled back her other arm, obviously intending to deliver him a resounding slap. Herb reached out and clamped her wrist in an iron grip.

"Now, Mrs. Holmstead, that's no way—"

"Let go of me, you pig!" she hissed at him from between clenched teeth.

Meeting her husband's eyes over her head, Herb spoke again, his tone almost conversational. "No offense intended, sir, but if you need help . . ."

She was beginning to struggle. People turned to stare, cocktails poised. Her voice rose in pitch. "Tell this asshole to let go of me, John. Tell him what you'll do if he doesn't! These fuckers are wrecking our lives! First the charges against Jason, and now this. *Tell him*, John!"

Suddenly, John Holmstead nodded to Herb and both men lifted and carried her toward the door. Her feet thrashed and obscenities echoed in the air long after the three had disappeared.

Janice and Joe came up beside Dixie, each with two drinks in hand.

"My God," whispered Janice. "Did you cause that?"

"Not really, but I don't think I helped much, either." Dixie flashed nearby onlookers a bright, reassuring smile, and the hum of normal conversation resumed.

"Don't you believe her, Janice." Joe handed Dixie a glass of champagne, giving her an intimate look. "Probably just seeing her drove the poor woman wild. Dix is like that, drives woman wild with envy."

Janice laughed a tight little laugh, and though Dixie knew Joe had meant only to pay her a compliment, she wanted to stuff his tie down his throat.

Herb rejoined them, dusting his hands and grinning from ear to ear. "Looks like life is going to be a lot easier for a couple of our officers from now on. John Holmstead just told me he's going to drop those harassment charges that he and his wife brought against the PD after their son's little party."

Dixie stared at him. "I don't believe it. Just because you gave him a hand with his wife? He never struck me as the type—"

She stopped in midsentence as Herb pulled the tape recorder out of his inside pocket.

"Nice little gadget," he said. "You wouldn't *believe* the things you can pick up on one of these things."

"Herb!" Janice gasped. "That's *blackmail*!"

Herb's grin grew wider. "Yep."

Joe Kirk walked away from them, shaking his head. "Holy shit," he groaned under his breath, "I didn't see or hear anything. Not one damn thing!"

Herb put an arm around his wife's waist and took Dixie's elbow. "Close your mouths, ladies, and let's see if we can't find the famous Mr. Todd."

One had to give Bobby Todd credit, Dixie decided. Upon first seeing them, the artist did jump slightly and do a double take, but he recovered almost immediately. Either he was as innocent as a new day, or a very cool customer indeed. One thing was sure: he certainly could act. Watching him now, Dixie wondered again if he was a homosexual playing straight or simply a straight who had once played at being a homosexual. On this occasion, even in formal clothes, he looked masculine to the point of woodsy.

The crowd around him was finally beginning to thin. Checks had been written for nearly half of the twenty paintings on exhibit. It was almost midnight, and Todd was glowing like a neon sign, his eyes bright and happy as he shook hands with Dixie. He ignored Herb.

"You're not exactly who I expected to see here tonight," he said, "but welcome all the same."

"Looks like it was a real success, Mr. Todd." Dixie extracted her hand. "Congratulations. Mind if I ask how all this came about?"

"Not at all." Nothing seemed to dampen the artist's spirits. "Some time back I did a portrait for a woman, someone
Charles put me in touch with, as a matter of fact. I believe
you know of her, now at least—Mrs. Pearlman. She showed
my work to some people from the San Francisco Art League
and one of them, Mrs. Marks, introduced my work to Milton
Forsythe. Things just kind of snowballed from there. God,
I'm still in a state of shock!"

For just a moment he looked downcast, but only for a
moment. "It's too bad Mrs. Pearlman couldn't be here tonight."

"The wages of sin," Herb muttered.

"She was a nice lady, Officer Woodall, regardless of how
it might look to you. The episode with Charles . . . he had a
way of . . . oh, it hardly matters now, does it? But for what
it's worth, Mrs. Pearlman was devoted to her husband, I
know that for sure. She and I became quite close while I was
working on that painting."

"It was your wages I was referring to, Todd,"—Herb still
did not like the artist—"and your sin. Seems to have paid off
pretty well. I just can't help wondering if this isn't part of
Bouchard's little blackmail package. You know, like 'Give
me the money, and throw a show for my friend'?"

Bobby Todd sobered now. His eyes became murky with
anger. "I would never use blackmail to further my career."

"Why not? You've used just about everything else."

The two men stared at each other and the tension wasn't
broken until Rose approached with Janice and Joe in tow.
Janice's eyes were watering slightly and Joe smothered a
yawn.

"Would you believe I found them sitting down in the lobby,
nearly asleep? Shame on you two for running off and leaving
them."

A smile lightened her face as she looked at the artist.
"Don't be insulted, Mr. Todd. I'm sure it wasn't boredom,
just the hour. It is late. Even Milt's beginning to look a little
faded. He just accepted another check, though, and said to
tell you that he and your mother will meet you in the cocktail
lounge. I see you've already met my daughter."

Bobby Todd stared at Dixie and his mouth fell slightly ajar.
A whole portfolio of expressions passed over his face in close

succession until, finally, he began to smile, and then to laugh outright. The others looked at him in question.

"You'll have to excuse me, Mrs. Marks, but the coincidence is just too uncanny for words. I've met your daughter before. As a matter of fact, she was in my studio when I was working on the painting you bought, *Spring Dream*. After seeing her, especially with the sun on her hair, I couldn't resist altering the complexion of my model."

Herb snorted in his inimitable way. Dixie shook her head and smoothed her locks self-consciously. Rose looked at her daughter, smiled, and felt another stab of guilt. *Next time*, she thought, *next time I really will be nice.*

But then she thought again of Dixie's job, of the danger. *I'll be nice, but I'll never give up!*

At one time, the Junipero Serra Freeway won an award for the scenic splendor it offered on its route from San Francisco through San Jose. Winding past a large mountain reservoir and then up and down through the hills, it made the long drive for thousands of commuters a pleasant experience, better by far than the exceedingly ugly stretch of Highway 101, more commonly known as Bloody Alley.

Just past the San Francisco International Airport, Joe cut across on the interchange connecting the two freeways. In these wee hours he chose Route 280 for safety and expedience rather than ambiance, but the Junipero Serra, like most of the peninsula, labored under a blanket of fog. At first, visibility was only minimally hampered, and the sleepy foursome talked in desultory spurts. In the rear seat, Janice and Herb carried on a mild, good-humored argument over whether or not they might one day purchase a Todd lithograph. Herb insisted it would never happen.

But as they traveled on, entering the rugged and sparsely populated stretch of miles connecting the two metropolitan areas, silence took the place of conversation. Fog thickened and choked the road. Joe was forced to slow the car until eventually it was moving at little more than a crawl, inching through a tunnel of gray mist that bounced the headlight beams back into their faces. Weariness and the mild lull of champagne was replaced by a helpless tension only the elements can produce.

"Maybe we should pull off," Janice said. She was leaning forward, gripping the back of Dixie's seat. "I can call the sitter and tell her we're staying over. She'll keep Amy."

"I don't think we'll find anyplace, honey, not out here," Herb said, trying hard to waylay his own fears. "As soon as we get out of these hills the going will be easier."

Silence closed around them once more as Joe maneuvered a wide turn. It was impossible to tell in which lane they were traveling.

Dixie was the first to look over her shoulder and see the set of headlights sliding up behind them. She scowled as the lights came closer, moving faster than safely allowed.

"Joe—"

She had no time to say more before the impact came, a resounding crash of metal against metal that pitched her forward, straining her seat belt to the limit. Janice had not fastened hers and Dixie felt her hit the back of the seat. Joe's forehead crashed down on the steering wheel, opening a small gash between his eyebrows. Herb remained unscathed.

"What the hell's the matter with them?" he swore. "They must be drunk!"

The Jag had rolled onto the soft shoulder of the road and Joe applied the brakes. He kept shaking his head back and forth, obviously trying to clear his thoughts. Janice groaned and began pulling herself back onto the seat.

Dixie and Herb unfastened their seat belts at the same time. They also turned in unison to see the car which had rear-ended them moving away, backing slowly down the freeway. One of its headlights was missing now, shattered in its violent contact with the Jag.

"If that son of a bitch thinks he's going to leave here, he's got another think coming," Herb growled and reached for the door handle. "We're lucky he didn't kill—"

"My God, he's coming back!" Dixie couldn't believe her eyes. The single headlight was rushing them, a cyclops barreling through the swirling mist with a roar and a wild screech of tires.

She braced herself and heard Janice scream as the Jag

shuddered. The other vehicle had come at them from the side this time, and for several moments the Jag was flooded with glare, lighting Joe's bloodied face. The attacking car continued to shove, slamming against them over and over again until there was nothing left but the sickening crunch of metal against metal, and finally metal against brush and soft earth as they tipped over the steep embankment. It was a nightmare—the sensation of flying—falling—the tumble of bodies as the Jag was temporarily airborne. Dixie felt her shoulders and the back of her head connect with the headboard just before the wheels of the Jag hit solid ground again. Joe howled in pain as the car swayed and bounced crazily, scraping its way ever downward through the thick undergrowth. At last it stopped.

The night was eerily silent, broken only by the soft hiss of radiator steam and, from somewhere in the distance, the sound of a car engine, growing fainter with each second.

At first, Dixie lay very still, afraid to move from where she was curled like a fetus beneath the dashboard. She could see Joe, his hand limp and dangling over the steering wheel. He was motionless, his face turned away from her.

"Janice?" Herb's voice rasped into the silence. "Janice?"

He was answered by a soft, almost inaudible groan, and at the same time Joe lifted his arm, bringing a hand to his head.

Slowly, Dixie tested her body, legs first and then arms. She felt bruised all over, like she'd been pressed through the ringer of an old-fashioned Kenmore washer, but all of her parts seemed to work. She gingerly unfolded herself and crawled up to the seat. "Joe, are you all right?"

He turned to look at her and she gasped. The cut on his forehead was still oozing, veiling his face in gore, and one eye was already beginning to swell shut. When he attempted to move the effort made him moan. "I think I've broken some ribs, Dix. Are you hurt?"

Her voice shook violently. "I don't think so."

There was movement in the backseat and she turned to see Herb. The left rear window was shattered and his face was cut along one cheek, but not too deeply, for it wasn't bleeding heavily. His hair fell down over his forehead. The Jag's lights were still on, blazing into the fog, and she could see his expression clearly. A terrible fear gripped her chest. His eyes

were wide and panic-stricken, his mouth moving without
sound. Janice was gathered into his arms, her face pale and
still.

"We . . . we've got to get help!" He was barely able to
speak. "She's hurt, Dix. Janice is hurt bad!"

Joe heard and tried to move only to moan again.

"I'll go," Dixie said.

She was already clutching the chrome handle, pushing
against the door, forcing it open through a tangle of scrub oak
and madrone. Her hair and clothing caught on the bristle of
undergrowth as she scrambled out and began clawing her way
uphill. Her arms were covered by the light wrap she'd worn,
but she couldn't see, and soon the fog left a sheen of moisture
over her face. She wasn't sure how far she had gone when
she heard the crash of feet coming toward her. Someone was
moving down, half sliding, half running. She started to call
out and then stopped, furiously trying to remember any sound
she'd heard right after the Jag rocked to a stop.

Had the other car pulled away?

Panic seized her. Her handbag was back in the car, and
with it her gun. Stranded this way, gripping the brush for
support, there was no way she could protect herself or the
unsuspecting people she had left behind.

"Hello! Is anybody down there?"

Dixie began to shake with relief. Tears of joy sprang to her
eyes as she tried to answer the friendly voice, but for several
moments all that came out of her mouth were sobs.

CHAPTER 16

THE EMERGENCY ROOM at Stanford Medical Center was busy. Nurses and green-clad technicians moved through on quiet, rubber-soled shoes at a dizzying pace. The smell of alcohol permeated the air. Dixie brought a paper coffee cup to her lips. Her hair was disheveled in spite of the combing she had given it, and her gown was soiled and ripped in several places. She watched and listened as the California Highway Patrolman standing nearby finished talking to the man who had come to their rescue.

The man was young, probably not more than twenty, and he hadn't bothered to remove the straw cowboy hat from his head upon coming indoors. Western shirt and jeans covered his lanky frame and he wore lizard skin boots which he alternately buffed on the back of his trouser legs every few minutes. At the moment, Dixie thought he was one of the most beautiful men she had ever laid eyes on.

"Like I said, Officer," he said with a twang, "I'm real sorry I can't tell ya more, but I wasn't about to smear my ass all over the freeway tryin' to catch that crazy bastard, not when I knew there was a car over the side. Seemed like getting to them was more important, so I called in on my CB for help and then started down the hill. *She-e-e-it!* That little lady near scared the crap out of me! I almost stepped on her!"

183

"But you're sure the car was red?" The patrolman was filling out a form attached to a clipboard.

"Uh-huh." The young man nodded. "The paint was all oxidized, I think, you know, real dull. But it looked red to me, and I'm pretty sure it was a Chevy. A piece of shit, I'm tellin' ya. Real scrungy."

"You could see the driver?"

"Hell, man, I was lucky to see the car! That's the worst fog I've ever been in! When I saw that Chevy bangin' the other car over the edge, I thought maybe I'd fallen asleep and was having a doozy of a bad dream. I still can't hardly believe it! Me and Lizzie almost had a wreck ourselves!"

The officer stopped writing and looked up. "There was a woman with you?"

The cowboy laughed. "Not hardly. Lizzie's my truck. Like her better'n I do most females."

There seemed to be little more he could add, and soon he was excused to leave. He came and stood just in front of Dixie, who sat huddled in her chair. "Real sorry about your friend, Miss. I hope she'll be okay."

"I hope so, too." She swallowed the lump in her throat. "There must be some way for me to thank you. If you hadn't come when you did, I don't know what might have . . ." She rubbed a hand over her forehead, unable to finish.

"You already thanked me plenty, Miss. You just take care, ya hear?" He waved and sauntered through the automatic doors.

The highway patrolman approached and sat down beside her. "I know you've answered my questions, Sergeant Struthers, and I don't want to be a pest when you're so worried, but I do have one more."

"Yes?"

"This accident, could it have any connection with something you and your partner are working on?"

She had anticipated the question. The answer left an acrid taste in her mouth. "I'd say that's a very good possibility, Officer Mendez. There've been a couple of other incidents, but until now I wasn't sure they were related."

She briefly outlined the accident she had on the day she and Herb had left the home of Ruth and Bobby Todd, an "accident" neither had connected to the Bouchard case at the time. She also related the later incident that had occurred on her own property. As she spoke, something began to churn deep inside her, starting in her stomach and working its way up, until she felt ready to burst. It wasn't confusion or fear, but a rage so intense that it left her nearly breathless.

Seeing her expression, the patrolman stood and nodded his good-bye. "I'll be sending you copies of these reports," he said. "I assume you'll be taking it from here. We'll give you all the assistance we can."

He had been gone only a few minutes when Joe came out into the waiting room. A large bandage was plastered across his forehead. His left eye was little more than an purple slit. He sat down, wincing at the pain engendered by his tightly wrapped ribcage. "I called a friend. He said he'd come pick us up."

"You didn't have to do that. Pop's on his way in the pickup." Dixie placed her hand over one of his, but there was no response.

Joe answered slowly, almost as if speech was painful. "This will probably work out better anyway. I figured you'd want to stay, but the doctor ordered me home. He gave me some codeine and I think I'll take a handful. It'd be nice to sleep for about fifty years."

Dixie nodded and noticed he was avoiding her eyes. "Where's Herb?" she asked.

"In one of the rooms with Janice. The doctors tried to get him to come out here, but he won't. I can't say I blame him." He hesitated, took a deep breath, and then obviously decided to say what was on his mind. "My guess is he's feeling just a little guilty."

She felt her spine stiffen. "I hope not, because there's no reason he should. This wasn't his fault."

"Maybe not, but if something happens to his wife you're both going to have to live with that bit of painful reality for a very long time."

Dixie snatched her hand back and glared at him. "Joe Kirk, if you weren't already such a mess I'd beat your face in. Herb and I are partners! Do you hear me, *partners*!"

"I've never doubted that for a minute, Dix. I wasn't

implying you were anything else, though I don't think Janice is quite so sure. What I *am* saying, right out, is that your jobs might not be worth the price Herb and his wife will have to pay."

Joe was finally looking at her, meeting her blazing green eyes with an anger of his own. "Correct me if I'm wrong, Sergeant Struthers, but does or does not this tie in with your present case?"

"Listen, Joe, we all have our jobs to do, you and Herb and I." Suddenly, she found herself almost pleading, begging him to understand. "We all feel the same way about—"

Joe cut her off. "Well, your job stinks, especially for a woman. Maybe what I'm really saying is for *my* woman. I'm not going to have a wife who gets knocked on her ass every month or two. And I'm not going to live with a woman who worries the hell out of me every time she walks out the front door. You're going to have to make up your mind right now about what kind of life you want, Dix."

She came to her feet slowly. All of her anger came rushing back but, looking down at him, she forced herself to speak in a calm, steady voice. "Joseph Winston Kirk, you've never asked me to be your wife—and if this is a proposal or a suggestion that we cohabit, I find your taste and timing just a little off kilter. I have a job that satisfies my personal needs and offers me a chance to do something worthwhile. You should understand that better than anyone."

"Dixie, use your head!"

"Be quiet, Joe. My head is just fine, and this is probably as good a time as any for us to set the record straight. You don't want to be married to a cop, but you've never asked me if I wanted to be married to an attorney—a politician. A senator, maybe? Someday? A president?"

"Listen, Dixie, maybe we should wait until—"

"No, Joe, you listen; I don't want to wait. I've thought about it, have been thinking about it, for some time, and I've made my choice. Perhaps I should have shared my thoughts, my doubts with you when I first began . . ." She looked deep into his eyes. "No, that would have been a bit presumptuous on my part—after all, you never asked me, and I didn't want to . . . oh, Joe, never mind. It really doesn't matter, not like it should.''

She looked away from him. She didn't want to talk to him anymore; she didn't want to see him. And all at once it occurred to her that, at the moment, she didn't even want to be in the same room. Turning, she walked out to the vending machines in the corridor. Worry for Janice filled her mind, pushing thoughts of Joe to one side.

A short time later she looked up and saw Stan Mitchell, another DA and Joe's best friend, enter the waiting room. When the two men came back out together, she saw Joe hesitate. For a moment their eyes met, and then he walked away.

Patrick watched Dixie pace back and forth until he was sure the tile floor would be worn clear through. She was like a cat, all wound up and ready to leap on the first person who got too close.

And it's not going to be me, he decided. There was no reaching the girl when she was in such a state. The only thing that could calm her now would be to see her partner walk through those doors saying that Janice was going to be fine.

It had been many years since Patrick prayed, but he did so now, the litany he'd learned in childhood running through his brain like a long forgotten friend: *I beseech you, O Lord, to hear my prayers and in your goodness have mercy upon our souls. For this, O God, I pray. Amen.* His lips moved silently.

When he opened his eyes, Dixie was standing in front of him, still at last. Her face was tender.

Taking hold of her hands, he drew her down into the seat next to him. She made no move to resist as he put his arms around her and eased her head against his chest. ''Methinks there's more here than meets the eye, *mouverene*. Where's Joe? I expected to find him here with you, if he could still stand up.''

''Oh, Pop, it's not just Joe. It's the whole thing!''

''Janice will be just fine, Dix. Stop your worrying and talk to me. It'll clear your mind and there's nothing else to do until Herbie comes.''

Dixie laughed shakily and straightened. "Don't ever let him hear you call him that or he'll wring your old neck!"

He smiled at her. "Now, that's more like it."

Her levity was spent. "I don't know what he'll do if anything happens to Janice, Pop, I really don't." She looked toward the doors of the emergency room proper. "What's taking so long!"

"Settle down, girl. Don't you remember the time I took you into the hospital with your big toe all bleeding from lettin' Jackie McPherson use your foot for target practice? It took hours for them to get around to you."

She gave him another fleeting smile. "Yes, and you acted awful! You bullied every nurse in sight."

"Well, I had to do something to let off steam," he retorted. "More so because it was *you* I wanted to kill. What would make a girl stupid enough to let a boy chuck a knife at her foot, might you be tellin' me after all these years?"

Patrick spoke in a slight brogue, and Dixie remembered all the times he had used the same ploy to bring her out of the doldrums or to distract her from some painful situation.

"I'll be tellin' you nothin', you ol' poop, except that Jackie McPherson was the cutest boy for a hundred miles, and he promised he wouldn't stab me. We were practicing to become a famous knife-throwing team."

"Oh, Lord!" Patrick chuckled. "Too bad you didn't stick to your plans. It would have been safer by far, I'm thinkin', than what ya be doin' now."

The sound of voices came to them from just beyond the doors. They both stood, and a moment later a gurney was pushed through. Herb was walking alongside, holding Janice's hand. She was pale and there were dark smudges beneath her eyes. Heavy sedation had obviously been given, and the lower half of her body was covered with a sheet that molded the outlines of a plaster splint on her left leg. She looked incredibly small. Her voice wavered as she called for the attendant to stop.

"Dixie." Janice released Herb's hand and reached out.

Tears impaired Dixie's vision as she took the hand and felt its gentle pressure.

"Please do me a favor." Janice smiled weakly. "Grab

hold of this ape and take him home. They've given me some lovely stuff, and all I want to do now is *sl-e-e-e-p*.'' Her brow puckered. ''I don't know what I'm going to do about Amy—''

''Will you please stop worrying?'' Herb bent over and put his face close to hers. ''Amy's going to be fine for a few days. I'll talk to Margaret next door. Or, better yet, I'll stay home with her myself. I've got a little time off coming—''

Janice's eyes opened wider, and she struggled as though she intended to sit up. ''Oh, no, Herb! You can't do that. He's got to be caught, that mad man, he might try—''

Herb pushed her gently down by the shoulders. ''Okay, okay, so I'll ask Margaret.''

Patrick cleared his throat and when he spoke his eyes were suspiciously bright. ''You'll do no such thing, Herb. Reversa and I can manage the munchkin just fine. Now Janice, you best be letting this gent haul you up to bed. Your lids are lookin' a might droopy.''

Her eyes closed all at once then, and she fell asleep smiling as the attendant rolled her away.

Herb stood looking out into the corridor for a long time after the gurney disappeared. ''One of her legs is broken in three places,'' he said, almost in a whisper. ''They're going to have to operate. Her pelvis and collarbone are fractured and she has a mild concussion.'' His shoulders hunched. *''Damn!''*

Dixie lightly touched his arm. When he turned and she saw his eyes, her arms went around him.

''She's going to be all right, Dix.'' He sounded like a little boy, incredulous, not quite daring to believe. His chest and shoulders shuddered once and then the tears came.

Dixie had often wondered what it would be like to have both a child and a career. Amy Woodall soon gave her an opportunity to find out. Janice had been scheduled for surgery the afternoon following the accident, and Herb came by with his daughter about noon, his face haggered and worried.

Reversa was waiting and gathered the little girl into her ample arms at once. ''Come here, dumplin'. I've been bakin' cookies all mornin' long. Now I need some hungry somebody to help me eat 'em.''

Confused by the whole situation, Amy's voice was shy. "What kind?"

Reversa pursed her lips and scratched her head. "Well, lemme see. There's chocolate chip, and a dozen or so peanut butter, and hmmm . . . oh, yes! A batch of ginger crinkles. You might not like those, 'cause they're covered with powdered sugar."

"Yes I will!"

"I don't know . . ."

"I will! Promise!"

"Okay then, if you're sure. You want to give it a try?"

The child nodded solemnly and then twisted to look at her father. Herb gave her a kiss. "You be a good girl now, all right?"

Amy bobbed her head up and down. "Will Mommy come home tomorrow?"

"No, but soon." He kissed her again.

Dixie walked him to the car. "You look like death," she said.

"Thanks a lot. I feel like I've been jerked through a knothole backwards."

"I know the feeling." She grimaced and put a hand on the small of her back, stretching her agonized muscles. "But my face is prettier than yours. Cut yourself shaving?"

Herb touched the long gash on his cheek, the result of flying glass and his only obvious injury. "Yeah. Just clumsy, I guess. Speaking of cuts, how's Joe this morning?"

Dixie concentrated on a hollow redwood tree which stood close to the house. "I don't know. Fine, I hope."

"Fine?" He placed a finger under her chin and forced her to look at him. "You hope?"

"Not now, Herb. Later maybe, but not now."

"Good enough." Opening the door of his station wagon, he hesitated. "Dix, about the way I've acted over the past few days—"

"Will you get out of here!"

He slid behind the wheel then and looked up at her through the open window. "You're some kind of lady, Struthers. Keep it up and you might even make a decent detective."

"Drop dead." She grinned. "Call me after Janice gets out of surgery."

He started the motor and had already turned around when he stopped the car and called back. "I'll pick Amy up as soon as I can."

"No, you won't; just phone and talk to her. I promised Reversa and Patrick they could keep her for the next few days. I expect you to be bright-eyed and bushy-tailed tomorrow morning." She pointed a finger down the driveway. "Now go! We'll talk tonight."

Every joint creaked, every muscle protested as she climbed the stairs to the deck. Upon getting up that morning, she had discovered a multitude of bumps and bruises she hadn't noticed the night before. They all seemed to be throbbing now. She went through the house to the kitchen and looked out a rear window. Patrick was working in the garden with Reversa and Amy perched on the step as observers. Every now and again the housekeeper would call out an insult and Patrick would shake the hoe at her, antics which sent Amy into throes of laughter.

"Three kids, that's what I've got," Dixie grumbled.

She knew she should go to her desk and start scratching out some notes, but for once she couldn't put her thoughts into any kind of logical order. Her outrage at the attack was temporarily smothered by a strange, almost paralyzing lethargy. Suddenly, she wanted nothing more than to lie down and sleep, and with that thought in mind she climbed yet more stairs to her bedroom. By the time she reached that shady sanctuary her eyes were almost closed. Falling across the satin coverlet, she was instantly asleep.

It seemed no more than minutes had passed when her nose began to itch. Something warm and heavy lay across the side of her neck and a soft breeze touched her cheek. She opened her eyes and nearly screamed, for there, just inches from her face, appeared a giant and unblinking blue eye.

"Hi," said Amy, moving back just enough to put her twinkling orbs into proper perspective. "You were sleeping."

"I was," Dixie agreed.

"You've got some freckles on your eyelids."

"Do I?"

"Yep. And when they wrinkle up you look just like a lizard."

Dixie digested this unflattering revelation and decided that at the moment she didn't care if she looked like a Columbian toad. "Where's Reversa?" she asked.

"Making lunch." Amy's arms tightened around Dixie's neck until they were nose to nose once more. "Know what Reversa told me?"

"No, what?"

Amy giggled. "Your *real* name."

Damn Reversa's hide, Dixie thought, but decided a casual approach might work better with a child. The housekeeper she could strangle later. "My real name is Dixie."

"No sir."

"Yes sir." Dixie felt five again, not to mention slightly ridiculous.

"Does Reversa tell fibs?" Amy looked very serious.

"Not exactly."

"Daddy says a fib's a fib."

Oh, screw Daddy, Dixie thought. *He doesn't know everything!* But she kept the comments to herself. She was still feeling sluggish and half asleep as she tried to think up an answer which would both satisfy the little girl and, at the same time, seal her lips forever.

"Well?"

"How many names do you have, Amy?"

Amy backed away again and held up three small fingers, ticking them off one at a time. "Amelia Jannette Woodall. Amelia was my grandmother's name. She's dead now."

"I'm sorry to hear that." Dixie breathed a sigh of relief, hoping the name business was going to get lost in a more emotional topic.

"Just like you got your great-grandma's name," Amy continued. "Reversa says shame on you."

Dixie groaned and for the first time in her life seriously considered firing the bossy black woman.

"I like your name," Amy said. "It's real pretty. T—"

Dixie clapped a hand gently over the little girl's mouth.

"That's my middle name, sweetheart, just like yours is Jannette. Do you want people to call you Jeannie?"

Her hand was pushed firmly aside. "No."

"Well, see! I don't want people to call me by my middle name, either. Okay?"

Amy shrugged. "Okay, but Daddy wants to know. I heard him and Mommy talking about it. Mommy said maybe it was Teresa. Daddy said no. He thinks it's something more stranger, Talul—Talu—" she scowled.

"Talula?"

"That's it!" Amy giggled again. "Silly, huh?"

Dixie sat up and pulled the child onto her lap. "Look, darling, let's make a deal; I won't tell anyone your name is Jeannie if you don't tell them my name is—"

"I don't care if people know." A sly look was coming into Amy's eyes, one which gave Dixie the chills.

"But I *do* care."

"Oh, all right." Amy leaped from Dixie's knee and ran to the door. "I won't tell—promise."

"Thank you very much, sweetheart. It makes me happy to hear you say so."

"That's okay." The small blonde head tilted prettily to one side, but Amy's grin was still impish. "Can I sleep with you tonight?"

Blackmail! Dixie decided it must run in the family. "Certainly." She smiled.

CHAPTER 17

HERB LOOKED RESTED and crisp. The successful surgery on Janice's leg and a full night of sleep had removed the circles from beneath his eyes. And while there wasn't actually a spring in his step, he seemed able to move without wincing.

Dixie looked like death on a soda cracker.

It had been a rough night. Amy had tossed and turned and mumbled in her sleep, thrashing her legs out every hour or so to deliver a series of quick, rabbity kicks to Dixie's midsection or the small of her back. Some psychological relief might have been provided had Dixie been able to feel some animosity toward the child, but in truth she felt none at all. To awaken and see the small sleeping face next to hers elicited a quite different set of unbidden emotional stirrings. That, combined with the memory of Joe and his ultimatums, did nothing to improve her mood as Herb picked her up that morning. Worse, in his elation at seeing Amy and knowing that Janice would soon be home, Dixie's partner seemed not in the least tuned in to her grouchiness.

Dixie Struthers had known relatively few of "those" days in her life, but now it was her turn—in spades. Her hair felt like it had been styled with a vacuum cleaner nozzle. She had nicked her calf while shaving. And she was already in the office when she noticed a set of small, jellied fingerprints across one leg of her pale yellow gabardine slacks.

Going to the women's restroom, she tried to repair her hair, an act of futility. It still looked like a red fuzz bomb. She used a damp paper towel drenched in liquid soap to clean her pant leg. In short, there could not have been a worse time for her to return to the squad room and see Art Cochran sitting casually beside her desk. Her first reaction was to turn and run, this followed by annoyance, and finally by a hot flush that turned her cheeks and the tip of her nose a bright red as she remembered they were supposed to meet at the airport on Sunday.

Her color deepened as she wondered how long he had waited for her to show up. Now she was sure she had been suffering some kind of posttraumatic shock.

Art came to his feet when he saw her. "A fine howdy-do." He grinned. "I trust a woman enough not to get her phone number and she leaves me standing at the airport."

The huge wet circle on her slacks seemed to work like an eye magnet. She saw Art look at it and then quickly away.

"I don't know what to say, Art, except that I'm sorry," she stammered. "It was one hell of a weekend."

"So I've heard."

Dixie glanced at Herb, who seemed absorbed in the paperwork scattered over the top of his desk.

"He called me last night," Art offered. "Seemed to think he owed me some kind of apology, though I can't imagine why."

"I'm the one who owes you an apology. Please believe me when I say that I've never stood anyone up before—not ever."

"Gee, nice to know I'm the first." He was still smiling. "As a matter of fact, I'd like to maintain that status—being the first, I mean—not being stood up."

She met his eyes and saw they were far from laughing. Suddenly, the mood she had labored under all morning lifted, to be replaced by a feeling of awkwardness which was even less characteristic. There was something about the pilot which gave her an unsettled, not entirely unpleasant sensation in the near region of her stomach. "Will a raincheck do by way of an apology? It's the only thing I can come up with unless you're heavy into flowers and chocolates."

"I was hoping for some chocolate-coated caramels, but I'll settle for the raincheck, gladly. How about tonight?"

Dixie shook her head. With the evaporation of her foul disposition, her brain was beginning to function on all pistons again. The question of how Charles Bouchard had been murdered no longer seemed more than secondary. The red Chevrolet, the tapes—those were the leads to be pursued, for they were the most likely to provide the *who*. Moreover, the incident on Junipero Serra gave clear evidence of the urgency involved.

"I'm going to be tied up for the next few days, Art, you understand."

"I do?"

The memory of Joe's obstinance and subtle attempts at manipulation flashed through her mind again. She gave the pilot a level look, her confidence suddenly and firmly in place. "I'm afraid you'll have to."

Di Franco paced the length of the squad room. The door leading into the corridor was closed and Dody, much to her disgust, had been excused to take a coffee break. All six investigators sat at their desks. The lieutenant had their undivided attention. A variety of expressions were mirrored on their faces, and looking at them Dixie felt a warmth akin to love seep through her. Delaney chewed the end of his ever-present cigar with ill-concealed ferocity. Brooks was doodling on a notepad, but his eyes were narrowed and glittering. Mike Davis and Jake Spatlin were statue-still, black and white totems with set jaws, folded arms, and dangerously bland faces. And though Di Franco never looked at her once, he, too, radiated a suppressed fury, an outrage that his officers had been attacked and at the injuries done to Herb's wife.

"We're through screwing around with this Bouchard thing," he said. "The mayor says she wants action and, like it or not, that's exactly what she's going to get. By tonight I fully expect she'll be calling the chief to complain that some of her leading citizens are being harassed—and if she doesn't I'm going to want to know why. I want every door within a three-mile radius of that Mystique joint knocked on. Spatlin and Davis, you pay a visit on Esquire Holmstead—make it two or three visits if you get any crap like we had over his son's party. Enriquez is already complaining, so, Delaney, I want you to talk to his wife real pretty, and while you're at it interview everyone who saw her between the time she says she left the salon and the time she showed up with her husband at the political banquet. You handle that while Brooks goes over to Todd's. I'll take care of Michael Dreyfus myself, and I want no statements issued to the press without my permission.'' He stopped and looked at Herb and Dixie. ''You two, come into my office.''

Dixie wasn't sure what she expected. Certainly it was unreasonable to hope that Di Franco was going to open his arms and suddenly embrace her into the fold. On the other hand, she had hoped, when he called them in, that maybe their silent and bloodless war was near mediation—as it turned out, a hopelessly optimistic conclusion. The lieutenant turned one steely glance on her and then gave his full attention to Herb. She suddenly became the Invisible Woman.

''We've sent Janice some flowers, Herb. And the guys thought the best gift they could come up with would be a housekeeping service. We found a good one that's in your area. As soon as Janice comes home, she'll have all the help she needs, with the house and with Amy. Most of the guys in the Bureau pitched in, several from Patrol Division, too.''

''You didn't have to do that. Janice won't know how to thank you.''

''I hope she won't try.'' Di Franco smiled. ''It's one thing for you to get the stuffing knocked out of you, but Janice isn't paid for that sort of thing. She's a great little gal.''

As the lieutenant continued to beam at him, Herb began to shift in his chair. To see Di Franco playing Papa Pope after all that had happened over the Bouchard case and Dixie's part in it was like waiting for the other shoe to fall. ''What about Dixie's car? It's probably totaled.''

''If this was a job-related incident, it'll be covered by the PD. That would have to be established beyond doubt, of course.''

''You as much as said it was job-related two seconds ago, and out in the squad room,'' Herb protested. ''She's going to have to buy a new set of wheels.''

"I'm not arguing with you, Herb. It's just like I said—
proof. Unless Struthers can prove that the accident was directly related to the Bouchard case the city won't reimburse.
For all they know it could have been one of her former
boyfriends." His voice became patronizing. "You've got to
admit it is possible, if only remotely. Up until the other night
the attacks have been aimed directly at her, not you."

Dixie was doing a slow burn. Being ignored was one thing,
but to have someone talk about her in the second person,
almost gossip about her, went beyond a simple lapse in
courtesy.

"I don't have any former boyfriends who are unbalanced,
Lieutenant Di Franco." Her voice was icy.

"How can you be so sure?" He wasn't exactly looking at
her, more like in her general direction. "You never know
when someone might be holding a grudge. Surely a good-
looking little lady like you has plenty of admirers. They can't
all be perfect."

Good-looking little lady? All the muscles in her stomach
were twisting into knots. Unconsciously she balled her hands
into fists.

Herb had his antennae out. He saw those glittering green
eyes narrow to catlike slits and knew an explosion was forthcoming unless he did something. The first thing he could
come up with was a cough. It wasn't a very original idea, and
the first hack was a little weak, but he managed another and
another until his eyes were watering. He had Di Franco's
attention, but Dixie was looking at him strangely, her coppery
head tilted to one side.

"I'll get you a drink." The lieutenant stood and hurried
from the office.

Herb's attack subsided instantly.

"Don't do that," Dixie said. "Quit running interference
for me, Herb. In case you haven't noticed, I'm all grown up
now. I can take care of myself."

"Glad to hear it, because attacking a two-hundred-pound
lieutenant can be mighty dangerous, to your health as well as
your career." He resumed his coughing as their superior
came back through the door.

After watching him drink, Di Franco sat down again.

"Look, the reason I called you two in here is to tell you that I'm separating you."

The other shoe had indeed fallen, and the choking sound that came from Herb was genuine this time. He swallowed several gulps of water to get himself under control and then put the glass down on the floor next to his feet. "What in the hell are you talking about, Tony? We need to stick close more than ever now."

"No." Di Franco's arms were folded across his chest. The expression on his face was implacable. "Herb, I'm putting you to work with Delaney. She can work with Bill Brooks. I don't want either of you on duty alone, but I don't want you together, either."

"Damn it, Tony, this is bullshit!" Herb exploded. "Dixie and I started this thing and we'll finish it—together."

"You're going to see Janice tonight?"

The question seemed so far in left field that Herb frowned. "Yes, of course. Why?"

"Give her my love."

They had been given a dismissal. Clean and to the point. Moreover, Herb had known the other man long enough to recognize the expression on his face. Tony had made up his mind, and it would take no less than a major earthquake rattling down from Chief Quinn's office to change it.

"Am I to assume this is a temporary reassignment, *sir*?" Herb's voice was stony.

"I haven't decided yet."

The two men stared at each other for several long moments before Herb stood. To his grave worry, however, Dixie made not the slightest move to leave. She leaned forward, resting her elbows on her knees. Her hands were pressed together just in front of her face, her fingers forming a temple that masked her mouth and chin. When he hesitated, she spoke without looking at him. "I'll be out in a minute, Herb. See ya."

Again, seeing her eyes with those dangerous pinpoints of light dancing just beneath the surface, he felt a brace of chills run the length of his spine. He stepped out into the squad room and closed the door softly behind him.

*   *   *

"Well?" Di Franco finally looked at her, but his eyes moved from her cheeks to her forehead, very careful to avoid her unblinking gaze. When she didn't speak immediately, he shifted in his chair. "I don't have all day, Struthers."

"I'm working alone." She said it softly.

His eyebrows shot down. "You'll do what I tell you to do, Sergeant. Brooks is your new partner."

"No, I'm working alone." She sat back and crossed her legs at the knee. "You cut off your options when you mentioned my 'former boyfriends,' Tony. My job doesn't allow for an invasion of privacy, or slander. Nor do I believe for a moment that you would have made such a suggestion to a male officer. I've never seriously considered a discrimination suit before, but you've managed to change my mind. I'll not only encourage a suit, I'll help put one together. I've just joined the ranks."

"Ranks? I don't know what the hell—"

"Yeah, Tony, the *ranks*." She was smiling now, not very prettily. "There are at least six women in the department who would love to see you hanging from the police garage by your testicles, Di Franco. Now there are seven. I'm the luckiest of all, though, because I'm the only one who's had the opportunity of actually working for you. Jackie Randall *wanted* to work for you—until she overheard one of your conversations with the Deputy Chief. You really shouldn't talk in the hallways, Tony. Everyone on the PD knows you don't want any 'split tails' working for you. And maybe you remember Paula Moore? She's the one you patted on the ass at the drinking fountain about three months ago. If memory serves, you told her to buy a girdle. Marlene Humphrey loves you, too. You might not know who I'm talking about because you never use her name. Seems you tagged her with 'Humps' when she attended one of your academy classes. It stuck like glue. She's had the name ever since."

"This is a bunch of petty crap, Struthers, and you know it."

"You're absolutely right. It all adds up to one big petty picture. Hasn't anyone ever told you women are like that?" She stood up. "I'm working alone, Lieutenant. That way, if one of my wacko boyfriends comes after me again, he'll have a clear shot.'

Di Franco also came to his feet and walked around the desk where he towered over her. "I'm not one of your Mystique patrons, Sergeant Struthers. Blackmail doesn't scare me."

Even in the high sling pumps she was wearing, Dixie's head came just below the level of his jawline. She tipped her chin back and looked into his eyes. "Which car shall I use?"

"As you well know, there aren't any extras."

"The burglary unit has one free. Guess you'll just have to borrow."

Di Francio bent slightly, putting their noses just inches apart. His voice came out in a whisper. "I'll have your ass before the month is out, Struthers."

She laughed, causing him to step back a pace. "Not likely, sir, but anyone can dream."

The unmarked car borrowed from the burglary unit didn't have air-conditioning. It was hot and stuffy when she got in. The ashtray was filled with cigarette butts, giving off a dry, putrid aroma that did nothing to help her nausea. Now, finally out of the squad room and free of the need to maintain a breezy facade, Dixie allowed herself a moment of misery. Her shoulders drooped and she rested her head against the hard, hot plastic of the steering wheel.

There had been no victory back there in the lieutenant's office, not for Tony Di Franco and not for her. At best, she had set her limits in a way he could clearly understand. At worst, she had created enough animosity to last her entire career. The war would rage on. She had wanted desperately to prove herself to him—as an officer and as a better-than-competent investigator. To fall back on her sex in that crucial moment seemed to her the ultimate cop-out. And yet there seemed no other avenue. He had pushed her to the wall and heaped on a mountain of small indignities which left her feeling trapped and enraged.

"Your temper has done it for you again, D.T.," she mumbled. "When are you going to learn?"

A tap against the car window caused her to jump. Herb smiled at her through the glass, that crazy lopsided smile she liked so much. Seeing it now made her want to cry. Slowly, she rolled the window down.

"Hi." Her voice sounded tinny and false to her own ears. "You and Delaney headed for the Enriquez place?"

The burly senior homicide detective, Pat Delaney, was there, too, standing a distance away but not out of earshot.

"No," Herb said. "*We're* going—you and I."

"Forget it, partner." She adamantly shook her head. "We've got enough trouble without going off half-cocked like a couple of rebellious kids. Go with Pat, and this time see if you can't talk to Michelle Enriquez and her mother together. Maybe you'll luck out and find our charming councilman gone from the premises. Maybe he'll even have taken the dragon, Christina, with him. You can always hope."

"What about you?"

"Time too fry the little fish, I think." She put on a smile. "The Mystique receptionist, Megan Severson, for starters."

"Her background's clean as a whistle, Dix."

"Goddamn it, Herb—except for Hobden everybody is clean! If we didn't know better, we'd have to swear the real killer was Bouchard himself!"

"Don't bite my head off." He reached through the window and put a hand on her shoulder. "This will be over soon. There are six of us now, and I think the other four guys want this case closed almost as bad as we do."

Pat Delaney stepped closer, the omnipresent cigar still clamped between his teeth. "Herb's right," he said. "We all feel like we've got a stake in this. Not just us, either. You know how it goes—word about what happened the other night is spreading. Cops don't like seeing other cops pushed around. The troops are up in arms."

Looking at him, Dixie felt a portion of that special warmth seep back into her bones. Delaney looked like a long-haul truck driver. Pug nose. Thick neck. A little heavy around the midsection. He usually didn't have much to say. A sit-back-and-watch type who made his decisions slowly and with extreme care. His voice was raspy and rough, but more often than not it was indeed the voice of the troops, the rank and file of policemen.

"Thanks, Pat," she said. "We need all the help we can get."

She addressed them both. "No matter how you cut it, this case keeps coming back to those tapes—or at least that's the way I see it. A woman, a young woman, made the call that tipped us. That makes me more than a little curious about Michelle Enriquez, Megan Severson, and even Deborah Lorry. That's what I'm going for, because it's all I've got."

Herb was shaking his head. "A guy. I tell you it has to be a man, Dix. Can you picture a lady driving the car that rammed us? And it sure as hell wasn't Michelle Enriquez who jumped you in your driveway."

"Hold on," she said. "The attack on me doesn't necessarily connect. That could have been a random thing, a kook."

"True, but are you willing to eliminate it?"

"We're going to eliminate nothing," Delaney said. "You go on, Dixie, check out the broads . . . er . . . the ladies. But I just finished reading the reports. Lots of things don't match. No marks on Bouchard's body, for one thing. Why? He didn't crawl into that spa without some help. So I'm inclined to agree with Herb. I don't think a woman could have done that, though I guess it's possible. And I wonder if you've given enough thought to those darn gloves?"

Herb and Dixie looked at Delaney as he scratched his head, a head covered with a thatch of thick brown hair which belied his fifty-odd years. He laughed and his jowly face was transformed. "I've never told anyone this, and if either of you lets out a peep I'll shoot ya, but I take a trip to the bee-u-ty parlor myself from time to time. You ever watch them put that dye glop on?"

Herb was staring at the other man's hair like a cobra-transfixed rodent. Dixie put a hand over her mouth, not quite suppressing a giggle.

"Go ahead," Delaney barked. "I could give a shit if you split a gut laughing! Do you want to hear about the friggin' gloves or not? I'm surprised you haven't tumbled already, Struthers. Don't you ever get yourself done up?"

"Sure," she answered, "but I'm too young to dye my hair."

"Very funny. How many times have you seen some dame . . . er . . . lady getting her hair colored? Did the beautician use two gloves?"

"Sometimes, but . . ."

She stopped speaking as a picture of Gregory, Mystique's head stylist, returned full force. He had been coloring a patron's hair on the first day she interviewed the salon employees. And he had been wearing gloves, or rather *a* glove, only on the hand he used to work in the color solution.

Pat Delaney saw the expression on her face and nodded his head. "Uh-huh."

"That means there could have been two people applying solution to Bouchard's hair."

Herb still seemed confused until the other man explained.

"After I read your lab reports, I called the gal who does my hair." Delaney scowled and chomped down hard on his cigar. "Stop with the shit-eating grin, Woodall. Everybody's got a right!"

"Okay, okay, your hair's lovely—now go on."

After a few mumbled and highly unflattering expletives the detective continued. "The beautician I go to said she likes to leave the other hand free because it gives her more dexterity. That hand usually doesn't come in contact with the color anyway, only with the outside of the applicator bottle and the handle of the comb she uses to work different sections of the hair."

"Remember what Judith Enriquez said, Dix?" Herb was nodding now. "She said Charles didn't *do* hair."

"Yes, but that doesn't mean he wouldn't have done his own. I can't see him letting one of his employees dab him down, not all over his body. Too much vanity."

"My point exactly," Delaney agreed. "I think he probably had one of the stylists do the hair on his head—someone he didn't give a shit about impressing—and then finished the job himself."

Dixie's lip turned down wryly. "Well, that narrows it down to just about everyone who worked at the salon. Bouchard didn't give a rip for anyone who couldn't do something for him."

Herb tapped the roof of the car with his fingertips. "It's better than nothing. At least we've got a little bit more direction. I'll talk to the stylists again, Dix. You go ahead with the receptionist."

"Don't forget you're supposed to be paying a call on the Enriquez family. I don't think it would be such a hot idea to alter Di Franco's grand plan, do you?"

"I suppose not. But this glove theory really intrigues me. Think I'll call over to the lab and see what I can find out."

Delaney cleared his throat and scuffed one foot against the pavement. "Ah, don't bother. I already told Di Franco about it. He was calling the lab just as we left the office."

Dixie and Herb gave him hostile stares.

"Hey, that's the way it goes. He's interviewing Dreyfus, and he's the boss, whether you like it or not. Personally, I like it just fine." He looked at Dixie and shrugged. "Sorry, Struthers, but the truth is Tony's a good man—just a *man's* man is all. It's going to take him a while to get used to having a powder puff in the unit. Don't look at me that way! No insult intended. The rest of the guys don't mind having you around."

"Good for them." She smiled and reached for the ignition key, hoping that if she backed out quickly enough she might be able to run over his toes. Unfortunately, it didn't work—he jumped back too soon.

The two male detectives stood in the parking lot, watching her pull into the street and drive away.

"Thin-skinned, ain't she?" Delaney rolled the cigar to the other side of his mouth. "She's gotta get over that if she wants to be a cop."

Herb looked at him. "She *is* a cop, Pat, a damn good one. But let's not get into that; I've got a question."

"Yeah?"

"Next time you take a piss can I come watch? I'm just dying of curiosity—does that beautician of yours do your whole—"

He ducked just in time to avoid contact with Delaney's ham-size fists.

CHAPTER 18

SEEING MEGAN SEVERSON in her own nest reminded Dixie of Bobby Todd. Both the artist and the receptionist could have written novels about leading a dual existence.

The apartment complex that housed the receptionist was like a thousand others that seemed to have been virtually air-dropped into the Santa Clara Valley over the past decade. A jungle of two-story cracker boxes, it was equipped with a small swimming pool, a recreation center, and tennis court, which allowed the owner to jack the rent heavenward. A large sign facing the street stated in bold letters that Whispering Pines catered only to adults. Following the winding aggregate pathway to apartment 243C, Dixie counted a total of three rather debauched-looking pine trees.

Upon opening her door, Megan displayed no animation, a commodity she obviously reserved for her workaday world. The short bob that had framed her face with such curly verve at Mystique de la Femme now stood on end, spiked, punk-rocker style. She wore no makeup and when she saw who had come to visit, her pale lips uttered a single, all-encompassing greeting.

"Aw, fuck."

"Nice to see you, too, Miss Severson. May I come in?"

"Have I got a choice?" Megan didn't wait for an answer but opened the door wider. "You can't screw up my life much more than you already have. Mystique has been shut down. I've been beating the bushes for two weeks and I still can't find a job. To work for Mystique used to mean class, man—really uptown status. Now it's the kiss of death. Every place I go people act like I walk around with a microphone between my tits.''

Dixie followed her down a narrow hallway. A doorway to the right showed an efficiency kitchen that looked anything but. Soiled paper plates, open cartons, and empty beer cans littered the Formica counters. It smelled like a sack of sour sponges. The small living room was only slightly more appealing—the nightmare of Baghdad. A low table cluttered with headshop paraphernalia and a set of tarnished brass candlesticks was surrounded by huge dusty cushions in varying faded hues. An Almaden wine bottle stuffed with peacock feathers and dried baby's breath sat on top of the television, lending a touch of dubious distinction to the poster-plastered walls. The drapes covering a sliding glass door were closed, allowing a single floor lamp draped with a red silk scarf to work its magic. Dixie suddenly felt like she had fleas.

"Sit wherever." The girl waved a lackadaisical hand.

"I won't take much of your time." Dixie remained firmly on her feet. "Just a few questions."

The receptionist shrugged and dropped down to sprawl across a particularly infested-looking black fur cushion. Dixie had the distinct impression she had selected it purposely, for it neatly set off the zebra-striped housecoat she wore. Her knees came up at once, revealing an expanse of unshaven leg below her ragged underwear.

"You might as well give up on me, Sergeant. I don't know crab shit about what was going on at the salon. I keep telling everyone that. I don't think it was a real big shock to the others, but it was to me. Charles always treated me kinda nice—said I oughta go to school and become a stylist. He promised he'd let me start right there at Mystique if I did—as an assistant, of course."

"Did he ever come on to you, Megan?"

"He was working up to it." The receptionist giggled. "I think the old fart was convinced I was a virgin. He was beginning to sniff around real good just before he got axed. I was hoping maybe he would spring for beauty school, damn it!''

"A lot of older men are like that, I guess."

"Sure are! Always after a young piece of ass. Hey, you want some tea? I've got all kinds."

Dixie suppressed a shudder at the idea of consuming anything from the kitchen she had just viewed. "No thanks, I'm full of coffee already. Were you surprised when you found out how old your employer really was?"

"A little, but I knew he was older than he looked. Michael told me about the fancy dye jobs." She sighed a little. "Now that's a guy I could go for. Too bad he and Gregory are so tied up."

"But I thought—"

The girl laughed again. "Yeah, I know. Everyone thinks Mike's as straight as an arrow. He even had me convinced for a long time. He's got a wife and two kids, looks like a fuckin' high school coach."

"Maybe you're mistaken."

"No way. Charles was gone one week and I caught Mike and Greg up in the apartment going at it like crazy." Her plucked brows raised. "You ever see two guys get it on?"

"Oh sure, in an art film or two." Dixie prayed the white lie would forestall any vivid descriptions.

"God! Really somethin', huh?"

"What about Eric?" Dixie asked about the other male stylist.

"Nope. He's straight for real. His squeeze is one of my best friends. They're supposed to be getting married soon." She threw Dixie an accusing look. "If he can find another job. He was thinking of trying to make some kind of deal with Max Hobden, but the Mystique thing won't work anymore, not under the management of anyone who used to work there. We're all going to have to forget about using it as a reference—everyone except Manuel. No one gives a shit about gardeners and janitors."

Manuel Ortiz! Suddenly, Dixie wanted to leave. It fit too well to be a coincidence. The janitor would have had access to the salon and to Bouchard. And his real boss, Max Hobden, had a motive! That left only the voice on the phone to account for. The murder of Charles Bouchard was beginning to reek of conspiracy. She looked at Megan Severson.

Part of a trio, perhaps?

Megan, seeing the detective put away the notebook she had been scribbling in, came to her feet. "That's it?"

Dixie nodded and started toward the hallway, saving her last inquiry until she reached the door and had her hand on the knob. "Did Charles ever let you help out in the main salon, you know, to encourage you?"

"Once in a while, but it was a drag. Mostly I just cleaned up after everyone. I never even got to mix the colors or do shampoos. Mrs. Pearlman let me wash her hair once, though. Too bad about her, she was a nice lady."

'Who usually mixed your boss's hair formula?"

Megan narrowed her eyes. "Michael Dreyfus already told you—Charles did it himself."

"Wouldn't that have been a little difficult?" Dixie's expression was guileless. "I can see him doing his chest and the rest but not his head."

"Guess he thought his dye jobs were a big secret, Sergeant. Sensitive about being an old geezer. Lots of people are like that. It's what keeps Clairol and L'Oréal and the rest in business."

Dixie thanked her and opened the door only to jump back immediately. Facing her, hand poised in the air, was a tall, gaunt-featured young man with a spiky bristle of blond hair. His complexion was pale, almost ghostly in comparison to the dark mascara on his lashes.

"Hi, Bert." Megan looked up at him wtih ill-disguised admiration. "Come on in."

Bert brushed past without speaking. When Dixie stepped into the corridor the door closed behind her, but not before she heard the receptionist bitterly complaining.

"That's one of the cops I told you about, Bert. Damn it, I had it made until that fucker Bouchard went and got himself murdered . . ."

At first Herb and Pat Delaney thought they had indeed lucked out. The plump little housekeeper, Lupe, who had greeted Herb on his second visit to the Enriquez home, the visit he had made without Dixie, answered and courteously ushered them through the house and into the backyard. Neither the councilman nor his secretary put in an appearance.

The two detectives, both dressed in slacks, sports jackets, and ties, felt hotter still upon seeing the huge pool set into a mosaic patio. Judith Enriquez sat beneath a wide umbrella reading the latest issue of *The National Enquirer* while her daughter lounged nearby, sunning herself in a scant bikini and sunglasses.

"Jesus," Delaney whispered, "now I know how James Mason felt." He tilted his head in the direction of the girl. "*Lolita!*"

Herb agreed. Michelle Enriquez might lack the bewitching blondness of Sue Lyon, but her body was more lush, smooth, and curved over muscles toned and limbered by years of horseback riding, tennis, and water sports. Her skin glowed a deep natural honey. Hearing Lupe speak to her mother, she came up on her elbows and smiled. The movement caused her thighs to separate and Herb heard Delaney groan under his breath again.

"Hello, officers." Mrs. Enriquez put on a cheerful face, though without Michelle's spontaneity. "Come, sit down. Lupe will bring something cool."

The older woman was also clad in a swimsuit, a blue and white one-piece with slanted vertical stripes that narrowed her waist by several inches. Her tan was light but sufficient to complement the golden hair and ingenue eyes. Had it not been for the comparison with her offspring, Herb was sure Judith would have captivated Delaney's admiration quite completely. And there was no trace of manufactured effervescence about the councilman's wife on this occasion, no alcohol-brightened eyes or clumsy speech.

"Is this nasty Bouchard thing still unsolved?" she asked, her brow puckering. "The whole thing is getting a bit tiresome. So disgusting to find out that horrid man was snooping on us!"

Herb looked at her speculatively. "I would imagine it was a bit more than just tiresome to some of your lady friends, Mrs. Enriquez—probably more like *worrisome*."

Her eyelashes lowered but only for a moment, and when they came up again her eyes met his without wavering. "I suppose you're right. I'm also beginning to think Charles Bouchard got just what he deserved." There was a hard edge of finality to her tone that gave her the full attention of both men. "What he did to Lucille Pearlman was terrible! If that poor woman didn't murder him, she should have!"

"Mrs. Pearlman wasn't at Mystique on the day Charles Bouchard was killed," Delaney said. "She was at the hospital with her husband. We checked."

Judith Enriquez looked at Herb. "Where's that nice lady officer who was here before?" she pointedly asked.

A flush crept up Delaney's face, but Herb smiled. "She's out on another interview, Mrs. Enriquez, but she said to tell you hello."

"How sweet! She certainly is a pretty little thing."

There was the sound of a window opening just behind them and Herb turned, squinting into the shadowy interior of the house. It took a moment for him to make out the figure behind the window screen, but he didn't need clear vision to recognize the crisp and decidedly lofty tones of the councilman's secretary.

"Your father would like you to come inside, Michelle. He does not feel you are dressed appropriately for visitors."

Herb turned back. The transformation on Michelle Enriquez's face was amazing. Her clean youthfulness seemed to evaporate under the secretary's censure. Deep creases appeared on her forehead and her lower lip curled scornfully downward.

"Tell my father to—"

"Michelle, that will be quite enough." Judith Enriquez scowled, but her tone softened almost immediately. "Why don't you run in and put on that cute little outfit we got yesterday? While you're inside you can see what's keeping Lupe." She looked at the figure still standing at the window. "Perhaps Al would like to join us, Christina. Would you please ask him?"

"Your husband is busy, Mrs. Enriquez. He's on the phone with the Mayor." The window closed with a snap.

"Probably on the phone to his stinking lawyers," Michelle mumbled. "Fucking hypocrite! I hope old Caesar fries Dad's ass—Christina's, too!"

"Michelle, go inside at once!"

The girl stood. Her hands were clenched into fists. But

instead of stalking into the house as Herb expected, she whirled and ran for the pool.

Judith Enriquez expelled a long worried sigh. "Please excuse her. She's been under a terrible strain over the past few weeks. Her grades aren't up to par, and she's not sure whether or not she will even make it into a state university."

"Too bad. She seems like a bright kid." The conversation was turning in exactly the direction Herb had hoped it would.

"Oh, she is bright. In fact, she was always on the honor roll until last semester. Her boyfriend died recently—one of those terrible drug things that scares us all—and Michelle has been miserable over it. I thought she was too young to be really in love. Maybe I was wrong."

"Don't worry, Mrs. Enriquez." Pat Delaney had tucked his cigar into his coat pocket. My girl is fifteen and every break-up is a tragedy with her. Kids heal pretty fast."

"Perhaps you didn't hear me, Officer. I didn't say she and her boyfriend split up—I said he was *dead*. And Michelle isn't getting over it quickly at all."

The cigar came back out and went smack dab between the middle of Delaney's front teeth.

"Is that why you didn't tell us Michelle was with you at Mystique that Thursday afternoon, Mrs. Enriquez?" Herb asked. "Were you afraid we might upset her?"

"Not at all, Officer Woodall. Actually, Michelle *wasn't* there for very long. All she did was take a quick swim and then leave. It just didn't seem important."

"Yeah," Michelle called from the edge of the pool. She was pulling herself out of the water. Her skin glistened in the sun. "I left all right—left *her* stranded." She pointed at her mother. "The next time I saw her she was frothing at the mouth."

The older woman came to her feet. "Michelle, you go into the house this minute."

"I'll go when I'm good and—"

"Michelle Belinda Enriquez!" The patio door slid open and Albert Enriquez stood framed there, his face dark and threatening. "Come here!"

Once more, the girl's entire demeanor changed. Her shoulders slumped and she walked to her father with her head bowed, trailing water behind her.

"Look at you!" The councilman held a large towel which he draped around her. Seemingly satisfied with her acquiescence, his tone softened, became almost tender. "Go around to the back door. Lupe is waiting for you."

Herb and Pat were on their feet, already anticipating Enriquez's next words. He didn't disappoint them.

"You will leave my house," he said "I suggest you return to your office at once. Your supervisor will wish to see you."

"Oh, goody!" said Delaney in a loud and exaggerated whisper. "Looks like we're gonna make the grade. There's been a complaint. After work the drinks are on me!"

Judith Enriquez's expression was hidden behind the hands she had placed over her face, but her husband looked close to apoplexy.

Hobden's office was closed. No cars in the parking lot. No secretary in the front office.

Dixie checked her notes for the address of Deborah Lorry and then made a wide U-turn, pulling back onto the Almaden Expressway. She had only gone a few blocks when the rearview mirror caught her attention. Traffic was relatively light, much more so than it had been a few minutes before. She watched as a small Honda Scrambler whipped in and out between the cars behind her. The motorcyclist wore a helmet and sun visor that hid his face.

Thinking back, Dixie was almost positive she had seen the vehicle earlier, as she pulled away from the Whispering Pines apartment complex. To make certain, she now made a quick left onto a neighborhood street and then another. The motorcycle kept its distance, but stuck to her like glue.

At first her heart thumped faster. Sore in body and spirit, the idea of another altercation turned her insides to ice. Then, all at once, the anger came flowing back. If the man behind her had traded his red Chevy for a new toy, he'd better know how to ride it very well indeed!

She almost smiled as she cruised leisurely out of the residential area and headed for the Nimitz Freeway. Rather than taking a direct thoroughfare, she made variations along the way, turning quickly and zipping through small industrial centers—slowing and speeding up, always making sure her

tail was able to keep her barely in view. The freeway offered
more opportunities. She drove off and on several times,
looping across an overpass and then streaking down into the
fast-moving lanes, going in the opposite direction. The devi-
ous route finally took her onto Highway 9 and into the
picturesque and quiet little suburb of Saratoga. The quaint
main street called for cautious speed. The cyclist was a good
block behind her, and when she pulled into a curbside parking
slot she saw him do the same.

Getting out of the car, she walked into the cool interior of
the Plumed Horse. It was a good restaurant—one she knew
well. She stood just inside the door, surrounded by the dark.
The foyer was papered in crimson and dimly lighted. Most of
the luncheon customers had gone and she could hear the
sounds of tables being cleared and reset in the dining room.
Soft music drifted out from the cocktail lounge. The bartender
was speaking to someone about a banquet scheduled for that
evening. No one appeared or seemed to have noticed her
entrance—a fact that suited her plans better than she had
hoped. She waited, hoping her pursuer would take the bait.

She didn't have long to wait. There was a flash of sunshine
as the door quickly opened and closed. A man stood uncer-
tainly, waiting for his eyes to adjust. A motorcycle helmet
was tucked beneath his left arm. Dixie was ready, the snub-
nosed Detective Special out of her purse and firmly in her
hand. But instead of planting its barrel in the small of his
back as she had intended, she swore. "Oh, for pete's sake!"

The exclamation was appropriate. Startled by her voice,
Pete Willis stumbled back and dropped his helmet.

"Damn, Sarge! You scared the hell out of me!"

"You ass!"

The voices in the cocktail lounge had come to a stop. Dixie
put her gun away and beat a hasty exit. Pete retrieved his
helmet and followed, only to have her turn on him again once
they were outside.

"You idiot! What in the blazes do you think you're doing?"

The patrolman's cheeks were red. He looked like a three-
year-old, caught with his hand in the cookie jar. "I knew you
burned me, saw me following way back there someplace. I
tried to catch up and let you know I was only . . . ah . . . er

. . .'' He looked at her miserably. "Shit, man—I can't do *anything* right!"

Dixie was scowling up at him. "Oh? And just what are you trying to do? Scare the crap out of me?"

"No."

He had answered so softly that she had to lean closer to hear him. "Who put you up to this, Willis? Di Franco? I thought you and I were friends!"

His shoulders straightened. "I wouldn't follow you around for anybody—especially not for the brass! What do you think I am, anyway? I'm no snitch! I just like to pay my debts, that's all. Everyone knows you're in trouble."

"Oh, for cryin' out loud." Dixie shook her head and then, seeing his discomfort, put a hand on his arm. "Look, Pete, the concern is appreciated, but I'm a cop, too—remember? I don't need a guardian angel, no matter how well intentioned. You're not even on regular duty status yet. Are you trying to break your neck or what?"

He dug at the pavement with the toe of his tennis shoe. "I just wanted to—"

"I know," she interrupted. "What I really wish is that you'd forget what happened to a certain rookie cop in a doughnut shop last year. Okay?"

At first he didn't answer. But when she continued to gaze at him, he finally nodded.

Pete watched as she got back into her car and drove away, giving him a breezy wave of her hand. And he remained standing there for a very long time afterward. People walking past began to slow and peer at the intent glower on his face. Finally, he limped back to the Honda.

Dixie knew something was up before she reached the squad room. There was a hum about the entire Detective Bureau, a buzz of voices and excitement that virtually touched her as she moved down the corridor from the elevator. Still, she was hardly prepared for the sight that greeted her upon entering the squad room.

Anthony Di Franco was perched behind Jake Spatlin's desk. His own office was not big enough to accommodate the camera equipment and reporters surrounding him.

"Touching, isn't it?" Herb was leaning against the door frame. He kept his voice low.

"What's happened?" Dixie blinked against the glare of lights.

"Dreyfus was popped again—this time for first-degree homicide."

"Di Franco got a confession?" She couldn't believe it.

"He didn't need one. Right after we left this morning, he followed up on Delaney's theory. Got the lab to run a computer enhancement on those prints inside the gloves. They were used by two different people. Bouchard wore one on his left hand. Guess who wore the other?"

She spoke with difficulty. "Michael Dreyfus." It came out in a whisper. Dixie decided it was most assuredly one of "those" days.

Herb nodded. "You win the prize. There were nice latent left thumb and index prints inside the other glove." He sounded as disgusted as Dixie felt.

Moving to a vantage point beside him, she leaned against the wall and watched Di Franco. He was stretched far back in the chair, smiling broadly.

"We've already filed charges with the District Attorney's office," he pontificated. "They'll be added to the former ones."

"Have you found the blackmail tapes, Lieutenant? At one time, Sergeant Struthers seemed to think there might be a tie-in between the two crimes." The reporter came up close with his microphone.

"Sergeant Struthers is a good investigator"—Di Franco smiled expansively—"but she's new at this and it's been a rough case. We haven't found the tapes, but of course there may be no connection at all between them and . . ."

His eyes fleetingly met Dixie's before she turned and walked out of the squad room. She stood in the corridor for several minutes, fighting the urge to throw up.

CHAPTER 19

SHE LEFT THE office at noon on Friday. The remainder of the week following Di Franco's big bust had been dead, with everyone except herself laid back and easy. Homicides in the city seemed to have come to a near standstill. No stabbings. No shootings. Jake Spatlin and Mike Davis had the only real case—a transient found bludgeoned beside the railroad tracks. There weren't any leads and no relatives to care one way or the other if the John Doe rotted in the morgue.

Dixie had seen Herb only intermittently over the past work days, a fact that did little to cheer her, though she understood the necessity of his spending a great deal of time traveling between San Jose and Stanford Medical Center.

Janice's quick recuperation was the single bright spot of the week—that and Amy's indomitable presence.

"Sergeant Struthers?" the child had asked just that morning. "Can I have you for an Auntie?"

So it had been decided. The formal address of Sergeant Struthers had been happily and immediately swapped for "Aunt Dixie."

To wake and find Amy curled next to her each morning was becoming routine—a pleasure she knew would soon be missing, for Janice was scheduled to return home on Saturday.

"Maybe we should keep her for another week or two," Dixie had hopefully suggested to Herb. "It's going to be hard

217

for Janice to get around in a wheelchair, even with someone to help.''

''Not a chance!'' Her partner had laughed. ''Your offer is appreciated, but I alredy know what Janice'll say. The thought of seeing that little crumb-grabber is what's pushing her to get well.''

God, Herb was *up*!

She strongly suspected his elation was brought about in part by a mental shakedown, a ''reprioritizing'' of his values—a renewal of his love for Janice. In a way, the accident had produced some very positive results and Dixie was glad for them both.

Still, on a more personal level, she couldn't shake the vague cloud of depression that hung over her. Amy would soon be gone. Her beloved and trusted Jaguar was a total loss, now only a heap of scrap iron atop thousands of other auto skeletons. The car had been a gift from her grandfather Sean upon graduating from high school, an elaborate and far too generous gift for an eighteen-year-old girl, perhaps, but with its passing a part of her life also seemed to be coming to an end.

Now, driving the Mustang she had rented up through the mountain roads, she keenly felt the loss. Her frustration over the Bouchard case did little to lift her spirits. She was unable to feel any joy over the arrest that Di Franco had so quickly made.

Was it professional envy that prompted the doubt she felt? Or perhaps her personal dislike of the lieutenant?

Her foot pressed down on the accelerator and the tires whined around the last curve leading to her own driveway as she gave herself an emphatic answer.

No! The arrest of Michael Dreyfus left too many loose ends. But everytime she attempted to point one of them out she was met with accusing looks from the other officers. *Tsk* those looks said—*don't be a poor sport. Chalk this one up to good ol' Tony.*

Let them think what they want, she decided. Come Monday she planned to conduct her own interview with Michael Dreyfus!

With this resolution she felt a semblance of calm return

Amy was waiting, and for this afternoon, at least, Dixie determined to leave her work behind.

The Mustang did not make its way over the ruts and gullies of the unpaved driveway with the same grace as her former conveyance, but that depression she also put aside as she drove into the clearing and saw Poke. The poor beast made no move to gallop toward her with his usual rollicking gait, for he was hampered by the flaxen-haired rider perched on his back. Amy was waving and grinning from ear to ear, pressing her heels into the dog's ribs. Poke solved this problem by lying down and rolling over. The little girl went tumbling.

"I think Poke needs a saddle," Amy said as Dixie got out of the car.

"Dogs don't like saddles." She bent and dusted Amy's face and hands. "Have you had lunch yet?"

"Nope."

"Good, I think we need to ask Reversa for a picnic basket."

"Goody!" Amy ran for the house while Poke stood and lumbered toward his mistress, tongue lolling from between his jaws. He looked up at her with large martyred eyes as she stroked his fur.

Half an hour later, comfortably dressed in a pair of jeans and a turtleneck jersey, Dixie watched the housekeeper pack a small wicker hamper.

"I don't think children usually eat Scottish eggs, Reversa," she said, careful to keep her tone free of critical overtones.

The black woman straightened and scowled. "Who's fixin' this do—you or me?"

"My, aren't you a prickly pear today. Have you had too much babysitting this week?"

"No! I think it's just plain dumb to go scootin' that little one home before her mama is up and around. No tellin' what kind of a woman those po-leece hired. Shoot, probably can't even cook!"

"Oh," Dixie laughed, "so that's it!"

Reversa went back to her work. "Nothin's *it*, Missy. I just want to see the child taken care of like she oughta be." She put in a stack of sandwiches and closed the lid. "And you don't have to worry about her eatin' Scottish eggs. I made

them for you. There's peanut butter and jelly for Amy—and
Kool-Aid—and cookies, and bananas—''

"Hold it! My God, I don't want her to be sick!"

"Sick?" The housekeeper laughed, a deep rumbling baritone from deep in her chest. "You haven't been watchin'.
That child has hollow legs!"

Amy stuck her head in the kitchen. "I put on my jeans,
Aunt Dixie." Her voice was a little shy at the unaccustomed
familiarity. "But I didn't need to. I already told you, remember, I don't catch poison oak. Mommy does. Daddy don't and
I don't, but Mommy catched it one time when we went
camping—right on her privates!"

"Lordy!" Reversa hid her mouth behind her hand.

Dixie decided no comment would elicit the least elabora-
tion. Picking up the hamper, she stood and shot Amy a
dubious smile, wondering at the same time if she was indeed
missing anything in her blissful lack of progeny.

A mournful Poke stood on the deck watching them go. He
whined and wagged his tail, started for the stairs, and then
changed his mind. In the end, the huge dog obviously decided
to forgo a romp with Dixie if he had to suffer Amy's intrusive
presence.

The forest was alive, bursting with color—lush green ferns,
blooming dogwood, patches of wild mustard flowers set against
the backdrop of soft redwood bark and pungent manzanita.
Dixie led the way, as familiar with the rugged landscape as
she was with the lines of her own face. Watching for the
distinctive outcroppings of moss-covered boulders that showed
her the way, she soon found Amy clinging to her free hand
with eyes wide and cheeks flushed.

"It's dark here," the little girl whispered. "Like in my
Hansel and Gretel book. Does a witch live here?"

"Only me."

"Oh."

At one point Dixie put down the hamper and knelt. Wrapping an arm around Amy's shoulders, she pointed out a
squirrel scampering through the foliage and before long the
forest worked its special magic. The child lost her fear and
began to enjoy the wonder of wildlife around her. The afternoon became an enchantment for them both. Though Amy

had been removed from the hard hustle of big city life to the slower-paced mountain community of Scotts Valley, her contact with nature had been thus far limited to family camping trips. The brief forays taken with her parents had been along marked and well-traveled trails. Those hikes were nothing like this. The day also wove a spell for Dixie, luring her, making her forget all but the small hand in hers.

Amy's normally bubbling and rowdy exuberance was replaced by a hushed reverence. Her steps were slow and her questions soft until they made their way into a clearing, at which time she literally squealed with delight.

Dixie laughed, for this was her favorite place and had been for as long as she could remember. Even now, when the weather permitted, she made her way to this stream to enjoy the peace and listen to the small series of waterfalls that trickled their way over boulders and fallen trees to fill a shallow pool.

"Can I swim, Aunt Dixie? Are there fishes in there? Is this where the squirrels drink? Are there skunk houses close to here?"

The questions came tumbling out of Amy's mouth, but she waited for no answers before she sat down on the flat surface of a large rock and began peeling off her shoes and socks.

"Hold on, stinker! Let's eat and then you can wade. If you look into the water, you'll see some tiny, little fish—minnows— and pollywogs, which grow into frogs."

"Like Kermit, on *Sesame Street*?" Amy plopped onto her belly and stared into the pool. Rippling reflections danced over her face.

Spreading the yellow-and-white-checkered cloth Reversa had packed and setting out lunch, Dixie mused. To have Amy close, as she had over the past days, was an unusual experience for her in many ways. Ryan had not been born until she was nearly twelve. Even then she had continued much as an only child might have, sharing her time between her grandparent's diverse households and that of her stepfather. By her own choice her friends had been close but few, and as a result her childhood had been, for the most part, spent with adults rather than other children. To have a man as a husband and companion had always been part of her aspirations, but after the pain of divorcing Donald that dream was carefully relegated to the distant future.

But to have a child?

The farsighted Reversa had tucked a towel and washcloth in among her victuals and after dipping the cloth in the cool mountain stream, Dixie wiped away traces of jelly and a red Kool-Aid mustache from Amy's face. She wasn't sure she liked the nesting instinct that was surfacing in her nature. It was unsettling.

Rolling up the legs of their jeans, they foraged into the pool together. An empty mayonnaise jar served to net a small school of pollywogs which Amy intended to take home and nurture into full-grown leapers. The afternoon was warm, abuzz with dragonflies and other insects. After a while Amy began to yawn and rub her eyes.

"We'd better get you home for a rest," Dixie said, with a twinge of regret. "Can't have you falling down in the water for a nap, now can we?"

To Dixie's surprise, Amy turned and circled her upper legs in a fierce hug that nearly threw her backward. "Don't let's go yet! Please, Aunt Dixie!"

Dixie's heart did a funny little skip. A reprieve seemed in order—from returning to the house at least—if not from a short rest. With the food cleared away the tablecloth made do for a blanket. They both stretched out and Dixie began to tell a story that very soon set Amy snoozing, shoulders rising and falling in an rhythm which seemed to match the timbre of the waning day. Dixie also began to drift, her eyelids heavy, her thoughts lackadaisical for once, blurred by the sweet peace surrounding them.

She wasn't sure if she'd actually been sleeping or simply daydreaming when she was roused by the sound of footfalls coming through the woods.

Whoever it was seemed hesitant, starting and stopping again after each few steps, as if listening. Every muscle in Dixie's body suddenly tensed, her somnambulant mood falling away in an instant. She quickly glanced down to see Amy undisturbed, curled into an almost fetal position, trusting and completely oblivious.

Dixie rolled over and came onto her elbows. The steps sounded again and she squinted toward the trees.

It could not be Patrick or Reversa, she thought. Both would have called out. Their tread would have been firm. They knew this spot well.

Once more there was the crackle of bracken. Dixie came to her feet and swore silently. There was no way for her to protect herself and Amy from an attack. Her gun had been left behind with her other worries. She looked around, her eyes frantically searching for a makeshift weapon—a broken branch, anything! But it was futile. She would have to go into the cover of the trees to secure any kind of usable club. The rock formations were limited to well-entrenched boulders and loose pebbles. There was nothing she could do but wait for the intruder to appear and pray she could hurtle her own body with enough force and surprise to gain the advantage. With that thought in mind, she stealthily moved to station herself behind a large tree that marked the only logical entry from the heavy cover of forest. The memory of that horrible night she was attacked on her own property washed over her, causing her heart to quicken, and she cursed her own complacency. Not once since the arrest of Michael Dreyfus had she felt any real conviction of his guilt. Now, more than ever, she was sure that if indeed he had murdered Bouchard it had not been a lone act. Someone had helped—the woman on the phone perhaps, or another man—someone who handled a red Chevrolet with all the lethal aptitude of a crack marksman. Michael's lover, Gregory? The Mystique janitor?

Dixie crouched, hearing the steps just feet away, and made ready to spring.

The man who emerged into the clearing had no time to scan the banks of the stream or pause before he was knocked completely off his feet. Air whooshed from his lungs in a painful grunt as Dixie rammed him with lowered head and shoulders, knocking him backward. He hit the ground and yelped as she scrambled over him. He tried to roll away. It was too late. Dixie's bent knee burrowed into his throat and he found himself helplessly pinned as she straddled his upper chest. If he had any breath to spare, the intensity of those glittering green eyes staring into his would have taken it away.

Dixie gasped. "Art!"

At first she was only startled and confused, but when he tried to grin, an effort almost entirely lost in a grimace of pain, a hot flush of color rushed into her cheeks.

"Help!" he croaked.

She tumbled sideways, falling onto a small mossy knoll, and came quickly to her knees.

Art clutched his throat and groaned. "Water!"

Seeing the convulsive expression on his face she jumped up and ran for the hamper and then down to the pool, filling a plastic cup and bringing it back with all haste. For a moment she thought he had passed out. He was still, his chest barely moving, his eyelids closed without a flicker. She dropped down beside him and lifted his head. When he still didn't move, she felt a moment's panic. "Oh, Art, I'm sorry!"

The pilot's chest began to quiver. His eyes opened. "Well, I should hope so." He laughed.

She abruptly dropped his head and leaned back on her haunches. "Here, drink this before I pour it all over you."

He sat and as a precaution took the proffered glass before she could make good her threat. He drank deeply and handed the glass back. "My God, this place in a veritable booby trap! First I'm nearly attacked by that horse you keep for a watchdog. A black Juno meets me at the door with all the hospitality of a porcupine, and then some old character named Patrick refused to allow me across the threshold until he called Herb and had me checked out."

"That old character is my grandfather."

"I know," he grinned. "Herb warned me."

Amy was sitting up in the middle of the tablecloth rubbing her eyes. "Is my daddy here?"

"No, darling." Dixie stood and went to her. "Did you have a nice rest?"

"Who's that?" Amy pointed at Art.

Art was coming to his feet, not without a due amount of moaning and groaning.

"This is Mr. Cochran, Amy, a friend of your dad's," Dixie answered.

"I thought I was a friend of yours, too," the pilot grumbled.

"Who hurted him?" Amy asked. "How come he's got all those leaves in his hair?"

An unintelligible stream of masculine grumbles came from Art as he began picking leaves and small twigs from his hair and clothing.

Dixie started to laugh, and once started found it hard to stop. His look of offended pride only heightened her glee. Soon Amy was also infected and they both giggled uncontrollably.

"Women!" Art swore, but he was grinning, too, a kind of rumpled and boyish grin that Dixie warmly noted in spite of her laughter.

He helped them gather the remnants of their happy afternoon and took charge of the hamper as they all started homeward. Amy walked contently between the two adults, looking up from time to time to watch their expressions.

"I can't understand why Patrick didn't show you the way," Dixie said. "It's almost impossible to give directions."

"He brought me part of the way, but when I told him I wanted to surprise you, he pointed in the right direction and went back."

Her mouth turned down at the corners. "You surprised me, all right. I bet I'll find ten gray hairs tonight!"

"Well, if you depend on me for them you'll never get any more. That's my first and last surprise, *Missy*." Art placed definite emphasis on the last word. He was grinning.

Dixie stopped in her tracks. Her own eyes narrowed to slits.

Amy looked up at Art and began to giggle again. "Good name, huh, Mr. Cochran?"

"Amy . . ." There was real menace in Dixie's voice now.

Art nodded enthusiastically. "Better than Pansy or Petunia."

Amy was nearly dancing with glee, positively aglow at the idea of having someone with whom to share her secret. "Better'n Rose or Daffodil—that's what Reversa says!"

"You two stop it, this instant!"

"Yep, yep, yep." Art's eyes sparkled. "Better than Lilac, or Jasmine, or Magnolia."

"Shut up, Art!" Seeing they had no intention of stopping

or shutting up, she strode ahead of them, tramping over the ferns. She was the first to come out into the clearing where her house stood. Glaring up at the deck she saw Patrick and an all-too-innocent-appearing Reversa. The housekeeper threw Dixie a sickly sweet smile.

" 'Bout time you three got back, Missy Tulip. Supper's been fixed for nearly half an hour.''

Dixie shook her fist and then cringed at the gales of laughter coming from behind her.

Dixie Tulip Flannigan!

Not for the first time, D. T. Struthers groaned and fleetingly wondered what she had done to deserve such a fate, or such a name.

CHAPTER 20

NOT IN A million years would Dixie have invited Art Cochran to stay for dinner after the fiasco brought on by the revelation of her middle name. Patrick and Reversa could not be prevented, however, and so she was forced to a show of hospitality.

Leaving the pilot to the temporary ministrations of her grandfather, she took Amy upstairs where they bathed and changed together. She cared not in the least that Reversa grumbled and groaned about the food getting cold. Likewise, she dropped her jeans into the clothes hamper and prayed the housekeeper would develop a sudden allergy to the poison oak she had tramped through.

Amy was sober as Dixie bathed and silently dressed her. "I'm goin' home tomorrow, huh?"

The question caused Dixie a sharp pain that made her face sterner still. She nodded.

"And I'm not gonna come back."

"Of course you are." Dixie concentrated on slipping a nightgown over the damp flaxen curls.

"No sir, 'cause you're mad and you won't let me!"

"I'm not mad!" The pain was becoming deeper, more intense.

Amy was quiet for several moments, obediently turning to be buttoned and slipping her feet into a small pair of furry scuffs. When she spoke again, her voice was quavering. "I'm sorry."

Dixie saw the tears, and her arms went around the little girl. "Oh, sweetheart, I'm not angry with you. I'm just sad because I'll miss you so much!"

It was a tearful reconciliation and private farewell that made them both feel much better. Returning to the living room, their faces were serene and happy. Art's eyes appreciatively took in Dixie, now dressed in a forest-green shirt and soft suede slacks with matching boots and vest. On any other woman the outfit might have looked masculine, but not on the small curvy figure descending the stairs. Dixie's hair cascaded over her shoulders in a riot of bright auburn curls. The gold Bismarck chain, and a large square-cut emerald ring with matching earrings, were somehow not at odds with the casual attire she wore. Rather, they lent just the right touch of femininity.

Dixie read Art's expression and felt a rush of pleasure. Her more expensive clothing and jewelry were never worn to work but she was not without her small share of vanity. A ring or bracelet, a fur jacket, or perfume priced like liquid gold gave her as much pleasure as the next woman. Just before coming downstairs she had stood before the mirror and critically examined herself, and to now see the result of her care brought her close to purring.

After dinner, a meal which Reversa served with uncharacteristic acquiescence, and having seen Amy safely to bed, Dixie led Art onto the wide front deck. The night was warm and it seemed a neutral choice; better than remaining indoors under the apologetic bustling of Reversa, and less intimate than the dark and narrow back porch.

Dixie chose to sit in a cushioned redwood chair, a chair with room for one, while indicating another for her guest. Art looked wistfully at a matching loveseat, then shrugged and sat, expelling an exaggerated sigh.

"You're a very hard lady to figure," he said.

She looked at him for several long minutes. "So I've been told."

"Do you take some kind of pride in that?" All bantering was put aside as an edge of irritability came into his voice. "I'm not sure what to make of you. One minute you're a tough little cop who's all business and the next someone or something I can't quite put my finger on.''

"I'm not intentionally perverse, if that's what you mean." She responded to his directness without rancor. "Just what is it you were expecting, Art?"

"Hell, I don't know. At first I thought you were just like . . ." His voice trailed away and he flushed.

"Like what?" she coaxed.

"Okay, like all the others I guess, eating the corn I was dishing out when we first met."

"Surely the woman you come in contact with aren't all so gullible, Art. Perhaps they choose to be that way simply because they like you." She was smiling at him.

He threw back his head and laughed. "See what I mean? Anyone else would be telling me what a chauvinist pig I am."

"I don't care for the *pig* thing much." She chuckled. "And if you're through asking questions, maybe you won't mind answering one."

"I haven't even gotten started yet, but go ahead."

"What made you come up here without calling first?"

"Didn't have your number."

"My address either. I assume Herb gave you both."

"Yes, bless his soul."

"Well?" She continued to look at him with a level gaze.

"Okay, a straight answer to a straight question. I was curious. Nothing about you fits, Dixie. I wanted to see how you live and," his voice dropped again, "I wanted to see *you*. That Bouchard case was over on the last day we talked. You're sure taking your sweet time about giving me a raincheck."

"Is your curiosity satisfied?"

"Do I get my raincheck?"

"Tomorrow good enough?"

They were both laughing as Patrick came out with a tray of mugs and three bottles of beer.

"Can't see you swapping blarney without some brew," he said. "Hope I'm not butting in."

The atmosphere was relaxed. The men carried on a lazy conversation and while they did so, Dixie gave Art her close but casual scrutiny. She had the distinct impression the pilot had never taken a relationship seriously before. No doubt he liked the challenge he imagined she presented. He was intrigued. But she wondered if it went beyond that. One thing was certain: she found Art Cochran physically appealing— almost overwhelmingly so—a fact that surprised her. Normally, she preferred men with dark curly hair, tall and well muscled, a description that missed him by a mile. The short sand-colored hair looked almost unkempt, with a stubborn cowlick at the crown. His eyes were a murky gray-blue and she doubted if he stood over five foot ten. His frame was muscular but lean and somewhat lanky.

So what was it?

She decided it must be the devil-may-care swagger and the humor that seemed always to hover beneath the surface of his face, ready to break through in an impish grin at the drop of a hat. Life with a man like Art would never be dull. Or serious?

Her musing was interrupted when the screen door opened again. Reversa stuck her head out. "Telephone, Miss . . . Missy. It's Amy's daddy. He asked to talk to the child first, but she's been curled up in the middle of your bed, fast asleep, for an hour now. Told him I wasn't gonna wake her. Told him we oughta keep her here for a while, too, but he's bein' stubborn as a mule!"

Dixie shook her head. It was hopeless. Nothing in the world would ever change the incorrigibility of her headstrong housekeeper.

Going indoors, she picked up the phone and caught the tail end of the conversation Herb was having with someone else.

"It does make a difference. I'm not at all sure Dreyfus is—"

"Herb?"

"Oh, hi, Dix. Just thought you'd want to know I got another one of those calls tonight—just before I left the office. You know, the woman."

"About the tapes?" Dixie felt her pulse quicken.

"Yeah. Weird, just like the last time only worse. She was laughing and I'm sure she was loaded on something, booze maybe, but probably drugs. A regular space cadet."

"What did she say? Did you get her name? Where are you?"

"Hold it! I couldn't get her name, but she kept doing her

poetry thing, remember? About Bouchard? And some way-out ditty about 'rocks with locks.' She's nuts! Wanted to talk to you, said the only good pig is a girl pig.''

''Sweet.''

''Thought you'd like that.''

''You still at the PD?''

''No.'' His voice lightened. ''They released Janice early. I brought her home tonight. She's tired but she wanted to talk to Amy.''

''I'll go wake her. Sorry about Reversa.''

''Don't bother. The old bossy britches is right. We can wait; Janice is tired, too. I'll come get Amy first thing in the morning.''

''I'll miss her. We had a great time today, but, damn, I wish I'd been at the office when that call came in!''

''I'm willing to bet you'll get another one. She kept saying something about your present—or she'd like to give you a present—or something like that. Make any sense to you?''

Dixie shook her head and then realized she hadn't spoken. ''No, nothing. What kind of present?''

''Beats me. You know what I keep thinking about? 'Sorry' presents.''

''Cripes!'' She saw again the agonized face of Lola Hobden distorted by bitterness and grief.

''My sentiments exactly. And according to our mystery caller, Dreyfus isn't guilty.''

''Sounds to me like she did quite a bit of talking, Herb.''

''Not really. Just a bunch of disjointed sentences and those crazy jingles. I'm tellin' you, Dix, she's looney. And that loud background music was there again. In fact, I think it was the same music as before.''

Dixie's face was thoughtful. ''Did you happen to catch any of the words?'' She searched her own mind, trying to remember the music that had played in the background of the first strange call, but she couldn't. During that call, she'd been too intent on the slurred voice.

''Only a couple of words—something about seasons or reasons—hell, I don't know. That stuff all sounds the same to me. I'm a country and western buff myself. I don't think it was a new song, though; maybe one of those oldie but goodie

things. The kids are listening to a lot of that now. Nostalgia
for the good old days. You know, the rebellious sixties.''

She said nothing. Song titles and lyrics were rushing through
her mind. Seasons. Reasons.

''You there?'' Herb asked.

''Uh-huh.''

''I smell smoke coming over the line. You come up with
something?''

''No, but damned if I'm going to let this go. First thing
Monday, Di Franco is going to listen to me. The Dreyfus
arrest is all wrong—I feel it. The whole business reeks like
the back of a paddy wagon on Saturday night.''

Herb groaned. ''Graphic, Struthers. Ugh!''

''Appropriate. And I'm beyond caring if Di Franco gives a
BFD about my rocking the boat or not. The collar he made on
Dreyfus just doesn't work, computer enhancement or no.''
She hesitated. ''You going to back me up?''

For a moment there was only silence. ''To reopen the case,
you mean?''

She said nothing.

There was a deep sigh on the other end of the line. ''Shit,''
he moaned. ''Might as well. The way I see it I'm out on my
grits come shift change anyway. That's what comes from
having a powder puff for a partner.''

''Herb?''

''Mmm?''

''I love you.''

He chuckled and hung up.

Dixie couldn't sleep.

Amy wasn't keeping her awake this time. It was her own
inability to remember something she knew might be very
important. Had Herb not mentioned the music playing in the
background of his phone call, she would never have wondered about it. But the fact that the music was the same, and
that she had heard it once before, niggled at her, gnawed at
the edges of her sleep like a sharp-toothed rat.

She tossed and turned until finally, close to daybreak, she
gave it up. Slipping out of bed, she padded to the closet and
put on a bathrobe. It was going to be one very long day. She
almost wished she hadn't made the date with Art.

Thinking about the pilot, she felt a little guilty. When she'd returned to the deck last night, she had been quiet. Sensing her distraction, Art had risen to leave. She had walked him to the battered pickup he'd arrived in, but it wasn't until after he left that his last action registered on her busy mind. Leaning toward her, he had obviously intended to move in for a good-night kiss, a signal completely lost on her at the time.

Sitting alone in the dawn-washed kitchen, sipping a cup of coffee, she shook her head in self-disgust. Now, more than ever, Art would be convinced she was playing hard to get.

She got up and turned on the radio but soon turned it off again. The music was irritating and shattered her train of thought.

When Reversa came into the room an hour later, Dixie was sitting at the table, still scowling, massaging her temples.

"Laws! You look like you've been eatin' prunes and buckshot, Miss Tulip!" She grinned mischievously—a flash of white teeth in her cocoa-colored face.

Dixie glared at her. "If you don't stop it, I'm going to start salting your oatmeal with ground glass."

The housekeeper laughed and shuffled to the stove, obviously frightened out of her wits. By the time she had a fresh pot of coffee brewed and a thick buttermilk flapjack batter prepared, Patrick and Amy were also up. Shortly afterward, Herb arrived and the kitchen was noisy with talk and laughter. Breakfast was finished in high spirits.

Not without regret, Dixie helped Amy pack her things and brought them downstairs for Herb to take out.

After submitting to a round of syrupy kisses, the little girl scrambled into Herb's station wagon, already firing a hundred questions at him about broken legs and casts and wheelchairs and crutches.

Reversa and Patrick were misty-eyed, but Dixie, having said her good-byes the evening before, managed to keep up a cheerful facade. Just before getting into the car, Herb looked at her closely and then put an arm around her shoulders.

"You look beat, Pard. Amy wear you to a frazzle?"

Dixie shook her head. "No, it's that stupid song you told me about. I'm going crazy trying to remember."

"Well, forget it for today. On Monday morning we'll hit Tony with both barrels."

"And if he won't go along with us?"

He met her inquiring eyes. "He will. I've been dragging my feet on this thing, Dix, I admit it. Just thinking about that night we were knocked over the . . ." His voice caught and several moments passed before he was able to continue. "I've been fooling myself because I wanted Dreyfus to be the one. I didn't want to think about having some guy—some *other* guy—still running around trying to stop us. The arrest took the pressure off and it just seemed . . . easier . . . safer." His mouth turned down ruefully. "Not much of an excuse, huh?"

"No, but a hell of a good *reason* when you think about Janice."

They both smiled.

"You going to get some rest now, put it aside until Monday?" He frowned at the faint smudges he saw beneath her eyes.

"I'll put it aside, but I doubt if Art would appreciate my catnapping on our first date."

"So he did find his way up here. Sure can be a pushy cuss when he wants something. Hope you didn't mind my giving out your address. I kinda got the idea you liked him." He wasn't looking directly at her any longer, and he began to shuffle his feet.

"I might," she said. "I haven't really decided yet."

Herb opened the door and got in. "Nice guy—I guess. Watch out for him, though. He was a real lady killer in high school."

"Don't worry." She smiled. "He'll stay in his cockpit and I'll stay in mine."

The station wagon pulled away to a chorus of good-byes and thank-yous, Patrick and Reversa waving until it disappeared.

Dixie busied herself getting ready, and at the same time did her best to keep the promise to Herb by not thinking about the strange phone call. It wasn't easy. She caught herself lapsing now and again, straining to grasp the threads of old rock tunes with appropriate lyrics. *Seasons. Reasons.* Once more the words went around and around in her head.

Was it just the one word or both? So far she'd come up with several songs but none matched the sentimental lyrics she seemed to remember vaguely.

When she arrived at Reid Hillview Airport, Art was waiting, pacing up and down the terminal. He was looking at his watch as she came through the door.

"O ye of little faith," she chided.

An easy grin split his face and the color of his eyes seemed to brighten by several shades, turning them almost blue. "It's about time, Tulip. Whatcha say we go upstairs and get some lunch before we take off—that is unless you think you'll get airsick in the Stearman."

Dixie lost her smile. Her gaze was steady and her tone slightly caustic when next she spoke. "Arthur Blatworth Cochran, I refuse to take the heat for my ancestor's frivolity. I'm Dixie because it's my only option, or D.T. if you prefer, or *Hey, you*—or whatever. I am *not* Tulip."

"Blatworth!" he exploded and then began to sputter. "How in the hell . . ."

Dixie's lower lip twitched. "Computer file checks turn up all kinds of interesting things. You live at 569 Soquel Way at LeSelva Beach. You were born on April 23, 1952, with the name—"

"Truce! It's my mother's maiden name, no fault of my own. You win, but you don't play fair!"

"Lunch sounds great." Her lashes fluttered at him.

"Good." He was obviously relieved to drop the topic of names. "Thought you might want to look at this even though your case is finished." There was a long cardboard tube tucked under his arm which he now held up. "Especially since I went to the trouble of getting it."

"An aerial map?" She kept several in her own plane at Buchanan Field.

"Nope, just a map. A friend of mine works at the county assessor's office. This one shows who owns what up in my neck of the woods. Still interested?"

"You bet!"

Settled once again in a comfortable booth in the Red Baron, they ordered lunch. After the waitress brought coffee, Art extracted the map and spread it over the table top. To Dixie's surprise, three areas had already been outlined in red.

"I read about these two characters in the papers," he said, tapping the map with his fingertips. "We both know about this one.'' The area he indicated was half a block of industrial property in the city of Santa Cruz. Another area which had been outlined was very small, surrounded on all sides by larger land holdings. Every piece of property in the county was neatly marked with the name of the taxpayer, the legal owner. The first area listed Max Hobden as owner.

Art tapped the second area. ''Robert Todd. I figured that might be the fellow I read about in the papers, the one who found the body.''

She nodded. ''In this case the Robert probably means his father, who passed away not too long ago. But it certainly doesn't look like an agricultural holding in any case. No crop dusting would be done there.''

''No. I flew over. Looked like a vacation house, not real big but nice. It's about a mile and a half from the beach.'' His hand moved in a circle. ''But there's farming all around. Surely the Todds have friends who keep the nasty kind of goodies you're looking for.''

''This interests me a lot more,'' she answered, indicating the third land area he had marked off. The bright red lines enclosed a huge block of acreage—flat, fertile farmlands—all owned by Albert D. Enriquez.

Art nodded. ''It's leased out,'' he said. ''I dust that whole area, but I'm contracted by four different farmers. Two are Japanese, one named Yoshioka and the other Inoue. Both of them are nice guys. Hard working.''

''What do they raise?''

''Between the four of them, a little of everything: artichokes, cauliflower, strawberries—even some flowers. The other parcels are leased by Sam Crites and Tom Blake—farmers, too, of course. And there's a small landing strip right in the middle of the four farms, a good one, well maintained.''

Art leaned back. ''Surprised me a little to find out who owned that property. Isn't Enriquez supposed to be champion of his Chicano brothers or something?''

''So?''

''So, Blake and Crites are in trouble up to their eyeballs with the United Farm Workers union. Caesar Chavez has thrown pickets up around both places. It's been going on for quite a while, and things have gotten ugly more than once.''

"Do tell!" Dixie whistled softly. "I'm sure Enriquez's opponents would just love to hear it. Something like this could blow his political platform to bloody hell."

Art nodded. "After I saw this, I made it a point to talk to the farmers," he offered. "Crites and Blake were closed-mouthed all the way, but Yoshioka and Inoue finally told me a couple of things you might find interesting. Enriquez flies in and out of there a couple of times a month from what I understand. He has a Bonanza he just sets down on the strip—that way he never has to cross the picket lines. I doubt if the workers even know why he's there—or maybe think he's just making a show of support—negotiating for them or something."

"He arrives alone?"

"Sometimes, but usually with his wife or secretary. Blake told me he even brings his daughter once in a while—she likes to hike down to the beach that borders the property. I don't know if all this helps you any."

His shoulder was touching hers now. It felt warm and strangely natural. She smiled. "Thanks, Art, it might help a great deal. Remind me that I owe you one."

"Well, since you mentioned it, I did get this speeding ticket the other day . . ."

Dixie made as if to hit him and he cringed. They were both laughing when the waitress brought their food.

The restaurant was busy, filled with weekend flying enthusiasts. The buzz of voices and tinkle of silverware almost drowned out the piped-in music, an easy rock radio station, which suddenly captured and riveted Dixie's undivided attention. Art stopped eating and looked at her strangely as he felt her freeze, a fork full of salad poised midway between the plate and her mouth.

"We had joy, we had fun, we had seasons in the sun . . . and the hills that we climbed were just seasons out of time . . ."

The chorus shot through Dixie's brain like a bolt of lightning. She laid down the fork, her eyes wide.

". . . Good-bye, Mama, it's hard to die when all the birds are singing in the sky . . ."

Art was shaking her arm. "My God, Dixie, what is it?"

The music played on as she grabbed her small leather handbag, opened it, and snatched the notebook she always carried. Her hands were shaking as she rifled through the pages. Finding the one she wanted, she began sliding out of the booth, ignoring Art's protests. The only sound which registered on her mind as she flashed into the lobby, heading for the telephone, was the voice of Terry Jacks, singing an oldie but goodie.

"*. . . Good-bye, Michelle, my little one . . .*"

People had turned to stare accusingly at Art as the small redhead bolted and ran from him. His cheeks flushed. Emerging from the booth also, he threw down a twenty, snatched up the map, and stalked out.

Dixie was talking into the phone as he approached. Her face was intent, her voice almost pleading. ". . . I know you want to talk to me. Please, I'm coming over right now." She listened and then spoke again. "No, no, don't do that. If they come back, just go to your room and wait. I'll be right there. Don't cry, Michelle. It'll be okay."

She turned to see him glaring at her with eyes like the Arctic Sea. She tried a bright smile. It didn't work.

"Another raincheck, Sergeant Struthers?" His voice was colder than his eyes, and the boyish grin was nowhere in evidence.

"I have to go, Art. Try to understand."

Looking at the earnest pleading in her eyes, his expression softened a fraction. "God knows I am trying, Dixie, but—"

The smile she turned on him then would have dazzled a Sphinx. Coming very close, she brushed his cheek with a kiss. He barely had time to react before she was gone, rushing down the open flight of stairs and out of the building. He stood watching through the window and saw her enter the parking lot at a dead run.

CHAPTER 21

SHE WAS DRIVING parallel to the white coral fence facing the main road when she saw the horse, Death Song. The beautiful roan moved like a work of art, muscles rippling, coat glistening in the early afternoon sunshine. But even the majestic animal could not compare with his rider. Michelle Enriquez was springtime itself, straight in the saddle, her cheeks bright. Her long hair flew out behind her, whipped by the wind. She was waving frantically. Dixie pulled the car onto the shoulder of the road and turned off the ignition. Upon getting out and coming closer, she saw that Michelle's eyes were wild. The girl kept looking over her shoulder. Her words came out in fast gasps.

"They're home! He's going to take me away, put me in a hospital so I can't tell! I went to my room, just like you told me, Sergeant Struthers, but I came out again. I heard them talking!"

The girl was close to complete and unreasoning hysteria. Dixie moved with caution. Approaching slowly, she reached over the fence and gently patted the gelding's velvet nose. The animal whinnied and pawed the ground, made nervous and restive by his rider's panic.

"Come with me, Michelle." Dixie spoke slowly. "This isn't a good place for us to talk."

"I can't . . . I can't . . ." Again she looked toward the house.

"I want to help you."

Michelle whirled her head back around, but now her eyes were narrowed. The full, softly pouting lips thinned and stretched back over her teeth. She nearly snarled. "Help! That's what they keep saying. 'We want to help you—come take your medicine like a good girl or we'll call Dr. Benson again.' They did call him, too. He's here already. They hate me! They're going to take me away where I can't tell anyone!"

The ugliness left her face as suddenly as it had appeared and she smiled at Dixie. "And *you* want to put me in jail."

"No, Michelle."

"Yes!" the young woman hissed. "You want to throw me in jail, put me away, just like they do. They'd have done it already if they could, but they want the tapes." A high keening laugh tore from her lips, raising the hair on Dixie's nape. Then her voice changed, dropping several octaves. Her words slurred and once more Dixie heard the strange sing-songy jingle. *"There are tapes, you know, and they will show who killed the—"*

Shouts caused them both to look out across the acre of pasture. Three people were running toward them. Two were men, one whom Dixie didn't recognize, and the other Albert Enriquez. Close behind the men ran the tall, lithe figure of Christina.

Michelle let out a blood-curdling scream of rage. Her mount pranced and reared, kicking forelegs violently into the air. Dixie stumbled back in alarm, expecting to see the girl thrown. Instead, Michelle leaned forward, her head close to the horse's neck. Mount and rider moved in unison, and an instant later the gelding was streaking across the flat, green surface, heading straight for a far fence that bordered the hillside. A single flying leap and they were free of the Enriquez estate. Within moments they were gone, lost in the shadows of drooping oaks and towering eucalyptus trees.

At first, the three figures froze in the middle of the field, shading their eyes against the sun. Then they turned hostile eyes on Dixie. Albert Enriquez was the first to move, and even from that distance she could see the menace on his face.

Guided more by instinct than conscious thought, she ran for the car. Throwing herself in, she turned the ignition and closed the door at the same time. The motor roared to life. The rear tires spun once, spewing a shower of gravel before they caught. The Mustang jerked forward and bounced onto the road. Dixie made a tight U-turn and sped away. Looking into the rearview mirror, she saw her pursuers just as they reached the fence.

The last look Dixie glimpsed on Michelle Enriquez's face had been wild—panic-stricken and ghostly pale. There was no telling what might be going through her unbalanced mind. The girl felt trapped. Boxed in on one side by her father's threats and on the other by her fear of arrest, she had taken flight into the hills.

Rounding a wide curve, Dixie slowed the car, driving along the iron-fenced perimeters of Mystique de la Femme. Every few yards she caught a glimpse of the mansion. Sitting as it was, deserted and seemingly devoid of life, it looked almost sinister, nothing at all like the enticing salon it actually was—or had been until a few weeks before.

Slowing still more, creeping the car past the high gate, she saw it was securely bound with chain and padlock.

Coming here had been a long shot, but worth a try. The distance between the Enriquez estate and Mystique was over three miles by road, but far less for Michelle. Mounted on Death Song, she could easily top the hill and work her way back down the other side, entering the salon property from the rear, where it was not fenced.

Dixie rolled the Mustang a few yards beyond the entrance and turned off the motor. How lucid was the girl? she wondered.

One thing was certain: Michelle Enriquez saw Bouchard's tape recordings as her ace in the hole—protection against her father. It suddenly seemed plausible that she might have hidden them somewhere up on that hillside.

Getting out of the car, Dixie looked at the fence. Forbidding. A series of close-set iron bars. Impossible to squeeze through.

Up and over was the only way, she decided, grateful she wasn't wearing her more feminine work attire. The sage jumpsuit would make what she suddenly planned to do a great deal less complicated.

After extracting the snub-nosed Detective Special, Dixie tossed her purse back into the car and clipped the holster to her belt. Approaching the barrier, she jumped. The muscles of her arms quivered, unaccustomed to the strain she placed on them as she pulled her weight upward to hook her right heel over the crossbar. She swayed for several seconds, struggling for balance. Perspiration beaded her forehead as she shifted her weight and grabbed with her right hand for one of the sharp, spearlike rails. The afternoon was hot and still, with only the sounds of birds and insects.

Thankfully, there was no one to see her perched there like an oversized gibbon, easing herself around. She'd nearly managed the delicate maneuver when the sound of hoofbeats reached her ears.

Her hands, already moist and unsteady, slipped and she tumbled over backward, crashing into a giant camellia shrub. She lay still for a second, trying to catch her breath and quiet the pumping of her heart. One of her pant legs had been ripped. There was a long, deep scratch on her forearm and another across her cheek. Her hair was tangled in the brush. It took several moments to extricate herself, but once free she didn't pause to assess the damage either to her person or to her ego. Looking up the wide slant of lawn toward the mansion, she began to walk, almost run, toward it.

The front door was locked tight. There was no sign of life inside. No noise. Not until she skirted the south side of the building and worked her way back. Then a soft nicker sounded.

Death Song stood on a wide, open patio where the patrons of Mystique de la Femme had once lounged after a refreshing swim or dip in the spa. But there was no furniture now, none of the modern tubular lawn chairs or round umbrella tables. The gelding's head drooped down, his coat mottled with sweat.

One of the heavy double doors leading into the pool area stood propped open. There were no interior lights and Dixie stood motionless, staring into the maw of darkness.

Her hesitation was short-lived, for in the next instant she heard a strange tumbling sound and then a splash. She moved forward cautiously, approaching the door sideways. Slipping quickly inside, she flattened her body against a cool, mosaic wall. The air was humid and heavy with the smell of chlorine.

Another noise, the sound of rocks being moved, accompanied by labored breathing, caught her attention. Her eyes gradually adjusted and she was able to make out the figure of Michelle Enriquez scrambling up the small hillock of lava stones above the spa. The waterfall had been turned off and as she reached the top of the jagged formation, she dropped down on her knees. Every now and again a low moan escaped her lips, a kind of muffled sob. Reaching before her, she grasped a large slab of stone and began to strain, pushing it up and away from her. Smaller pieces of rock were dislodged and plunked into the water below.

Slowly, one foot at a time, Dixie worked her way closer, keeping against the damp wall and whenever possible taking advantage of the leafy cover provided by intermittent potted plants. She was within a yard or two of the spa's edge when she stopped.

Michelle was weeping in earnest now, her shoulders heaving as she reached down out of sight. When her hands came up again, they brought with them what appeared to be a large cloth bundle wrapped in several layers of transparent plastic. She inched backward, using elbows and knees for balance.

The girl was less than halfway down when Dixie gasped in surprise. She stiffened and held her breath, realizing someone else was in the huge room. At first glance it seemed only an illusion, a swift streak of denser shadow shooting out from behind a palm in the far corner, beyond the swimming pool. But then the meager light from the open doorway struck something silver and bounced a brief reflection off the wall just above Dixie's head. Faster and faster the shadow moved, a man running on silent feet, with a pitchfork poised before him like a jousting lance. Again there was a flash as light hit the lethal prongs pointed directly at Michelle's unsuspecting back.

"Look out!" Dixie's warning rent the air and echoed off the walls.

Michelle whirled and screamed, the bundle flying from her hands. It hit the tiled floor and she toppled. Her arms windmilled helplessly just before she pitched forward. Her head dashed against the edge of the spa and then, by some miracle, she sprawled sideways, missing the water.

The man froze at the sound of Dixie's yell, but now he moved forward again. Advancing on the girl's inert figure, he brought the pitchfork above his head.

"Stop!" Dixie pulled her revolver. Dropping onto one knee, she took aim. "I'll shoot!"

She still couldn't see his face clearly. For a moment he stood poised like a menacing statue, arms raised. The room was deathly silent until, finally, he lowered his weapon. The pitchfork clattered to the floor.

"Step back!" Dixie moved to a crouch, both arms braced forward, the gun firmly in her hands. When he didn't respond immediately, she spoke again, the words hissing out from between clenched teeth. "Move, you son of a bitch, or you're dead meat!"

She was very close now, and as he stepped back she was able to make out his features. The dark eyes of Manuel Ortiz glared at her.

She yelled again. "Lie down and spread out!"

There wasn't time for conjecture. Kneeling, she was forced to take one hand from the gun as she reached for Michelle. It was impossible to see clearly and dangerous to look away from the man spread-eagled on the tile floor. She had to rely on her sense of touch.

Michelle was alive, but unconscious, her respiration shallow. Her forehead was cut and bleeding heavily. Dixie stood slowly.

"On your feet," she ordered. The gun was leveled at him. "Pick her up and bring her outside."

The dark head came up off the tiles and again Manuel pinioned her with narrowed, reptilian eyes. His hesitation vanished as she brought the gun still nearer his face.

He scraped himself up with jerky, barely controlled movements. The muscles of his shoulders bunched into massive knots as he lifted Michelle's limp body and lumbered toward the door.

It wasn't hard to understand why he paused just before stepping out. In contrast to the cool darkness of the pool area, the afternoon sun was blinding. He stumbled slightly, almost dropping his burden. What Dixie didn't expect as she came through the doorway herself was to feel talonlike nails dig into her forearm. The gun was snatched from her hand and she froze as the cold steel of its barrel was suddenly pressed into the soft, vulnerable flesh of her right temple.

"Thank you very much, Sergeant Struthers."

Dixie turned her head with infinite care to see Christina smiling at her. The expression was poorly suited to the secretary's haughty face and did nothing to melt the snapping ice in her black eyes.

Funny, the things one noticed, Dixie thought. She felt suddenly and inexplicably detached—like an observer rather than a participant of the scene unfolding around her. She noticed how the two front teeth of her captor were slightly crooked, one lapped a fraction over the other, and the tiny beads of perspiration above Christina's upper lip.

Keeping gun and attention trained on the detective, Christina spoke to Manuel. He was still holding Michelle.

"Throw her over the horse." An unpleasant laugh came from deep in her throat. "I've always preferred Alberto's name for El Bravo, but suddenly I've changed my mind. I do believe Death Song is more fitting."

The groundskeeper did as he was instructed, but when he had finished arranging Michelle's dangling upper torso across the saddle and turned back, he was frowning. He ran a nervous tongue over his lips. "You're not going to get me into this one, Christina. I already told you—"

"You already are in, *hermano*—like it or not."

Dixie's eyes widened. *Hermano?* The word brought her back to reality. Had the Spanish word for brother been used in the literal sense, or as just the haphazard endearment so currently in vogue?

Christina saw the question register on Dixie's face and laughed again. "That is correct, Sergeant. Manuel is my youngest sibling. He is what you gringos would call our *black sheep.*"

Manuel obviously found no humor in her barb. "Forget this shit," he hissed. "I'm not killing no cop!"

"Shut your mouth!" Christina spat back. "Go now, bring Diablo from around back. There is no time for argument."

The stocky young man still balked, but only momentarily. When Christina fired a rapid staccato of vehement Spanish at him, he moved quickly, disappearing around the mansion. In a few seconds he was back, leading a huge jet-black stallion. The horse possessed flared nostrils and demonic eyes.

Dixie suppressed a shudder of relief as Christina removed the gun from her temple and backed away.

"We are taking a trip," the secretary informed her, "a very short trip. I would allow you the luxury of riding, but Diablo is a bit selective about who sits upon his strong back." She walked to the stallion and proudly rubbed the sleek coat. "Beautiful, is he not? Alberto is very good to those who serve him."

"No doubt,' Dixie drawled. "I'm sure our illustrious councilman will buy you a silver saddle when he sees what your brother has done to Michelle."

"He will see nothing—except, of course, what *you* have done. A tragedy for the Enriquez family to have their poor, sick daughter shot down by the lady pig."

As if protesting the premature plans for her funeral, Michelle groaned.

Christina spoke to Manuel in rapid Spanish again, sending him back inside the building. When he emerged, he was holding the plastic-wrapped bundle which he gave her in return for the gun—a gun he kept aimed directly at Dixie. He smiled also now and motioned toward the hillside. "It is your turn, *puta*—move!"

The filthy name caused Dixie to stiffen in indignation, but he closed the gap between them and shoved her.

Christina walked to Death Song and pulled the lax reins over the gelding's head, leading him close to her own horse. Once mounted on Diablo, she jerked her head and spoke to Manuel. "Bring her."

The hillside was steep, and while there were no actual bridle paths, Dixie could see that narrow strips of earth had been bared and hardened beneath hoofbeats. This was not the first time Mystique de la Femme had been paid a call via horseback. As she struggled upward, following close behind Michelle's mount, her mind worked furiously. Manuel Ortiz prodded her in the back every minute or two. When her steps faltered or slowed, he pushed harder. At one point she stumbled and went sprawling.

Christina reined to a stop and twisted in the saddle. "You really must be more cooperative, Sergeant." Her voice was silky. "It is growing late and I must return to my employer. He is most anxious about his daughter."

Dixie pulled herself up and automatically dusted her clothes. One arm throbbed where a wide swath of skin had been scraped away. She ignored the pain. Her head tilted back and she met the other woman's malevolent gaze with eyes of green fire. "You're a fool, Christina. No one is going to believe I killed Michelle—and even if they do, how are you going to explain my death?"

The laugh that came from the secretary was chilling. "I will need to explain nothing. Like everyone else, I will be shocked. The newspapers will be avid—a real tragedy, so sad. The beautiful but disturbed daughter of Councilman Enriquez pursued into the hills. Terrible how she was shot just before her horse reared and trampled the equally beautiful policewoman."

Christina smiled sadly. "Tragic, is it not? Hooves can leave unbelievable wounds. A shame to disfigure a face as pretty as yours, but how else to cover the wound my brother will make on your head, eh?"

Seeing Diablo prance restively, Dixie's mouth went dry. Christina was right. A blow on the head with the pistol butt or even a rock might easily go undetected under evidence of a killing by those deadly sharp hooves. In a desperate gamble, she turned to the Mystique caretaker.

"So you do your sister another small favor, eh, Manuel? I suppose it makes little difference—you can only visit the gas chamber once."

She saw the man's tongue flick over his lips again. His eyes darted toward his sister. He seemed about to speak when she silenced him with a chop of her hand and a spew of Spanish too fast for Dixie to follow.

Another groan from Michelle brought the unintelligible flow to a halt. The girl moved this time, her arms flaying the air, knees bending. Her body began to slither off the saddle. Manuel leaped forward to catch her.

A primitive instinct for survival rather than premeditation prompted Dixie's next move. As Manuel rushed past her, she

lowered her upper torso and hurtled her full weight into his
midsection. He grunted and air whooshed from his lungs,
followed immediately by a bellow of rage as her teeth sank
into his wrist. The gun dropped from his grip and hit the
ground, sliding into the bracken.

The next moments were pandemonium. The horses reared
and whirled on the uneven hillside. Michelle, still only partially conscious, thudded to the earth and tumbled limply,
rolling over several times until her body wrapped around a
tree trunk. Christina swore and tried to dismount. Half on,
half off the startled Diablo, she finally jumped clear.

Dixie was a flurry of teeth and claws. Flat on his back, his
upper chest straddled, Manuel brought up one arm to protect
his face and attempted to throw her off with the other. It was
like grappling with a wildcat. Finally, arching his spine, he
managed to unseat her.

Never in her life had Dixie known the desperation which
now flooded through her. Thrown onto her side, she tried to
scramble away only to have him grasp her ankle and drag her
back. She kicked wildly with her free leg. Her first thrust
glanced off, but she continued to pummel his muscular chest.
His grip was like iron. At last, lurching and striking out with
a deliberation born of terror, she aimed higher. Her boot heel
made firm contact. A sickening crunch was immediately followed by a violent spurt of blood as Manuel's nose flattened
and was ground to a pulp.

Once free, Dixie was on her feet. Her chest rose and fell as
she stared down at the man below her. Manuel Ortiz emitted
a series of gurgled moans.

A crackling sound caused Dixie to turn—but not quite fast
enough. She had time for only a brief glance at Christina's
hate-filled face before the butt of her own revolver came
crashing down on her head. A burst of pain thundered through
her brain and the world went black.

CHAPTER 22

"Stupido!"

Christina lashed out at her brother in searing contempt. He was a fool—a bumbling idiot—just as he had been all of his life!

Why must she always be forced to suffer the stupidity of those around her?

First there had been her parents—ignorant—with dirt-grimed fingernails and the dreams of peasants. Even now they could envision nothing beyond their cheap, little east-side home with its plastic-covered furnishings. Her older brothers were no better. Construction workers! Grocery clerks!

No ambition!

Manuel had been born to her parents late, when Christina was already fifteen. She had hoped he would be different. But no, he was even more stupid and lazy than the rest, running with other members of his ridiculous Chicano gang and getting himself in trouble over and over again. She had been wrong to depend on him.

If there was one thing Christina had learned early, it was to depend only on herself. In school she had gotten good grades and then gone on to business college, finally going to work as a staff secretary in the mayor's office. During all that time she never gave herself to anyone—not until she met Alberto Enriquez. So handsome he was—and so unbelievably rich!

She could see he liked her right away, but when he first offered her a job she had been very careful to decline. Above all, she had decided, he must be convinced of her loyalty and value as an employee. Only a little at a time, over candlelit dinners, did she tell him what he wished to know about his political opponent. In those days he had thought he would become mayor, not realizing how fast his career would move, how quickly he would become a candidate for senator.

Then, when the time was exactly right, Christina had given herself to him with a passion that left him gasping for more.

That had been three years ago—three years of working and watching and waiting. Alberto needed her more than ever. Someday, soon, she would be more than his secretary. Though he had not said it yet, the councilman, soon-to-be state senator, needed Christina as a wife!

The soft blonde *puta* to whom he was presently wed was an embarrassment! Judith Enriquez was a lush. She talked far too much—and to Christina's ultimate delight she was being blackmailed by Charles Bouchard!

Yes, wonderful, Christina thought—until she learned the whole story. Keeping Alberto's books, she had very soon noticed the drain on his bank account, and upon going to his silly wife she learned the truth. The proprietor of Mystique de la Femme had recorded some rather graphic and titillating encounters between Judith Enriquez and Kathryn Holmstead.

Such a discovery did not shock Christina. Rather, it filled her with glee. Now everything would be easy. She, with Judith's help, would manage to buy the telltale recordings once and for all—an outright purchase which would insure Alberto a quiet divorce.

At first glance, the situation had seemed perfect, but that had been before Christina's meeting with Bouchard. The salon owner was more shrewd than she expected. Not only did he have on tape the courtship of Judith and Kathryn, but also the complaints of the former against her husband— including Alberto's clandestine affair with Christina and reams of dialogue on his political hypocrisy.

Yes, Charles Bouchard knew it all, and he had no intention of releasing the tapes, not until he squeezed Judith Enriquez completely dry. The man had laughed in Christina's face—a mistake that had finally cost him his life.

Retribution had not come immediately, of course. It had taken several months and all the cunning and foresight at Christina's command. First, she had to become friendly with the empty-headed receptionist. But once she learned about the true ownership of the salon, the rest came slowly but satisfactorily.

Manuel's fresh release from prison and his fortuitous connection with M.O.R.E. simplified matters. An earnest plea to Alberto had easily convinced him to call Mr. Hobden and arrange a job at the salon for her brother.

Manuel soon provided her with just the little details she needed: how Michael Dreyfus disliked his employer; how the salon manager hated his bimonthly ritual of applying hair color to Charles Bouchard's graying head. Every other Thursday night Manuel was obliged to wait later than usual before cleaning the main salon and pool area. He was thus delayed so that the master might strip down and do his body hair, relaxing undisturbed while he awaited the desired youthful effect.

Oh, yes, Christina had once thought, so good to be a woman of ambition and intelligence. So easy to dilute the leftover hair color. So satisfying to watch Charles Bouchard twist and turn, his eyes begging for mercy as Manuel held him down. He had still been begging when they lifted and carried him to the spa, convulsing in agony as the poison attacked his nervous system.

So smooth it would have gone, too, had it not been for the surprise of Bobby Todd's arrival—and the unexpected complication of Michelle's unrequited love and vengeful grief!

Now, looking at the fluttering eyelids of Alberto's daughter, Christina was filled with a white-hot rage. Always this child stood in her way!

Michelle Enriquez had been pampered all her life. Everything she wanted was instantly provided. She had only to pout her lips and squeeze out a tear or two. But even the doting Judith and Alberto had been unable to pacify their child when her equally spoiled boyfriend had been found dead—found by Michelle herself. From that day on she'd grown increasingly

demented, babbling about suicide when the whole world knew
it had been simply another case of idiocy. The boy, Jeff, been
typical of the young rich. Bored and self-gratifying, he
had finally gone too far in his quest for excitement. Christina
had been as convinced of this as were the police and the
Enriquezes, and all the other horrified parents of Los Palamos.

Yes, Christina had been convinced that the stupid boy's
death was accidental, until after the fateful passing of Charles
Bouchard. And from that time onward, luck seemed to flee
her every effort. All her plans and dreams and schemes began
to evaporate.

First, she and Manuel had been surprised by the arrival of
Todd. What a fright that had been! Worse than having to hide
like cowering rats was being unable to search out the tape
recordings. For that she and Manuel were forced to wait until
after the authorities left. And then—*caramba!* They had torn
the place apart, all for nothing!

For days Christina had worried. Not about the police who
came snooping around—they could be dispatched—but about
the recordings that could destroy Alberto's career. Over and
over again she had sent Manuel to look, carefully of course,
since the salon was once more in business. And over and over
again she had silently damned Judith Enriquez for her loose,
drunken lips.

But it wasn't until the night Christina overheard Michelle
on the telephone, speaking to the policewoman, that she
learned the truth. How she had wanted to slap the girl!

Since that night she had alternately cursed herself and
Michelle. Had she, Christina, only left things alone Michelle
would have accomplished the job for her. Distraught and
crazed, the girl had been creeping into the salon night after
night, slinking about the mansion, watching Bouchard with
malevolent, vengeful eyes. All that while Michelle had been
savoring the death she herself had planned for the salon
owner! The death *she* planned for him!

"Let's get out of here, Christina." Manuel was speaking to
her now, whining like a frightened dog.

"*Stupido!*" She said it again. "How many times will you fail?
This *gringa* would be dead already if you were not such a fool!
Now we cannot go, not until we have done the job properly."

Michelle Enriquez was pulling herself up. Leaves were caught in her hair and blood caked her forehead. She blinked and stared at them. At first her eyes were dull, uncomprehending, but then they cleared and narrowed.

"You killed him!" she was on her hands and knees. A tangle of hair fell over her twisted, death-white face. *"Cheat! Cheat! Cheat!"* Her voice was high and shrill.

"Calm yourself, Michelle." Christina spoke in the same cool, condescending tone she always used when addressing Alberto's daughter, and at the same time she advanced. From the corner of her eye she could see her brother. He was holding a blood-soaked handkerchief to his shattered nose, but when he saw what she was doing his lower jaw gaped. His eyes widened as Christina unfastened the snaps on her shirt, one at a time. Slipping her left arm out of the sleeve, she transferred the gun to her right hand until she had discarded the garment completely. Overhanging trees dappled shade over the olive smoothness of her skin. Her breasts swelled around dark coppery nipples. She began methodically wrapping the red-and-white-checkered shirt around the barrel of Dixie's .38 caliber Detective Special.

Michelle had come to her knees now, almost as if she were praying or begging. Ghostly pale, she watched Christina's movements with the fascination of a mesmerized rodent staring into the eyes of a deadly cobra.

Christina smiled and fired.

For a moment death didn't register. Michelle remained kneeling upright, her lips parted slightly before her soft cinnamon-colored eyes glazed over. The small round hole in her forehead bled very little. Calves pinned beneath her, she fell straight back, shuddered once, and was still. The back of her head was gone. Patches of hair and bloody brain fragments clung and oozed down the tree trunk behind her.

"She-e-e-it!" Manuel's eyes were like saucers.

Christina stood looking at the body with a bland expression. When she finally spoke, her voice was a monotone. "Go back to the salon," she told him. "Set the rocks back in place and leave. Return to the home of our parents until I call you. You must take a trip for a while, but not in that disgusting car of yours. The police will be watching for it. I will buy you a bus ticket to someplace far, far away.''

''But I can't leave,'' he protested. ''They will suspect me. If I try to get rid of the car, they will trace me . . . and there is my probation officer!''

''You will do as I say!''

He paled at the gun she swung on him. He began to back away.

It was exactly what she had expected. Men were spineless— all of them, even Alberto. A man was nothing without a strong woman. *Nothing!*

She waited until her brother's hurried, stumbling steps died away before going back to Diablo. Death Song stood higher on the hill, his withers twitching nervously.

A *gelding*! Christina's lips curled in contempt. She pre-ferred an animal with *huevos*. Her Diablo was such a one— spirited, full of fire.

As if divining her admiration, the stallion snorted and pawed the ground. She touched the velvet of his nose once and then took the reins and mounted. After securing the plastic bundle which contained the tape recordings, she slipped the revolver into the waistband of her denim pants. Her shirt was a loss, powder-burned and torn where she had used it as a silencer, but it would do. She would rip it and tell Alberto she had fallen. She was about to put the shirt back on when she saw Dixie move. Not much of a movement, just the slightest unfurling of her legs where a moment before she had been crumpled into a heap.

Christina clicked her tongue and coaxed the horse very close, bringing his hoofs just inches from Dixie's auburn curls.

''Now, my lovely Diablo,'' she crooned, ''a few moments more and we shall go home.'' Her hands tightened on the reins. She was just raising the sharp heels of her boots when the sound of breaking branches caused her to freeze.

The man who came through the cover of scrub oak was a *gringo*, fair-skinned, with hair like straw and light eyes— very tall. He held a gun.

''Get down!'' he ordered.

For all the emphatic harshness of his command, Christina clearly detected an undertone of certainty. She didn't move.

"I said get down!" He was coming forward, limping slightly, raising the gun higher. Rivulets of sweat poured down from his hairline.

Christina inhaled deeply and then inwardly smiled as she saw his glance dart to her breasts. At the same time she drew the gun and pulled back hard on Diablo's reins. Her hair had worked loose and flew about her in disarray, a midnight avalanche of blue-black flames. The horse reared.

The man yelled and fired—not once but three times.

Dixie awoke to a cacophony of noise and pain. At first she couldn't move. The agony in her head transmitted itself to her stomach. She groaned, but the sound was lost in the thunder of hoofbeats and reverberating gunfire. Then, eerily, the world went silent and still. She felt herself sinking into blackness again and struggled to open her eyes. A wave of nausea threatened.

"Sarge?"

A frown puckered her brow. She must still be unconscious or only asleep after all. Dreaming the voice was somehow vaguely familiar, an echo from her past.

"Can you move, Sarge?"

A man's voice. Distraught.

Dixie's eyelids fluttered. At first the only thing she saw was an ocean of dusty green. One side of her face was pressed into the fallen eucalyptus leaves and the pungent, oily smell of them caused her stomach to lurch again. She rolled over and the pain increased.

A strong, incredibly gentle arm slid under her shoulders and neck, supporting her head. She felt her upper torso being lifted and looked up to see the pale and anxious face of Pete Willis.

"Don't tell me,"—she tried to smile—"you always pay your debts."

CHAPTER 23

"I'D LIKE TO choke you with my own two hands!" The high color on Herb's face as he towered over her gave his threat credence. "If you had to go off half-cocked, you could've at least called me first!"

"I've already told you, I was only playing a hunch." She threw aside one of the blankets on her bed. The weather was too warm for convalescence. Her bedroom felt claustrophobic and stifling.

"Bullshit! Are we partners or not?"

"I don't know, Herb—are we? Di Franco seems to have other plans!" Irritation crept into her voice. Her head was pounding unmercifully and her stomach was still upset. There were bruises all over her arms and legs. She had been in bed for less than twenty-four hours and already she felt itchy and thin-skinned.

His tone softened. "As long as we're both in the unit, we're a team."

"How long do you suppose that'll be? God damn it, will you please sit? It hurts my neck to keep looking up!"

Herb stared at her in surprise. There were tears in her eyes. "Aw, Dix." He sat down in the chintz-covered chair beside her bed. "I didn't mean to yell at ya, please don't—"

"Will you shut up!" She turned away from him.

They were both silent for what seemed an eternity. Her

wanted to say something—apologize for coming on like a Sherman tank, but he couldn't find the words. Instead, he sat wishing he could dissolve into the carpet. Her back was to him now, but every second or two he saw her shoulders hunch and quiver. When she finally spoke, her voice was low and thick.

"I'm a lousy cop, Herb."

The statement was so unlike her that he momentarily forgot his own remorse. "God, don't say that! You're the best partner I've ever—"

"I let her die. Michelle Enriquez is dead and if I'd just . . . just . . ." Her voice broke.

"Just what?" He reached out, touching her shoulder, and felt the muscles beneath his hand tense. "Look at me, Struthers. Please, turn around."

She obeyed slowly. There was no makeup on her face. Her nose was bright pink. The Mount Everest–size lump on the crown of her head made brushing painful and her hair was in a riot. Herb decided she'd never looked more beautiful.

"Michelle Enriquez was a very sick girl," he said. "I don't think anyone could have helped her—not really. She probably wasn't right even before her boyfriend killed himself."

"You're sure that's what he did?"

Herb nodded. "Michelle's parents gave me a note they found in her room, the one she found when she discovered Jeff Chambers's body. It was laid out in black and white. He had evidently picked up Michelle at Mystique a couple of times, and I guess that's all Bouchard needed to set the lure. The kid must have been a latent homosexual. From reading the note, it was pretty clear he'd only slept with the old reprobate once, but he couldn't live with himself afterward."

"Poor kids." Dixie thought of all the secrets Charles Bouchard had collected—all the lives he had destroyed. "He was really wicked, Herb. I don't use the word often, but it suits him perfectly. Really and truly *wicked*."

"Yeah. Charlie Phelps and Christina Ortiz would have made a delightful pair."

He saw the shudder ripple through her. "Come on," he coaxed. "It's all over now."

A knock at the door caused them both to turn. Patrick put his head in. "You've got another visitor, sweetheart."

Dixie quickly wiped her eyes. All she needed now was for Art to come traipsing in. She looked like warmed-over death!

Her grandfather stepped in, but to her greater horror it wasn't Art who followed. Rather, framed in the doorway, stood Anthony Di Franco, with a huge floral bouquet in his hands. He lifted the flowers a little higher and gave her a lame smile. "The guys thought you might like these."

Dixie blinked several times, hardly able to credit her own vision, and then shot a look at Herb. Her partner was grinning from ear to ear.

Flowers. They were everywhere—every variety imaginable. The chapel was heavy with their mingled scents. A huge spray of ferns and ribbon and yellow roses draped the ebony casket. But the people gathered were surprisingly few in number. Family. Close friends. An inconspicuous reporter or two.

Dixie occupied the last pew alone. The recessed lighting just above her head had been dimmed almost to darkness. It was difficult to sort out the emotions which had driven her to come.

Guilt?

No, she decided, not guilt but an overwhelming remorse. The memory of Michelle's fresh, youthful face tore at her with unrelenting intensity.

People did die. Old people. Young people. Rich. Poor. A fact beyond denial or argument. But the cold-blooded violence of this death made it unconscionable.

There were people she recognized in the room. The smooth coiffure of Kathryn Holmstead. Every now and again the woman's hand came up and plucked nervously at the collar of her dark silk blouse. On her right sat her attorney husband. He was still, as if he'd been carved in stone. Her son, Jason, leaned forward on her left, his arms and head resting on the pew in front of him. A few other young people were scattered throughout the chapel, their faces starkly pale, unbelieving.

All heads turned in unison as Albert and Judith Enrique emerged from the small alcove set aside for immediate fam

ily. The councilman and his wife came forward to stand
before the casket of their only child. A wide gap separated
them.

Suddenly a sob rent the air. Albert Enriquez began to sway
slightly, listing toward the casket and then backward again.
His wife turned hesitantly toward him, her facial expression
hidden behind the drape of a black veil. Ever so slowly,
almost tentatively, her arm came up. She stepped closer and
touched his shoulder. In the next moment they were holding
each other, sharing the overwhelming grief that would remold
the direction of their lives.

Dixie left the chapel before her presence could be noticed.
She was almost back to the rented Mustang when she saw a
familiar station wagon parked next to it. Her jaw muscles
tightened as she recognized the two tall figures sitting in the
front seat. Herb and Pete were talking quietly and didn't see
her until she approached and spoke through an open window
on the passenger side. Pete leaned away from the vehemence
in her face and voice.

"Now listen here, you two, I've just about had it! If you
insist on playing Lancelot and Galahad, go find yourself
another maiden in distress! I gave up the role last week!"

Herb looked at Pete and shrugged. "Excitable—just like I
told you—but don't worry, you'll get used to it."

Both men smiled at her and she felt the anger slowly ebb
away. "What are you talking about, Woodall, or should I
ask?"

"You shouldn't. Just get in your car, or rather that hunk of
junk you rented, and follow us to the nearest cup of coffee."

They both looked like little boys, brothers who'd just
collaborated on an expensive Mother's Day gift. Five minutes
later she was sitting with them in a booth at Denny's—the
nearest cup of coffee.

"The roster has just been posted for shift change," Herb
informed her. "Di Franco is doing some body swapping."

Had it not been for the twinkle in her partner's eyes Dixie
would have felt a moment's apprehension. "Oh, for pete's
sake, will you spit it out!"

"There she goes, using my name in vain again," Pete said. "Can you break her of that?"

"*We* can try," Herb answered.

Dixie looked from one to the other. "Don't tell me—"

They nodded at the same time, their heads bobbing like little plastic dogs in a low-rider's rear window.

"But Pete's just off probation," she protested. "I can' believe Di Franco would—"

"Believe it," Herb interrupted. "He decided Mike Davi needs a little career developing—sent him packing back t patrol. Pete's coming in as Jake Spatlin's new partner."

While not a formal promotion, coming upstairs as an inves tigator was most definitely a status jump, unheard of for first-year patrolman. Dixie extended her hand in congratulations

"Welcome aboard," she said and then looked at Herb "Does this mean—"

Again he anticipated the question before it was completed "Yep." He nodded. "Like it or not you're stuck with me Now, I think it's about time we get you home. The docto said a week's rest, remember? Patrick was pacing the floo when we dropped by to tell you the good news."

She opened her mouth to argue, but suddenly changed he mind. The depression that had been with her for days wa gone, but her body was still in mild agony from the abuse had taken. For just this once she decided to let them play o their self-appointed roles as her knights in shining armor.

CHAPTER 24

To BE AT the controls again felt wonderful. Dixie banked the plane gently to the right and swooped down over a small, picturesque valley. From four thousand feet, the colorful patchwork of farms and ranches was spectacular. Mountains of billowing clouds served as a breathtaking backdrop to the lush green and vivid gold quilt that crept up to the sparkling blue Pacific.

Dropping altitude, she circled over Watsonville, the sleepy town around which the agricultural community revolved. Seen at ground level or from the air, it was not a sight without charm: the town square, complete with outdoor pavilion and small cannons; the brick walls and towering steeple of St. Patrick's Church; the Victorian elegance and lacy trim of historic Tuttle Mansion—they all gave the town a nostalgia, a grace that echoed with bygone and, perhaps, better days.

Adjusting her sunglasses, Dixie began searching the skies around her, checking for other air traffic as she prepared to land.

Once a World War II training base, and larger by far than Reid–Hillview, the Watsonville Airport boasted no control tower. Cows grazed lazily in fields around its perimeters.

"I hope you know what you're doing, young lady." The voice of her passenger and erstwhile copilot cut across her concentration.

Dixie glanced quickly to her right to see her mother also busy, visually checking their air space.

"Looks fine," the older woman said and settled back in silence while Dixie circled again and then brought the Beech Baron in for a neat landing. Once they had taxied safely onto the runway apron, Rose continued her mild reprimand.

"Really," she sniffed, "I still can't believe this—to think of your chasing about after a man when you only have to snap your fingers—"

"Please, Mother!" Dixie tried to curb her irritation. After all, she had invited her overbearing parent to come along, knowing full well she would probably be subjected to a lecture and reams of unasked advice.

Serves me right, she thought; that's what I get for being a coward!

It was true. The idea of flying here alone to see Art made her insides quiver. She wondered if she'd done the right thing. Her insides were still shaking like crazy.

Rose unfastened her seat belt and sniffed again. "Have it your own way. I'm going to call Heddy Redgrave. It's been a long time, and I think maybe she'd like to catch up on things over a nice, long lunch."

Dixie shook her head in disbelief. "Is there anyplace on earth I could take you where you don't have friends, Mother?"

Rose smiled sweetly. "I don't know, dear. You'll just have to keep trying."

Dixie had spotted Art's blue Stearman from overhead and hoped her timing and the information she had squeezed from Herb weren't wrong. The field seemed deserted.

A mild breeze ruffled her hair as she and Rose made their way to the main building, a small restaurant quaintly dubbed the Belly Landing. They were almost to the entrance when Dixie, furiously scanning the planes tied down off the field, spotted the ungainly lines of a black and yellow Pawnee parked farther away, close to a tin Quonset hut. The shoulder wings and odd fuselage of the craft made it slightly jarring to the unaccustomed eye. A man dressed in fatigue pants and scuffed leather jacket was tinkering about the propeller.

Turning back, Rose saw the direction of her daughter'

gaze and the expression on her face. "Oh, forever more," she muttered, "don't tell me *that's* the one!"

Her disdain wasn't hard to understand. Even from a distance Art looked most decidedly scruffy. His hair, swirled into cowlicks, was badly in need of cutting and his loose-fitting clothes were oil-stained.

"Don't be so quick to judge," Dixie pleaded. "After all, he's been working. Come, let me introduce you. I'm sure once you've— "

"Oh, no you don't," protested Rose, who had very definite ideas about protocol. "I'm going to make my phone call, and then I'm going to enjoy a nice cup of coffee. You can bring your . . ."—she waved an airy hand—". . . whatever he is inside after you've presented your little peace offerings."

She indicated the objects Dixie held—a box of chocolate-covered caramels in one hand and a small bouquet of tulips in the other. She resignedly shook her head at the younger generation's strange mating habits. "When you're ready, I'll be inside."

Thus putting the conversation to an end and feigning a breezy indifference, the older woman entered the restaurant.

Rose Marks waited just inside the doors for several minutes, watching through the tinted glass as her daughter walked away. Once assured her voyeurism would go undetected, she stepped out again. Opening her large handbag, she quickly extracted the mother-of-pearl opera glasses she always carried. She trained them on the figure of Art Cochran.

At first she saw only the back of his unruly head, but as Dixie drew closer the pilot turned. His mobile face went through a whole series of changes: a disbelieving frown, an incredulous uplift of brows, and finally a slow, lazy smile.

Rose looked more closely, squinting into the lenses. Yes, it was a rather attractive face—and rather more than a nice smile.

She knew she should lower the glasses at that point, but she didn't. Instead, she focused on Dixie and saw her hold out those silly little gifts. It was the kiss that finally stopped Rose's spying, a meeting of lips that caused Dixie to drop both flowers and candy onto the hot asphalt.

Rose gasped and lowered the glasses, still suffering a delicious case of goose bumps as she went inside to dial the phone.

Heddy Redgrave's cheerful voice answered at once and Rose smiled. "Hello, darling," she chirped. "I know it's a bit untimely, but how would you feel about an overnight guest?"

All the same, Dixie's indomitable parent wondered just how Art Cochran felt about women in police work.